FIRE
&
SWORD

HARRY SIDEBOTTOM

THRONE OF THE CAESARS

FIRE
&
SWORD

THE OVERLOOK PRESS
New York, NY

This edition first published in hardcover in the United States in 2017 by
The Overlook Press, Peter Mayer Publishers, Inc.

141 Wooster Street
New York, NY 10012
www.overlookpress.com

For bulk and special sales, please contact sales@overlookny.com,
or write us at the address above.

Cataloging-in-Publication Data is available from the Library of Congress

Manufactured in the United States of America

ISBN 978-1-4683-1436-6

2 4 6 8 10 9 7 5 3 1

To Richard Marshall

An empty pageant; a stage play; flocks of sheep, herds of cattle; a tussle of spearmen; a bone flung among a pack of curs; a crumb tossed into a pond of fish; ants, loaded and labouring; mice, scampering and scared; puppets jerking on their strings – that is life.

MARCUS AURELIUS, *MEDITATIONS* VII.3

CONTENTS

THE ROMAN EMPIRE
IN AD235–8

.... Provincial borders
1. *ALPES GRAIAE*
2. *ALPES COTTIAE*
3. *ALPES MARITIMAE*

Dvina

Borysthenes

Marcomanni
Quadi

Iazyges

GOTHS

Olbia

Tanais

Panticapaeum

KINGDOM OF THE
BOSPORUS

PANNONIA
INFERIOR

Mursa

DACIA

ROXOLANI

Istria

Black Sea

Phasis

COLCHIS

IBERIA

Viminacium

Durostorum

Tomis

MOESIA
INFERIOR

Sinope

Artaxata

ARMENIA

Sirmium

Naisus

Novae

MOESIA
SUPERIOR

Serdica

THRACE

Byzantium

BITHYNIA-PONTUS

GALATIA

CAPPADOCIA

PERSIAN
EMPIRE

Tigris

MACEDONIA

Cyzicus

EPIRUS

ASIA

Ephesus

Samosata

MESOPOTAMIA

ACHAEA

Athens

CILICIA

Antioch

SYRIA COELE

Emesa

Euphrates

Palmyra

LYCIA
PAMPHYLIA

SYRIA PHOENICE

n   *e   a   n*   *S   e   a*

SYRIA PALESTINA

Alexandria

ARABIA

CYRENAICA

EGYPT

Nile

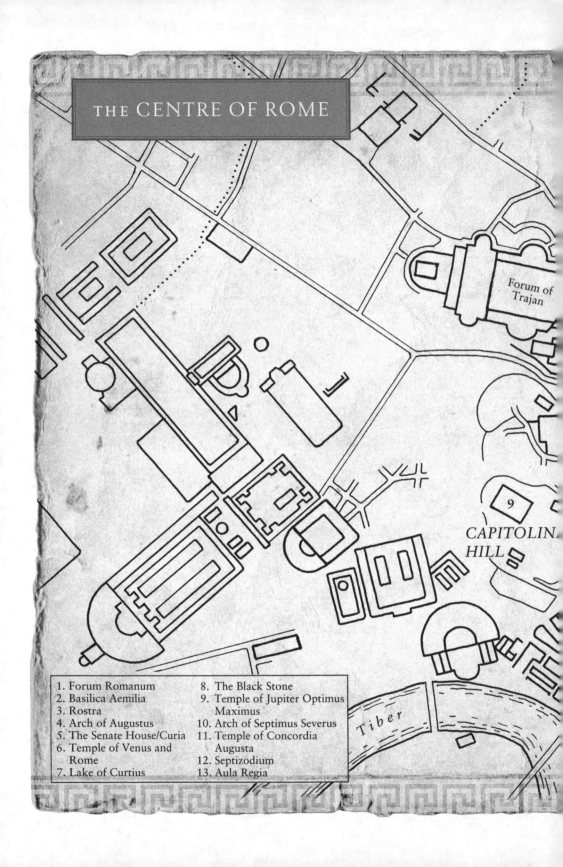

THE CENTRE OF ROME

Forum of Trajan

9

CAPITOLIN
HILL

Tiber

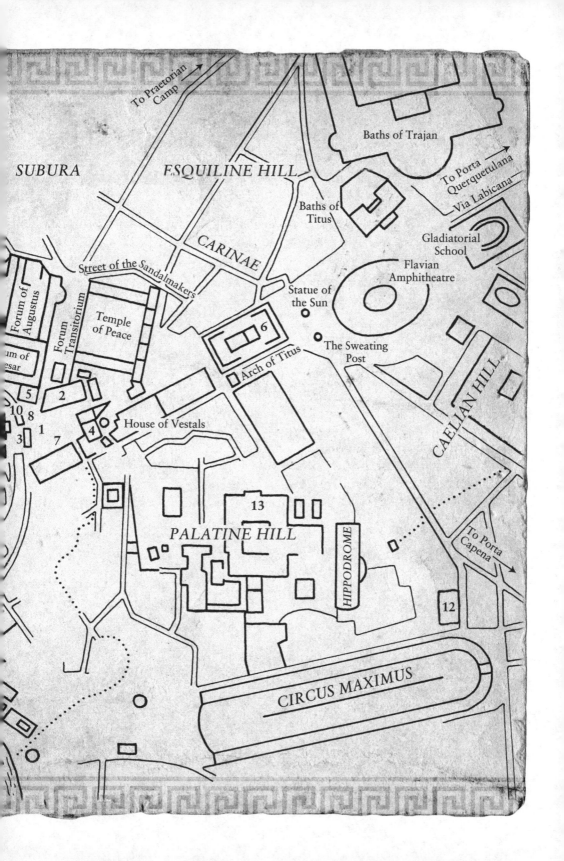

SUBURA

ESQUILINE HILL

To Praetorian
Camp

Baths of Trajan

To Porta
Querquetulana

Via Labicana

Baths of
Titus

CARINAE

Gladiatorial
School

Street of the Sandalmakers

Flavian
Amphitheatre

Statue of
the Sun

Forum of Augustus

Forum Transitorium

Temple
of Peace

6

The Sweating
Post

um of
esar

5

2

Arch of Titus

CAELIAN HILL

10

8

1

4

House of Vestals

3

7

13

PALATINE HILL

HIPPODROME

To Porta
Capena

12

CIRCUS MAXIMUS

THE NORTHERN FRONTIER

0   50   100   150   200 miles
0   100   200   300 kms

N W E S

GOTHS

C a r p a t h i a n s

Tisza

• Potaissa
• Apulum

IAZYGES

Sarmizegetusa •

T r a n s y l v a n i a n   A l p e s

• Istria

NIA
OR

• Sirmium

Pincus Fort

DACIA

ROXOLANI

Pontes •

Viminacium •

• Tomis
• Durostorum
• Marcianopolis

Danube

Novae •

MOESIA
INFERIOR

*B l a c k
S e a*

Nova

MOESIA SUPERIOR

• Naissus

• Serdica

THRACE

• Philippopolis

• Hadrianople

Perinthus •
• Byzantium

MACEDONIA

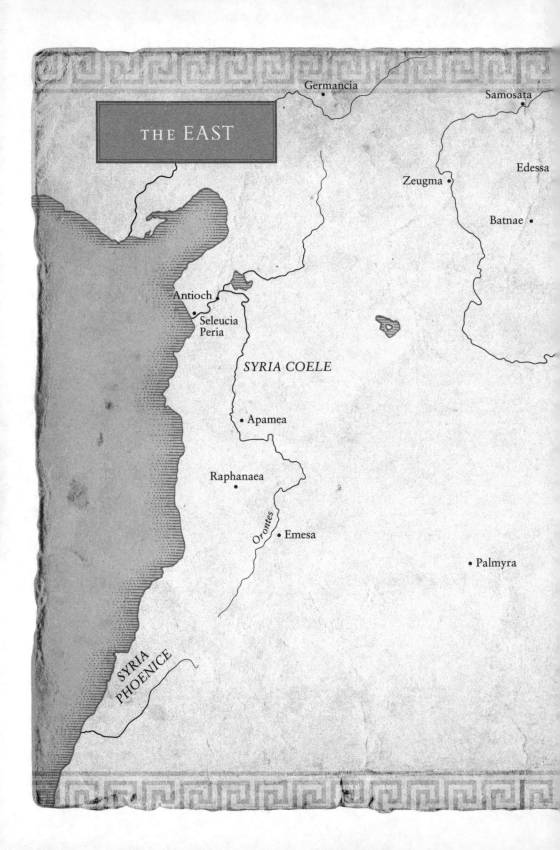

THE EAST

Germancia

Samosata

Edessa

Zeugma •

Batnae •

Antioch •
• Seleucia
Peria

SYRIA COELE

• Apamea

Raphanaea
•

Orontes

• Emesa

• Palmyra

*SYRIA
PHOENICE*

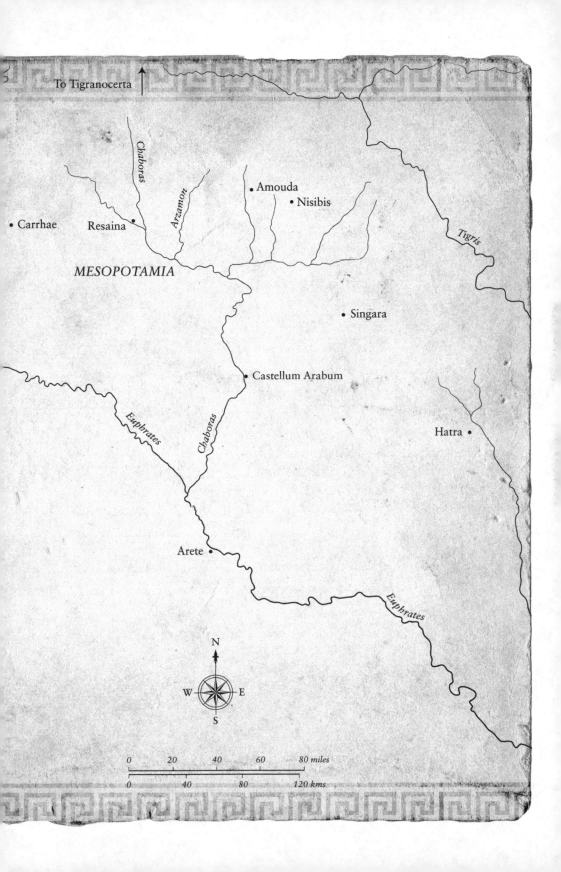

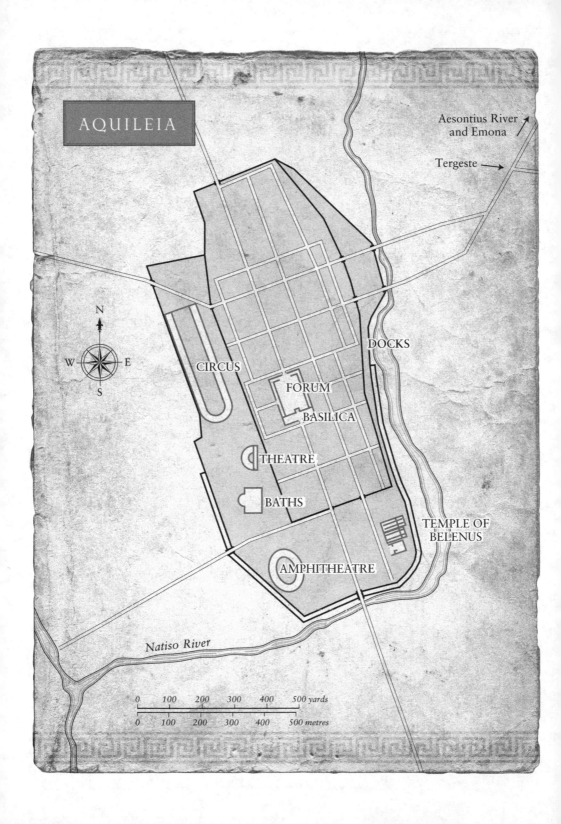

AQUILEIA

Aesontius River
and Emona

Tergeste

DOCKS

CIRCUS

FORUM

BASILICA

THEATRE

BATHS

TEMPLE OF
BELENUS

AMPHITHEATRE

N
W E
S

Natiso River

| 0 | 100 | 200 | 300 | 400 | 500 yards |
| 0 | 100 | 200 | 300 | 400 | 500 metres |

CAST OF MAIN CHARACTERS
(A COMPREHENSIVE LIST APPEARS AT THE END OF THE BOOK)

IN ROME

Pupienus: Prefect of the City
Pupienus Maximus: His elder son
Pupienus Africanus: His younger son
Balbinus: A patrician of dissolute ways
Gallicanus: A Senator of Cynic views
Maecenas: His intimate friend
Tranquillina: Ambitious wife of Timesitheus
Maecia Faustina: Daughter of the late Emperor Gordian the Elder, and sister of the late Emperor Gordian the Younger
Marcus Junius Balbus: Her young son
Caenis: A prostitute in the Subura
The Die-cutter: Her neighbour and client, a workman in the Mint

IN AQUILEIA

Menophilus: A Senator of Stoic persuasion, co-commander of the defence
Crispinus: Another Senator with a philosophical demeanour, the other commander of the town

IN THE NORTH

Maximinus Thrax: The Emperor
Caecilia Paulina: His deceased wife
Verus Maximus: His son and heir
Apsines of Gadara: Secretary to Maximinus
Flavius Vopiscus: A general
Anullinus: Praetorian Prefect
Volo: Commander of the *frumentarii*
Julius Capitolinus: Equestrian commander of the 2nd Legion
Parthica
Dernhelm: A young barbarian hostage, beginning to be called
Ballista
Timesitheus: Equestrian official, a prisoner on his way to
Maximinus
Honoratus: Senatorial governor of Moesia Inferior on the Danube
Iunia Fadilla: Wife of Verus Maximus, on the run

IN THE EAST

Priscus: Equestrian governor of Mesopotamia
Philip: His brother
Catius Clemens: Governor of Cappadocia, long-term supporter of
Maximinus
Ardashir: Sassanid King of Kings

PROLOGUE: AFRICA

The City of Carthage,
Eight Days before the Kalends of April, AD238

'Lay down your arms!'

As he spoke, Capelianus turned in the saddle, took in the enemy. On both flanks their levies were running, back under the aqueduct, pelting through the tombs towards the illusory safety of the walls of Carthage. His own auxiliaries, all discipline gone, were chasing them, hacking at their defenceless backs. Here in the centre, half of their regulars had put down their standards and weapons, and stretched out empty hands in supplication. Only a thousand still stood against him; the Urban Cohort, and the young men formed into the sham Praetorian Guard of the two usurpers. Win them over, disarm them, and victory was complete. Africa would be won back for Maximinus, the revolt of the Gordiani crushed. Not a battle, but a massacre.

'Lay down your arms, fellow-soldiers. Your fight is done and over.'

Frightened eyes stared at him over the wall of shields a few paces ahead. They were outnumbered two to one. These

1

locally raised Praetorians were not real soldiers. There was no sign of the younger Gordian.

'Your pretend Emperor has fled. Those who led you astray have fled. No mounted officers remain under your standards.'

Still the enemy did not move.

'Return to your military oath. You were misled. The clemency of your true Emperor Maximinus is boundless. I am merciful. There will be no retribution.'

A stirring in the ranks opposite. A tall, heavy man, pushing his way to the front. He was bareheaded.

Capelianus realized his mistake. His opponent had not fled.

Gordian the Younger stepped forth, like some terrible, martial epiphany.

The din of the killing was distant. Into the unnerving silence, here in the eye of the storm, Gordian shouted.

'We will stand together to the end!'

Gordian drew his sword, levelled the blade at the man who had come to kill him.

'The coward Capelianus has put himself at our mercy.'

Gordian was just a dozen paces away; big, powerful, clad in armour, exuding menace.

'Some god has blinded him. Kill the cuckold, and the day is yet ours. With me, brothers.'

Capelianus felt his limbs clumsy with fear. Only four ranks of legionaries between him and those terrible man-killing hands.

'Are you ready for war?' Gordian called, the words booming through the lines.

Ready! Caught up in the intoxicating ritual of blood, the enemy shouted as one.

Ready!

On the third response, they charged, heedless of the odds against them.

At a run, Gordian crashed, shield to shield, into the foremost legionary. The man staggered back, fell to the ground, unbalancing those behind. Gordian was in their midst. Steel flashed in the sun. Men flailed and screamed. The tumult stunned the senses. Through it all, remorseless, heavy-shouldered, Gordian drove forward. An officer at his side cut down another legionary.

A mere three ranks shielded Capelianus. He felt his courage slipping away. Your heart shrank when you were past fifty, shrank until it was no bigger than that of a child.

Gordian chopped down a man to his right, took a blow, cut down the legionary in front.

Two ranks between Capelianus and Nemesis.

This was insane. Capelianus turned the head of his horse. The battlefield was his, except for here. No point in throwing his life away, not when victory was in his grasp. His cavalry had routed the opposing horse on the left. Only a handful of the enemy had broken through, and escaped to the south. Now his Numidian tribesmen were galloping wildly to the city in pursuit of plunder and rape, and the pleasures of killing the unresisting, but the regulars were rallying. Canter over there, watch from the safety of their formation, as the overwhelming numbers of his legionaries ground down Gordian and the last of the rebels.

As Capelianus hesitated, he saw Gordian take a blow to his unhelmeted head. Bloodied, but seemingly impervious, as if some deity inhabited him, Gordian thrust his blade through his assailant. Gods below, where had the degenerate acquired this energy? Was there no stopping him?

One rank remained. Prudence dictated withdrawal. Capelianus gathered his reins.

No. Everything hinged on this moment, this fleeting, unstable encounter between what had been and what would be. If they saw him flee, the morale of the legionaries would break. Panic would spread like wildfire through his whole

3

army. Gordian would be left with the last ordered infantry in the field. With that tiny, ragtag force, the unworthy sot of a pretender would have won the most improbable of victories, would have defeated the 3rd Legion Augusta, the only legion in Africa. Gordian would process into Carthage in triumph. They would throw flowers at his feet. Gordian and his odious father would continue to wear the purple.

Capelianus tugged his sword from its scabbard. The bone hilt was slippery in his palm, no comfort. He yelled at his men, his voice unsteady.

'Kill him! Cut him down!'

There was still some fight left in the legionaries. A slashing blade near severed the neck of the rebel officer next to Gordian. A spray of blood, bright in the sunshine. The officer vanished under the stamping boots of the melee. And suddenly Gordian was alone, ringed with steel.

'Kill him! Just one man, finish him!'

For a moment they hung back like dogs around a bear brought to bay in the arena.

Gordian shifted his sword and shield this way and that, covering himself, gathering his strength, searching for an opening, a way to Capelianus. Blood was running freely down Gordian's face, getting in his eyes.

'For the gods' sake, it is just one man. He is wounded. End him!' Capelianus was hollow with fear.

A movement behind Gordian. A legionary jabbed his sword hard between Gordian's shoulder blades. Gordian stumbled forward. Another swung at his head. Gordian brought up his splintered shield. Too slow. The sharp, heavy steel cut into his jaw, snapping his head sideways.

'Finish him!'

Gordian was on his knees. A blow to the back of his head dropped him to all fours, and then they were on him, like a pack of wild dogs breaking up their prey.

Capelianus howled in exultation. 'Cut him to pieces. Dismember the drunken bastard.'

Gordian was dead! So much for comparing himself to Hannibal, to Alexander. He was dead! The posturing fool was dead!

'Chop off his head. Trample his body.'

The unconsidered words were a spur to action. Yes, he would trample his enemy in the dirt. Vaunt over him like a hero of old, a hero from Homer. Capelianus sheathed his unused sword, went to climb off his horse.

A hand gripped his arm. Firmanus, the *Primus Pilus* of the 3rd Legion. How dare he put his hands on a superior officer? Capelianus would break him to the ranks, have the skin off his back. The old Centurion was saying something.

'Gordian the Elder.'

All the Furies, how had the senile goat slipped his mind? Capelianus had waited half a lifetime and more for his revenge. It would not escape him now.

Festina lente. Capelianus mastered himself. *Hurry slowly*. First the field must be secured. The revenge of the gods grinds slow but certain.

With the death of the younger Gordian, his remaining men had begun to surrender. Already the seasoned legionaries of the 3rd were surrounding them. Capelianus gave Firmanus his orders, his voice low and confidential.

'Disarm them. Separate the Praetorians from the men of the Urban Cohort. Execute all the former. Keep the latter for decimation. Have the four Cohorts who came over without fighting retake their oath to Maximinus. Keep your legionaries under the standards. They can join the looting tomorrow. They will have a donative to make good their losses.'

Firmanus saluted, and went off to enact the commands.

Capelianus was satisfied. The youths enlisted in the bogus Praetorians had instigated the revolt. It was right they should pay the penalty. The regular soldiers of the Urban Cohort had done no worse than choose the wrong side. Decimation was enough. Discipline would be restored when one in ten had been beaten to death by his tent-mates. Old-fashioned Roman morality. The spectacle would be edifying. Maximinus would approve.

Off to the left, Capelianus' cavalrymen were rounding up their defeated opponents. The majority of these prisoners were civilians who had risen against their rightful Emperor. Implicated in treachery and sacrilege, they too must die. Their numbers demanded all of Capelianus' horsemen as a guard.

Capelianus regarded his staff: Sabinianus the traitor, two tribunes, and four troopers. In the distance the gates of Carthage were still clogged with the slaughter. Further organized resistance was improbable. Seven mounted men should ensure his safety. Now for Gordian the Father.

'With me.'

Capelianus set off towards the aqueduct and the city.

Gordian the Elder would not escape. For three decades Capelianus had nurtured his hatred. He had been a young Senator of promise, tipped for great things. Until his whore of a first wife had cuckolded him with Gordian. Against all justice, the priapic old man had been acquitted of adultery. In the Senate, among the imperial courtiers, Capelianus had become a figure of mockery. The inadequate who could not control or satisfy his wife. His career had stalled. Eventually he had mortgaged his estates to raise the money to buy the Consulship. Then he had re-mortgaged them to obtain the governorship of a province. Rather than Asia or Africa Proconsularis, wealthy provinces where he could have made good all the bribes and recouped his fortune, he had received Numidia. Flyblown deserts and barren mountains, intractable natives and savage tribes, scorching in summer and freezing in winter; a host of mundane duties, scarcely rewarded; an

6

office for junior Senators who would climb no higher. The bitterest draught was swallowed when old Gordian had been installed in Carthage: an aged Silenus lording it over the second city of the empire, reaping the riches of neighbouring Africa Proconsularis.

They rode under the aqueduct, and through the necropolis. Fresh corpses were strewn among the resting places of their forebears, like blood offerings in some barbaric religion. The small cavalcade passed a pretentious, half-finished tomb in white marble. Capelianus had given Carthage over to the soldiery. For three days they could do as they pleased. It gave Capelianus a grim satisfaction that the bereaved family might never again have the means to finish the tomb. If any lived to attempt the task.

The Hadrumetum Gate was blocked with the dead and dying. They reined in. Some auxiliaries were energetically stripping bodies. The corpses were pallid things, all humanity gone. Capelianus shouted at the soldiers to clear a path. Reluctantly they turned to the unwanted and unremunerative task, heaving and shoving as they handled the recalcitrant sides of meat.

'Faster, you dogs, unless you want to feel the lash.'

Gordian the Elder must not escape. Capelianus turned to Sabinianus.

'Will he try and get away by the harbour?'

Sabinianus took his time answering. 'I do not think so. They trusted to their numbers. There was no provision for flight. No ship was readied.'

Nothing appeared to ruffle the patrician assurance of Sabinianus. Late last night, he had crept out of the city, deserted the Gordiani. In the camp of Capelianus, to prove his change of heart, Sabinianus had cut a prisoner's throat. The prisoner had been his closest friend. It was said Sabinianus had loved Arrian like a brother.

7

No one could trust such a man. Sabinianus had revealed the ambush set by the Gordiani: the five hundred horsemen hidden among the warehouses and walls of the Fish Ponds beyond Capelianus' left wing, poised to take his army in the flank, to roll up the line. Without the intervention of Sabinianus the battle might have had a very different outcome. Capelianus looked at him with loathing and contempt. *Love the treachery, detest the traitor.*

'What will the old man do?'

'Make a stand in the palace.'

'A stand?' Capelianus failed to keep the anxiety out of his voice. 'They kept troops in reserve?'

'A handful.' Sabinianus smiled. 'Nothing to bother the conqueror of Carthage, the new Scipio.'

Capelianus had granted Sabinianus his life. Yet the decision could be revoked.

The way clear, they clattered into the town.

It was a vision of the underworld, Tartarus, where the wicked endure their eternal punishments. Bodies, slumped and naked. Old women and young children wailing. Smashed heirlooms, desecrated homes. A smell of spilt wine and burning, a reek of vomit and excrement.

They rode up the Street of Saturn, between the Temples of Venus and Salus. As if to mock the divine assurances of *Love* and *Safety*, a young matron ran pell-mell from an alley. Hot in pursuit, a dozen or so Numidians.

Despite himself, despite the urgency of his mission, Capelianus stopped to watch.

The Numidians caught her on the steps of the Temple of Salus. As they stripped her, there was something arousing about her sharp, desperate screams. Her body was very white, even her legs and arms; a well-brought-up young wife, sheltered from the sun, modest and chaste.

She lashed out, but they forced her down, bent her over

8

a low balustrade. Her buttocks were pale as marble, her sex dark and desirable. The heat of the climate inclined Numidians to rape, their loose, unbelted tunics facilitated the act. When their leader mounted her, she called some appeal to the men on horseback.

Capelianus smiled. 'Health and great joy to you.'

The men laughed.

This would not do. Capelianus had an infinitely more pressing desire. Not lust, but vengeance.

They entered the Forum, passed the white altar of Peace and the bronze tablets inscribed with the ancient laws of Rome. At the far end soldiers and tribesmen promiscuously went to and fro among the pillars of the governor's palace.

A Prefect, the commander of one of the auxiliary Cohorts, came down the steps.

'Gordian the Elder is in a small dining room, the one they call the Delphix.'

'Alive or dead?'

'Dead.'

Before dismounting, Capelianus addressed the Prefect. 'Your Cohort broke ranks, disobeyed orders, chased the rebels. After the three days of licence, there will be punishments.'

The officer saluted. 'We will do what is ordered, and at every command we will be ready.'

The chastened Prefect led them into the corridors of the palace. From deeper in the labyrinth, muffled by inlaid doors and heavy curtains, came the sounds of bestial revelry. Capelianus half-remembered a passage of Polybius from his schooldays. The Greek historian had been much impressed by the order with which the Romans sacked a town. No soldier turned to looting until he was given the command. All the plunder was heaped in one place to be distributed according to rank and merit. No man kept anything back for himself. But that was long ago. Things were different now.

Discipline and virtue were only words. The way of the ancestors, the *mos maiorum*, all forgotten, no more than an
expression.

In the Delphix a semi-circle of troops stood like a tragic
chorus around the hanged man. An overturned chair and a
pool of liquid beneath the dangling feet of the corpse. The
front of Gordian's tunic was wet. It was said a hanged man
ejaculated. By the smell, it was just urine.

Capelianus studied the bulging eyes and protruding tongue.
A coward's death. Not the steel, but the rope. A woman's way
of suicide. The dissatisfaction habitual to Capelianus consumed
his thoughts. There had been a prophecy that the Gordiani
would die by drowning. Capelianus had looked forward to
making that come true. A butt of wine would have been
fitting. Father and son had both cheated him.

'We have captured one of their friends.' The young Prefect
was eager to make amends.

The man was pushed forward. He was battered, his clothes
torn, his arms and legs laden with chains.

'Name? Race? Free or slave?' Capelianus intoned the
traditional beginning to an inquisition.

The prisoner did not answer. He was staring at Sabinianus.

'Name?'

Now the man gave his attention to Capelianus.

'Mauricius, son of Mauricius, town councillor of Thysdrus
and Hadrumetum.'

Capelianus knew of him. 'The catalyst of this evil revolt.
An arch-conspirator.'

Mauricius drew himself up in his chains. 'Friend of the
late Emperors, Prefect of the Horse Guards of Marcus
Antonius Gordianus Romanus Africanus Augustus, Father
and Son.'

'A traitor.'

'No traitor, but a true friend.' Mauricius looked again at

10

Sabinianus, with hatred. 'A friend loyal to death. We should have known from the start. The signs were there. We should have listened at Ad Palmam when you said you would sacrifice anyone for your safety.'

No emotion showed on the face of Sabinianus.

'Coward! Oath-breaker with the heart of a deer!'

'You realize you will die.' Capelianus cut off the imprecations.

'What is terrible is easy to endure.' There was a smile on the face of Mauricius, its reason unknowable.

'You will be tortured.'

'You cannot hurt me.'

'The claws will tear your flesh.'

'They cannot touch my soul.'

A local festival, the Mamuralia, occurred to Capelianus. 'You will be whipped through the streets of Carthage. Outside the Hadrumetum Gate, by the Mappalian Way, you will be crucified.'

'I am a citizen of Rome.' There was outrage in Mauricius' tone, yet somehow his self-possession held.

'No, you are an enemy of Rome. As a *hostis*, you will die. Take him away.'

Mauricius did not struggle, but he shouted as they dragged him from the room. 'Death to the tyrant Maximinus! Death to his creatures! You are cursed! The Furies will turn your future to ashes and suffering!'

Capelianus turned to the Prefect. 'What of the others close to the pretenders?'

'All of rank dead on the battlefield, apart from Aemilius Severinus, the one they call Phillyrio. He was ordered south some days ago to gather the Frontier Scouts. Together with those *speculatores*, he was to rally the barbarians beyond the frontier.'

'We will hunt him down. We will hunt down all their

11

followers, high and low.' Capelianus felt a stab of pleasure. He had always loved the chase; men or beasts, it made no difference.

'Some of their household – Valens, the *A Cubiculo*, and some other freedmen and slaves – escaped. They had a fast ship waiting by the mole of the outer harbour.'

Capelianus rounded on Sabinianus. 'You told me they had no ship ready.'

Sabinianus said nothing.

'You brought us here. Were you trying to let him escape?'

'No.' Sabinianus' downturned mouth twitched slightly. 'Last night I gave proof of my change of heart.'

Had the tiny involuntary grimace betrayed the patrician? Capelianus could not be sure. Sabinianus the traitor needed watching, but for now Capelianus put him out of his mind.

The corpse was still there.

'Get him down.'

The soldiers bustled about the task, teetering on chairs, holding the legs of the corpse.

Capelianus wondered what could have induced his old enemy and his wastrel son to have bid for the throne. Certainly not justice or duty. They were archaic concepts, suitable back in the days of the free *Res Publica*, but outmoded and unfitting in the debased age of the Caesars. Capelianus knew what motivated men under autocracy. Nothing but lust and greed. The latter was far the stronger; greed for power as well as for wealth. At his advanced age perhaps the father had considered there was little to lose, that it would be no small thing to die clad in the purple. As for the son, his thoughts had been addled by wine and debauchery, his reasoning unsound. Yet even so, they must have appreciated in moments of clarity that they would fail. No legion was stationed in the province of Africa Proconsularis. The secret had long been revealed that Emperors could be made

12

outside Rome. But never without the backing of thousands of legionaries.

The corpse was down.

'Cut off his head. It will go to Maximinus.'

A soldier set about the butchery.

But would the head reach Maximinus? Against all likelihood, the Senate in Rome had declared for the Gordiani. Italy had gone over to the rebels. The fleets at Misenum and Ravenna controlled its ports. The head would have to travel up the other shore of the Adriatic, go ashore in Dalmatia, then journey overland to seek out Maximinus on the Danube frontier.

Decapitation was never easy. Sawing away, the soldier was slipping in a welter of blood.

And what remained for the Senate now? Traitors to a man. Maximinus was born a Thracian, brought up as a common soldier. Forgiveness was not a virtue cultivated by either group. The Senate could expect no mercy. Executions and confiscations, a holocaust. Few would survive. Great houses would be extinguished. The proscriptions of Sulla or Severus would be as nothing.

The head was off. Blood pooled across the marble floor, soaked into the fine rugs.

'Preserve it in a jar of honey. Maximinus will want to gaze on his face.'

The Senate could expect no mercy. All its accumulation of experience and expertise in subtle negotiation would do no good. The Senate would have to acclaim another Emperor. Thessalian persuasion; necessity disguised as choice. But who would it clothe in the purple? Surely a governor with troops at his disposal. Maximinus was with the Danubian army. Decius in Spain was his dedicated supporter. So would the Senate turn to a governor on the Rhine or one in Britain? Or would it send a laurelled despatch to one of the great commanders in the East? Or possibly, just possibly, might its gaze focus nearer to hand? To a man proven in the field, a man who had overthrown Emperors, a man who held all Africa in his hand?

'Throw the rest of him out into the Forum for the dogs.'

Some considered ambition was a vice, others held it a virtue. Capelianus inclined to the latter view. Yet to be Emperor was to hold a wolf by the ears. Better by far to be the man who stood behind the throne of the Caesars. Capelianus looked over at Sabinianus. Traitors had their uses.

PART I:
ITALY

CHAPTER 1

Rome

The Temple of Concordia Augusta,
Six Days before the Kalends of April, AD238

'Dead? Both of them? Are you certain?'

Standing before the Senate of Rome, the old freedman was unabashed by the Consul's brusque questions.

'Gordian the Younger died on the field of battle. When Gordian the Elder ordered me to convey what remained of his household to safety, his mind was set on suicide.'

Licinius Rufinus leant forward on the Consular tribunal. 'Was his bodyguard with him?'

'He was alone.'

'You did not see him take his life?'

This was pointless. Pupienus sat back, let his gaze shift around the huge interior of the temple, run over the myriad sculptures and paintings, part obscured by the gloom. Valens had been *A Cubiculo* to Gordian the Elder forever, since before the flood. He had served well when his master was alive, and would do the same now his master was dead. There was no doubting his evidence. The Emperors that the Senate had

17

acclaimed were dead. No amount of juristic interrogation could bring them back.

Opposite Pupienus a painting by Zeuxis hung over the heads of the Senators. Marsyas was bound to the tree hand and foot, naked, already twisted in agony. At his feet the Scythian slave was sharpening the knife, looking up at the man whose skin he would peel from his living body. With the Gordiani dead, every Senator in the temple could expect some similar fate when Maximinus came down from the North and took Rome. Maximinus was a Thracian, a barbarian. They were no different from Scythians; strangers to reason and pity. Clemency was not in their nature.

Valens was dismissed, and walked out. Pupienus envied the aged ex-slave. The very obscurity of his station might prove his salvation. There was no such hope for himself. No hope at all for the man appointed Prefect of the City to oversee Rome in the name of the Gordiani. None whatsoever for the man complicit in the killing of his predecessor, Sabinus, Maximinus' appointee. Too late for a change of heart, and compromise was not an option. Some other, desperate course must be taken.

As presiding magistrate Licinius called on the Conscript Fathers to give their advice.

In the nervous silence, Pupienus turned the ring on the middle finger of his right hand, the ring containing the poison.

To the relief of all, Gallicanus sought permission to address the meeting.

Pupienus regarded the speaker with disfavour. A tangle of unwashed hair and beard, a homespun toga, no tunic, bare feet; an ostentatious parade of self-proclaimed antique virtue. All it needed was a staff and a wallet for alms, and he would have been Diogenes reborn. Pupienus thought Cynic philosophers were meant to abstain from politics; certainly they should not possess the property qualification of a Senator. He trusted his distaste did not show on his face.

'A tyrant is descending upon us. A monster stained with innocent blood. Conscript Fathers, we must recover our ancestral courage.'

All true enough, although Pupienus considered that more than rhetoric was needed. Specific proposals were required at this desperate pass. The Senate hated Maximinus for killing their friends and relatives, for the continual exactions to pay for the unwinnable northern wars. They loathed him for the lack of respect shown to their order. Since his elevation, he had never set foot in the Curia, or even visited Rome. Ultimately they despised him for not being one of them. When news came of the revolt of the Gordiani in Africa, it had seemed a gods-given salvation. The Senate had voted them the purple, had denied Maximinus and his son fire and water, had declared them enemies of Rome. The Senate had acted hastily. It had gambled, and it had lost. There was nothing for it now but to gamble again. One last throw of the dice: elect a new Emperor.

'A ravening tyrant is coming from the savage North. We must defend our families, our homes, the temples of our gods. We must stand in the ranks ourselves. To elect another tyrant in the hope that he will defend us from the one already approaching is insanity.'

The words irritated Pupienus. No candidate had yet been nominated. It was too early for personal invective. Unless . . . surely Gallicanus was not going to propose the mad scheme he had aired in Pupienus' house three years earlier, when the news had come that the Emperor Alexander had been murdered?

'Place a man above the laws, and he will become lawless. Power corrupts. Even should a man be found with the virtue to resist temptation, a man who would rule for others not himself, history has shown that the heirs to his position will be tyrants, ruling for their own perverse pleasure.'

19

The small philosophic coterie led by Gallicanus' especial friend Maecenas shook back the threadbare folds of their togas and applauded. The majority of the Senators, all better apparelled, sat in silence.

'I am not suggesting anything new, anything foreign. The gods forbid we should institute a radical democracy. The Athenian past demonstrates how quickly such a constitution slides into mob rule. I do not even propose we Senators take power, rule as an aristocracy. Every such state inevitably has been deformed into an oligarchy, where a few rich men trample down their fellow citizens. No, I argue we should return to our ancestral government. Rome became great under a free Republic. Every order of men knew their duties and their place. The Consuls embodied the monarchic element, the Senate the aristocratic, the assemblies of the people the democratic. All was balanced in harmony. As a Republic, Rome defeated Hannibal. As a Republic, Rome will defeat Maximinus. We have already elected a board of twenty men to prosecute the war. We have no need of an Emperor, no need to set the boots of an autocrat over our heads. Conscript Fathers, we need do nothing to restore the Republic. The providence of the gods who watch over Rome has made the Republic live again. Let us seize our liberty! Let *libertas* be our watchword!'

Gallicanus, archaic probity personified, glared defiance at the unmoved togate benches. Maecenas came forward, and put his arm around the shoulders of his *amicus*, said something soft in his ear. Gallicanus smiled, no longer a barking Cynic dog, but, despite his more than forty years, an unsure youth seeking approbation.

Pupienus was mildly surprised when Fulvius Pius took the floor. Inoffensiveness, not ability, had seen Pius rise to the Consulship then the Board of Twenty. His career had been marked by neither independence of thought or action, nor much display of courage.

'Fine words for a lesson in philosophy, fine words to address two or three pupils. Utterly inappropriate to this august house.'

Since his election to the Twenty, not only had a certain initiative surfaced in Pius, but an unexpected asperity.

'I will not enter into a philosophical dialogue with Gallicanus. This is not the time or place to debate the tenets of the schools. Instead we should face realities. No one regrets the passing of the free Republic more keenly than me. The busts of Cato, Brutus and Cassius have pride of place in my house. But the free Republic is nothing more than a pleasant memory. If we could not see that for ourselves, long ago the historian Tacitus taught us that the rule of an Emperor and the continuance of our empire are inextricably linked.'

Still locked in an embrace, Gallicanus and Maecenas glowered at the speaker.

'Only a handful of men, beguiled by the high-sounding words of philosophy, want the return of the long dead Republic. The majority of all orders desire the status quo. The provincials can appeal to the Emperor against unjust decisions of their governors. The *plebs urbana* look to the Emperor to give them the sustenance of life, and the spectacles that make it worth living. The soldiers receive their pay from the Emperor, and give him their oath. What of the Praetorians? Their sole reason for existence is to guard the Emperor. And what of us, Conscript Fathers? With no Emperor to restrain them, the ambitions of certain Senators would again tear the Republic apart. A welter of civil strife would consume our armies. The barbarians would pour over the frontiers, sack our cities, drown our dominion in blood.'

'Not if we return to the ways of our ancestors,' Gallicanus shouted.

Pius smiled, as if patiently correcting a schoolboy. 'The *mos maiorum* was no defence against Caesar or Augustus. We do

21

not live in Plato's Republic. Let us face facts as statesmen. We must have an Emperor to lead our defence. The fate of the Gordiani shows that the man elected must command legions. As the armies in the North are with Maximinus, let us send the purple to a governor of one of the great provinces in the East, begging him to march with all haste to save Rome.'

Gallicanus bellowed defiance. 'Cowardice! The gods may never grant us another opportunity for *libertas*!'

Amidst an outcry of disapproval – *Sit down! Leave the floor!* – Maecenas pulled his friend back to his seat.

'Conscript Fathers.' Licinius struggled to be heard over the clamour. 'Senators of Rome!'

Eventually the house heeded the Consul.

'Conscript Fathers, the distinguished Consular Fulvius Pius has given us good advice. In all but one respect. The very practicalities he urges mitigate against the election of an eastern governor. Their allegiance is unknown. Indeed the governor of Cappadocia, Catius Clemens, was one of the men who put Maximinus on the throne.'

Pupienus was not alone in looking at Clemens' younger brother. Catius Celer sat modestly a few rows back, among the ex-Praetors and other Senators who had not yet been Consul. His face betrayed nothing. He had been quick to acknowledge the Gordiani. Many great houses had the foresight to survive times of troubles by having relatives on both sides.

'That aside, there are factors of distance and time. With favourable winds, a despatch might reach Syria in days, but by land or sea an army could not return for months. Maximinus will be upon us long before. We must acclaim one of our own. The Senate already has elected the Board of Twenty to defend the *Res Publica*. The choice should be made from among their number.'

A low murmur of speculation filled the temple.

Licinius continued. 'A decision of this importance is not to be taken on a whim. I propose to adjourn the house, to allow time for careful consideration, to seek to discern the will of the gods, and to allow us to mourn the Gordiani with due piety. The Senate will reconvene on a propitious day, when the auguries are good. Conscript Fathers, we detain you no longer.'

The doors of the temple were opened. Light filled the *cella*, banishing the dark to rafters, corners, and seldom-frequented spaces behind the statuary.

Pupienus wholeheartedly believed in the traditions of the Senate, but he needed to be alone. He told his sons to accompany the presiding Consul home as his representatives, and requested his close friends to join him later for dinner.

It took time for the near four hundred Senators in attendance to make their way out into the sunshine. Some lingered, talking in little groups, covertly eyeing the members of high standing and influence. Intrigue and ambition, two things at the heart of their order, had, at least for the moment, driven out fear. Many looked at Pupienus as he sat unmoving and alone.

Pupienus regarded Marsyas: naked, racked, ribs lifted high, skin stretched, taut and vulnerable. No escape from the knife. Marsyas had challenged Apollo. It had been his downfall, brought him to his hideous end. Marsyas was not the only one destroyed by ambition. Some philosophers castigated *ambitio* as a vice, others held it a virtue. Perhaps it was composed of both qualities. Pupienus was ambitious. He had risen high. Yet was the ultimate ambition – the throne itself – too dangerous for a man whose life was predicated on a lie? Pupienus knew that if the secret that he had guarded all his life were revealed his many achievements would be as nothing, and he would be ruined and broken.

The temple was almost empty, just a few attendants clearing away the paraphernalia of the meeting. Pupienus' secretary, Fortunatianus, was waiting on the threshold. Pupienus beckoned him.

Fortunatianus knew his master. Without words, he handed Pupienus the writing block and stylus.

Pupienus opened the hinged wooden blocks, regarded the smooth wax. His mind worked best with something on which to focus, some visual mnemonic. There were only nine of the Board of Twenty in Rome. On receipt of the news would ambition drive others to desert their posts and rush to the city? What of Menophilus at Aquileia, or Rufinianus in the Apennines? Best leave them aside, deal with such circumstances if they arose. For now there were only nine men eligible for election in Rome, only nine men in this strange situation thought capable of empire. He ordered them, and wrote a list, annotated only in his thoughts.

Capax imperii

Allies
Pupienus – Prefect of the City, experienced and resourceful, accustomed to command, yet a novus homo, standing on the edge of a precipice
Tineius Sacerdos – a respectable nobleman, father of the wife of Pupienus' elder son, loyal, but lacking dynamism
Praetextatus – another nobilis, ill-favoured father of the ill-favoured new bride of Pupienus' younger son, a more recent friend of unproven fidelity, apparently without competence

Opponents
Gallicanus – a violent, hirsute, yapping Cynic
Maecenas – his intimate, somewhat better groomed, yet still rendered intransigent by philosophic pretentions to virtue

Three, including himself, who could be expected to favour the candidature of Pupienus. It could be assumed that Gallicanus and Maecenas, beguiled by dreams of a dead Republic, would oppose any aspirant to sole power. Pupienus needed to win over two of the remaining four. Yet it was not just the men themselves. Everything depended on the votes they could bring. The issue would be decided by decree of the whole Senate.

Which two must he attempt to bring over?

Much would tell against Licinius among traditional Senators: his Hellenic origins – *Greeks were naturally untrustworthy* – his early employment – *a secretary at another's beck and call* – even his intelligence – *Greeks were far too clever for their own good, and always, always talking.*

Fulvius Pius had a long career behind him, and was distantly related to the Emperor Septimius Severus. Familial ties and propinquities of office might sway a few to his side in the house, but nowhere near enough.

Valerian had been at the heart of the brief, doomed regime of the Gordiani. The death of the principals would have robbed their faction of appeal to the majority of Senators. Yet there were issues to weigh beyond the Curia. Pupienus himself commanded the six thousand soldiers of the Urban Cohorts. All the other military forces near at hand – the thousand Praetorians and seven thousand men of the *vigiles* in Rome,

25

and the thousand swords of the 2nd Legion in the Alban Hills – were led by equestrian officers, every one of whom was bound by the ties of patronage to the *Domus Rostrata*, the noble house of the Gordiani. If Valerian was in his camp, Pupienus could put a noose of steel around the Senate House.

And then there was Balbinus. A porcine face on a corpulent body, both bloated by a lifetime of indulgence and perversity. A soul where stupidity vied with low cunning, and profound indolence with vast ambition. It was impossible to measure how much Pupienus despised the man. Yet Balbinus was a kinsman of the divine Emperors Trajan and Hadrian, a member of the Coelli, a clan that went back to the foundation of the free Republic, and, by their own account, beyond history itself, all the long way to Aeneas and the gods. Irrespective of his character, centuries of familial wealth and public honours, an atrium filled with smoke-blackened portrait busts, endowed Balbinus with a status that could command the votes of many Senators.

In politics often emotion must be set aside. Pupienus would have to stomach the patrician's sneers and jibes. *Rome is less your lodging house than your stepmother. Beguile us with your ancestry; tell us the great deeds of your father.* But what bait could Pupienus dangle before those slobbering jaws, what prize so glittering that it could pierce Balbinus' lethargy, and induce him to prevail on his relatives, friends and clients in the Curia to vote imperial honours to a man he regarded as an upstart, little better than a slave?

The honours of an Emperor. Pupienus reviewed the purple, the ivory throne, the sacred fire. In a private enterprise one could press on or draw back, commit oneself more deeply or less. But in the pursuit of an empire there was no mean between the summit and the abyss. To be Emperor was to live on the stage of a public theatre, every movement and word visible. There was no mask. One's inner being and past were

26

stripped bare. Certainly too close a scrutiny for a man with a secret lodged less than two hundred miles from Rome. If he were to proceed, Pupienus would have to go one last time to Volaterrae, and bury his past. It was a task he had prayed never to have to undertake. Everything decent cried out against it. But to bid for the throne all emotion must be set aside.

CHAPTER 2

Northern Italy

The Aesontius River, Two Days before the
Kalends of April, AD238

If they went on, any scout or spy concealed in the farm
would see them. Menophilus had halted his small column
well back from the treeline. They would wait and watch.
There were about three hours of daylight left. This close to
the enemy, unnecessary risks were to be avoided. Quietly,
he told his men to dismount, take the weight from the backs
of their horses.

The farm was still in the spring sunshine; red tiles and
whitewashed walls, black holes where the doors and shutters
had been removed. Big, round wine barrels, all empty. No
animals, not even a chicken pecking in the dirt. No smoke
from the chimneys. No sign of life. Menophilus thought of
his home, and hoped war never came to distant Apulia.

A small unpaved road ran to the farm from the south,
then turned north-east and disappeared into the timber.
Menophilus had avoided it, instead leading his ten men
laboriously up through the woods that bordered the river.

The going had been soft, progress slow, and the horses were tired. The rest would do them good.

A movement in the yard. A figure walked from the barn and went into the house. Although the distance was too great to make out the individual with certainty, he had the bearing of a soldier. It could not be otherwise. All civilians had been forcibly evacuated on Menophilus' orders. Despite the destruction of the bridge, at least a part of the army of Maximinus had got across the Aesontius.

The hostile piquet was not an insurmountable complication. They could not be much more than half a mile from the site of the demolished bridge. Menophilus gave the *Optio* the watchwords – *Decus et Tutamen* – and his instructions. Two of the most reliable men were to lie up and observe the farm. The junior officer and the rest of the troopers were to lead all the horses back to a clearing; the one with a tree that had been hit by lightning. Let the horses graze, but they were to remain saddled, their riders with them, ready to move out. Menophilus and the guide would continue the reconnaissance on foot. If they had not returned by dawn tomorrow, the *Optio* was to withdraw the way they had come. When he got back to Aquileia, he was to inform Crispinus that the Senator had sole command of the defence of the town.

Menophilus thought about Crispinus. In Rome his initial impression of his fellow member of the Board of Twenty had not been completely positive. It had been difficult to see beyond the long beard, with its philosophical pretentions, and the ponderous, over-dignified ways of moving and talking. Although Crispinus had much experience of command, political necessity rather than military expertise had saddled Menophilus with him as joint commander of Aquileia. Yet as the two men had prepared to defend the city against Maximinus in the name of the Gordiani, a certain respect had grown between them. If Menophilus fell, Aquileia would remain in safe hands.

The thud of hooves was deadened by the leafmould under the trees, but no body of cavalry moved silently. The breeze was from the north, and Menophilus doubted that the creak of leather and the clink of metal fittings, the occasional whicker of a horse, would carry.

When there was just the sound of the gentle wind in the trees, he gave his attention to the way ahead. The farm stretched towards the Aesontius: the house, then the yard with the massive wine barrels, the barn and some sheds, a tiny meadow, and a steep track cut down through the trees to the river. There was no cover to cross the track, but the incline and the outbuildings might obscure the view from the dwelling to the riverbank.

Menophilus checked that his guide was ready. Marcus Barbius smiled, tight-lipped. The youth had every right to be nervous. It would have been better to have a soldier. But none of the men of the 1st Cohort Ulpia Galatarum, the only troops in Aquileia, knew the country. The young equestrian's family owned these lands. In more peaceful times, the farm was occupied by one of their tenants.

The two of them graded down through beech trees and elms until they were among the willows by the stream. The Aesontius was running high and fast, its green waters foaming white where they surged over submerged banks of shingle.

When they reached the path, Menophilus crouched and peered around the trunk of a tree. From down here, only the red roof of the farmhouse was visible over the barn. Of course, if men were stationed in the outbuildings, they would have an uninterrupted view down to the river. The nearest shed was no more than fifty paces distant.

Menophilus stood. 'We will walk across. They may assume we are two of them.'

Barbius did not speak, but looked dubious.

'If we run, it will arouse suspicion.'

Barbius still said nothing. He appeared little reassured. Perhaps fear had robbed the youth of speech.

Both of them were wearing tunic, trousers, and boots, and had sword and dagger, one on each hip. They looked like off-duty soldiers. To move quietly, before leaving, Menophilus had removed the *memento mori* – a silver skeleton – and the other ornaments from his equipment. Now he took the long strap of his belt, and twirled the metal end, as was the habit of soldiers at their ease.

With his left hand, he took Barbius by the elbow, and propelled him out across the path.

Let us be men.

One step, two, three. The strap-end thrumming. *Let us be men.* Not looking up at the farm. At every step, the fear of an outcry, or the terrible whistle of an arrow. Five steps, six.

Eight paces, and they were back in cover.

Menophilus dropped to the ground. Heart hammering, he crawled back to the edge of the path.

Once again, he gazed up from behind the bough of a tree.

Nothing moved. Utter stillness.

He watched for some time. From this point on, the piquet at their backs, escape would be infinitely more difficult.

At length, somewhat satisfied, heart beating more normally, he wriggled backwards to where Barbius waited.

They went cautiously up the bank, flitting from tree to tree through the dappled shadows.

Ahead was a blaze of light where the road meandered through the woods.

Again, Menophilus stopped, took cover, and watched and waited.

The backroad was grey, dusty, and empty. A pair of swallows low over it, banking and swooping. A sign of bad weather to come.

Telling Barbius to watch both directions, Menophilus walked out onto the byway, studied it. The distinct marks of military hobnailed boots. No impressions of hooves or hipposandals. The surface was powdery, not tramped down. Only a few of the enemy had gone up to the farm, all of them on foot.

Returning to the shade, Menophilus and Barbius went through the trees parallel to the road.

Soon the road joined a grander, paved version of itself. The Via Gemina was the main route from Aquileia to the Julian Alps, and on to Emona and the Danubian frontier. When war did not threaten, there would be many travellers. Today it was deserted. There were no guards at the junction.

A final rise, and the Via Gemina dipped down to the Aesontius. The river here was very broad. Usually shallow, now it was swollen with spring melt from the mountains. All that remained of the central sections of the Pons Sonti were the stubs of piers, the water breaking around them, tugging at their loosened stones. On the far bank was the beginning of a pontoon bridge. The first two barges were in place. A large body of soldiers was manhandling the next down the bank. Around them was the bustle of disciplined activity. Gangs of men braked wagons down the descent, and laboured to unload huge cables and innumerable planks.

Below Menophilus, at the foot of the slope, a small rowing boat was moored to the near bank. Here all was quiet. A detachment of troops, no more than a hundred, lounged in the shade. An officer had a detail of ten men standing in the road, about fifty paces from their resting companions. Menophilus cast about, and found a tangle of undergrowth from which to observe.

The shadows lengthened, and across the river the work went on. On the near bank, the soldiers passed around wineskins. From time to time, individuals wandered a little downstream to relieve themselves. Menophilus unhinged a writing block, and made occasional, cryptic notes.

It was in moments of inactivity that his grief threatened to unman him. What was the point of this reconnaissance? Of any of it? The risk and the striving; all for what? His friends were dead. Gordian the Father and Gordian the Son, both dead. Of course, he had known they were mortal. Death was inevitable. Friends were like figs; they did not keep.

Philosophy was a thin and inadequate consolation. If they were his friends, they would not want him in misery. But they were beyond that. They had escaped. The life of man was but a moment, his senses a dim rushlight, his body prey to disease, his soul an unquiet eddy, his fortune dark; a brief sojourn in an alien land.

True, they had lived as they wished, and they had met their deaths well. Gordian the Son struck down on the field of battle, opposing the forces of the tyrant. Gordian the Father by his own hand, the decision his own. The world was wrong to see the rope as womanish. Everywhere you looked, you found an end to your suffering. See that short, shrivelled, bare tree? Freedom hung from its branches. What was the path to freedom? Any vein in your body.

Life was a journey. Unlike any other, it could not be curtailed. No life was too short, if it had been well lived. Menophilus knew he should not rail against what could not be changed. Instead he should be grateful for the time he had been granted with his friends. But the pain of their loss cut like a knife.

The shadows were lengthening. Dusk had fallen down at the waterside. Torches sawed in the breeze, as men continued to labour in the gloom.

Menophilus had gathered some useful intelligence. It was carefully noted in his writing tablet. From the bull on their standard, he had learnt that the men on the near bank were from the 10th Legion Gemina, which was based at Vindobona in Pannonia Superior. Evidently they had been ferried over a few at a time by the one little rowing boat. There were not yet many of them on the Aquileian side of the Aesontius. From their demeanour, they were relaxed and confident. They knew that the rebels had no regular army to bring against them in the field. No attack was expected. On the far side of the water, the prefabricated materials of the pontoon bridge, and the proficiency of their assembly indicated that it belonged to the imperial siege train. Another twenty-four hours should see its completion.

What he had discovered was not enough. He needed to know what other troops accompanied the 10th Legion, or, at least, form some idea of their numbers. He would wait. The night might provide more answers.

Darkness fell, and the wind picked up. It had shifted into the south-west. From that direction it often brought rain in these regions. A downpour would further swell the river, hamper the bridge-building. A difficult business manoeuvring the barges in a strong current, and there was the danger of debris swept downriver. If it rained heavily, the pontoon might not be ready for a couple of days. Menophilus committed that to memory; it was too dark to write.

Clouds, harbingers of a storm, scudded across the moon. The wind soughed through the foliage, creaking branches together. The woods were alive with the scuttling and the choked-off cries of nocturnal predator and prey.

Down by the river, streamers of sparks were pulled into the air from the campfires of the enemy. Across the Aesontius the trees were dense, and the riverbank high. Most of the fires were over the crest of the slope. No way of gauging their number from the glow in the sky. Something bolder was demanded.

Menophilus outlined his plan to Barbius. In the ambient light, the youth's eyes were white and round with fear.

34

'Watch my back,' Menophilus said. 'Leave everything to me.' He affected an assurance he did not feel. Stoic training helped.

Menophilus got up, and stretched, working the numbness out of his limbs. When he felt ready, he patted the young man on the shoulder, and set off. Barbius followed close; being left alone possibly seeming the worse of two evils.

They went down crabwise, peering at the ground. With each step, Menophilus first put down just a little of his weight on the side of his foot, feeling for twigs which might snap, stones which could turn, before transferring the whole onto the sole of his boot. Often he paused to listen. Staring through the trees, taking care not to look at the fires glowing between the tree trunks, he tried to ascertain their position.

An owl glided overhead on silent, pale wings.

Menophilus remained still for a time after its passing, before resuming his painstaking descent, angling a little downstream.

In a wood at night, fear in your heart, time and distance lost all exactitude. For eternity the river remained as far as ever, then they were standing on its brink. They retreated a few paces uphill. Each pressed hard against a willow, trying to merge into their shapes, as if hoping to effect some unlikely metamorphosis.

Menophilus could smell the fish in the river, the mud and decayed leaves along its bank. He schooled himself to patience. A brief sojourn in an alien land.

Someone was approaching through the trees. In the dark, Menophilus gazed to the side of the figure, the better to see.

The soldier passed by closer than a child could throw a stone. He went down and stood on the riverbank, fumbled with his belt and trousers.

Softly humming a tune – an old marching song – Menophilus stepped out from behind the tree trunk. He made no attempt to be quiet as he walked down.

The soldier half turned; a stream of piss arcing in front.

'*Ave*,' Menophilus said.

'*Ave*,' the soldier grunted, and returned to concentrate his aim into the water.

Menophilus unsheathed the blade, and had it at his throat in one movement.

'No noise.'

'Please, no. Please, do not kill me.' The soldier spoke quietly, fighting his terror.

'Death is your last concern.'

'Please . . .'

'Answer my questions. No one will know. It will be as if this never happened.'

'Anything . . .'

Menophilus was aware of Barbius nearby, but hanging back.

'What other troops are with the 10th Legion?'

The soldier hesitated.

Menophilus let the edge of the blade slide over the soft flesh.

Any resolve broken, the man started to talk. 'Detachments of all the other three Pannonian Legions; about four thousand swords.'

'Who commands?'

'Flavius Vopiscus.'

'Where are Maximinus and the rest of the field army?'

'Still on the far side of the Alps.'

'Where?'

'At Emona.' For his life, the soldier would volunteer anything he knew. 'They will not march until they get word the pontoon is ready. Supplies are short. Better the forces are separate.'

Menophilus calculated distances, rates of march. If the bridge was finished tomorrow or the day after, another day for a messenger to ride post-haste to Emona, perhaps four more days for the main force . . .

36

The blow took him unawares. He doubled up, clasping his stomach.

The soldier was off, crashing through the undergrowth, clutching up his trousers.

Menophilus dragged air into his chest, tried to get enough to shout at Barbius to stop the soldier.

The young equestrian was rooted, like some autoch-thonous warrior half-emerged from the soil.

'Enemy in sight! Spies!' the soldier was yelling as he ran.

Menophilus got his breath. Too late. He straightened up, hissed at Barbius: 'Run!'

Barbius was off like a hare.

Menophilus, sword still in his right hand, gathered up the scabbard in his left, and set off after.

Roots clutched at his feet. Branches whipped his face. The hot sting of blood on his cheek. A searing pain in his chest.

Barbius was in front, a little higher up the bank.

They fled south.

From behind came the ring of a trumpet sounding the alarm, the bark of orders.

Menophilus burst out onto the track. No time to look up at the farm. Too busy watching his feet. Barbius already gone into the trees beyond.

Once Menophilus stumbled, almost fell. When he looked up, there were two soldiers ahead off to the right, indistinct in the gloom. The men watching the farm? No, there were too many, four or five.

'This way!'

Menophilus angled away from the soldiers.

Barbius ran straight towards them.

'This way, you fool.'

A sword cut from nowhere. Menophilus blocked awkwardly. The hilt slipped from his grip. He grabbed the wrist of his assailant's sword arm. The man had him by the throat. They wrestled, boots stamping for purchase. An ungainly, macabre bout.

Slammed back against a tree, Menophilus' fingers closed on the dagger in his belt. He tugged it free, punched it into the man's flank.

The soldier went down, cursing, hands plucking at the embedded blade. Not dead yet, but no further threat.

Menophilus was free. Unarmed, but free.

Through the wood, he could see Barbius. The youth was ringed by soldiers.

Menophilus scrabbled across the forest floor, hunting his sword.

Barbius had dropped his blade, was sinking to his knees, begging.

The metal pommel, the worn leather back in Menophilus' hand. He looked across at Barbius. Five to one; no hope in those odds. Menophilus stood, irresolute. The life of the youth, his own life, weighed against the cause.

Barbius' eyes were bright with terror. He stretched out his hands in supplication. It did him no good. A soldier hacked down at his head.

Menophilus turned, and ran.

A lightning-blasted tree, shimmering white.

'*Decus*,' came the challenge.

'*Tutamen*,' Menophilus gasped the response.

Strong hands helped him into the clearing. Most of the troopers were in the saddle. The *Optio* gave him a leg up.

'We will do what is ordered, and at every command we will be ready.' The junior officer was good.

'Aquileia,' Menophilus said. 'Not the way we came. Due west, across the open countryside.'

Once clear of the treeline, there was no imminent danger. The enemy had no horsemen. They went at a canter, skirting orchards, clattering between the pruned-back lines of vines and the huge, round empty barrels. It was near dawn. The stars fading.

Barbius was dead. Menophilus would have to tell his father. There were practicalities to consider. The father had charge of the walls of Aquileia.

The youth was dead, because Menophilus had abandoned him. Another thing on his conscience, another repulsive stain on his soul. There were more than enough already. Gordian had ordered him to kill Vitalianus, the Praetorian Prefect. He had gone so much further. On his own initiative he had murdered Sabinus, the art-loving Prefect of the City; he had beaten his brains out with the leg of a chair. No one had instructed him to release the barbarian hostages, to send Cniva the Goth and Abanchus the Sarmatian to unleash their tribesmen on the Roman provinces along the Danube. All in the name of freedom, in the name of a cause. Freedom bought at the price of innocent blood. A cause left leaderless by the death of his friends.

He had to believe it was worthwhile. Maximinus was a tyrant. Mad, vicious, beyond redemption, it was Menophilus' duty – as a Stoic, as a man – to tear him from the throne, to free the *Res Publica*. Perhaps Vitalianus and Sabinus had not been irredeemable, but they had supported the tyrant. They had to die. The warriors of Cniva and Abanchus would draw troops away from the army of the tyrant, make possible the overthrow of Maximinus. Duty was a hard taskmaster, war a terrible teacher.

As they neared Aquileia, the sun came up. Menophilus wondered where his duty lay now. His friends were dead. The Senate would elect a new Emperor from among the Board of Twenty. Doubtless, on receipt of that news, some members of the Twenty would abandon their posts, and ride for Rome. Menophilus would not. He would remain, defend

Aquileia to the last, do his duty. Remain like a headland against which the waves would break; he would stand firm, until the storm subsided, or he was overthrown and found release.

CHAPTER 3

Northern Italy

*The Julian Alps, The Day before the
Kalends of April,* AD238

Timesitheus stumbled on the uneven surface of the track. The
long loop of chain dragged the heavy manacles down on his
grazed, bloodied wrists, but that was as nothing to the pain in
his damaged hand. It was eleven days since he had been
captured and for the last three of them he had been herded
along this mountain path towards Maximinus, like a beast or
a runaway slave being returned to a vengeful master.

The mission should not have ended in this way. The Board
of Twenty had instructed Timesitheus to report on the defen-
sibility of the Alpine Passes, and attempt to win the locals
over to the cause of the Gordiani. There had been no intention that he should expose himself to danger. The presence
of an old enemy in these mountains had changed everything.
It was an ancient enmity, its causes almost lost in time, but
still strong, very strong. Timesitheus had let personal hatred
override his rational mind. He prided himself on his ration-
ality. His life should not have ended that way.

At first, after he had killed Domitius, the tyrant's Prefect of Camp, he had thought he would get away. In the inn, he had not been dismayed; not when he had found the gladiator, his one follower, had disappeared into the night, deserting him, not even when he had been disarmed and shackled by the soldiers. He was a Hellene, trained in rhetoric. Next to no one could resist the powers of persuasion wielded by such a man, certainly not a handful of simple, leaderless soldiers. He had money and influence, and greed and vanity were strong passions among the ill-educated. For days, in the remote *mansio*, he had talked, low and earnest, to Maximinus' four legionaries. He had mustered every conceivable argument and inducement. They should not be deceived by appearances. Of course, he was not alone. The roads through the mountains were held by troops loyal to the Gordiani. The soldiers were cut off. If, against all odds, they succeeded in reaching Maximinus, the cause of the Thracian was doomed anyway. Better to go south by easy stages. The Gordiani would welcome those who came over, reward handsomely the men who brought to safety a high-ranking official such as himself. The saviours of the Prefect of the Grain Supply would experience the full range of imperial benefaction; not just wealth, but rapid promotion and social advancement. They would all wear the gold rings of the equestrian order before a month had passed. And they should think of their families. The 2nd Legion's base in the Alban Hills was but twelve miles from Rome. If they chose the wrong side in the civil war, what would happen to their wives and children? Who would protect them?

It would have worked – Timesitheus was convinced – but for one thick-set, bearded brute. The legionary had been intransigent and aggressive from the beginning. It was he who had chained Timesitheus. Swearing at his companions, he had urged them to ignore the poisonous treason of 'the little Greek'. He had prated about the military oath, dwelling on the binding and sacred nature of the *sacramentum*. Loyalty was everything in the army. Maximinus had doubled their pay. The big Thracian was one of them, a soldier, nothing like this yapping, shifty *Graeculus*. Finally the legionary had won the argument by recourse to violence. Each time he heard Timesitheus trying to corrupt his tent-mates, the legionary would cut off one of the Greek's fingers. Timesitheus had seen no option but to persevere, and the hirsute soldier had carried out his threat.

Taking a grip on his courage and every emotion, Timesitheus had battened them down. Somehow he had managed to place his left hand on the block. If he struggled, if they held him down, the damage might be worse. He had looked away, shut his eyes. He had heard the blade slicing through the air, the sickening sound as it chopped through bone and cartilage and flesh. The agony had come a moment later. To cauterize the wound, they had had to seize him, grapple him to the floor, pinion him tight. Stupid with pain, Timesitheus had watched the white-hot steel press into the severed stump of his little finger. Even as he screamed, he knew the dreadful smell would never leave him.

The mutilation had ended all hope of persuasion. It had bound the other soldiers to the bearded ogre. Even the stupidest of them now realized that if they went over, rather than hand out rewards, Timesitheus was honour-bound to have them all killed.

All his honeyed words and subtle threats, all his Odysseus-like cunning, had won Timesitheus nothing but a brief delay. The hairy savage – now the acknowledged leader of the soldiers – had believed the lies about the forces of the Gordiani holding the main passes. Stupid, but resourceful, he had found a local guide who, for the promise of a substantial sum of money, had agreed to lead them over the Alps to

43

Maximinus. They would take a seldom-frequented shepherds' path, one traversable only on foot.

For two days, they had trudged north, through the foothills, passing between oak, beech and juniper. This morning, they had turned east, climbing a switchback route into the mountains. Staggering along, cradling his left hand against the tug of the chains, Timesitheus had seen the deciduous trees give way to pines. The resinous smell mingled with the stench of his own charred flesh.

These wild mountains were the haunt of a rich landowner turned brigand called Corvinus. Promising him the earth, only days before, Timesitheus had induced him to pledge his support to the Gordiani. It counted for nothing. Before he died, Domitius would have extracted from Corvinus the same promises to the other side. Safe in his fastness, the bandit chief would sit out the conflict, then emerge to claim his undeserved recompenses from the victors. To hope for rescue by Corvinus was to set to sea on a mat.

Weak with pain and fatigue, his left hand useless, unarmed and his wrists chained, Timesitheus could see no way to effect his own escape. He should summon a Stoic fatalism. No point in railing against things which could not be changed. What did not affect the inner man was irrelevant. The torment of his hand undermined such attempts. Philosophy was not his way. Better to stare into the black eyes of fear, to force that rodent to scuttle back into the darkness. Meet his death like a man, take comfort from the things he had achieved. From relatively humble origins, he had risen high; governed provinces, advised Emperors. 'The little Greek' had become a potent man, feared by his enemies. He regretted being caught, but he did not regret killing Domitius. Theirs had been a considered and mature hatred, nurtured over time. Often the Prefect had expressed the desire to eat Timesitheus' liver raw.

'We will spend the night here.' The guide pointed ahead.

By the track was a rustic, dilapidated inn. A stopping place intended for shepherds, it had no stables, instead an empty pen for their flocks stood next to a solitary, large hut. Built out of logs, with a steep-pitched roof against the snows of winter, it promised no privacy, and little comfort.

Inside there was just a single, smoky room, the kitchen occupying one end. The landlord, in the high-belted leather apron of his profession, showed them to the middle of the communal table. His demeanour evinced no surprise at the arrival of four soldiers escorting a chained prisoner in this remoteness. He and the guide spoke in some unintelligible dialect.

Interrupting in loud army Latin, the heavily bearded legionary demanded wine and food: the best on offer, or the old man would regret it. Let him have no thoughts of holding anything back, or cheating them. With a strange look on his face – it might have been avarice – the landlord moved to do their bidding, grunting instructions at two slatternly slave girls by the fire.

The four soldiers eyed the girls. As the slaves moved to prepare the food, it was obvious they wore nothing under their stained tunics. The drink would provoke the lechery of the soldiers, and later, all bedded down together like animals, sleep would be hard to find.

Tired and disgusted, Timesitheus looked away. Six shepherds sat at the far end of the table from the fire. When the newcomers had arrived, they had stopped talking. Now they resumed, a low murmur in the uncouth tongue employed by the innkeeper. Like all of their wandering kind, they were armed, and exhibited an air of suspicious watchfulness. By the one door, a lone traveller, a bulky man wrapped in a cloak, and with a broad-brimmed hat pulled down over his face, was asleep on a mattress of straw. The room was bare

45

of all ornaments, with the odd exception of a single large red boot placed on the ledge over the fire.

Lacking any distraction, Timesitheus found his gaze resting on one of the slave girls. As she stirred the pot, her buttocks shifted under the thin stuff of her tunic. An image of Tranquillina came into Timesitheus' mind. She was naked, laughing, in the private baths at Ephesus. Her hair and eyes so very black; her skin marble white. The lamps were all lit. After her wedding night, no respectable Roman wife would allow such a thing. Tranquillina was ever bold, untroubled by convention, in the intimacies of the bedroom, as in the round of public life. It was something Timesitheus loved, yet almost feared, about her.

How would she hear of his arrest? Who would break the news to her? Would she learn nothing until after his execution? She would take the news bravely. The thought brought him no comfort. He had never deceived himself that she had married him for love. The daughter of a decayed senatorial house, she had wed a rising equestrian officer for advantage, plain and simple. Yet they had enjoyed each other's company. He hoped that over the years he had inspired more than an iota of affection.

Timesitheus thought of their daughter. Sabinia would be eleven in the autumn. A beautiful, trusting girl, she showed no signs yet of her mother's wilful independence. What would she do without a father? But, of course, Tranquillina would marry again. She was still young, still in her twenties. Her aspirations would not die with him. The prescribed months of mourning, and another man would enjoy the pleasures of her company, of her bed, be driven by the spur of her ambition. Timesitheus hoped – he would have prayed, had there been gods to hear – that Sabinia's stepfather would treat her with kindness.

The girls brought over the food and drink. Sure enough, as they served, the soldiers pawed them, made crude comments. The girls exhibited a resignation, and a contempt for externals, that would have been envied by a Stoic sage.

Timesitheus tried to cut some mutton. It was difficult with one hand. He had no appetite anyway. His hand throbbed. It was strange that he could still feel the severed finger. It hurt terribly. He felt light-headed and sick.

The boot over the fire caught his eye. It stirred some deep memory, but, exhausted and in pain, he could not bring it into focus.

How long before they reached Maximinus? The Thracian had condemned him to death even before he killed Domitius. What would Maximinus do to him now? There were awful rumours of the Palace cellars. The rack, the pincers, the claws, wielded by men with ghastly expertise, men lacking any compassion. As there was no likelihood of escape, Timesitheus should seek to take his own life before they arrived. It would not be easy, but what was it the philosophers said? *The road to freedom could be found in any vein in your body.*

The door opened, and a well-built man in a hooded cloak entered. The garment was expensive, pinned by a gold brooch in the shape of a raven. Garnets were set in the gold. The man's face was obscured by the hood.

The soldiers regarded the newcomer with hostility. He ignored them, walked to the fire, said something in dialect to the room at large.

The landlord picked up a poker. He took a couple of steps to the middle of the table, and brought it down on the nearest soldier's head.

Schooled in violence, the remaining three soldiers reacted fast, scrambling to their feet, drawing their weapons.

The stranger was by the innkeeper, a blade in his hand. At the far end of the table, the shepherds were up, swords out. The big man who had been sleeping was blocking the doorway, dropped into a crouch learnt in the arena.

'Put down your weapons.' The stranger's tone was calm, educated.

'Fuck you!' Obdurate to the end, the bearded legionary glared around, searching for any improbable line of escape.

'Death comes to us all,' the stranger said.

The legionary spun around towards Timesitheus. 'One step, and the *Graeculus* dies.'

Timesitheus threw himself backwards off the bench. He rolled, landed on his feet. The legionary surged at him. Timesitheus swung the chain that held his wrists. A rasp of steel and the thrust was deflected. The stranger stepped forward, and drove his blade into the soldier's back. The legionary looked uncomprehending at the tip of the sword emerging from his chest. He crumpled, and fell.

The last two soldiers were on the floor, the shepherds finishing them off.

The room was splattered in blood. It reeked like a slaughterhouse.

The stranger pushed back his hood.

Timesitheus recognized Corvinus.

'You look surprised.' Corvinus smiled. 'I thought Maximinus' boot would have given you warning.'

Timesitheus could think of nothing to say.

'I am sorry you lost your finger,' Corvinus said.

'It is of little consequence. It was not my wife's favourite.' Timesitheus had always recovered fast. 'How?'

'No one travels the mountains without me knowing. Your gladiator found me.'

The hat discarded in the doorway, Narcissus approached, grinning, like a big, dangerous dog expecting a reward.

Timesitheus told the gladiator to find something to remove his manacles, then addressed Corvinus.

'You kept your word. Your loyalty to the Gordiani will be rewarded.'

'They are both dead.'

Now Timesitheus was adrift. If the Gordiani were dead, everything was changed. 'Then why?'

Corvinus was cleaning his blade. 'You promised me a wife from the imperial house. I intend to marry Iunia Fadilla.'

'Maximus' wife? The daughter-in-law of Maximinus? All for love?' Timesitheus' laughter sounded high and unhinged to his own ears.

'Living in a wilderness does not rob a man of all finer feelings.'

Blood was seeping through the bandages wrapped around Timesitheus' hand. The pain returning. He was shaking.

'Although there are more prosaic reasons.' Corvinus was composed, as if on the hunting field, or at a symposium. 'The Senate is to elect a new Emperor from among the members of the Board of Twenty. In the name of the Gordiani, as well as an imperial bride, you offered me Consular status, a million sesterces, tax exemption for me and my descendants in perpetuity, and houses in Rome, on the Bay of Naples, and an estate in Sicily. The wealth of Croesus is not to be thrown aside. I need you to go to Rome, and ensure that the promises are kept by whoever next wears the purple.'

CHAPTER 4

Northern Italy, Beyond the Alps

*The Town of Emona, Four Days before
the Nones of April, AD238*

The heifer, garlanded and with gilded horns, was led into
the Forum, past the serried ranks of the soldiers, and up to
the altar of Fortuna Redux. The Emperor Maximinus took
a pinch of incense, and let it fall into the fire. The flames
crackled; blue and green. Enveloped in the smell of frank-
incense and myrrh, he made a libation of wine. The ceremony
had begun, and it would run its stately course.

Maximinus was impatient. The gods must be honoured.
It would have been wrong for an Emperor returning to Italy
not to make offerings to the divine fortune that had brought
about his safe return. Yet the endless ceremonies and delays
that had to be endured frustrated him beyond measure. He
wanted his enemies in front of him, within reach of his
strong hands. He had been at his arms drill when the news
arrived of the deaths of the Gordiani. The jolt of pleasure had
been brief. He recalled the whey-faced messenger stammering
out that the Senate intended to elect one of their own as

50

another pretender. Maximinus had not harmed the messenger. Paulina, his wife, dead nearly two years, would have been proud of his self-control.

The heifer lowed, unsettled by the crowds.

Once, the Senators of Rome had understood duty, had been men of virtue. They had remained on the Capitol, composed in the face of the inevitable, as the Gauls swarmed up the hill. The Decii, father and son, had dedicated themselves to the gods below to ensure the victory of their armies. Self-sacrifice and courage, long marches and hard duty had comprised the life of the Senators. But that had been long ago. Centuries of peace, of wealth and luxurious living, had corrupted them beyond redemption. In marble halls, under the gaze of the portrait busts of their stern forebears, they disported themselves with painted courtesans and depilated catamites. They were dead to shame, to the way of their ancestors. To them the *mos maiorum* was no more than an archaic expression.

Paulina had been right. The Senators would always hate and despise him as a low-born usurper. They were too far from virtue to understand. Maximinus had never wanted to be Emperor. Since he had ascended the throne, nothing he had done had been for himself. Everything had been for the safety of Rome. From their palatial residences on the Esquiline, and their villas on the Bay of Naples, they could not see the terrible threat of the northern tribes. Everything – private estates and fortunes, even the treasures stored in the temples of the gods – must be sacrificed for the war. If it was lost, the barbarians would stable their horses in the temples, and tear down the empire.

Maximinus tipped wine over the heifer's brow. As the liquid splashed down, the beast dipped its head, as if agreeing to its own sacrifice. Maximinus took a handful of flour and salt, and sprinkled it over the heifer. Then, with the iron knife only to be wielded by the Pontifex Maximus, he made a pass over the victim's back, intoning a prayer of thanks for the blessings already received, and asking for the deity's favour in the trials to come.

Stepping back, Maximinus nodded to an attendant. An axe swung in the sunshine, thumping down into the nape of the heifer's neck. The heifer collapsed, stunned, its soft, gentle eyes unfocused. Two assistants pulled back its head, and one, with the assurance of long practice, cut its throat. Another of the *victimarii* moved to catch the blood. Some went into the jar, more gushed onto the ground, spattering up the man's bare legs. Bright red blood ran in the cracks between the paving stones.

The trials to come. What had given the Senators the unexpected courage to continue the war? With the deaths of the Gordiani, they had lost the resources of Africa. Italy was virtually unarmed. Perhaps a thousand Praetorians remained in their barracks in Rome, and roughly the same number of legionaries of the 2nd Parthica in their base on the Alban Hills. As the majority of their fellow-soldiers were with Maximinus, the loyalty to the senatorial cause of those left in Italy must be suspect. Of course there were six thousand men with the Urban Cohorts, another seven thousand in the *vigiles*. But the former were better at controlling the crowds at the spectacles than standing in the line of battle, and the latter were no more than armed firemen. The fleets at Misenum and Ravenna had turned traitor, but their marines were of little account on land. Against these inadequate, motley forces, Maximinus was bringing the might of the imperial field army. With Maximinus here at Emona were over thirty thousand veterans. Already Flavius Vopiscus, with an elite detachment of another four thousand men from the Pannonian Legions, was over the Alps, and across the Aesontius river.

How could the Senate hope to resist such a force; an

overwhelming force which could draw reinforcements from all the armies stationed throughout the provinces? The thought brought Maximinus a stab of doubt. Was there something else? Was the Senate gambling on some further treachery, as yet unknown? Capelianus had proven his commitment by crushing the rebellion in Africa. From Spain, Decius dominated the West. No one was more loyal than Decius, an early patron of Maximinus' career. Nothing untoward had been heard from Britain, and nothing was to be expected from that dismal, damp backwater. The only credible challenge could come from the great armies stationed on the Rhine, the Danube, and in the East.

As the *victimarii* went about their business, Maximinus considered the problem.

From Cappadocia, Catius Clemens oversaw the other governors in the East. Clemens was a hypochondriac, forever dabbing his nose, complaining of this and that fever. Yet at the battle of the Harzhorn, he had fought like a Senator of the free Republic. After the death of Paulina, mad with grief and drink, Maximinus had punched Clemens in the face, knocked him to the ground. No Roman with any spirit would forget such an insult to his *dignitas*. Clemens had been one of the instigators of the plot which had killed Alexander and put Maximinus on the throne. Having overthrown one Emperor, Clemens had the nerve to strike down another. And Clemens need not act alone. His younger brother was in Rome, while his elder brother was governor of Germania Superior. Combined with the authority of the Senate, the armies of the Rhine and the East could shake the world.

Then there was the Danube, watched by Honoratus from Moesia Inferior. Absurdly beautiful, Honoratus looked as if the noise of a symposium would frighten him. Yet he also had proved himself on the battlefield in Germania, and, of course, he was the second of the three complicit in the death of Alexander. Honoratus had been reluctant to leave the imperial court, and take up a post in the distant North. It was not beyond the bounds of possibility that he might attempt to return to the centre of power by force.

Perhaps, Maximinus thought, it might be best to remove them from office. But that begged the question who should replace them. Flavius Vopiscus was wracked by superstition; always clutching amulets, or trying to foretell the future from random lines of Virgil. Yet he was resourceful and determined. Maximinus, however, could not spare him. He was needed for the campaign in Italy. Anyway, Flavius Vopiscus was the final member of the triumvirate that had overthrown Alexander. There were many high-ranking men in the imperial entourage. Maximinus' eye fell on Marius Perpetuus, a Consul of the previous year. But what was to say any of them would prove more trustworthy? And might not an order dismissing Clemens or Honoratus provoke the very uprising it was designed to prevent?

Paulina had been right; an Emperor could trust no one. At least no one of wealth and status. Maximinus trusted his soldiers. Some spark of antique virtue still lived in simple men; the sons of peasants and soldiers, born on the farm, or in the camp, uncorrupted by city life. Although rations were limited, and remounts in short supply, the army was rested, ordered, and ready to march. Cross the Alps, join with Vopiscus at Aquileia, take that city, then march on Rome. A speedy campaign, reward the troops, and punish the guilty with exemplary severity. That was the way to stamp out any sparks of rebellion before they flared.

A fable of Aesop came into his mind; one of those his mother had told him. A lion and a bear fought over the carcass of a fawn. When they were bloodied and exhausted, a fox stole the prize from under their noses. Maximinus dismissed the idea. This would not be a long campaign. The army only had to set foot across the Alps for almost everyone to come, holding out olive branches, pushing forward their children, begging for mercy and falling at their feet. The rest would run away because they were cowards.

The *victimarii* had rolled the corpse of the heifer onto its back, had slit open its belly. Arms red to the elbows, to the armpits, they cut and sawed at the innards. Soon they offered the slimy, steaming products of their labours to their Emperor. Maximinus might be impatient, but if any of the organs were deformed he would order another sacrifice. The gods were to be treated with all reverence. Without their approval, nothing could prosper. Turning them in his hands, one by one, he inspected the liver, lungs, peritoneum, and gall bladder. There was a shadow on the heart, but nothing to cause concern. He announced the sacrifice propitious.

As Maximinus washed and dried his hands, he noticed spots of blood on the white of his toga. Such things happened, it signified little.

He had never desired the throne. Duty demanded that he crush this revolt, then make one last campaign into the forests of Germania. Then, the empire secure, he could set aside the purple. He would return to Ovile, the village of his birth, there to be reunited with Paulina, his dead wife. A sharp sword, an end to troubles. He would go as willingly as this sacrificial animal.

Yet what of the succession? Unlike Sulla the Dictator, or Solon the Athenian lawgiver, Maximinus could not walk away, leave it to chance. The *Res Publica* needed a strong hand at the helm.

Maximinus gazed across at his son. Verus Maximus stood, sulky and bored, not bothering to feign interest in the sacrifice. The breeze played with the boy's artful curls. His son was beautiful, but weak and vicious. How had he and Paulina bred such a creature? At the moment of conception had she

55

looked at something ill-omened? Or had there been witch-craft, a malignant daemon, or some terrible conjunction of the stars? Verus Maximus could not be allowed to inherit.

The soothsayers had predicted a dynasty of three generations from Maximinus' house. His only male relative was a second cousin. Rutilus was serving as a junior officer with Honoratus on the Danube. The youth had promise, but lacked experience. Maximinus would not wish on him the lonely, awful eminence. The soothsayers may well be mistaken. The will of the gods was hard to discern.

More and more Maximinus' consideration turned to Flavius Vopiscus. In a long series of commands, the Senator had shown courage in war, ruthless efficiency in peace. He was capable and ambitious – too ambitious, even? Could he rein it in, govern for the benefit of his subjects? Or would he be a slave to his own desires, treat the *Res Publica* as his private possession and become a tyrant? The question was unanswerable. No man's soul was completely revealed until he was above the law, beyond all restraint. At least his amulets and collections of oracles demonstrated that Flavius Vopiscus feared the gods.

Maximinus realized that he was still staring at his son. Verus Maximus would not meet his eyes. A coward as well as cruel. It was no wonder that his wife had run away. The imperial spies had reported the beatings. When Iunia Fadilla was found – how could a lone woman evade detection? – he would send her somewhere safe, away from Verus Maximus. Of course, when he retired, she would be safe. Before abdication, there would be one last, stern duty. Like a Roman of old, Maximinus would execute his son.

A hubbub broke into Maximinus' thoughts. In the deepening gloom, men were shouting. The soldiers were clashing their weapons on their shields, the trumpets were sounding.

The sun! The sun!

As Maximinus looked, the sun vanished.

In the darkness soldiers lit torches, beseeched the gods, lamented their fate.

If the sun falls, it warns of desolation for men, the death of rulers.

Maximinus' heart shrank, his courage deserting him. The treasures from the temples. It had not been sacrilege. He had not seized them for himself. Every last one of them had gone to pay for the war, to protect the temples themselves, to protect the homes of the gods. The secretary Apsines, all of the council, had said the gods offered him the treasures. There was no sacrilege. The gods should not turn against him.

The desolation of men, the death of rulers.

Apsines stepped forward. The Syrian had his hands raised like a herald at the spectacles calling for silence.

'Soldiers of Rome.'

Those nearest quietened.

'This is a terrible portent – terrible not for us, but for our enemies!'

The troops shifted in the dimness, as unconvinced as Maximinus.

'Soldiers of Rome.' Apsines had the voice of a trained Sophist, skilled in dominating an audience. 'Soldiers of Rome, remember your heritage. On the day Romulus founded the eternal city the sun failed. You march to Rome. When your Emperor Maximinus has scoured the Senate, cleansed the seven hills of traitors, exiled vice and restored virtue, it will be as if Rome was refounded.'

A sliver of light in the sky. Maximinus' spirit lifted. Perhaps the Syrian was right; he was an educated man.

'Follow Maximinus Augustus, the new Romulus, to found Rome anew. Thank the gods for this sign. Rejoice! You are the instrument of their will.'

In the gathering daylight, the troops gave a ragged cheer.

To Rome! To Rome!

57

PART II:
ITALY

CHAPTER 5

Etruria

The Hills outside the Town of Volaterrae,
Four Days before the Nones of April, AD238

Nothing separated humanity from the beasts except self-control. No one had greater need of that quality than a man who had hidden his own history. More than half a century of lies and evasions, of subterfuges and half-truths had left their mark. Pupienus knew that he had been shaped by the long decades of iron discipline, the ceaseless guard against an unconsidered word. Today he would cut the last link to the past. The severance would demand every ounce of his self-control.

The plebs thought him gloomy and aloof, even forbidding. Pupienus had nothing but contempt for their views. During the eclipse earlier, as they passed through Telamon, he had watched the plebs running here and there, howling and wailing. Surely even the meanest intelligence could grasp that it was nothing more than the moon passing between the earth and the sun. The plebs had no self-control.

The small cart rattled up the narrow track into the hills.

Pupienus turned the ring on the middle finger of his right hand, the ring containing the poison. His wife and sons, all his household, thought he was visiting the estate on the coast south of Pisae. It had been bought for that purpose. He would go there afterwards; talk to the bailiff, inspect the fields, act as if nothing had happened. Looking out at the wooded slopes, Pupienus found it hard to believe that he would never make this detour again. As ever, he travelled with just his secretary Fortunatianus. The latter drove the cart. There would be no other witnesses.

It was a bad time to be away from Rome. The next meeting of the Senate would be held in five days. In politics there was always more that could be done, but Pupienus' preparations had been thorough, indeed meticulous. He thought he could count on enough votes. The inducements he had offered should be enough to sway both the faction of the Gordiani as well as the avaricious patricians clustered around Balbinus. For the former, Valerian was promised a senior post with the imperial field army, and his brother-in-law Egnatius Lollianus the province of Pannonia Superior. Before the latter had been dangled the prospects of Rufinianus becoming Prefect of the City, and Valerius Priscillianus a travelling companion of the Emperor. Although the stroke of genius had been the mouth-watering delicacy Pupienus had set before the greed of Balbinus.

The cart lurched around a bend. Not far now. Since setting out, Pupienus had tried to fortify himself with examples of men who had put the *Res Publica* before their families. Nothing useful had come to mind, nothing Roman, or edifying. Instead the old story of Harpagus had haunted his thoughts. Harpagus had offended the King of Persia. Invited to a royal banquet, Harpagus had eaten his fill. At the end of the dinner, the King ordered a salver uncovered to reveal what Harpagus had consumed. Under the cover was the head of the courtier's beloved only son. Asked how he had liked his meal, Harpagus had managed to reply, 'At a King's table, every meal is pleasant.' That was how one ate and drank at the court of a King. One must smile at the slaughter of one's kin.

One last rise, and they were there. Pupienus told Fortunatianus to stop. He got out, and looked down on the little homestead tucked away in a fold of the hills. The simple dwelling, the yard with the cistern and the small forge. The drystone walls of pebbles from the river bound with clay. The smoke drifting over the red tile roofs. The ringing of the hammer on the anvil. It seemed impossible that he would never come here again. What he had to do was unfeasible. It was against nature. But in the pursuit of an empire there was nothing between the summit and the abyss.

Pupienus walked down the slope, and went through the gate. The aged dog lying on the dung heap recognized him, and did not bark. Getting to its feet, it came unsteadily over. Wagging its tail, it licked his hand.

The forge was as Pupienus remembered. The slave boy was standing, pumping the tall bellows, forcing air into the furnace. The aged blacksmith was perched on a stool by the small anvil. He had the head of a hunting spear in the pincers, was working it with a hammer. Pupienus noticed the hammer was lighter than his last visit.

Seeing him, a look of delight appeared on the face of the smith; quickly suppressed. Telling the boy to go and prepare food, the blacksmith quenched the spearhead, then got up, agile despite his more than eighty years. Fortunatianus had remained outside. They were alone.

Pupienus embraced the old man, inhaling the familiar scorched smell, feeling the strength that remained in the muscles of arms and shoulders.

'Health and great joy, Father.'

Not letting go, the smith leant back, regarded him.

'What is wrong?'

Pupienus took a deep breath – charcoal, hot metal, dust – and tried to find the words. 'The Gordiani are dead.'

'Even in this remote backwater, we heard.'

'The Senate intends to elect a new Emperor from the Board of Twenty.'

His father smiled, sadly. 'And you are a candidate.'

'Yes.'

They stood without speaking, holding each other like men on the edge of some disaster.

Pupienus' father broke the silence. 'You know that I never wished to be parted from you. Your brothers and sisters were dead. I had buried your mother. You would have died too. I had nothing. The man I sold you to was not unkind.'

'No, my master did not mistreat me,' Pupienus said. 'And our kinsman Pinarius soon saved the money to buy my freedom, took me to Tibur, brought me up as if I were an orphan. I have never blamed you.'

His father disengaged himself. 'But an ex-slave cannot hold a magistracy, let alone aspire to the throne. Give me the ring.'

'No!' Pupienus was shocked despite himself. 'There is no need. Apart from the two of us, only Pinarius and Fortunatianus know. My old master has been dead for more than three decades. Your slave thinks that I am an old patron of yours.'

'Give me the ring.' His father's voice was gentle. 'I am old, my strength failing. Would you deny me a peaceful release?'

Pupienus could not speak.

'My mind begins to wander. I talk to myself. Words escape my mouth unintended.'

The slave boy knocked on the door. The food was ready.

They walked across the yard to the house with its bare earth floor, sat on rustic benches. The boy sent away, they ate alone: bread, cheese, cold mutton.

'I know you cannot come here again,' his father said.

Self-control, Pupienus told himself. He could not let his discipline desert him now. He took the ring from his finger, and handed it to his father.

That was how one ate and drank at the court of a King.

CHAPTER 6

Northern Italy

The Aesontius River,
Four Days before the Nones of April, AD238

Menophilus was back at the bridge over the Aesontius, gazing down at the Pons Sonti from almost the same place. But the circumstances were different. Last time it had been night, now it was day. Then he had ten men, now four hundred. Then he had been hunted, now he was the hunter. The gods had looked graciously on his endeavours.

It did not do to tempt fate. If the day went well, if he survived, he would make an offering. Nothing extravagant, not an empty show of ostentatious wealth, but give the gods something he valued. The small, silver *memento mori* of a skeleton would serve. He had worn it on his belt for years, thought it brought him luck. He would dedicate it in the Temple of Belenus in Aquileia. Menophilus smiled. Once he had thought he was on the path to Stoic wisdom, now he accepted that he had not advanced a step. Far from a sage, he was still a fool mired in superstition.

If the gods had not had a hand, a strange combination of

efficiency and negligence on the part of his enemy had given Menophilus this opportunity. With the competence of years in the field, Flavius Vopiscus had built the pontoon bridge, got the siege train across the river, and marched off towards his objective. All had been accomplished with alacrity, yet, displaying a carelessness that could only have come from an utter contempt for those ranged against him, Maximinus' general had not thought it necessary to bring any cavalry. It had made the task of Menophilus' scouts simple. Operating in pairs – one from the 1st Cohort, and a local volunteer – they had kept their distance. Menophilus had no wish to disturb the complacency of Vopiscus. All he needed to know was the whereabouts of Vopiscus' main force.

The four thousand or so Pannonian legionaries that comprised the advance guard of the imperial army were camped, along with the wagons carrying the disassembled siege engines, ten miles to the west on the Via Gemina, about six miles north-east of Aquileia. Informed of that, Menophilus' strategy had been obvious. A night march from the city, east along the Via Flavia to reach the river, and then follow the stream north. Get behind Vopiscus, approach the bridge without his knowledge. The farm had been a worry. Half a mile from the site of the Pons Sonti, when Menophilus had been here before, it had contained an enemy piquet. They could warn the garrison of the bridge. Extraordinarily – yet more evidence of lax overconfidence – the guard had been withdrawn from the farm. The house, barn, sheds, and huge wine barrels were all empty. Now Menophilus' auxiliaries were resting in the farmstead, eating cold rations as an early midday meal, waiting for his signal.

Menophilus himself was back in the woods, lying, wrapped in a dark cloak, among the beech trees and elms, under whose boughs young Barbius had been hacked to death. He pushed the thought away. Guilt served no purpose. What

67

could not be changed was an irrelevance. The youth's father would not see it, but death was nothing. It was a release.

The river was even higher than before. Its waters surging through the roots of the willows on its banks, breaking white over the remains of the piers of the demolished stone bridge, tugging with immeasurable force at the pontoons of its replacement. The little rowing boat had gone; perhaps, if carelessly moored, it might have been swept downstream by the force of the current.

Waiting was the hardest part of battle. Menophilus did not fear death. What was life but standing in the breech, awaiting the barbed arrow? Nothing was certain in war – one should never take the favour of the gods for granted – but he had few doubts about the outcome of the day. Below him less than a hundred men of the 10th Legion Gemina still guarded the nearer, western end of the bridge. There were more enemy troops at the far end; among the trees, their numbers could not be gauged, but there was no reason to think them any greater. Menophilus outnumbered the foe, by two to one, or more. Surprise was on his side. Wait for the right moment, when the legionaries were at their most unready, a sudden charge, seize the bridge, and sever the cables securing the pontoons. The river would do the rest. Vopiscus, the advance guard and the siege train, would be isolated on the Aquileian side of the Aesontius. Maximinus and the main army left stranded on the other. It would not win the war, but it would delay and frustrate the enemy.

The eight men who would wield the axes and cut the bridge were volunteers. Menophilus had consulted an engineer, a sardonic individual called Patricius. Part the cables holding together the two central pontoons, and the river in spate would tear the rest of the structure apart in moments. The volunteers had been promised great rewards, comparable to those first over the walls in the storming of a city. Their names were all listed, as were those of their dependants. In the myth Horatius, the bridge demolished behind him, had swum the Tiber in full armour. Today, Patricius assured him, many, perhaps all of the men with axes would be claimed by the Aesontius.

Menophilus watched the grey-green water rushing past, inexorable and carrying all manner of flotsam. His eyes rested on a branch, a drowned cat, another branch; always changing, always the same. When he had been here before, his duty had seemed clear. The Gordiani were dead. His post was at Aquileia. Who the Senate placed upon the throne was none of his concern. He would remain at Aquileia, defend it to the best of his ability, defend it to the last. Now he was not so sure. Had grief warped his judgement? Maecia Faustina and the boy Junius Balbus remained in Rome. Young Gordian had never been close to his sister or nephew, but they were his blood. With a new regime, the relatives of the old rulers were at risk. The house of the Gordiani was wealthy, its stored-up treasures might provoke the cupidity of any new Emperor. Should Menophilus have left the defence of Aquileia to his colleague Crispinus? Should he have gone to Rome to safeguard the *Domus Rostrata* and its inhabitants, to protect a widow and her child?

What of the pitiful remnants of the *familia* that had escaped from the disaster in Africa? With old Valens the Chamberlain had come Gordian's concubine, Parthenope. She was pregnant. If Parthenope had not been a slave, and if the child she carried was a boy, he would have been heir to the throne. For a Stoic, freedom and slavery were not defined by the laws. Inside every individual was a spark of the divine *Logos*. If his soul was servile, the King of Persia was a slave, while, if such was his nature, the lowest slave in chains could be a King. Outside Rome, in the Villa Praenestina, there were already many slaves fathered by the younger Gordian.

Somehow this unborn child was different. Menophilus had dined and laughed with Parthenope. It did not seem right that his friend's posthumous child should live in servitude.

Down by the river, smoke was curling up from the cook fires. The legionaries were beginning to mill about, starting to prepare food. Only ten of them still stood to arms, a few yards out in the road. It was time.

Menophilus turned to Flavius Adiutor, the Prefect of the 1st Cohort.

'Bring up your men. The show should begin.'

With heightened senses, Menophilus tracked the departure of Adiutor; the chink of his armour, the snap of each twig, the suck of mud at his boots. It had rained very hard in the night, but the blustery wind from the south-west had blown away the clouds. The sun shone from a ceramic blue sky, dappling the road where the trees overhung. Yet if the wind remained set, it would bring more storms.

No body of troops ever moved in silence. You could order them to muffle their arms, wrap their boots in rags, but it was almost impossible to convince them of the necessity of removing the good luck charms from their belts. What was the point of silence, if it might occasion your death? Menophilus was in no position to judge them. He heard the jingle of ornaments of Adiutor's men before the tramp of their feet. Eyes never leaving the legionaries down by the bridge, he could not help grinning at his own prescience. The customary levity of meal times – the shouts and songs, the clatter of utensils – would mask the sound of the approaching auxiliaries. The timing was perfect, and his men were fed, the enemy hungry. An empty belly sapped a man's courage.

Menophilus warned himself against taking pride in his fore-sight. Do not tempt the gods. Worldly success was worthless.

Slipping back through the wood, Menophilus waited for

the auxiliaries around the bend in the road, out of sight from the bridge. They came into view. Five Centuries, steel helmets, mailcoats, weather-beaten faces above oval shields; these were hard men, veterans transferred from the East by Maximinus for his northern wars. Now they would fight against the Thracian. All men were bound to fate, like a dog to a cart.

They halted, and Menophilus went through the plan once again with Adiutor and the Centurions. One Century was to remain here, as a reserve. The others were to go down to the river. Around the corner, it was less than a hundred paces to the Aesontius. They should charge at a jog, maintain silence, keep their order, shout their war cry just before contact, chase the guards away. Two Centuries were to stay on this western bank, no unnecessary killing, accept the surrender and disarm any legionaries who had not fled. The leading two Centuries were to follow those who escaped across the bridge, drive off the troops at the far end, then return. They should leave behind just two *Contubernia* on the eastern side. Twenty men should suffice – the walkway of the pontoon was no more than eight paces wide. Menophilus would send in the men who would cut the bridge. When it was about to give, the two *Contubernia* would be recalled.

The volunteers with axes fell in behind Menophilus, at the side of the road. The officers returned to their stations. No trumpet calls or bellowed orders – these troops knew their business – just a nod from Adiutor, and they set off.

Menophilus moved through the trees parallel to the column to find a point of vantage. The forlorn hope hefted their axes, and followed him. It was best not to think about them.

The leading auxiliaries were around the bend, clattering twenty or more paces down the incline, before the alarm was raised.

71

Enemy in sight! Many voices were shouting at once.

The ten legionaries in the piquet raised their shields, shuffled together, all the time yelling for support, and glancing over their shoulders. Their companions ran here and there to snatch up their weapons. They were getting in each other's way, cursing and shouting, stumbling and tripping over cooking pots and all the other impedimenta of a camp in uproar.

Watching from above, Menophilus did not let himself smile. Never tempt fate.

Ulpia Galatarum! Menophilus' men shouted as one.

When the war cry of the auxiliary Cohort rang out, the legionaries broke. Taken unawares, in complete disorder, faced by an avalanche of steel, they could not be blamed. Some ran into the woods on either side. More dropped their arms, held out their hands in supplication. Yet the majority turned and rushed to the bridge. There they jostled and fought to get onto the pontoon, and then, casting shields into the water, they ran pell-mell across.

The two designated Centuries of auxiliaries were hard on their heels.

With more warning, the legionaries at the far end of the bridge had time to form up, shoulder to shoulder, shields overlapping, blocking the walkway. But it was their own tent-mates who crashed into them, hauling their shields aside, desperate to get away. Like a badly made dam, the shieldwall held for a moment, then collapsed under the pressure. On the eastern side of the Aesontius, figures vanished up the bank, into the woodland. Resistance was at an end.

Going down to the bridge, Menophilus and the volunteers waited for the troops to stream back across. Adiutor was everywhere, roaring commands, rounding up prisoners, restoring order. The operation could not have gone better: a bloodless battle, a victory without tears.

Walking out onto the now empty bridge, Menophilus'

boots sounded hollow on the planks. A few feet below those thin boards, he could sense the rush of the river. The pontoon seemed a fragile, impertinent thing in the face of such power. Reaching the centre, he took stock. The post of twenty auxiliaries at the eastern end, Adiutor getting the remainder, and the thirty or so prisoners, under control on the western bank. All was in hand, but there was no reason to delay.

As Menophilus turned to the waiting men a cloud darkened the sun.

'Cut the cable holding the anchor of this barge.'

The men did not move. They were staring at the sky.

'There is no time to waste.'

The nearest soldier dropped his axe, raised his arms to the heavens. Another sank to his knees. They all began to shout; incoherent, terrified prayers.

It was getting darker; more like night than day.

Menophilus looked up. The sun was vanishing. Not a cloud, but an eclipse.

If the sun falls, it brings desolation to men! The soldiers were wailing and sobbing like women. *Desolation and death!*

'It is nothing,' Menophilus called, 'an eclipse, a shadow.'

Lost in dread, the men ignored him.

'It is not a portent. It is just the moon passing between the earth and the sun.'

Pray to the gods, pray for the return of the sun!

Menophilus took off his cloak, held it in front of the eyes of the nearest soldier. 'Is this alarming? Is this a terrible omen?'

He whisked the cloak away. The man stared at him, open-mouthed, not speaking.

'What is the difference, except the eclipse is caused by something bigger than my cloak?'

In the murk, the soldiers stopped weeping. They stood, trembling like frightened animals.

'You are soldiers of Rome, not irrational barbarians, or effete easterners. Master yourselves, remember you are men, recover your discipline.'

His words were greeted by an uncertain silence. Not all men were amenable to reason.

'The gods control the cosmos.' Which was true in a sense. 'When we return safe to Aquileia, we will sacrifice an ox to Helios, the sun god, another to the god of the river. See, the moon is passing from the face of the sun, the light returning.'

With the daylight, the men's courage returned. Some looked shamefaced, but others were still evidently shaken. Hard labour and the very real dangers of the river in spate would take their minds off the eclipse.

The downpour in the night had combined with the spring melt from the mountains to make the Aesontius rise dangerously. The barges were riding higher than allowed for by the engineers who had built the bridge. The anchor of the central one on which Menophilus stood had dragged. Its cable was now at an angle of no more than forty degrees; not enough to hold against the stream were the barge not lashed to those on either side. The others were much the same. The anchor of one, however, had caught. It was now dragging the prow of its barge down towards the surface. The pontoon was under intense stress, yet it would stand, unless something intervened. Menophilus gave the order to cut the anchor rope.

As two of the men clambered onto the prow, and prepared to wield their axes, a messenger ran back from the advance post on the enemy side of the river. There were troops moving in the woods to the east. Menophilus kept the runner with him. He could not see the enemy yet. Anyway, there was nothing to be done. The handful of men on the far bank would have to hold.

The axes bit down into the cable. It was thick, waterlogged, taut as if woven of steel. The impact of every stroke vibrated through the barge. Suddenly, like a clap of thunder, it parted. One end shot away into the river like a water snake. The other narrowly missed the legs of one of the axemen. The decking shifted under Menophilus' feet, the barge wallowed, lurched backwards. The screech of tortured ropes and wood was loud over the roar of the river. The additional strain pulled at the cables that ran laterally from barge to barge, and up the risers to the banks.

Originally Menophilus' plan had been to sever the bindings from the Aquileian bank. It would have been infinitely safer for those doing the cutting. Yet, Patricius had told him there was the possibility that the pontoon would swing like a hinge, and many of the barges might come to rest against the far bank. If undamaged, they would allow Maximinus' men to quickly repair the bridge. Menophilus had taken the engineer's advice, and made the hard decision to break the centre of the structure.

The runner was sent to recall the outpost from the far end of the bridge.

Menophilus spotted a flash of movement in the treeline on the opposite shore. The enemy had rallied fast, much faster than he had expected. There was not a moment to lose. The bridge must be destroyed before it could be retaken.

The men of the piquet ran past, boots drumming on the woodwork. Menophilus told the axemen to turn their attentions to the ropes securing the barge to its neighbour. They hefted their blades. He hesitated, trying to think of something to say. Nothing came to him. He turned, and ran after the others, towards safety.

Looking back from the bank, the scene was set out like some grand spectacle in the Flavian Amphitheatre: the dark green hills beyond, the pale line of the pontoon crossing the roiling waters of the river. There were two ropes at the prow of the barge, two at the stern. The men worked in pairs, legs braced, blades flashing in the sun.

Now there was a new audience: a Century of enemy legionaries on the far bank. Their Centurion, marked out by his bronze helmet with its jaunty transverse crest, was belabouring them with the vine stick of his office. Again and again he brought it down on their backs, trying to force them to move out onto the bridge. Enduring his blows and imprecations, they would not budge.

A crack echoed above the noise of the river. A rope at the prow of the barge whipped back, dashed one of the axemen to the decking. The rope next to it parted. Another man went down. With an awful inevitability, the pontoon began to give, bowing downstream. The men on their feet dropped their axes, started to run back towards Menophilus and safety. Two loud reports, and the ropes at the stern snapped. The bridge parted, the force of the floodwater forcing its sides apart.

The decking heaved and swayed under the feet of the running men. They staggered, reeling side to side, as if drunk. One went sprawling. Green water spumed up between the planks. Fifty paces to go. Behind them, a barge ripped free, ropes hissing murderously through the air. Then a second, and a third. Thirty paces. The men lurched, fell to their knees, scrabbled forward. Then the walkway in front of them splintered and tipped, and the whole pontoon came apart, unstitched along its entire length.

The heavy barges spun, ramming into each other, crushing everything in between. All of Menophilus' men were gone, except two. In the chaos of wreckage, they clung to an upright barge. Their shouts could be heard above the din. The barge swung out into midstream, turned side on to the torrent. Slowly, very slowly, it tilted, and overturned. And there was no more shouting.

'The men are ready, the prisoners secured.' Adiutor's voice was flat, betraying no emotion or criticism.

'Have the men form column of march.'

'We will do what is ordered, and at every command we will be ready.'

Menophilus looked out at the Aesontius, at its waters as they swept the debris downstream, and he felt the relentless, remorseless pounding of guilt. It was like the river; it never stopped.

CHAPTER 7

Rome

The Temple of Jupiter Optimus Maximus,
Eight Days before the Ides of April, AD238

The eunuchs were dancing in the Forum. It was a bad omen.
Wailing, clashing cymbals, they capered away from the armed
guard. The eunuchs were everywhere, the streets full of their
cacophony. It was the third day of the festival of Magna
Mater. The courts were closed, and the Senate should not
convene. Yet there were few days in April without one festival
or another. Even an Asiatic deity, an immigrant like Cybele,
accepted that in an emergency the *Res Publica* took precedence. And it was the anniversary of Caesar defeating the
Numidians; that, at least, was auspicious.

Pupienus walked under the Arch of Septimius Severus.
In the crowded reliefs above his head, the Emperor made a
speech, his troops took cities, battering rams shook walls,
barbarians surrendered, and gods looked on in approval. The
scenes of overwhelming triumph were timeless, all the more
powerful for being divorced from narrative. Severus had been
a fine Emperor; certainly stern, and a terror to his enemies

at home and abroad. Pupienus owed much to Severus, and would keep his example in mind.

As Pupienus and his entourage ascended, their progress was hindered by gangs of plebs drifting up to the Capitol. Unlike the eunuchs, the sordid plebs did not leap aside. Some stood, with dumb insolence, until the guards shoved them out of the way. As Pupienus passed, the plebs – men and women – regarded him with silent hostility. Pupienus knew they thought him harsh, blamed him for the deaths in the Temple of Venus and Rome the previous year. The plebs were fools. There had been only a few killed. As Prefect of the City, he had ordered the Urban Cohorts to use cudgels, not their swords. He had left the side gates clear for the rioters to escape. If it had not been for him, the Praetorians would have been sent in, and massacred everyone in the holy precinct. As it was, his clemency had cost him his office. Maximinus had dismissed him for *insufficient zeal in his duties*. Now he was Prefect of the City again, and, if the gods were kind, by dusk he would be something greater. He put the plebs out of his thoughts. They were not worth considering.

They came out onto the summit of the Capitol by the altar of Jupiter Optimus Maximus. Behind it loomed the huge temple of Rome's patron deity. The gilded doors and roof of the home of the *Best and Greatest* god glittered in the sun.

There were more of the plebs up here. Off to one side, they clustered around the statue of Tiberius Gracchus, the long-dead demagogue and would-be tyrant they regarded as their martyred champion. It had been erected on the spot where he had been beaten to death by patriotic Senators intent on saving the *Res Publica*. The plebs did not concern Pupienus. Let them wait outside the doors, while their betters decided the fate of the empire.

Pupienus walked up the steps, through the tall columns, and, leaving his bodyguards at the doors, into the inner sanctum. The *cella* was tall and dark. Already there were several hundred Senators murmuring on the ranks of benches set out along the sides. Looking neither left nor right, Pupienus walked the length of the chamber, and stopped before the statue of Jupiter. At a small, portable altar, he made a libation of wine, and offered a pinch of incense into the fire. Jupiter – seated, massive, and chryselephantine – gazed over Pupienus' head at the smoke coiling up to the ceiling.

Piety satisfied, Pupienus acknowledged the presiding Consul, Licinius Rufinus. He took his place on the front bench in the midst of his supporters. On either side were Praetextatus and Tineius Sacerdos; both also ex-Consuls and fellow members of the Board of Twenty. Their combined friends and relatives were ranked about them.

The opposite benches contained Balbinus, and his repellent coterie of patricians. Prominent among them was Rufinianus. It was contemptible, and utterly predictable, that Rufinianus, also one of the Twenty, had abandoned his assigned post defending the passes over the Apennines, and scurried back to Rome to see what personal advantage he could secure.

Pupienus lifted his eyes, let them wander over the golden eagles, whose wings supported the roof. It was in the lap of the gods. He had done all that he could. Balbinus was bought and paid for. His cruel, sensuous mouth had slobbered at the offer. Undoubtedly it would not stop him reneging on his word, if his greed spotted something yet more tempting on the table. The avarice and vanity of the other patricians had been accommodated; not that they were any more to be relied upon.

Returning his gaze to the floor of the hall, Pupienus sought out Valerian. Broad and solid, with an open, trusting face, he sat modestly some way from the tribunal of the Consul. Of course inducements had been offered and accepted, but Valerian was a dutiful man, and would do what he had been persuaded was best for the *Res Publica* in this time of danger.

80

By default leader of what remained of the faction of the Gordiani in Rome, Valerian brought with him the allegiance of the commanders of those troops in the city not already under the command of Pupienus himself. Yet Valerian had vetoed bringing soldiers onto the Capitol. Pupienus had conceded the point. The impression created would have been one of military tyranny. The guard of young men from the equestrian order was altogether more fitting. It evoked that of Cicero in his finest hour; when he saved the state, defending *libertas* from the conspiracy of Catiline.

The bodyguard had been the idea of Timesitheus. An equestrian himself, within hours, the *Praefectus Annonae* had raised a hundred stalwart youths from good families, equipped them with swords. The stock of Timesitheus stood high. The first in the field against Maximinus, he had slain the Thracian's Prefect of the Camp. He had organized irregular forces to harass Maximinus' communications and supply lines over the Alps, had risked his life and taken a wound escaping from the tyrant's men, and ridden post-haste to bring the news to Rome. The bandages on his left hand were widely regarded as a badge of honour. Pupienus did not trust him. There was no denying his capacity, but a strange light burned in the dark eyes of the Greek; a light of ambition unrestrained by any morality or compassion. Now Timesitheus had armed men at his beck and call, and, as *Praefectus Annonae*, he controlled the grain supply of Rome. Timesitheus needed watching very closely. Any Emperor might feel the need to be rid of such a dangerous subject.

'Let all who are not Conscript Fathers depart. Let no one remain except the Senators.'

The ritual words of the Consul were to be taken literally. This was to be a closed session. The clerks, scribes and other servants, public and private, filed out. Licinius ordered the doors shut and bolted.

81

'Let good auspices and joyful fortune attend the people of Rome.'

There were no windows, and the only light came from torches in archaic sconces on the walls. Shadows massed in the recesses, flitted across the walls; insubstantial yet threatening, like the souls of the dead. The air was close, sickly with incense. Pupienus was sweating, his chest tight. From long habit, he went to turn the ring which was no longer on his finger. The throne was almost within his grasp, the reward for a lifetime of endeavour and self-control, the culmination of his rise from obscurity. When his patron Septimius Severus ascended the throne, he had himself adopted into the imperial dynasty. Some wit had congratulated Severus on finding a father. No one would find Pupienus' father now. The familiar, terrible emotions of guilt and love gathered in the darkness at his back, and were now joined by an aching sense of loss.

'Conscript Fathers, give us your advice.'

At the Consul's words, two men got to their feet.

'I humbly request permission to address the House.' There was no humility in Gallicanus' harsh voice, and none whatsoever in his ostentatiously homespun toga, with its conscious air of antique virtue and moral superiority.

'Publius Licinius Valerian will address the house,' the Consul said.

Gallicanus raised his voice. 'In the name of *libertas*, I demand to speak to prevent tyranny.'

'Valerian has the floor.'

Gallicanus sat down. He wore a look of grim satisfaction on his face, as if yet again given evidence of the moral deliquescence of his fellow Senators.

'I am well aware, Conscript Fathers, that when events press, we should refrain from lengthy words and opinions.' The innocent, guileless face of Valerian shone with sincerity.

82

'Let each of us look to his own neck, let him think of his wife and children, of his father's and his father's father's goods. All these Maximinus threatens, by nature irrational, savage and bloodthirsty.'

Valerian had a natural dignity. Pupienus wondered if he was too credulous to sit on the throne.

'There is no need for a long speech. We must make an Emperor, to confront the dangers of war, to manage the affairs of state. We must choose a man of experience, an intelligent and shrewd man of sober habits. I recommend to the house the Prefect of the City, Marcus Clodius Pupienus Maximus.'

It is right, it is just. The shouts rang up to the roof. *Pupienus Augustus, save the Res Publica. Aequum est, iustum est.*

Pupienus composed his expression, and – weighty *dignitas* personified – rose to his feet.

It is right, it is just.

Pupienus noted that Balbinus could not bring himself to join in the acclamations. How Pupienus loathed and despised that bloated wine-sack that passed for a man.

'Conscript Fathers,' Pupienus tried to put Balbinus from his thoughts, 'to wear the purple is to wear the yoke of slavery; a noble slavery, but servitude all the same. The Emperor is a slave to the common good, to the *Res Publica*. Duty lies hard on an Emperor. The task is daunting, and, as Jupiter is my witness, not one to which I aspire. Yet when Maximinus, whom you and I declared a public enemy, is upon us, and the two Gordiani, in whom was our defence, are slain, it is my duty to accept.'

Pupienus Augustus, may the gods keep you!

Again Balbinus remained silent. Even the patricians around him chanted, but Balbinus did not so much as mouth the words. Centuries of privilege, countless generations of office, had created that monster of self-satisfied complacency and arrogance. A lifetime of indulgence and ease had

83

nurtured perversity and depravity. The pig-like eyes regarded Pupienus with malevolence.

Pupienus looked from Balbinus to Valerian; the latter honest and decent, the other a sack of faeces.

'In a time of revolution, the duties of an Emperor are too heavy for one man. Conscript Fathers, you must clothe two men in the purple; one to rule the city, one to go out and meet the tyrant with an army. When I take the field against Maximinus, Rome must be left in safe hands.'

There was silence now, all eyes fixed upon Pupienus.

'Conscript Fathers, I recommend to you a man of illustrious birth, a man dear to the state by reason both of his gentle character and of his blameless life, which from the earliest years he has passed in study and in letters.'

The bitter medicine must be swallowed; the unpalatable words said.

'You have my opinion, Decimus Caelius Calvinus Balbinus must be raised to share the throne, in all its powers and duties.'

Balbinus Augustus, may the gods keep you.

Balbinus' porcine features shone with undisguised triumph.

It is right, it is just. Balbinus and Pupienus Augusti, what the Senate has given you, take gladly.

Amid the uproar, few noticed the unbolting of the doors. Pupienus watched Gallicanus, his intimate friend Maecenas, and two other Senators slip out. Withdrawal could form the basis of a charge of treason. But let them go, let them play Thrasea or some other philosophic sage, who had courted martyrdom by their refusal to attend their Emperors in the Senate. Their resistance was puerile. They could achieve nothing.

'We present to you, Conscript Fathers, a proposal that imperial powers be voted . . .' The Consul began the formula that would free two men from all temporal restraint.

'And that it be lawful for them to issue orders to all

84

governors of provinces, by right of their overriding military authority, and that it be lawful for them to declare war and peace, and that it be lawful for them to make a treaty with whomsoever they should wish, just as it was lawful for the divine Augustus.'

Pupienus closed his eyes, let the sonorous words flow over him, and considered the tasks that lay ahead. He would go to Ravenna, raise troops there. With its lagoons and marshes, it was a good defensive site. If Aquileia fell, Maximinus would not be able to march on Rome leaving Ravenna behind unconquered. The Adriatic fleet could bring supplies and reinforcements into the town, and, in dire necessity, provide a means of escape.

Balbinus would remain in Rome, empowered to maintain order in the city. Most likely, he would relapse into torpor and vice. Should the patrician venture anything particularly ill-advised or detrimental to the public good, reliable men would be at hand to restrain him, or, at least, give Pupienus timely warning.

Defence alone would not win the war, or eliminate Maximinus. Nothing had been heard from the North. No word from Castricius, the knife-boy discovered by Timesitheus and sent by Menophilus to assassinate the Thracian. Either Castricius had been caught, or he had not made the attempt. If captured, the youth would have died in agony. If he had lost his nerve, the same fate would befall him if he were ever seen in Rome again. Likewise, the Procurator Axius had not yet seized control of the province of Dacia. Another initiative was necessary. Someone must be despatched to attempt to win over the governors along the Danube. Behind enemy lines, in the heartlands of Maximinus' support, the odds against success were long. There was a Senator called Celsinus. An ex-Praetor, his estates were mortgaged far beyond their value. Celsinus was desperate enough to put everything on one roll of the dice to restore his fortunes.

The East was more promising. Catius Clemens, the governor of Cappadocia, was the key. Clemens had been one of the triumvirate that had put Maximinus on the throne. Pupienus had spent long hours cloistered with Clemens' younger brother, Celer. The provisional arrangement reached might satisfy the family of the Catii. Young Celer would go from Rome to govern Thrace. While there he would be Consul *in absentia*. The eldest brother, Priscillianus, would retain Germania Superior for two years, with the province of his choice to follow. Clemens himself would leave Cappadocia. Returning to Rome, he would be enrolled in the Board of Twenty, and be entrusted with the defence of the eternal city.

Pupienus' close friend Cuspidius had agreed to travel to the East. It was a terrible risk. There was no guarantee that Clemens would not remain loyal to Maximinus, or even aim for the throne himself. In either event, Cuspidius would suffer an awful fate. Pupienus had no desire to be responsible for the torture and death of his friend. But with the throne came terrible decisions.

'And that whatever is undertaken, carried out, decreed or ordered by the Emperors Pupienus Augustus and Balbinus Augustus, or by anyone according to their command or mandate, they shall be lawful and binding, as if they had been undertaken according to the order of Senate and people of Rome.'

The thing was done. Now, according to tradition, the new Emperors should make offerings to the gods at the altar in front of the temple, then process down to the Forum, and speak to the people of Rome from the Rostra.

As the doors were opened, and the Senators arranged themselves in order of precedence, Balbinus waddled up to Pupienus. They shook hands. It was like grasping a fish.

'You had better keep your word.' Balbinus' breath reeked

of wine. 'I will not be inferior to someone like you in anything. We must both be Pontifex Maximus.'

'I gave my word.'

The drink had not dulled Balbinus' covetous nature. The compromises and unworthy innovations required to gain power sickened Pupienus. Never had two men held the office of Pontifex Maximus, never had there been a less fitting intermediary between Rome and the gods than Balbinus. If it should prove possible to remove him, without doubt the gods would applaud. The joint reign should not be long enduring. Kingship was indivisible.

Outside the light was bright. They paused for a moment at the top of the steps.

The plebs – hundreds, if not thousands of them – stood in a wide semi-circle. Nearer at hand, the young equestrians cheered. Few of the plebs joined the acclamation.

At the altar, Balbinus took it on himself to address his new subjects.

'The Senators, with Jupiter as fellow councillor and guardian of their acts, have vested in me the powers of an Emperor. One man alone cannot rule Rome and crush the bandits who march against us over the Alps. In my care for your safety, I have elevated Marcus Clodius Pupienus Maximus as my colleague. Rejoice, your troubles are at an end!'

The equestrians set up a chant.

Blessed is the judgement of the Senate, happy is Rome in your rule!

The massed ranks of the plebs greeted this with an ominous silence.

What the Senate has given, take gladly!

Obscured by the crush, men pushed through the midst of the crowd. To his left, Pupienus caught the white gleam of a toga, in another place got a glimpse of a slight, hooded figure that he half recognized. Near the latter, a man stepped forward.

'Only the people have the right to pass law. Only the people can elect an Emperor.'

The man shouting wore a leather apron, high-belted. An innkeeper, one of the lowest of the low.

'We do not want your cruel old Emperors. Let the people choose!'

Balbinus rounded on some of the equestrians. 'Arrest that criminal.'

'Jupiter is our only ruler!' Others took up the innkeeper's shout.

Three equestrians grabbed the innkeeper. He struggled.

Jupiter is our only ruler!

The first stone flew, then another.

Jupiter our only ruler!

The third missile hit Balbinus on the shoulder. He bellowed with pain, then screamed at the equestrians: 'Use your swords, kill them all!'

The mob surged forward, engulfed the innkeeper. The three equestrians were down, being kicked and beaten.

Behind Pupienus the good and the great stampeded back up to the comparative safety of the temple.

'Kill all the scum!' Balbinus howled.

Timesitheus was at Pupienus' elbow. 'Augustus, retire into the temple.'

With what *dignitas* he could maintain – stones rattling off the marble – Pupienus went back up the steps. Disappointingly, Balbinus blundered past. For a moment, Pupienus had hoped outraged stupidity might have left Balbinus to be torn apart by the mob.

Pupienus paused at the doors, looked back. Timesitheus and the equestrians, blades in hand, were backing up the steps. The hail of stones had ceased.

In the *cella*, all the Senators were talking at once, like a flock of frightened birds.

Balbinus came up to Pupienus, grabbed the folds of his toga. 'This is all your fault. There is no way out. We are trapped.'

Pupienus disengaged the grasping hands. The doors were not shut, but blocked by the armed young men. Pupienus went over to Timesitheus. 'Do you think you can get through them?'

'I am not a Senator. They should not harm me.'

'Go and summon the troops.'

A strange light danced in Timesitheus' eyes, like a candle behind glass. 'Trust me, Augustus, and see what will happen. I will save you all.'

CHAPTER 8

Rome

The Temple of Jupiter Optimus Maximus,
Eight Days before the Ides of April, AD238

Caenis wanted to see them elect a new Emperor. She had gone to watch the eunuchs dancing in front of the Temple of Cybele the day before, but had not got tickets for the theatre, and it was days until the next festival.

She had packed a simple meal – bread, cheese, a couple of hard-boiled eggs, some lettuce, and a flask of wine – and invited the old die-cutter to go with her. Although sometimes she let him into her bed for free, she had no great affection for her neighbour. Yet long experience had taught her that she would be bothered less if she were accompanied by a man. To the same end, she had dressed like a respectable woman: a long, plain gown, bands in her hair, sensible sandals, no jewellery or make-up. Many girls would be working the streets during the Festival of Magna Mater, but Caenis had not applied for a permit. It was not that she did not need the money, rather that she thought she had found other ways to raise what was necessary to escape her life, leave Rome, and reinvent herself.

They walked through the Forum, under the arch to some dead Emperor, and started up towards the Capitol. Although it was early, there were many others going up the hill. The die-cutter was still limping from the wound he had taken in the knife fight in the Street of the Sandal-makers. She let him carry the blanket and the basket.

'Clear the path!'

A solid phalanx of well-dressed men was coming up behind them.

'Make way for the Prefect of the City!'

The young equestrians in the vanguard were shoving the plebs to the side of the path.

The die-cutter took her arm, and drew her out of the way. He muttered something about turning the other cheek.

Ringed by armed guards, Pupienus, the *Praefectus Urbi*, swept past. He was a stern-looking old man, with a long, forked beard. Some of the bystanders hissed him. Men had died when he had used the Urban Cohorts to clear demonstrators from the Temple of Venus and Rome. Just as they never forgot their heroes, the plebs of the city were very slow to forgive a man who had harmed them.

Despite his past, and his grim demeanour, Caenis thought Pupienus had gone some way to redeem himself. He had taken a stand against Maximinus. That counted for something. Maximinus was nothing more than a barbarian tyrant. In the three years since he had taken the throne, not once had he come to Rome, let alone shown himself to his people. Worse still, Maximinus had limited the number of shows and spectacles, and used his soldiers to plunder the treasures stored in the temples of the gods. All the money he had stolen had been squandered either on his pointless northern wars, or on deifying his ugly dead wife; a woman that many said he had murdered with his own hands.

It was right that Maximinus should be overthrown. Caenis

hoped that Pupienus and the other Senators would choose a good Emperor; someone young and beautiful, amiable and generous. The plebs wanted an Emperor who would live among them in Rome, not with the army on some distant frontier. They wanted an Emperor who would restore the spectacles and, attending them in person, would listen to the demands of his subjects, and grant them with an open hand. Menophilus, the young Senator she had once seen make a speech in the Forum, would make a good Emperor. He was handsome, would look good in the purple.

Coming out onto the square dominated by the great Temple of Jupiter, Caenis and the die-cutter went across to a small sanctuary on one side where the throng was less dense. Finding a space on the steps, Caenis busied herself spreading the blanket, opening the basket, unwrapping the food. She felt like a young matron with an older husband.

'The sanctuary of Abundance, a good place to eat,' the die-cutter said.

Caenis said nothing.

'The women gather here for the Saecular Games held every hundred years. Heralds go through the lands inviting people to something they have never seen, and will never see again.'

'How do you know these things?'

'I read books. My eyesight is good close to, things further away are a problem.'

Caenis did not reply. Other people's knowledge always struck her as an accusation against herself. It was not her fault she was illiterate. She had not chosen her life. She had been twelve, and still called Rhodope, when her mother sent her to her first man. It was a hard world. You learnt that earlier, or you learnt it later. It made no difference. She did not blame her mother. When her father had died, her mother had sold his anvil and hammer, all the rest of his tools. After that money ran out, her mother had earned a pittance by weaving. They had survived in one room, in a tenement in a poor quarter of Ephesus. Her mother had waited for her one remaining asset to mature. A daughter's good looks, like a dead husband's possessions, were there to be sold.

Caenis spread the food and drink before the die-cutter. He took only some bread and a little lettuce. He did not touch a drop of wine. His abstinence must be a religious thing, some form of fasting. The die-cutter was unaware that Caenis knew that he was a Christian. There was an illicit thrill in sitting with an atheist who stood outside the law. The knowledge that his life was in her hands was exciting. She could inform against him – he would be executed – and she would be rewarded. Perhaps, before that, he could be put to other uses. Musalia, the other girl who worked in the bar, would think such thoughts were wrong. But Musalia was a tender-hearted fool. Everyone in life made their own choices.

Caenis had left Ephesus after her mother died, when a pimp had tried to control her. All the money in the world flowed into Rome. She had thought that she would get more for her body there. Booking her passage, she had ceased to be Rhodope, instead calling herself Caenis: *Bitch*. A hard name for a hard world.

Since childhood, she had never been as happy as on the voyage. Sailors were superstitious. Sex brought bad luck on a ship. No one had pestered her. She remembered the sun and the spray, the odd pitching motion, the strange smells of salt and tar, mutton fat and bleached wood. She remembered the islands, the semi-circular harbours, the white houses on the hills beyond, tranquil in the sun. Their names were poetry: Zacynthos, Cephalonia, Corcyra.

More and more people came up to the Capitol. The crowd hung back from the altar of Jupiter, but clustered thickly around the statue of Tiberius Gracchus. When the golden doors of the great temple were closed for the meeting of the

Senate, the plebs murmured unhappily. There was a tension, an air of expectation. Individuals moved with purpose through the throng, talking insistently to groups here and there. Sometimes there were brief chants of *Libertas, libertas.*

Caenis smiled at the die-cutter. 'Stop looking so gloomy. You may not be the best-looking man that has ever visited my bed, and you are far from young, but you still have your vigour. Besides, you are lucky. The gods have favoured you with a skill. You make good money. Senators come to talk to you at the Mint. It must be interesting.'

The die-cutter continued to peer, myopically at the shining doors of the temple.

'As an artist, they must admire your work.'

The die-cutter did not look at her. He shrugged. 'The magistrates in charge of the Mint, the *Tresviri Monetales*, are not yet Senators. They are the children of great houses. They know nothing. They are pampered, ignorant fools.'

'But Menophilus came to see you. He was a friend of the dead Emperors.'

'He was better than most. He knew what he wanted on the coins. He did his duty to his friends.'

Caenis put her hand on his thigh. 'He is very handsome. As you have met him, you could attend for the morning *salutatio*, become one of his clients.'

'He is away, defending Aquileia.'

'When he returns. You could take me.'

The die-cutter did not take his eyes off the entrance to the temple. 'He might not welcome a man who works with his hands and a whore.'

Caenis slid her hand up, near his crotch. 'At times every man needs a whore. We will do the things a well-bred wife will not.'

The die-cutter was frowning at the temple. 'Is something moving?'

94

The gilded doors had opened wide, and a procession of Senators was descending the steps. It was headed by old Pupienus and the grossly fat patrician Balbinus.

Caenis and the die-cutter stood, the better to see and hear.

The procession halted at the altar.

Balbinus was making a speech. Only snatches of what he said carried. 'Jupiter as fellow councillor . . . powers of an Emperor . . . bandits who march against us . . . care for your safety . . . elevated Marcus Clodius Pupienus Maximus as my colleague . . .'

The young equestrians were chanting – *What the Senate has given, take gladly!* – a thin noise against the silence of the immense crowd.

Caenis saw men worming through the throng. Four of them wore togas – broad purple stripes like blood on the gleaming white. Among these Senators was Gallicanus, the hairy fraud who pretended to a rough, manly virtue. He was speaking to a youth muffled in a hooded cloak. She knew that thin figure, knew him intimately.

An innkeeper, distinctive in the leather apron of his trade, was bellowing something incomprehensible.

Three of the equestrians went to grab him. A scuffle broke out. The first stone was hurled, then another.

Jupiter is our only ruler! The crowd were chanting, like a well-drilled chorus.

Caenis saw Balbinus reel, as a stone hit him.

The mob surged forward, swallowing the equestrians and the innkeeper.

Clutching up the folds of their togas, precious *dignitas* forgotten, the Senators turned and fled up the steps. A rain of stones clattered all around them. The mob jeered, and bayed for blood.

Caenis was pushed in the back, as men rushed to join the riot. She would have fallen, been trampled on the hard marble, had the die-cutter not caught her. Shouldering against the flow of humanity, he dragged her back into the shelter of the shrine of Abundance, pushed her into a corner, shielded her with his body.

When the noise died down, they came out of their refuge.

The doors of the Temple of Jupiter were still open, but blocked by the young equestrians. They had swords in their hands. From the foot of the steps, the dense mass of plebeians watched them. An uneasy truce held.

Their meal had been trodden underfoot. The wine flask was gone. Caenis busied herself packing the remnants into the battered basket. She was scared, and weary, very weary of always being afraid. The threat of brutality and casual violence was ever present in the slums of the Subura. She wanted more than anything to leave, escape from Rome, from squalor, leave her life of *infamia* behind. All she desired was to live a modest, respectable life on one of those peaceful, sun-drenched islands; Cephalonia or Corcyra.

'We should go,' the die-cutter said. 'If the troops come, there will be a massacre.'

'We would never get through the crush.'

The die-cutter grunted. She was right.

A lone figure emerged from the temple. He wore a tunic with a narrow purple stripe. His hands were empty, one of them bandaged. He walked down the steps. An unarmed equestrian; the mob would tear him limb from limb. Then Caenis recognized him: Timesitheus, the *Praefectus Annonae*. Under his management the grain supply had increased. He had been wounded fighting Maximinus. His popularity might save him.

Timesitheus stopped in front of the crowd. Caenis could see him talking, but not hear what he said. After a few moments, a way opened up through the crush, and he was lost to view.

'Before the stones, was that Castricius in that hood?'

'No,' Caenis said, 'your eyesight is getting worse.'

She did not want him to know that the knife-boy had returned to Rome. She did not want anyone to know. After his arrest, against all probability, Castricius had appeared at her door late one night. He had told a wild story of surviving some secret mission to the North. She had not believed a word of it. What she did know to be true was that Castricius had murdered a man in the Street of the Sandal-makers. The authorities would pay if she gave information which led to his capture, if she bore witness against him. The money would be useful, but, even with what she could make by denouncing the die-cutter, it would not be enough.

Gallicanus the Senator was the answer. Gallicanus' slave had been a customer in the bar. The slave had been drunk, but he had sworn it was true. He served in Gallicanus' bed chamber. He should know the truth. What Caenis needed was to find a way to talk to one of Gallicanus' political enemies. It was common knowledge that there were more than enough of them in the Senate. Any one of them would shower wealth on the person who gave them the means to bring down Gallicanus. No career could survive that revelation. Gallicanus was the oldest story: public professions of austerity and virtue, masking private vice and perversity.

Yet the problem remained – how did a whore from the Subura gain admittance to the councils of a Senator?

Caenis sat down. Her mind shied away from the practical difficulties, and wandered instead through a happy dream of the opulent results. She would buy more decent clothes. Musalia could have the tawdry costume of her profession. No longer Caenis, but once again Rhodope, she would take a ship to Corcyra, or one of the smaller islands. Letting it be known that a dream sent by the gods had guided her to her new domicile, she would say that her husband was dead, and that she was an orphan. She would buy a small house, purchase a respectable maid, and a doorkeeper. Doubtless there would be suitors for a young widow with her own property.

Gordian! Gordian!

The crowd at the top of the path up from the Forum was moving. Men were chanting at the top of their voices.

Gordian! Gordian!

What was happening? Why were the plebs shouting the name of the dead Emperors?

CHAPTER 9

Rome

The Carinae,
Eight Days before the Ides of April, AD238

Never use a lie, unless it was necessary. Timesitheus had not lied to Gallicanus and his hired mob outside the Temple of Jupiter. He had not summoned troops. Instead he had called for gladiators, some tough slaves, and his wife. Timesitheus grinned to himself. If Gallicanus knew anything about women, he would have known that Tranquillina was far more dangerous than any soldiers.

Coming out into the Forum under the Arch of Septimius Severus, Timesitheus had given a street urchin his ring, promised him more money than he would see in a year if he fetched Tranquillina and the others. The boy had run off. Timesitheus had followed only a little more sedately; hurrying along the Argiletum between the Senate House and the Basilica Aemilia, down the length of the Forum Transitorium, across the Street of the Sandal-makers, and up the steep steps to the great houses of the Carinae. Now, breathing hard, he waited outside the *Domus Rostrata*, the mansion of the Gordiani.

Time was pressing. There was no telling how long the mob would keep the Senate blockaded. The equilibrium on the Capitol was delicate. Timesitheus did not think that the plebs would assault the temple, or attempt to burn the Senators out. Yet, despite Gallicanus, the mob might drift away, or, once they got news, Pupienus' Urban Cohorts, or other troops might intervene. Timesitheus had not lied to Pupienus either. He had not said he would fetch troops, just that he would save the two new Emperors and the Senators. And so he intended, although in a manner they would not expect, and certainly would not welcome.

For the moment there was nothing for it but to wait. Fear fed on inactivity. Timesitheus could hear the black rat feasting in the dark, could sense its sharp teeth. To occupy his mind, he retied the bandages on his hand. The missing finger throbbed, and the stench of burnt flesh was still there.

They came around the corner: Tranquillina, the two gladiators – Narcissus and Iaculator – and six strong-armed slaves. Her gown hauled up, Tranquillina marched at their head. Most women went out in a litter, attended by a *custos* and a maid. Not his wife. Tranquillina had the heart and soul of a lioness.

The urchin scampered up, and Timesitheus retrieved his ring and handed over the contents of his wallet. Coins would not be an issue after today; one way or another. The boy went and sat on the opposite pavement, wanting to see what happened.

In as few words as possible, Timesitheus described events on the Capitol, and what he planned.

'Once undertaken, there can be no drawing back. Everything we have ventured before by comparison was mere child's play.'

Tranquillina's eyes were dancing, torchlight on black water. 'You are a man. Do everything that becomes a man.'

'If we should fail?'

'We fail? The moment is auspicious. No time for delay.'

The doors of the *Domus Rostrata* were open. Timesitheus walked into the spacious vestibule. It was decorated with the beaks of warships that gave the house its name.

'Maecia Faustina is not receiving people.' It was Montanus the freedman.

'We have come to see her son, Marcus Junius Balbus.'

'The child is resting.'

'Where?'

'That is no concern of yours.' Montanus had all the haughtiness of an ex-slave with a position in a noble household.

'It is very much my concern.'

'I must ask you to leave.'

Timesitheus stepped very close to Montanus. The freedman recoiled. With his undamaged hand, Timesitheus pulled him back.

'You remember me.'

Montanus said nothing.

'I remember you; an insolent slave, scars on his back, arse like a cistern.'

Timesitheus drew his bandaged hand softly down Montanus' cheek. 'I have found out all about you. In the Palace cellars, they treat your sort worse than a murderer: the rack, the claws and the pincers. Soon enough burning like a human torch, half-choked, half-grilled to death. One of those calcined corpses they drag with hooks from the arena, a broad, black trail left behind in the sand.'

The freedman was pale with terror.

'Where is the boy?'

'In the painted colonnade.'

Timesitheus spoke to one of the gladiators. 'Iaculator, watch him. If he shouts or tries to run, kill him.'

They went into the house, across the wide atrium, with

its part-worked white sarcophagus. Servants flitted away like disturbed bats. On the walls of the colonnade innumerable animals – stags, elks, Cyprian bulls, chamois, Moorish ostriches – met grisly deaths.

The boy looked up from his play.

'Misitheus,' he lisped.

'Marcus.' A broad, guileless smile on his face, Timesitheus extended his good hand.

'What happened to your other hand?'

'Nothing; an accident of war. Marcus, you must come with me.'

'But my mother.'

'This is not women's work. Today you must be a man.'

'But Mother said I would not take the *toga virilis* until next year.'

'You will take it today.' The boy's delicate, triangular little face lit with pleasure.

Timesitheus turned to one of his slaves. 'Gather his toy soldiers, carry them carefully.'

Holding Timesitheus' hand, the boy crossed the atrium, past the part-finished tomb of his father.

'Where are you taking my son?'

Maecia Faustina stood in the doorway, tall and severe, flanked by two more freedmen.

'To claim his inheritance.'

'Marcus is a child. His place is at home with his mother.'

'He is thirteen. Today he will wear the toga of manhood. Marcus no longer, he will be Gordian.'

'His grandfather and uncle are dead.'

'And he is their heir. The people of Rome demand a ruler of their blood.'

'Never!' Maecia Faustina blazed like some stern, martial goddess. 'I will not have him killed too!'

'Stand aside, *domina*.'

'No, I will not! I have lost my husband, my father, my brother. My son shall not leave this house.'

'Let us pass.' Timesitheus remembered her freedmen: Reverendus and Gaudianus, two more Christians, two more in fear of the arena. They were easy to deal with; their mistress was more of a problem.

'Ha!' Maecia Faustina exclaimed, relieved and triumphant. 'Our cousin is here. He will put an end to this.'

Maecius Gordianus, the Prefect of the Watch approached. 'I am afraid, *domina*, Timesitheus is right. The boy must follow in the footsteps of his grandfather and uncle. The safety of the *Res Publica* must come before maternal affection.'

'Traitor!' Maecia Faustina spat. 'How much did it cost to buy you?'

'You insult me, *domina*.' The Prefect looked over at Tranquillina, and smiled. 'No money changed hands.' Timesitheus did not like that smile, did not like it at all.

'No matter.' Maecia Faustina was implacable. 'I will not move. None of you, not even a creature like you, or that stinking little Greek informer, would dare to manhandle the daughter and sister of the late Emperors.'

Tranquillina stepped past her husband.

'Get away from me.'

Tranquillina punched the older woman, full in the mouth.

Maecia Faustina reeled back, clutching her face.

The freedmen were bundled out of the doorway.

'You little whore!' Maecia Faustina's face was bloodied. 'Bring back my son!'

Outside, Timesitheus dried the boy's tears, spoke gently to him. 'Your mother will understand in time. This is not a thing for women. You must be a man. Think of your uncle. You must be brave, like him.'

'Time for that later,' Tranquillina said. 'We must move quickly.'

They halted briefly in the Forum Transitorium. Narcissus went into the Temple of Minerva, and came out with a purple cloak. Timesitheus put it on Marcus. He told Narcissus to hoist the boy on his shoulders.

As they passed the Senate House, Timesitheus started the acclamation: 'Gordian Caesar. Gordian Caesar.'

After a moment or two, the plebs milling about took it up.

Gordian Caesar! Gordian Caesar!

The noise rolled under the Arch of Septimius Severus, all the way up to the Capitol.

Gordian Caesar! Gordian Caesar!

SWORD, PART III:
THE PROVINCES

CHAPTER 10

Dalmatia

The Town of Bistua Nova in the Mountains,
Eight Days before the Ides of April, AD238

She had had to run. Despite the gnawing uncertainty and danger, despite the hideous discomforts, Iunia Fadilla knew she had made the right decision. Huddled in the rustic cart, as it descended towards the out-of-the-way town, she had few regrets.

Verus Maximus had beaten her on their wedding night. *If I have to marry a whore, I will treat her like one.* At first he had hit her thighs, buttocks and breasts; places covered by her clothes. Recently it had got worse. At New Year she had had to wear a veil. Maximus had claimed he could smell wine on her breath. *When a woman drinks without her husband, she closes the door on all virtues, opens her legs for all comers.*

When he was away with the army on the Steppe, she had prayed that a barbarian arrow would find him; not a clean kill, but something slow and lingering. The gods had not answered her prayers. It seemed Gordian had been right; the gods were far away, had no care for mankind. On his return, she had determined to kill Maximus herself. She had a knife, he was unconscious with drink, yet she could not steel herself to commit the act. To run had been her only resort.

She had never wanted to be Empress, surrounded by ceremony, her every move circumscribed. She wanted her old life back. A rich, young widow, her life in Rome now had the nostalgia of a golden age; her beautiful house on the Carinae, her friends, a round of recitals, dinner parties, the spectacles and the baths. If Gordian had proposed when her first husband, old Nummius, had died, if he had taken her with him to Africa, none of this might have happened. She might have been spared Maximus. But even that was uncertain. As a great-granddaughter of the divine Emperor Marcus Aurelius, she had a value in dynastic politics. Maximinus Augustus had chosen her as a bride for his worthless son to give some legitimacy to his upstart regime. The marriage had been an attempt to reconcile the nobility of the Senate. As far as she could see, it had failed.

Popular moralists thundered against the ease of divorce. You saw them on every street corner in Rome; hairy Cynics fulminating against lax morality. High on their list of the reprehensible were shameless women who cast off the restraints of husbands. A few words said in front of seven witnesses – *Take your things and go* – and a marriage was ended. Yet who would dare say those words to Caesar? The lowest slave could flee to a temple, claim the right of asylum. What priest would grant that to the wife of Caesar?

There had been nothing for it but to try and escape. Born of desperation, her plan had been simple. Accompanied just by her cousin, Fadillus, his servant, and her maid, she would head west in a fast carriage. *Diplomata* purloined from the imperial chancery would provide a change of horses at each Post House. They would outrun any pursuit. When they reached a crossroads marked on the map at a place called Servitium, she would have to decide her next move.

Ahead, in the Alps, was Corvinus. She had met the equestrian just the once, as they had passed at a bend on a lonely upland road. *Should you come this way again, my lady, accept my hospitality. My name is Marcus Julius Corvinus, and these wild mountains are mine.* He had given her a brooch; garnet-studded gold in the shape of a raven. Off to the south lay Dalmatia, the province governed by Claudius Julianus. She knew him well; decent and honourable, a lifelong friend of Gordian.

To entrust her future to either was a gamble. It was said that Corvinus was no better than a brigand. Only a foolish girl, the simpering heroine of a Greek romance, would mistake a passing invitation for a binding oath. What would be more natural than a brigand ransoming a female hostage back to her family? And what of Claudius Julianus? He was a quiet, unassuming man. Would he find the courage to defy Maximinus? The province of Dalmatia had no legions. Easier for a man of *quies* to be swayed by the proximity of the northern armies, and hand her over to a vengeful husband, find some way to salve his own conscience later. Men were good at that.

In the event, the decision had been taken from her by the unravelling of her plan. No sooner had they left Sirmium than they saw the detritus left by Maximinus' troopers: broken straps, shed hipposandals, empty flasks. Before the first town – a miserable place called Saldis set in a marsh – there were lame and foundered horses and dismounted stragglers in the road. Worse still, messengers spurred foam-flecked mounts past them in both directions. She knew little of armies on the march. It had never occurred to her that the road would not be empty; all Maximinus' men long gone. They could not continue west to Servitium. Now their only option was south towards Dalmatia. They had to get off the main road, and they had to do so without being seen.

109

Fadillus had found the answer. Although, as her tutor, her cousin was her legal guardian, he had never questioned any of her decisions about her property, or anything else. She had not thought of him as a man of much substance. Now, like Mark Antony, or some other Roman of old, in this crisis he had cast off his sloth and begun to show an unexpected resource.

They had changed horses at the Post House in Saldis, and rattled out to the west. As soon as they were out of sight of the town, and at a moment when there were no prying eyes, Fadillus' servant, Vertiscus, had jumped down, and set off back to town on foot, a wallet full of coins hidden inside his tunic. It was easier for a slave to slip unremarked back into Saldis. Fadillus had driven on until the road was bordered by woods. Checking that no one was watching, he had turned off into the trees, not halting until the vehicle could go no further, and they were deep in the forest.

They had passed the night all together in the carriage. The noises of the wildwood were unsettling; the whispering of the leaves, the creak of boughs, the scuttle and cries of predators and prey. Iunia Fadilla was frightened, for a long time unable to sleep.

Fadillus had woken her well before dawn. He stripped everything of value from the carriage, hid it with brushwood, turned the horses loose. When the carriage was found, it would be assumed that they were dead. As he said, the empire was full of tombstones bearing the words *interfectus a latronibus*; killed by bandits.

Through the dark night, he led his cousin and her maid south-east, across country. They had clambered over drystone walls, pushed through hedges, splashed across swampy meadows, waded small streams. Once a covey of partridges had clattered up. Nothing else betrayed their nocturnal wandering. Eventually, bedraggled and exhausted, they had

110

come to the backroad that ran south from Saldis towards the mountains. Covered in filth, unrecognizable, they had sat on the verge, like mendicant devotees of a god that had failed them.

In the grey half-light of the false dawn, the first wayfarer went by. A countryman on a donkey, he had two chickens and a sack tied behind him. Not long after, he was followed by a ramshackle cart piled with vegetables. Other rustics passed, all heading to the town. Iunia Fadilla had never known that peasants were about so early. One or two grunted greetings, most ignored the itinerants.

After sunrise, as if summoned into existence by the light, a wagon had come from the town. On the driver's seat was a man in a hooded cloak, a stout staff propped at his side. He peered closely at them, then reined in the two mules. Fadillus helped his cousin and the maid into the back, then climbed up beside Vertiscus. Together they had set off into the unknown.

For sixteen days, they had plodded on, across the plains, then into the foothills, and finally the mountains. Iunia Fadilla remembered country journeys of her childhood, trips to the Bay of Naples, or distant Apulia. Straight, white, well-made roads, at intervals the pillars marking the entrances to grand estates. Long, tree-lined drives, at their end, shimmering in the distance, elegant villas, with fountains, statues, shaded walkways. Villages of plastered houses, paved streets, and bustling market places. This bleak countryside held no resemblance. Set back on hills, hard of approach, the farms were small and square, built of unmortared stone, forbidding like tiny fortresses. Many had watchtowers. The hamlets were no better. Blank walls crowded winding alleys. At their centre, a muddy square, overlooked by squalid, rough-hewn shrines, which even the most rustic of gods would be ashamed to inhabit.

As a girl from a senatorial house in Rome, Iunia Fadilla had been brought up with a certain understanding of those who lived in the countryside. Hard work and fresh air made them strong and healthy. The frugality of their life, and their distance from the corruption of the city, made them honest. Antique virtue was to be found in their fields and sylvan glades. Her memories of the estates of her father and his friends tallied with this vision. Bailiffs standing in the sunshine before the main house, flanked by lines of farm-workers; all smiling, blowing kisses. Young girls offering the posies of flowers they had gathered. The songs of the vintage, the laughter as her father took off his shoes, and, barefoot, helped tread the grapes. Dinners by torchlight in the vine-yards, the music and dancing.

The countrymen of the upland borders of Pannonia and Dalmatia were a different species. Twisted and gnarled, tattoos showing through the dirt, they regarded the interlopers with silent suspicion. At the first two villages, they denied they had any food to spare. What the taxman had not taken, the soldiers had stolen. In the other villages, there was nothing but spelt and millet for sale. Iunia Fadilla had eaten spelt-cake at her marriage to Maximus. It was not a good omen. Nowhere was there an inn, no one offered them a bed for the night.

They slept in the wagon, went hungry. Up in the moun-tains, the cold wind sang in her ears. The road was flanked by slopes topped with freestanding outcrops of grey rock, like tattered sentinels. The tallest peaks were snow-capped, darkened by the clouds hanging on their shoulders.

Few of those they had met on the road acknowledged their existence. Those that did spoke in some barbaric tongue, or near incomprehensible Latin. Two encounters had brought sheer terror. First, they had seen a small patrol of cavalry in the distance, cantering north. Thank the gods, the country there had been broken, and they had turned off the road, and hidden in a copse. The troopers had not stopped, but scanned the verges as they passed. Just when Fadillus had said it was safe, although before they started to rejoin the road, a lone rider had galloped back, and vanished to the south.

The other meeting had been unavoidable, and far worse. Four horsemen had appeared, not uniformed, but reasonably mounted, and all armed. A drop on one side, a sheer cliff on the other; nowhere to hide. *Interfectus a latronibus.* Many travellers just vanished. The riders were dressed as civilians, but, as they drew near, the ornaments on their belts, the way they moved, had revealed them as soldiers. Deserters most likely. Freed from discipline, as cruel as wolves. Outlaws denied fire and water. Their leader had spoken to Fadillus. Questioned on who he had seen on the road, Fadillus had answered truthfully. There had been no reason to lie. Iunia Fadilla and her maid had sat very still in the back of the wagon. Despite their accumulated dirt, they had drawn the attention of the other riders. Fadillus had said Iunia Fadilla was his wife. An awful pause, before the leader had said the maid could entertain him and his men. Fadillus had protested that she was his property. The leader had said he could have a wineskin for her trouble. Iunia Fadilla got down from the wagon, and the men climbed up. Standing by the mules, she had tried to close her ears to the noises from the bed of the wagon. When the men had finished, they swung back into the saddle. The leader thanked Fadillus with mock courtesy, and apologized for his memory. Now he recalled that he had no wine to give. He turned his horse, and led his tatterdemalion troop away to the north.

Restuta had been silent, stony-faced since. But the life of a slave girl was hard; it bred resilience. The leader of the *latrones* had said that there was a town ahead, a place of reasonable size, with four inns, and a bath house. Iunia Fadilla hoped it might go some way to restoring her maid's spirits.

Bistua Nova was set in a wide plain, ringed by great,

hump-backed mountains. Beneath the notched skyline, pale green grassland and white rock showed against the dark green of the pine forests. Vertiscus walked, holding the halters of the mules, and Fadillus kept his boot on the footbrake, as they inched the wagon down the steep incline.

The first two inns could not have looked less inviting. The third, on the crossroads in the centre of town, appeared somewhat better. The mules stabled, and the wagon chained in the yard, Fadillus took lodgings. Told that the fires of the town bath house were not alight, he ordered water heated in the kitchens and a hip tub brought up to the room. He sat downstairs drinking in the common room with Vertiscus, while the women bathed.

The water turned black as Restuta washed her mistress.

'I am sorry for what happened.'

'It is of no importance,' Restuta said. 'Women are born to suffer and endure.'

Iunia Fadilla said nothing.

'You know that as well as any.'

Iunia Fadilla felt a flash of anger at the girl's presumption, then had to fight back tears.

'Let me dry you,' Restuta said.

'No, I can dry myself. Get in the tub.'

The towel, although threadbare, was clean. Iunia Fadilla watched as Restuta undressed. The girl was thin, but beautiful. Certainly as beautiful as Iunia Fadilla's vain friend Perpetua. A turn of the stars, an accident of birth, and Restuta could have been the toast of society in Rome, rich, young poets begging her favours, rather than a slave girl, with no choice what man took her. Gordian was right: either the gods did not exist, or they did not care.

Fadillus was enough his old self to demand fresh water when it was his turn to bathe. When the men came downstairs to eat, it did not look as if Vertiscus had bothered.

114

The innkeeper's wife served them. The mutton could have been more tender, and there were bits in the bread that crunched in your teeth, but both were delicious. The wine was fierce and warming. Iunia Fadilla could not recall a meal she had enjoyed more. She ate and drank more than a respectable matron should.

Full, and a little tipsy, they retired upstairs. Iunia Fadilla felt uncomfortable. There was one room, with one big bed. She and Fadillus would take the bed, there were straw mattresses on the floor for the servants. Her embarrassment was ridiculous; for nights on end they had all bedded down in the back of the wagon. In her shift, she slipped under the covers. She fell asleep wondering what it would be like if Fadillus drowsily rolled over, and made love to her. A half-remembered line of poetry: the servants listening as Hector mounted Andromache.

She woke with a start in the dead hours of the night. The door was open, Vertiscus standing over them.

'There are soldiers. They are searching the inns at the far end of town.'

In something close to panic, she pulled on her tunic and cloak, grabbed one of the two bundles of her meagre belongings.

'Which direction did they come from?' Fadillus was tense, but controlled.

'The north.'

'Then they are looking for us.'

'The wagon is unchained, the mules harnessed. We must go.'

'No. It cannot outrun men on horseback. Vertiscus, lead them off down the road to the west.' Fadillus wrapped Restuta in Iunia Fadilla's other cloak. 'The girl goes with you.'

There was no time for farewells. They clattered down the stairs, out into the starlit yard.

115

'Wait there.' Fadillus pointed Iunia Fadilla to a shadowed corner by the dung heap.

Lights were showing behind the shutters above them.

The two slaves climbed up onto the driver's seat. Fadillus unbolted the gate, hauled it open.

Vertiscus shook up the reins, cracked the whip.

As the wagon squealed out into the road, Fadillus peered around the gatepost.

A shout in the distance. Other voices took it up.

The sounds of the wagon turning at the crossroads, rattling away.

Iunia Fadilla felt an almost overpowering need to relieve herself. She cursed her weakness.

The drumming of horses' hooves, and the jingle of equipment grew louder, then receded, as the troopers raced after the wagon.

'Now!' Fadillus hissed.

Clutching her bundle, Iunia Fadilla went over to him.

'We do not have long. We must get clear of the town.'

Taking her elbow, he guided her out into the street.

They ran to the crossroads, and plunged down the road heading east.

The houses fell away behind them, but soon her lungs were scorching, and she could not run any further. Fadillus dragged her off the road, up a slope, and into the cover of some trees.

'Rest here a moment, then we will go on.'

And so it was, as the stars wheeled above them, they resumed their hapless odyssey.

CHAPTER 11

Moesia Inferior

The Banks of the Danube,
Four Days before the Ides of April, AD238

At this point the river was wide, almost a mile, and the northern shore was nothing but a low, dark line. Honoratus ordered the signal made to bring the envoys across.

What was he doing here? A man who had cast down one Emperor, installed another on the throne, stuck here at the edge of the world.

Honoratus pushed such thoughts aside. There was time for a final inspection. The troops were arrayed in a great crescent around the tribunal. In the centre were five thousand infantry, legionaries and auxiliaries, their shields and helmet crests uncovered, their armour burnished and gleaming. On each wing stood five hundred cavalry, horses groomed and tack polished. Mounted senior officers flanked the tribunal. More normally they would stand behind Honoratus on the platform itself, but as governor he embodied the majesty of Rome, and thought splendid solitude more imposing. The army made a bold demonstration of the disciplined strength of Rome. That was just as well, Honoratus had stripped the frontier of the province bare to gather nearly half of all his forces here outside the walls of the town of Durostorum.

The barbarians should be impressed. Military might, like everything else, had to be openly paraded before their eyes; abstract ideas were beyond them. Honoratus, however, was a good judge of character, of his own, as well as that of others. He accepted that his approval of the formal observation of rank and its attendant ceremonies was a weakness, one he perceived stemmed from his lack of assurance about the impression that he made on the world. Dignified parades, allied to his good looks and charm, had always served to screen his uncertainties. The command of Delphic Apollo, *Know yourself*, was imprinted in his soul.

Honoratus climbed the steps to the lofty tribunal, just a lone interpreter at his heel. He settled himself on the ivory chair of his high office. The standards were massed behind him – the golden eagles, images of the Augustus and Caesar, plaques showing the names of the units picked out in gold letters – all held aloft and displayed on poles sheathed in silver.

The big warship had put out from the far bank. Its broad, arrowhead wake, and the pools where its oars had cut the water, were the only marks on the glassy surface of the Danube. Sitting very still – a governor did not gawp around like a yokel – Honoratus let his eyes take in the view: the reed beds, the marshes, the whole pestiferous hinterland of this river at the edge of the world. Gods below, he hated this place.

The galley was approaching the near bank. As Honoratus watched, it turned, and began to edge, stern on, towards the jetty. As governor, he commanded the *Classis Moesiaca*, and had summoned the trireme *Providentia*, the flagship of the fleet, upriver from the sea. Nothing should be omitted that might overawe the barbarians.

118

The *Providentia* was made fast, and the boarding ramps run out.

Honoratus watched the barbarians disembark. There was Tharuaro, the high chief of the Tervingi Goths. On one side of him walked a priest, one of those they called a *Gudja*, on the other a young warrior Honoratus did not recognize. They were followed by three more Goths wearing the signs of royalty. Behind them came a dozen long-haired noblemen.

The barbarians had come to Honoratus. It was a sign of weakness to initiate diplomacy. The status and numbers of the envoys showed respect. So far, all was fitting. But barbarians only came when they wanted something. Honoratus hoped it was not permission for any of their number to cross the river and settle within the empire. Barbarians were irrational, and there was no foretelling their reactions to an unequivocal refusal.

Tharuaro walked up to the base of the tribunal with confidence. Ideally, barbarian envoys confronted by the might of Rome would be more abashed. Sometimes, it was said, they were struck dumb, abased themselves and burst into tears. This chieftain, of course, had been here before.

With dignity, Tharuaro bowed, put his fingers to his lips, and blew a kiss to the standards bearing the imperial portraits. His entourage likewise performed the adoration. Honoratus saw the evident reluctance of the young warrior.

'Hail, Honoratus, the general of Maximinus Augustus and Maximus Caesar.' The greeting was not fulsome. Tharuaro spoke the roughly accented Latin of the army. The interpreter would not be needed, unless the other barbarians contributed, and they lacked the language of civilization.

'Hail, Tharuaro, ally and friend of the Roman people, King of the Goths.'

Some of the other barbarians looked askance. *Rex* was the natural translation of *Reiks*, but there were many Kings

119

among the Goths, and no doubt the three behind Tharuaro also held that title. Tharuaro preferred to be styled *Drauhtins*, or Leader of the Tribe, but it was beneath the majesty of Rome for her representative to use such an uncouth word. At the cost of a certain offence, Honoratus had learnt which of Tharuaro's followers understood Latin.

Honoratus waited. It was not for him to speak first.

'You Romans know the Tervingi Goths well. You know our fidelity in peace, and our valour in war. The wide lands of the Goths hold the bones of many of your soldiers.'

Honoratus' thoughts drifted. It was the usual verbose and bombastic speech to be expected of a hairy, illiterate barbarian. Quite likely Tharuaro would spend an eternity singing the praises of his own ancestors, before he announced what he wanted.

'Giving us gold and silver as surety of your friendship, you avail yourself of the blessings of peace and harmony, and leave the business of war to us. The gods have decreed that war again has come to the lands of the Goths, and descends upon your frontier.'

Now he had Honoratus' attention.

'Cniva has returned.'

'He is a hostage in Rome,' Honoratus said.

'The hostage has returned.'

'How?'

Tharuaro smiled. 'Some believe he has been summoned by a *Haliurunna*, one of our Gothic witches.'

'Where?'

'Cniva appeared among the Carpi in the mountains, now he is with the Roxolani Sarmatians on the Steppe. He has much gold. His followers move among the Goths, buying support, seducing men from their true allegiance.'

Honoratus remained silent.

'A war-leader needs much gold to reward the courage of

his warriors, to bring noble fighters to his hearth-troop Rome is wealthy. To defeat Cniva calls for much gold, minted and bullion.'

Honoratus had no idea if the story was true. The provincial *fiscus* had been plundered almost empty to pay for Maximinus' endless northern campaigns. He marshalled his thoughts before speaking.

'The Emperor is master of uncountable wealth, and he shows favour to those who serve him well. I need to consult Maximinus Augustus about these matters. After three months, come here to this spot, and discover and receive an answer. Stand against Cniva, crush subversion in your territories, keep the peace with Rome; demonstrate by your actions that you deserve it, and you can be assured that you will bask in the limitless generosity of imperial benefice.'

Tharuaro did not look overjoyed. The young warrior at his side positively glowered.

'Now you will be my guests at a feast, and there you will find me open-handed.'

Honoratus stood, to indicate that the audience was at an end.

It was nothing but prevarication. Yet, at the cost of those slippery words, a few precious trinkets, and the deployment of his own charm, he thought he could purchase three months of peace. And when that time had passed, his forces would be ready, forewarned, the whole province on a war footing.

Honoratus walked down the steps, and was helped into the saddle of his waiting warhorse. A few moments later mounts – somewhat less splendid – were produced for the barbarians. The cavalry formed up around them, and they proceeded to the town.

As the cavalcade rode under the arch of the main gate, Honoratus noted with satisfaction the Goths' heads turning as they peered at the defences. The counter-weighted port-cullis, the machicolations, the torsion-powered artillery; the barbarians could neither copy them, nor force a passage through them. Even their limited intellect must comprehend their inferiority.

The feast was in the Basilica opening off the Forum. The Goths appeared reluctant to leave their weapons at the door – so much for their vaunted *fidelity in peace*, Honoratus thought – until told to by Tharuaro. Inside, they were further perturbed by the Roman arrangement of three-man dining couches. Well schooled, none of the Romans laughed as the barbarians clambered up, and uncomfortably reclined.

Honoratus took the place of the host in the middle of the top couch. On his right was Tharuaro, to his left the *Gudja*. The truculent young warrior, apparently a son of Tharuaro named Gunteric, looked both contemptuous and unhappy on a couch with two Roman cavalry officers some way down the hall. Honoratus had encountered few things stranger than eating with barbarians, especially with a native priest who had bones woven in his hair, so that they clacked when he moved. Some of the bones looked disconcerting; apparently it was not uncommon for a *Gudja* to perform human sacrifice.

To prevent the meal descending into farce or tragedy, Honoratus had told the kitchens to produce simple food – mainly roast meats – and ordered the cupbearers to dilute the wine with eight parts of water.

The *Gudja* did not speak, but crammed everything that came to hand into his mouth. Tharuaro put himself out to be companionable and expansive. He launched into an inter-minable account of the origins of the different groupings of the Goths. It involved elaborate genealogies, a great deal of wandering, and a bridge collapsing. Of course, Honoratus thought, if they had not been barbarians, they could have just rebuilt the thing.

Why was he still languishing here in Moesia, almost as if in exile? The poet Ovid had been right about this place.

Your open fields have few trees, and those sterile,
Your coast a no man's land, more sea than soil,
There is no birdsong, save for odd stragglers from the distant
Forest, raucously calling, throats made harsh from brine;
Across the vacant plains grim wormwood bristles –
A bitter crop, well suited to its site . . .

. . . no diet suited
To an invalid, no physician's healing skills . . .
. . . I am haunted
. . . by all that is not here.

Honoratus had done more than enough for Maximinus to earn a recall from this dangerous, unhealthy backwater. The Thracian owed him no less than the throne itself. It had been Honoratus who had first taken the terrible risk of talking treason with Flavius Vopiscus and Catius Clemens. Together the three of them had seen it through. Sometimes Honoratus wished that he had never been party to the awful scene in the imperial pavilion; the naked, fingerless corpse of the old Empress, Alexander's mother, the dog gnawing human remains in a corner.

Before the blood was cold, Honoratus had ridden to Rome. He had won the city over to Maximinus, secured the vote in the Senate which had given him legitimacy. He had campaigned with him in Germania, fought with distinction in the battles in the marsh and at the Harzhorn. The marriage of Maximinus' son to Iunia Fadilla had been his idea. If Maximus had been more presentable, the link to the Antonine dynasty would have reconciled the senatorial nobility to the new regime.

Back then, two years ago, Honoratus had accepted the need to come to Moesia. The province was overrun with barbarians. Honoratus had chased out their raiding parties, closed the frontier. When the imperial field army had arrived, he had marched with Maximinus out onto the Steppe. He had commanded the right wing in the victory at the Hierasos river. When the Emperor departed for the West, Honoratus had thought that a new governor would be appointed, and he would travel with the court. But no, here he remained in this wilderness.

Tharuaro was laughing immoderately, slapping his thigh, as he recounted the way some northern tribes liked to bugger their young warriors. Honoratus smiled and nodded, as if listening to the wittiest conversation at a symposium.

Perhaps this semi-exile was not the fault of Maximinus, but of Flavius Vopiscus. Honoratus had been relegated to the Danube, Catius Clemens to distant Cappadocia. Of the trium-virate who had clad Maximinus in the purple, only Vopiscus remained with the Emperor. Vopiscus was twenty years younger than Maximinus. If the latter's son inherited the throne, his vices would soon see him cast down. The thing was obvious. Yet the superstitions of Vopiscus would make him a dreadful Emperor. The *consilium* would be filled with astrologers and magicians; high decisions of state would turn on an alignment of the stars, or a random line of Virgil.

Better Honoratus himself made a bid for the throne. He had two legions. Anullinus, the Praetorian Prefect, had been one of those recruited to kill Alexander. Ammonius, the governor of Noricum, was another. There was more support to be gathered along the Danube. Faltonius Nicomachus and Tacitus, the governors of Pannonia Inferior and Moesia Superior, owed their posts to that revolution. If he could raise the money, rather than buying off Tharuaro or Cniva, he could add their savages to his cause. Maximinus had

124

squeezed the provinces hard, but more could always be raised. At the very least, the cities of Moesia Inferior would have to offer him crown gold if Honoratus were proclaimed Emperor, and imperial estates in the region could be sold. And, if he could gain the backing of his friend Catius Clemens, add the eastern armies to the Danubian, then victory would almost be assured. Of course, Catius Clemens might have aspirations to sit on the throne himself.

Tharuaro had moved on to telling a sad story of how some barbarian Prince had ransomed his friend at the cost of his own eyes. No more food was being brought out, and even the *Gudja* was eating more slowly. Soon it would be time to hand out some golden torques and arm-bands, and this pretence of conviviality could be drawn to a close.

Remember the Apollonian injunction; *Know yourself.* Honoratus accepted it was neither love of Rome, nor personal ambition, that prompted his thoughts. Instead, it was his overpowering desire to leave this loathsome place, leave it at any cost. When appointed governor, he had sent for his family. He should have known better. When he had served here before, as legate of a legion, he had left them safe in Italy. The poetry of Ovid was warning enough. Within two months of arriving, Marcus had taken a fever and died. Marcus was his only son. The boy had been seven.

A servant appeared at the foot of the couch, bearing an armful of golden trinkets.

Honoratus put on a brave face, smiled his beautiful smile, and prepared himself to give gifts to the assembled barbarians.

CHAPTER 12

Mesopotamia

North of Edessa, towards the Euphrates,
Three Days before the Ides of April, AD238

Gaius Julius Priscus, the governor of the province, lay on the hillside, face muddied, and wrapped in a faded, grey-green cloak, which was pulled over his head. The rolling, high country above Edessa was bare, almost treeless, but at this time of year it was green. The grass, in which Priscus was stretched, was studded with white flowers. Down the slope was a bank of yellow flowers. Priscus did not know their names, but he appreciated beauty – in nature, a poem, or a lover – even in this ghastly place.

Dust drifted up on the breeze. The forerunners of the army which Priscus had come to watch were straggling towards the head of the valley. It was time to put away other thoughts. Priscus had always prided himself on a fierce pragmatism.

With the hundred or so of his men he had saved from the fall of Carrhae, he had ridden west. The Persians, intent on pillage, rape, and killing, had offered no pursuit. Priscus had found his field army at Batnae; less than four thousand on foot, and a thousand mounted. It was an inadequate force. Two thousand of the infantry were recent recruits. Waiting, he drilled them in the mornings, and inspected their equipment in the heat of the afternoons. In the evenings he dined with his *consilium*, and discussed strategy. Some of his officers – including one or two of the more experienced, who should have known better – had expressed the hope that the Persians would retire to the east, sated with plunder. Priscus had been unsurprised when the scouts brought word of the approach of the barbarians.

The enemy were no longer led by Ardashir, the Sassanid King of Kings, but there were still more than ten thousand of them; too many to fight in an open battle. Priscus had left Batnae garrisoned by just one auxiliary Cohort and the local militia. Not wanting to abandon his province, he had not continued west to the bridge over the Euphrates at Zeugma. Instead, he had led his men north-east to Edessa. As he expected, the Persians had followed.

Edessa was placed in the hands of Manu, the heir to the abolished client-kingdom of Osrhoene. To defend what had been his late father's capital, the man they called Bear-blinder had the thousand regulars stationed there, and whatever inhabitants could wield weapons. When the Persians appeared before the walls, Priscus and the field army drew the majority of them off into the hills to the north.

They had gone by circuitous routes, the Sassanids dogging their steps, snapping at their heels. Every day there were skirmishes. Sometimes Priscus halted, formed up the army as if to fight, before slipping away again. He had long experience of fighting against the odds, and had the advantage of knowing the terrain. So the weary, dangerous days had dragged on, until they had come to this valley.

From captured enemy outriders and deserters, Priscus had

learnt that Ardashir, with the bulk of the barbarian horde, had gone to besiege Singara, far to the east, where an isolated garrison of legionaries held out. The Persians pursuing him were led by a young son of Ardashir, Hormizd of Adiabene. According to the reports – freely given, or extracted with the knife – Hormizd believed Priscus was intent on nothing but reaching the crossing of the Euphrates at Samosata, and retreating to the comparative safety of the neighbouring province of Cappadocia. That belief might yet be the undoing of Hormizd.

There was a keen irony in Priscus expending all his ingenuity, risking his life in this unequal, probably doomed, defence of Rome's eastern territories. He had been born out here, in a village called Shahba, a flyblown dump in the wastelands on the border between Syria and Arabia. He had grown up speaking Aramaic more often than Greek or Latin. Unlike his brother, Philip, he had no residual affection for the area. Priscus had worked hard to get away. As an equestrian officer, he had served all over the vast empire, in military and financial posts. Wherever he had been sent, Spain or on the Rhine, each place was better than here. He loathed the heat and the dust of the orient, the narrow, self-seeking parochialism of its contemptible natives. He had bought estates in Italy. His wife was in his house on the Caelian Hill, his son in the imperial school on the Palatine. With all his soul, he wished that he also was in Rome.

The vanguard of his army had entered the valley below. Sutlers and camp servants mounted on mules and donkeys, they carried the standards of the cavalry, and from a distance might be mistaken for such.

Priscus let his gaze roam over the folded crests on the far side of the valley. Fighting the Persians was like fighting the Hydra. You cut off one head, and two grew in its place. A victory meant little. Rout a Sassanid horde, and they sent another. Yet a single Roman defeat would be calamitous. Despite that, Priscus knew that he had to keep an army in the field. If not, the Persians could pick off the defended towns at their leisure. He had to fight today, and he had to win.

The main body of his infantry moved onto the floor of the valley. Porcius Aelianus, the Prefect of the 3rd Legion, had them strung out in a good simulacrum of disorder. In their wake, still out on the plain, what appeared to be the baggage train meandered along, screened by just a thin line of infantry. If the gods were kind, it would be an opportunity and a prize too tempting for the Sassanids to overlook.

Priscus had manned the wagons with picked veterans from both his legions. They wore rough cloaks over their armour, their weapons and shields were hidden in the beds of the carts, and their standards had been sent ahead further up the column. They knew what was expected of them, and they were commanded by Julius Julianus, the Prefect of the 1st Legion, a man of proven abilities.

The trap was set, and now Priscus could see the dust raised by the Persians coming up from the south.

If he was victorious today, he would have bought his province no more than a measure of time. Herakles killed the Hydra by severing its head. To vanquish the Persians called for an army which could defeat the King of Kings. March the whole imperial field army east, bring all the might the empire could gather, kill Ardashir, and decapitate the Sassanid beast.

Priscus had no doubt that Maximinus would crush the rebellion of the Gordiani. Africa was unarmed, Italy virtually as powerless. Equally, he was certain that Maximinus would never be diverted from his unwinnable northern wars. The Thracian was a fool. Priscus had served in Germania. The barbarians there could not be conquered. If a barbarian ruler there was contumacious, you used bribes and the threat of force to set the other chieftains on him, and bring him down.

In the East, you could unite the Kings of Armenia and Hatra, the rulers of Palmyra and the Arabs, every native dynast, and Ardashir would defeat them all.

Maximinus had to be dethroned, and if united the seven armies in Rome's eastern territories could bring that about. The key was Catius Clemens, the governor of Cappadocia. Clemens was one of the triumvirate that had clothed Maximinus in the purple. The governors of Syria Phoenice and Egypt were closely bound to the regime, and could be expected to follow the lead of Clemens. On the other hand, Priscus himself had Mesopotamia, and his brother-in-law held Palestina. The allegiances of the governors of the two remaining armed provinces, Syria Coele and Arabia, were less certain. If Priscus could remove Clemens, by whatever means, and take over Cappadocia, he would control three of the seven. The support of one more would give him a majority, with which he could bring the rest into line.

During this interminable march, another possibility had occurred. What was needed was a military leader who could win a civil war against Maximinus, then lead a victorious war against the Persians. Priscus himself had no desire for the dangerous eminence of the throne. Catius Clemens, however, had already shown the nerve and ambition necessary to depose one Emperor and create another. By all accounts he had acquitted himself well on campaigns in the North. For such a man, hearing the crowd acclaim him Augustus, being elevated above the law, might seem commensurate with his virtues.

Priscus had sent a messenger asking Catius Clemens to meet him in Samosata. Another despatch had requested Aradius, the governor of Syria Coele, to attend. In the high citadel of Samosata, overlooking the Euphrates, a decision would be made. Either Catius Clemens must wear the purple, or he must be eliminated.

The baggage train was lumbering into the valley, the Persians close behind. Priscus put speculation aside. First he had to survive this encounter, emerge victorious. One task at a time. Pragmatism, always pragmatism.

The Sassanid horse archers swerved across the plain like low-flying swallows. They never seemed to go anywhere unless at a gallop, or, at the least, a fast canter. Behind them, inhaling the dust of some eight thousand inferiors, came the ironclad noble cavalry, two thousand of the feared cataphracts. At the head of their column flew a battle standard; yellow and green, with an abstract design like an inverted trident. Under it rode Hormizd of Adiabene. He was confident, this son of Ardashir; no flank guards were deployed.

Excited, ululating cries came up the hillside. The light horsemen had seen the disorganized rear of the Roman army. They booted their mounts. Priscus tried to keep his eyes on the heavy cavalry with Hormizd. It was they who would decide the day.

Like a god looking down on Troy, the drama of conflict distracted him. The mounted bowmen were doing as their nature dictated. Cantering forward, they put two or three arrows in the air, skidded around, and shot another over their mounts' tail as they retreated. The same manoeuvre, repeated over and over, by thousands of men. The disguised legionaries, unshielded, cowered among the carts. Death and pain whistled all around them. There was nothing they could do, but help their fallen, and endure.

When Priscus looked back at the Persian heavy cavalry, he cursed his inattention. He was horrified to see that the cataphracts had halted. The big yellow and green standard, and the officers beneath it, advanced a few paces. Priscus could make out Hormizd. He was wearing a silver helmet, fashioned to resemble the head of a bird of prey. The Sassanid Prince looked up at the hillside, seemingly straight at Priscus, then turned his gaze to the far slope, the steeper one. Hormizd was not a young fool after all.

Behind the command group, chargers pawed the ground, sidled. Infected by the expectancy of their high-strung riders, they edged forward. Hormizd and the officers around him gestured for the cataphracts to keep back. They reined in their horses. But hereditary noblemen of any culture were hard to control. Put them together, and on horseback, the thing became near impossible. The great Nisean warhorses shifted forward. Like a landslide, they caught up Hormizd and those around him, bore them along. Hormizd was no fool, but his prudence had done him no good.

Heart soaring, Priscus watched the cataphracts ride into the valley. He waited until he saw them lower their lances, then, when he knew they were committed to the charge, he crawled back up the slope. Rolling over the crest, he got to his feet, and ran down into the hollow where his troopers were hidden; a thousand of them, drawn up in a line five deep.

'They have taken the bait.'

Sporakes, his bodyguard, gave him a leg up.

'Form a wedge on me. Advance at the walk, until I give the command. Keep your places, no trumpets, no calling out until just before contact.'

Priscus took his shield in one hand, gathered his reins in the other, and nudged his horse on with his thighs.

'These Persians were all born when the moon stood together with Mars in Cancer,' Ma'na the Hatrene said.

As the line paced up the reverse slope, Priscus gave Ma'na a puzzled look.

'Men with that conjunction of stars are doomed to be eaten by dogs.'

On Priscus' other side, Abgar of Edessa laughed. 'Then they will be happy. When Persians die, when they have finished fucking their sisters and mothers, murdering their

132

fathers, their religion tells them it will be best if their corpses are devoured by wild beasts.'

'Birds,' Ma'na said. 'The sister-fuckers prefer birds.'

'Dogs, birds, it is all the same. We are the instrument of their deity. We will give the reptiles the righteous end they desire,' Abgar said.

They were so young, and brave, and beautiful; nothing like easterners at all. With these Princes on either shoulder, and Sporakes at his back, Priscus could ride through the walls of Babylon itself.

They came over the skyline. Without stopping, they took in the scene down in the valley below. The legionaries had grabbed their weapons, formed the wagons into a rough defensive line. Some of the Sassanid nobles were in among them. Legionaries thrust and hacked at them from the carts. The majority of the cataphracts had pulled up short. They were at a halt. The impetuosity of their charge had left them wedged together, hopelessly intermingled with the horse archers.

'Charge!'

Priscus dropped his reins – guided his mount with his posture and weight – and drew his sword.

It was not above two hundred paces down to the floor of the valley, the incline gentle, very few rocks. They picked up speed. The ground trembled under them.

A babble of voices rose up. The faces of the Persian nobles were hidden by facemasks, aventails of mail, but there was no mistaking the fear in their sounds and gestures.

Ultio! Ultio! The shout went up from the Roman ranks. *Revenge! Revenge!*

Horsemen were spurring away from the Persian mass. Those at the rear fled back the way they had come. It was harder going for those on the far side, as they put their mounts to scramble up that steeper slope.

Priscus angled the charge towards the front of the enemy,

aiming at the warriors under the yellow and green banner.

The charge went home with a din that stunned the senses. All was noise, movement, stinging dust. The scent of hot horse and reek of rank sweat.

Panic had gripped the Persians. Next to no troops would stand if surprised by a determined charge to the flank or rear. Nobles and horse archers alike, they jostled and fought each other to win free of the tangle.

Priscus could see the trident standard drawing back up the far slope.

'With me!'

Ma'na and Abgar still flanked him, Sporakes had his back. They forced their way through the throng, only giving blows to clear the way.

When they were at the foot of the incline, the Persians saw them coming. The duty of the nobility rallied them. Each knew he could not return to the court of the King of Kings if he had left Ardashir's son to be cut down or captured. About fifty cataphracts turned and formed a line.

'Through them! Do not let him get away!' Priscus was half-aware that he was shouting.

The slope was against them, but the shaken Persians received them at a standstill.

A long lance jabbed at Priscus' face. He jerked his head aside. Kohl-lined eyes wide between helmet and hanging mail. Priscus was inside the head of the lance. He thrust at the Persian's chest. The tip of the blade skidded off the scale armour. The cataphract dropped the lance, dragged out his sword. Their horses circled. Priscus cut at the head. The Persian blocked. Hooves stamping, they went around. Perceptions narrowed to nothing but each other. The Sassanid's blade had the longer reach. He wielded it in a curious fashion, with his forefinger curled over the front of the crosshilt. He jabbed. Priscus took the blow on his shield.

He jabbed again, Priscus turned it with the edge of his blade. They resumed their watchful equine measure.

'Ahuramazda!' With a yell, the Persian thrust to the body. Again, Priscus took the blow on the side of his weapon. This time, he did not draw away. Steel rang on steel. Priscus forced his blade up that of his opponent. The Persian screamed as the sharp steel reached his forefinger. He dropped the weapon, clutched the wounded hand with his sound one. Dispassionately, Priscus chopped him from the saddle.

The green and yellow standard was nowhere to be seen. Hormizd of Adiabene had gone. Sassanids were still being butchered, but the fight was over. Priscus tried to collect his wits. He needed prisoners. He looked at Ma'na. No, he would not do. The Prince of Hatra hated the Sassanids, as did Abgar of Edessa. They would leave none alive.

'Sporakes, get the men to spare those who try to surrender. Have the Persians dismounted, their hands bound.'

The bodyguard looked vaguely defiant.

'I will be safe enough with Ma'na and Abgar.'

Sporakes saluted, but there was still an odd look on his face, as if he was put out, not by the specific instructions, but the fact of being given an order at all. Priscus put it out of his mind. There was so much that needed doing.

'Ma'na, ride and tell Porcius Aelianus to pitch camp.'

The young Prince of Hatra saluted, and spurred off.

Superstitiously – having said he would be safe with the two Princes – Priscus did not want to despatch Abgar. Looking around, he spotted a young tribune. What was his name?

'Tribune, take a hundred troopers, and set out a defensive line at the opening of the valley, in case any of the prisoners escape, or some of the Persians rally.'

The youth saluted.

'And, Caerellius' – it was important to remember the men's names – 'post piquets on the hills.'

Abgar handed him a flask, and Priscus drank the unmixed wine.

Hormizd had escaped, but the day was won. It would take time for Hormizd to regather his forces. Priscus could leave his army unmolested in the north of his province, while he crossed the Euphrates, to do whatever seemed best to him in Samosata.

PART IV:

Italy

CHAPTER 13

Rome

The Palatine,
The Ides of April, AD238

'Must you stand so close?'

Pupienus had never cared for too great a physical intimacy in public. It was beneath the *dignitas* of a Senator, let alone an Emperor. He could feel the pleb's hot, unseemly breath as he peered into his face.

'My apologies, Augustus.' The die-cutter stepped back. 'My eyesight is not good at a distance.'

The die-cutter limped back to his stool, and took up his drawing materials.

Balbinus belched. 'I told you this was ridiculous. The *Tresviri Monetales* should be left to run the Mint. It is a task for junior magistrates. No one, apart from a soldier or one of the unwashed, ever looks at the image on a coin.' Balbinus ruffled the hair of his bejewelled young slave boy. 'Do you study the coins I give you, my pretty one?'

They were in the Aula Regia, the great audience chamber of the Palace. Pupienus and Balbinus were enthroned, the near naked catamite at the feet of the latter, the old die-cutter on his low perch. The inescapable imperial entourage – courtiers, Lictors, Praetorians, freedmen and slaves of the *familia Caesaris* – stood at a decorous distance.

The stylus of the die-cutter scratched over the papyrus, as he captured the features of Pupienus.

Columns of purple Phrygian marble stretched up a hundred feet to where they supported the great beams of cedar of Lebanon which spanned the ceiling. From niches along the walls, the gods, huge and carved in a green stone from the deserts of Egypt, regarded the transitory ceremonies of humanity. Behind the thrones was a gigantic statue without a head. Maximinus had been decapitated, and instructions had been given to demolish the remainder of his image. It would be replaced by three smaller figures: Pupienus and Balbinus Augusti, and their Caesar Gordian III.

There was a doorway in the far right corner. Behind it were stairs which led to the unfrequented small rooms under the roof. Pupienus thought how good it would be to go up there on his own. From that point of vantage, he could look down on the Forum, take in the hills – the Capitoline, the Esquiline, and the Caelian – and survey the city which he ruled. But an Emperor was never alone, and Pupienus had only a share of power.

'If it pleases you, Augustus?'

The die-cutter stood further away, and proffered the drawing tentatively, like a man offering a bun to an elephant.

Pupienus regarded his portrait. The high forehead, straight nose, unsmiling mouth, and long beard – laureate, draped, and cuirassed – there was nothing frivolous or decadent. It was the bust of a mature Emperor who would order the affairs of state, military and civilian, with a calm, serious consideration. The forked beard evoked both the sternness of Septimius Severus and the philosophical deliberation of Marcus Aurelius.

Those divine Emperors had dealt with unworthy men who had claimed a share of the imperial authority. Severus put the severed head of Niger on public display, and trampled the corpse of Albinus under the hooves of his horse. After the event, Marcus said that he would have spared Avidius Cassius, but rumour claimed that he had quietly poisoned Lucius Verus.

Gordian! Gordian! The memory of the shouts of the mob surging up to the Capitol rankled. That fat fool Balbinus, quivering with fear, had jumped at the safety offered in investing old Gordian's grandson as Caesar, offering him a junior part of the imperial power. Under the circumstances, besieged in the Temple of Jupiter, with no troops to scatter the plebs, Pupienus himself had been able to see no course but acquiescence.

The snivelling boy himself – apparently he was thirteen, although he looked about ten – was nothing. The untrustworthy little Greek Timesitheus had thought to rule via the youth. But Pupienus had quashed that ambition. Oh, how cleverly he had brought that scheme to nothing. After the three rulers had appeared before their people, made a sacrifice at the altar in front of the temple, clasped hands as evidence of their concord, and promised both a large donative and lavish games, the plebs had dispersed. Once the Capitol was near deserted, Pupienus had proposed that an honour guard of Senators accompany the new Caesar back to the *Domus Rostrata*, his family home. Until Gordian reached a man's estate, he should be spared the chill formalities of the Palace, and the heavy duties of state. Even Balbinus' limited comprehension had grasped the sense. There had been nothing the treacherous *Graeculus* Timesitheus could do. Many of his armed equestrians were youths from senatorial families;

141

threatening the plebs was one thing, but none of them was prepared to turn their swords on the Senate. Pupienus and Balbinus had walked the covered passageways and tunnels to the Palatine, and young Gordian had been returned to the Esquiline.

The best of it had emerged only later. Gordian was restored to the care of his mother, the formidable Maecia Faustina. Apparently, when Timesitheus had abducted the boy from his house, the little Greek's wife, that wanton-looking bitch Tranquillina, had punched Maecia Faustina in the face. The latter now had banned Timesitheus from the *Domus Rostrata*. Pupienus graciously had stationed some men from the Praetorian Cohorts there to ensure that the house of the Gordiani was protected. Pupienus hoped the *Graeculus* and his whore had enjoyed their brief moment of triumph; retribution was coming, and he would ensure that it brought them no pleasure.

The die-cutter was scrutinizing Balbinus now.

'Make me look young and virile.' Balbinus stroked his slave boy. 'And I am virile, am I not?' The child simpered.

'Gordian is young,' Pupienus said.

Balbinus turned to his co-Emperor.

'A certain maturity is apposite for an Augustus,' Pupienus continued. 'It brings experience and wisdom. And a fuller physique is fitting.'

There was suspicion in Balbinus' porcine eyes.

'The body of the Emperor is the symbol of his reign. In his own person, he can proclaim a time of plenty.'

Balbinus took a drink, and told the die-cutter to get on with it. 'I have pressing duties,' he said, leering at his catamite.

Pressing duties. The old satyr had never acknowledged any obligations, except to his cock and his belly.

Meeting real duties involved awful decisions and sacrifice. No one had experienced that more intimately than Pupienus himself, no one except his own father. He pushed the thought aside, and steadied himself by marshalling his plans.

Pupienus had kept his promises to the patricians around Balbinus. Once secure on the throne, Pupienus had stepped down from the Prefecture of the City, and awarded the office to Rufinianus. A letter, sealed in purple, had gone to the western Alps summoning Valerius Priscillianus to become a travelling companion of Pupienus as Emperor. He had done what he could to fulfil his obligations to the faction of the old Gordiani. Valerian was named as another imperial tent-companion, and Egnatius Lollianus had been given the title of governor of Pannonia Superior. How the latter might be made a reality was uncertain, given that the province was behind Maximinus' lines, and held by the Thracian's chief supporter Flavius Vopiscus. In politics sometimes appointments could only be speculative. It was easy to give away things that belonged to someone else.

When Pupienus marched for Ravenna, the security of Rome would be a concern. Gallicanus' philosophical friend Maecenas was the member of the Board of Twenty with nominal charge of the defence of the capital. Maecenas was both unreliable and without capacity. That the Urban Cohorts were now commanded by Rufinianus was no reassurance. All the other troops in and around the city were led by clients of the Gordiani: Felicio had the Praetorians, Maecius Gordianus the Watch, and Serapamum the 2nd Legion out in the Alban Hills. None of them could be summarily dismissed without good reason.

Pupienus had done what he could. His adoptive father Pinarius had been made co-Prefect of Praetorians. The old man had demurred. A retired imperial head gardener from Tibur, he had no experience in politics or the military. An appeal to familial loyalty had won him round. Pupienus' other move had been more imaginative. He had gone to the camp of the *frumentarii* on the Caelian, and interviewed the Centurions stationed there. One of them, a veteran called Macrianus, had been wounded in Alexander Severus' Persian war. Now crippled in one leg, Macrianus was intelligent, unscrupulous, and deeply embittered; ideal qualities to be the new head of the Emperor's spies in Rome. Pupienus had instructed him to pry into everything, intercept the mail, place informants in the homes of all the leading men, and keep him informed of every rumour.

Weak foundations, but they might hold until Pupienus returned.

Away from Rome there had been news both good and bad.

Aedinius Julianus, the governor of Narbonnensis, the most southerly of the Gallic provinces, had offered his support to the new regime, if he were recalled to Rome, and made Praetorian Prefect. Pupienus had replied on the instant. Aedinius should have his wish, if he brought over both his province, and neighbouring Gallia Lugdunensis. It could kill two birds with one stone. The return of Aedinius would provide an ideal opportunity to remove Felicio from the Praetorians.

The other report was so alarming as to be incredible. As one of his first responsibilities, the lame Macrianus had inspected the diplomatic hostages held in the city. Two of them – Cniva the Goth, and Abanchus the Sarmatian – were gone. They had been set free at least a month earlier. The move had been clandestine. It was thought Menophilus had sent them to raise their tribes against the forces of Maximinus in the North. What desperation could have induced Menophilus to take such a disastrous and short-sighted decision? Whatever Emperor they acknowledged, the legions along the Danube were Romans, and it was not the soldiery, but civilians who would suffer most if the frontiers were

144

breached by hordes of savages. Once across the river, it could take years to drive the barbarians out. Tax revenues could not be raised from massacred peasants and burned farms. For all his Stoic principles, there was something irrational, even wild, about Menophilus. After all, in Rome he had murdered two opponents with his own hands. If he survived the defence of Aquileia, something must be done about Menophilus.

'If it pleases you, Augustus.'

The die-cutter hobbled across to Balbinus.

Gods below, was Pupienus to be surrounded by the deformed? He made a mental note to have the dwarves and other buffoons in the Palace sold.

'Hmm . . . handsome, sleek, well fed; a fine icon of an era of abundance.' Balbinus passed his portrait to Pupienus.

A heavy-jowled, fleshy face, with a look both complacent and disgruntled: the die-cutter had talent. Not the face of a man who should be allowed to debauch the imperial dignity for long. No longer than a weak child.

'The reverses of the coins should express the stability of the reign,' Pupienus said.

'If it pleases you, Augusti,' the die-cutter said, 'may I suggest clasped hands with the legend FIDES, and perhaps AMOR MUTUUS AUGUSTORUM.'

'Just so,' Pupienus said. The good faith, and mutual love of the Emperors. Just so indeed.

CHAPTER 14

Northern Italy

Aquileia,
The Ides of April, AD238

The condition of a man, if he could see it aright, was always that of a soldier in the breach: every moment might bring the bite of a barbed arrow.

The northern camp of Vopiscus was some five hundred paces from the town. The gate was open, and the first of the enemy were coming out.

Despite himself, Menophilus' breathing was shallow, his heart beating fast. There was no reason to be afraid. What was the worst that could happen? Death held no fear. The Demiurge placed a spark of the divine in each man, with death he took it back, and there was no more pain, no sentience at all. With no afterlife, there could be no punishment, and the pounding guilt must cease. Menophilus could imagine nothing else that would free him from the waves of remorse that haunted his nights, and threatened to undermine his every waking moment. Death was to be embraced.

From the wall, the land to the north stretched away. It

was utterly flat. The first four hundred paces were ravaged: stumps of trees where groves had been felled, insubstantial scatters of debris where suburban villas had stood, and where family tombs had flanked the Via Julia Augusta. The earth was gouged where the spoil had been dragged into the city. It had all been done for a purpose. The destruction ordered by Menophilus denied cover to the attacking forces, and, as a by-product, created an almost limitless store of jagged, heavy missiles to drop on their heads, and crush the life from their bodies.

The camp from which the Pannonian legionaries were marching was sited beyond the swath of devastation. Out there Menophilus' men had done no more than drive out the occupants, requisition everything edible, and tear the doors from all the buildings. Now columns of smoke rose across the plain. Finding the gates of the city closed against them, the summons to surrender rejected, the besieging troops of Vopiscus had turned their frustration against everything inanimate in their power. For the last few days, the defenders had watched them chopping down vineyards, torching farms. The embers of divine reason burned low in the common soldiery.

Oblivious to the human drama preparing below, a stork flew over the wall. Menophilus turned, and watched the great bird as it went to its nest high on the Temple of Belenus. Rebuilding sections of the wall, some nests had been destroyed. Menophilus was glad others remained. A local superstition linked the safety of the town to the presence of the birds.

The enemy standards were in plain sight, and from them numbers and affiliations could be estimated. Three thousand swords drawn from three of the four Pannonian Legions. After the destruction of the pontoon over the Aesontius, the advance guard of the army had proceeded with exaggerated

147

caution. Until Maximinus should arrive, Vopiscus lacked the troops to encircle Aquileia. He had entrenched his first camp well to the east, the Natiso river between it and the city. The imperial siege train remained there, protected by a thousand legionaries. The other three thousand had been led on a wide flanking march, crossed the stream miles to the north, and then warily edged down to construct this second set of field fortifications, from which they were now emerging.

Menophilus and his fellow commander Crispinus had made their dispositions. Menophilus had the north wall, with the five hundred auxiliaries of the 1st Cohort Ulpia Galatarum under their Prefect Flavius Adiutor. They were backed by two thousand of the civic militia led by their magistrate Barbius. About half of these levies were armed with bows or slings.

Down at the port, Crispinus guarded against any intervention from the enemy across the Natiso. The Senator had the majority of the crews of two Liburnian warships which Laco, the Prefect of the Ravenna fleet, had brought up the river. Although only eighty of them were marines, all the hundred and sixty rowers and sailors were armed and accustomed to military discipline. Another two thousand locals provided additional numbers.

Along the walls to the west and south, where there was no immediate threat, were distributed four thousand more levies. They were in the charge of the military Prefect Servilianus, and Statius, the other Aquileian magistrate.

In the Forum was a reserve of the final two thousand conscripted citizens. If there was some dire emergency, the utility of these bakers, porters, and other tradesmen was doubtful. If the fierce, veteran Centurion with them could get them to the walls at all, it was hard to imagine that anyone could induce them to stand up hand-to-hand to an onslaught by veteran legionaries.

Aquileia boasted twenty-four pieces of torsion artillery. Eight apiece of these light, bolt-throwing ballistae were on the northern and western walls, just four each to the east and south, where the Natiso curled around the town. They were manned by auxiliaries seconded from the 1st Cohort, aided by able-bodied labourers.

It was a ragtag force that defended the city. But Flavius Vopiscus had far too few fighting men to take the walls by storm. Maximinus' general was making a demonstration. His men were equipped only with scaling ladders, not the full paraphernalia of poliorcetic endeavour. He was gambling that the levies did not have the stomach to fight, would turn tail, and abandon their posts. Menophilus thought he might well be right; that the odds favoured the attackers.

What was life, but a brief sojourn in an alien land.

The Pannonian legionaries were drawn up in good order. Menophilus could see Vopiscus riding along the line, evidently making a speech. He would be praising their martial virtues, disparaging the civilians who opposed them, offering prizes to the first soldiers over the walls, plunder to all who survived. The faint sound of cheering came across the empty plain.

The sound, and the sight of the serried ranks were enough to put fear in the hearts of the armed townsfolk on the walls.

'There are an awful lot of legionaries,' Barbius said.

'Nowhere near enough.' Menophilus spoke more brusquely than he intended. He found it hard to talk to the town councillor. On the return from the reconnaissance of the Pons Sonti, the conversation had been difficult. *Your son died bravely. Surrounded, he cut down three, four of the enemy before he was overwhelmed. He died sword in hand. He will be remembered as a hero; a man who gave his life for liberty.* Menophilus had felt like a bad actor, stripped of mask and buskins, and forced on stage to mouth words of his own devising, lines he did not believe.

Barbius had not broken down. Instead, with infinite sadness, he had said he had another son.

Philosophy was no comfort to Menophilus; not even the sage words of Epictetus. If you take on a role that is beyond your powers, you not only disgrace yourself in that role, but you neglect the role that you were capable of fulfilling. What role was he fit to play?

Barbius' surviving son was a military tribune with the 4th Legion Flavia Felix, serving with the field army of Maximinus. It could only raise questions about the loyalty of the father. Menophilus needed to watch Barbius, watch the bereaved as if he were a traitor. War was a hard teacher. Civil war was degradation.

Trumpets rang out from the ranks of the enemy, their standards inclined forward, and they began their advance.

Five hundred paces, still out of range of the ballistae; there was all too much time to wait. Menophilus turned to a messenger. 'Go and tell Laco it is time for him to go. Although his two galleys have only a skeleton crew left aboard, the enemy are committed, and there is no one to hinder them.'

The soldier saluted.

'And tell him that if the naptha arrives in Ravenna, he is to try to run it upriver under cover of darkness.'

The Pannonians were nearing the band of devastated land.

On the battlements, while the auxiliaries waited stolidly, the levies fidgeted and chattered.

'Silence on the wall.' Menophilus had addressed his men earlier. He was unsure that it had done much to stiffen their resolve.

The enemy marched into the scoured land. There was no advantage in delay.

'Ballistae load.'

The *clack-clack-clack* of the ratchets, the high whine of sinew and wood under extreme tension.

'Loose.'

The *click-slide-thump* of the release, repeated from tower to tower, all along the wall.

Menophilus followed the bolt from the nearest ballista. A dark streak, travelling almost too fast to follow. It fell short, embedding itself harmlessly in the earth.

Clack-clack-clack. The artillerymen wound the machines back.

'Shoot at will.'

The second, ragged volley sped away. Off to the left the small figure of a legionary was plucked backwards, as if by the hand of a deity. Along the walls, the levies cheered immoderately, clutching at any shred of encouragement.

Disturbed by the noise, a stork flapped up from the top of one of the towers. It flew unhurriedly towards the north-east, to the upper reaches of the Natiso.

Unable to contain themselves, one or two of the militia shot arrows or slingshots. The range was far too great. The shower of missiles became a hail.

'Stop shooting,' Flavius Adiutor shouted.

Only a few obeyed.

'Loose at will.' Menophilus countermanded the order. He put his hand on Adiutor's shoulder, spoke so he alone could hear. 'It will keep up their courage. A busy man has less time to dwell on his fear.'

Out of habit, Menophilus scanned the entire field. There was nothing new, no other threat than the advancing line of legionaries. In solitary splendour, the stork circled over the distant, peaceful river.

The first of the enemy went down, struck by arrows and stones. They were within a couple of hundred paces.

The Pannonians closed ranks around their fallen, trudged inexorably onwards. They had no archers or slingers, no way of hitting back. The shields of the front rank bristled with

151

shafts. Yet they endured, and still they came; a silent and terrible phalanx.

The civilians were terrified, looking sideways at each other, eyeing the steps down into the town. A few stepped back from the machicolations.

Menophilus moved fast. Gesturing for the crew to cease shooting, he clambered up onto the nearest ballista.

'Hold your positions! There is no safety in flight. Remain on the walls. Push the ladders away, and they cannot reach you.'

Frightened faces stared up at him from both directions.

'Think of your wives and children. Be men. Hold the battlements, and you will be safe.'

The legionaries were at the foot of the wall; a solid line of shields and helmets, an armoured beast. As one they shouted: *Maximinus Augustus!*

A shadow passed over Menophilus.

Maximinus Augustus!

A civilian close to Menophilus dropped his bow, turned to run. Adiutor knocked the man to the ground. Two more bundled the Prefect aside.

The siege ladders reared up, swaying towards the wall.

'God is with you! See!' From atop the ballista, Menophilus pointed to the sky.

Those who had turned in flight paused, hesitated.

'See – your god Belenus gives you victory! His sacred bird returns to the city.'

The stork did not alight on its nest, but flew south over the streets of Aquileia.

'Belenus fights at your side!'

'Belenus!' Adiutor shouted. 'Belenus!'

Others took up the chant; first the auxiliaries, then the levies.

Belenus! Belenus!

Like men possessed, the townsmen threw themselves at the ladders, hurled chunks of masonry down at the soldiers.

Javelins whipped up from the troops below. Some found their mark. Unheeding, the militia strained at the ladders, dragged them sideways, past the point of no return.

Menophilus saw a legionary almost at the level of the battlements dashed from the rungs. He fell, limbs flailing, clutching at imaginary purchase in thin air.

Above the uproar – the screams and shouts, the crash of falling stone, wood, and armour – Menophilus heard the trumpets below sound the recall.

'Cease shooting.'

Again Adiutor's command went disregarded.

'Do not waste ammunition.'

The auxiliaries, like ploughmen at the end of a long day, put down their weapons, slumped down, backs to the battlements.

The armed citizens – full of the savage joy of killing, while in no danger – threw rocks, wielded their bows and slings as fast as they could, dealt death indiscriminately.

From his perch, Menophilus watched men die; pierced by cruel steel, brains dashed out by rocks. He pushed away his pity. It was nothing. Sparks of the divine returning whence they came. The defenders could retrieve the missiles in the night. Let the citizens of Aquileia get the taste of blood. They would need it in the days to come. And now they were committed. They could hope for no mercy.

CHAPTER 15

Northern Italy

The Aesontius River,
The Ides of April, AD238

There was the river, hidden by the trees, but a brooding, malign presence.

It had rained again in the night, and the ground was poached by the passage of the army. Maximinus led the imperial entourage down from the camp slowly. The mud sucked at the hooves of the horses. A slip or a fall now would be a bad omen.

Since the eclipse, many in the army thought the campaign ill-starred. *If the sun falls, it warns of desolation for men, the death of rulers.* Not everyone had been convinced by the interpretation of Apsines that the desolation would fall upon the enemy. The Syrian was an orator, not a priest. A Sophist would argue black was white; anything for advantage. Maximinus was not sure that he was convinced himself.

Other things weighed on their spirits. Since Emona, the army had been short of supplies, of food and fodder. Their descent onto the plains of northern Italy had not been as

154

Maximinus had foretold. The inhabitants had not appeared carrying olive branches, pushing forward their children, falling at the feet of the soldiers, and begging for mercy. Domitius had not been waiting with remounts; the Prefect of the Camp had disappeared without trace. The army marched through a sodden, empty land. The officers muttered it was as if the primordial flood of Deucalion had come again, and swept away humanity.

The isolation was complete. They had crossed the Alps without hindrance. But for days now they had heard nothing from the North. No messengers, stragglers, or supply trains had emerged from the mountains. All had vanished somewhere in the high passes.

And there was the river. The sun was out when they finally saw the Aesontius. With the vanguard, Maximinus had watched the German horsemen spurring down through the trees. Laughing, boasting their ability to cross in full armour, they had put their mounts into the water below the piers of the dismantled bridge. The Aesontius was not like their slow northern streams. Swollen by the rain and the snows melting in the mountains, it was a rushing torrent. They were not halfway across before they were in trouble. Maximinus had heard their screams of terror as the current took them. They floundered and turned as it swept them downstream. One by one, they went under. Of the twenty men and horses that went into the water, none had come back. Today the Aesontius would be placated with a sacrifice.

The cavalcade halted at the replacement pontoon bridge. A page held his horse's head, and waited for Maximinus to dismount.

The improvised bridge looked solid enough. It had been the notion of Volcatius, a Senator previously overlooked by Maximinus. Apparently he had seen similar in his native Gaul. Although the countryside had been stripped of

155

everything portable, there were a lot of empty, rounded wine barrels in the deserted fields. They were enormous, the size of a house. Watertight and hollow, they floated like ungainly boats. Laboriously, they had been manhandled into the water, firmly anchored, and lashed together. With brushwood laid on top of them, and soil piled evenly on top of that, a roadway crossed the Aesontius.

Maximinus inspected the troops drawn up along the bank. They looked tired, dirty, and hungry. But the soldiers, unlike their effete officers, were resilient. Although some had fallen by the wayside, there were still some thirty thousand with the standards. It was the most potent field army in the world. If Aquileia had not already fallen to Vopiscus, the town could not hope to resist such a force. Ravenna would not be saved by its marshes and lagoons. Then on to Rome. A steady, ordered progress, crushing all in its path. Vengeance meted out.

The gods willing, of course. Maximinus spat on his breastplate to avert bad luck. He knew the high-born officers at his back would be looking askance at such superstition. To Hades with them, and their condescension.

Maximinus swung down from the saddle.

Would Paulina have approved of the ritual he was about to perform? He had doubts. She had been the most gentle of women, kind-hearted. War was the work of men. And this he was about to do was time-hallowed, a venerable part of the *mos maiorum*.

It was not two years since she had died, but already he found it hard to remember her exactly. The harder he tried to recall her pale eyes, her delicate features, the more they slipped away. He carried with him several coins bearing her portrait. At times, on the march, or when meetings of the *consilium* dragged, he studied them. They bore only a passing resemblance to his memories. Whoever made them perhaps had no idea what she looked like. The long nose, the jutting

156

chin; they reminded him of a feminine version of himself. The two images merging into one. It was fitting; they had been as one.

Maximinus looked over at his son. There was nothing of himself in Verus Maximus. You heard of daemons fathering children on women in the guise of their husbands. But there was nothing of Paulina either in the weak, cruel youth. When Maximinus was very young, old women in the village talked of witches stealing infants, leaving some changeling in their cot.

Back in Emona, Maximinus had been saddened by the news that Iunia Fadilla's carriage had been found looted and abandoned. He imagined the misery inflicted by his son that had driven her to that desperate, doomed flight. It had taken courage. He did not like to think of her raped and murdered by bandits in some dark wood or dismal lair.

Verus Maximus, of course, had refused to believe she was dead. He had vowed to find her, to take a terrible revenge. In his ravings, it was unclear if his petulant, vicious retribution would fall on his errant wife or the brigands. It made no odds. Verus Maximus was too ineffectual to achieve anything by himself, and Maximinus had immediately called off the search. In a civil war, soldiers could not be spared to scour the hills of the backcountry for a corpse in a ditch.

'Imperator.' The voice of Anullinus brought him back.

Maximinus waved the Praetorian Prefect away. There was something feral about Anullinus, something wrong with his eyes.

Setting his massive shoulders, Maximinus stepped onto the bridge. He gestured for Apsines and Javolenus, his bodyguard, to accompany him. With those two on either shoulder, he felt reassured. Verus Maximus crowded his back. The rest of the entourage – Senators, equestrian officers and heads of chanceries – trailed after.

157

The soldiers had the prisoner waiting at the centre of the bridge. The animals and the sack were ready. It had been Maximinus' idea, although Apsines had advised him on the technicalities. Maximinus had rejected a hood for the prisoner. If a man had to die, even a traitor should have one last look at the light he was leaving.

Apsines had shown his worth. True or not, his words had calmed the soldiers during the eclipse. Since Paulina died, Maximinus often talked to the Sophist. There was no one else. Paulina was dead, the companions of his youth, Tynchanius and Micca, were dead. Maximinus was alone.

Apsines deserved the status and ornaments of a Consul which Maximinus had awarded. The Senators with the army complained that giving such honours to an equestrian subverted the *mos maiorum*. As if the ways of the ancestors could be reduced to formal ranks and privileges, rather than duty and virtue. And the Senators betrayed their arrogance and stupidity by not realizing that what they said in their tents in the presence of their slaves would be reported to the Emperor. The *frumentarii* of Volo were in every elite household. At court there was no privacy. There were informants everywhere.

Abanchus the Sarmatian was bound hand and foot. Stripped to the waist, his back was a bloodied mess from the scourge. There was dried blood in his long hair.

Maximinus remembered walking into the hut. He had been no more than a child. His family all dead. His mother and his sisters naked. It was not Abanchus' tribe of Iazyges that had done the killing, but all northern barbarians were the same; savage, irrational, less than human.

Verus Maximus pushed Apsines out of the way, stood by his father. The youth's eyes were alive with anticipation.

'This is wrong,' Abanchus said.

'You are a traitor, and you deserve to die.' Maximinus

still found it hard to believe that Menophilus, or even the little Greek Timcsitheus, would stoop so low as to invite barbarians into the empire. How could the most depraved citizens put their own interests above the good of the *Res Publica*? Thank the gods Abanchus had been caught trying to sneak through Pannonia. Honoratus would have to deal with Cniva the Goth on the Danube.

'Give me a sword.'

Verus Maximus laughed.

'Let me fight in the arena. Give me the death of a warrior.'

'An Emperor is the father of his people.' Maximinus had listened to what Apsines called political philosophy. 'An attempt on the life of an Emperor is . . .' – the word escaped Maximinus – 'is to try and kill your father. Punishment should fit the crime. Let the sentence be carried out.'

The cockerel was easy enough to get into the leather sack. Although its legs were tied, the dog was more difficult. The soldier carrying the viper wore gauntlets, and handled it with great caution. It had been impossible to get a monkey.

Abanchus was lifted off his feet, stuffed head first into the sack. When the neck was secured, it muffled the terrible sounds: the dog snarling, the man screaming.

Verus Maximus clapped his hands with pleasure.

The sack thrashed and bulged as it was dragged to the edge. A heave, and it splashed heavily into the river.

In moments it was gone.

Parricide – that was the word Maximinus had been hunting for – parricide.

CHAPTER 16

Northern Italy

Aquileia,
Two Days after the Ides of April, AD238

Menophilus walked out from the River Gate. With him were Crispinus, his fellow commander, and the two leading magistrates, Barbius and Statius. The entire town council followed. Menophilus could sense their indecision; the way their fear gnawed at their dignity and resolve. It was important the civilians were there. This was their town, and a show of unity was vital.

In the distance a small party of horsemen was leaving the enlarged eastern camp. They would be Maximinus' envoys.

The Thracian's army had arrived the day before. The great columns of infantry and cavalry had snaked across the plain, standards flying, purposeful and imposing. Their sheer numbers had terrified the townsfolk watching from the battlements.

The imperial field army had divided, and funnelled towards the two camps constructed by Vopiscus. All afternoon soldiers had laboured, digging ditches, building palisades, and erecting tents. It seemed impossible there could be shelter for all that multitude. At sunset a herald had approached the town walls, proposed a truce, and arranged this parley.

Menophilus stepped onto the bridge. The Natiso was fifty paces wide. Menophilus stopped where the central twenty paces of the span had been demolished. The water at his feet was very green, slow moving.

The envoys cantered down the road in the sunshine. Beyond them, beyond the camp, the plain stretched, green and flat, until it dissolved into a blue haze. All that could be seen of the mountains was a faint dark line of the foothills. White clouds piled up above the invisible heights.

Maximinus would not come himself. It was beneath the imperial dignity to bandy words with rebels. He would send some junior officers.

Menophilus looked downstream. When he had first arrived in Aquileia, the port had been bustling. Ships and barges moved in the roadstead, more made fast to the wharves. Stevedores, bent under their burdens, unloaded wine, olive oil, and luxuries brought from the south. The snap of whips as cattle and slaves were driven up the gangplanks, the creak as cranes swayed bales of hides down into holds.

Now the waterfront was silent and empty. All the ships had sailed, except for a few rivercraft which had been hauled up into the warehouses. The cranes had been dismantled, moved to other places, ready for some more bellicose use. The slipways were blocked, and the passages into the town bricked up. The walls and rectangular towers were a patch-work where they had been hastily repaired with anything that came to hand: broken statues and tombs, the drums of fallen columns. Above them, from between the crenulations, the townsfolk – women and children, as well as men – peered out anxiously. Even the soldiers, standing up there by the four ballistae, appeared nervous.

The riders were approaching the bridge.

161

Menophilus, affecting unconcern, let his gaze slide upriver, off to the north. There were three bridges over the Natiso, close together, all broken now. For the first couple of hundred paces the trees along the bank had been cut down. The water there flashed like a mirror in the sun. Further out dark poplars and lighter willows stood along the banks. The branches of the latter hung down over the stream, making a shaded, secret passage. The river ran not far from the other camp of Maximinus' army. Menophilus viewed the scene through a fog of fatigue and guilt; the climate of his life.

The envoys had arrived. There were six of them – a tribune, three Centurions, and two troopers. They dismounted. The troopers held the horses, and the others came onto the bridge.

'It is my son,' Barbius said.

Menophilus had feared this, and, now his fear was realized, found he had nothing to say. Words failed him around Barbius.

'Courage,' Crispinus said, and put his hand on the shoulder of the magistrate. 'We must all have courage.'

They stood on the far side of the gap. The tribune, Barbius' son, took off his helmet, the better to be heard.

'Maximinus Augustus, the Emperor to whom you have given your oaths, orders you to lay down your weapons.'

He was a fine young man, tall and composed. His gaze took in them all, only briefly resting on his father. Military command had given him a voice that carried well.

'You should receive him as a friend rather than an enemy. You should be occupied in making libations and sacrifices rather than preparing for bloodshed.'

His words were greeted with silence.

'Do not forget that your city is on the point of annihilation. It is in your power to save yourselves, your homes, your wives and children. Accept the offer of an amnesty and a pardon for your errors from our noble and merciful Emperor.'

Behind Menophilus the town councillors shifted and whispered.

'It is not the people of Aquileia who are guilty, but those who have led them astray.' Barbius' son chose his words carefully. 'Hand over the instigators of this treason. Only Menophilus and Crispinus will be punished.'

The muttering behind Menophilus was louder.

The tribune looked at his father. 'My wife and children are in our family home. Father, spare them. You have lost one son, left to die by Menophilus, the man you protect. Spare the rest of your loved ones.'

Menophilus had to say something. Nothing suitable came to mind. What use was his Stoic philosophy? Death is nothing. We are dying every day. Family and friends, life itself, all are like figs, they do not last. Menophilus knew himself a bad actor, with the wrong lines.

'Stay firm.' Crispinus turned his back on the envoys, addressed the townsfolk. 'Do not betray the Senate and the people of Rome. Earn yourselves the title of saviours and defenders of all Italy.'

Crispinus pointed back at the camp on the plain. 'Do not believe the promises of a tyrant who breaks his word and deceives people. How many defenceless men has he tortured and killed? Do not be enticed into surrendering yourselves to certain destruction.'

He walked without alarm among the councillors. Long-bearded, the broad purple stripe on his toga; Crispinus embodied senatorial *dignitas*. 'Do not be disconcerted by the size of their army. Those who serve a tyrant fight with no enthusiasm. You who fight for your own homes, for *libertas*, can expect the favour of the gods. You have stout walls, weapons in your hands, courage in your hearts. Defy the tyrant!'

The townsmen were silent. They looked at Crispinus, and

sidelong at each other. Everyone was waiting for a lead to follow.

Barbius stepped to the very lip of the broken span. There were tears running down his face.

'May the gods hold their hands over you, my son. But this thing you ask, it cannot be done. If we surrender, your brother died for nothing.'

'But, Father—'

'Enough,' Menophilus said. 'You have your answer.'

CHAPTER 17

Northern Italy

Aquileia,
Four Days after the Ides of April, AD238

From a point of vantage high on the aqueduct Maximinus could see the town and hinterland of Aquileia laid out like an intricate drawing by a land surveyor. He almost expected to see carefully inserted labels and numerals. The Via Julia Augusta and the aqueduct ran parallel and arrow-straight down to the walls near on half a mile away. From this distance the aqueduct looked undamaged. Only the last twenty or thirty paces of the arches had been demolished. Obviously the defenders had been worried by the possibility of soldiers using the watercourse to reach the walls. They had diverted the water far to the north. Where the line of the road and aqueduct could be seen again beyond the defences, they continued to the open space of the Forum. To the right was the Circus, its western wall forming part of the perimeter, and further on was the amphitheatre, set back in urban parkland. In the far left corner of the town stood the great Temple of Belenus. The Natiso bounded Aquileia

165

to the east; having been hidden by the town, the river reappeared running south to where, some five or six miles distant, the waters of the Gulf of Tergeste flashed in the deceptively peaceful sunshine.

Once, many years before, when on guard duty in the Palace, Maximinus had heard Septimius Severus tell of a dream which had revealed that one day Severus would hold the imperial power. A god had taken Severus to a high place commanding a wide view, and, as he gazed down from there on all the land and all the sea, he laid his fingers on them as one might on an instrument capable of playing wonderful music. The whole world had sung at his command.

Maximinus' own accession had been more mundane. No deity had given forewarning. All the supposed omens had been invented after the event. It had been on the Rhine. The recruits that he had been training had mutinied. Taken by surprise, Maximinus had been unable to stop them acclaiming him Emperor. The purple would have proved fatal within the day if Vopiscus, Honoratus, and Catius Clemens had not pledged the support of the legionaries they commanded. In hindsight, Maximinus suspected the uprising might not have been quite as spontaneous as it had first appeared. It gave him grim satisfaction to think that if the senatorial triumvirate had wanted a malleable ruler, their hopes had not been realized. Maximinus knew that the northern barbarians posed a mortal threat to Rome; everything else paled into insignificance. Desperate times demanded hard measures. To survive, savage wars had to be fought along the Rhine and Danube, the empire had to be run like an armed camp. This uprising was a distraction that must be speedily crushed. There was no time for delay.

'A pity the city did not fall to my first assault,' Vopiscus said, as if he could tell what his Emperor was thinking.

'Once the rebels had killed your legionaries, they knew

we must take revenge. The embassy of young Barbius was bound to fail,' Maximinus said.

'But it was worth me making the attempt.' There was the sound of a question to Vopiscus' self-justification.

'You did the right thing,' Maximinus said. 'Aquileia will fall today.'

High on his eyrie, the wind buffeting his ears, Maximinus gave the order to advance.

The trumpet note was picked up and repeated along the line below. The arms of the ballistae snapped forward, and thirty iron-tipped bolts shot away towards the battlements. There was no reply. The scouts had reported that the defenders had only eight pieces of artillery along this northern wall. Doubtless they would conserve ammunition, and keep those who served the machines below the crenulations until the attackers were closer.

The three penthouses on wheels which covered the rams groaned into motion. The engineers of the legions had assembled them the day before. The frames were locally cut green wood, bolted together with metal clamps from the siege train, the roofs and walls hides of freshly slaughtered cattle, plastered with wet mud from the river. One device advanced down the road towards the gate. The other two lumbered very slowly across the plain to the left of the aqueduct, aiming at two sections where the wall had been hastily repaired, and might be weaker. Each sheltered a crew of fifty. They would earn their pay today hauling the heavy, ungainly structures to the walls. And then earn it again with the backbreaking labour of swinging the metal-sheathed ram.

Alongside the rams, mobile screens, also of wood and hides, protected the hook-men, who would prise out sections of timber and stone dislodged by the siege engines. Behind the first line went yet more mantlets; these sheltering the archers who would clear the wallwalks. For now the massed columns of the assault troops waited out of range.

The troops were in good spirits. Last night they had feasted on the beasts killed for their hides. The soldiers who had arrived with Maximinus were anxious to prove that they could succeed where the Pannonians of Vopiscus had failed, and the latter eager to make amends.

There was one cloud in Maximinus' mind. All the cattle remaining with the army had been slaughtered. There were none to be found in the surrounding countryside. It should not matter. They would take all the provisions needed when the town fell. Aquileia was a prosperous emporium.

Maximinus went to the first of the ladders, Vopiscus followed, and they began the long climb down.

The imperial staff were waiting below: Anullinus, the Praetorian Prefect, with his unsmiling, cruel eyes, Julius Capitolinus, commander of the 2nd Legion Parthica, that Gallic Senator Volcatius, who had thought of using the wine barrels as pontoons. All were men driven by ambition; untrustworthy, strangers to duty and virtue. At the edge of the group was that young barbarian hostage, the son of Isangrim, ruler of the Angles. Maximinus wondered what the long-haired youth had made of the execution of Abanchus the Sarmatian. Severity was essential. Only fear made barbarians keep their word.

'Father?'

Maximinus ignored his own son.

The rams were making good, if slow progress. Maximinus called for the imperial entourage's horses.

'Father, is this necessary?'

'It is necessary,' Maximinus said. 'At the start of a siege the Emperor must show himself before the walls, demonstrate his contempt for their missiles. It instils fear into the hearts of the enemy, and puts an edge on the courage of his own men.'

'But all the high command, the horse guards; we make a large target. What if we were both hit?' Verus Maximus could not hide the apprehension in his voice.

'Javolenus will ride on my right, you on my left. No soldier fights well for a coward.' Maximinus did not try to hide his contempt. It would undermine his son in the eyes of the senior officers, but that was of no consequence. Verus Maximus would not sit on the throne.

Maximinus mounted Borysthenes, his favourite charger.

With evident reluctance, his son also got into the saddle.

'Here we are again, old friend.' Maximinus stroked Borysthenes' soft ears, inhaled the good sweet smell of warm horse. He touched the silver ring on his thumb, the gold torque around his neck; gifts from Paulina and Severus, reminders of trust and good faith, things worth fighting for.

'Unfurl the standards. Let them know who comes against them.'

The road looked long and bare and bright in the sun. Half a hundred fights, a lifetime of combat, and still that odd hollow feeling as it began. His bodyguard on one knee, his son the other, Maximinus nudged Borysthenes forward.

They picked up speed, and with a thunder of hooves, and a rattle of harness, cantered towards the town.

Maximinus! Maximinus! The chant went up as they passed the infantry. *Maximinus!* Never a shout for his son, the noble Caesar. Soldiers were not fools. They would never follow Verus Maximus.

The walls loomed ahead, tall and grey, silent and forbidding. Three hundred paces, two hundred. The horsemen veered off the road, passed the ram, clattered back onto the paved surface.

The breeze snapped the banners, whistled through the jaws of the dragon standards.

At a hundred paces, the battlements suddenly were empty

no longer. As if conjured out of thin air, armed men thronged the walls.

Maximinus watched the snub nose of a ballista on the gate turning in his direction, sniffing for his blood. He rode on, back straight. Death comes to a coward as certainly as to a brave man.

Arrows rained around them. Slingshots pinged and skittered up off the track. Maximinus paid them no attention. He would not go down to Hades until the gods willed.

He saw the recoil of the ballista, but did not catch sight of the bolt. Two seconds later it tore past, just over his head. Behind him a scream, human or animal, impossible to tell.

'Imperator, this is close enough,' Javolenus shouted.

Maximinus ignored his bodyguard.

'Father, this is madness!' Verus Maximus screeched.

Perhaps thirty paces from the gate, no further than a peasant could throw a stick, Maximinus reined Borysthenes to the right, gave the warhorse its head, and raced along the wall.

The defenders thronging the battlements yelled insults – *Tyrant! Murderer!* They called out the names of villains from myth and history – *Sciron! Spartacus!* Some of the abuse was aimed at his son – *Catamite! Cocksucker!* They jumped up and down in their hatred, and shot and hurled everything to hand.

The missiles hailed all around. Behind, men and horses were going down. Maximinus was unmoved. The hollowness was gone. Now he was calm. He felt the presence of the Rider God, the deity of his native hills, and knew that nothing would touch him.

With contempt Maximinus noticed that Verus Maximus had pulled his horse round to put his father and Javolenus between him and the wall. The youth's face was very pale. He was mouthing high-pitched obscenities.

Anullinus had closed up on Maximinus' left, partly shielding the Emperor.

A man stood on the machicolations, hauled down his breeches, bared his arse.

Turning his mount away, Maximinus laughed. He could not remember laughing since Paulina died.

As he galloped back to the waiting legionaries, Maximinus could not have been happier. The defenders were like children. They had dug no pits, planted no stakes, spread no caltrops. Smoke from no fires to heat oil hung over the battlements. They had not even lowered anything to pad the walls to absorb the impact of the rams. What could be expected from a rabble of civilians led by two effete Senators. Aquileia would fall like a ripe fruit.

When he reined in, he saw the rams had reached the walls. The one on the far left struck first. A fine dust filtered down from the wall.

'Soldiers of Rome.' Maximinus raised himself on the horns of his saddle to address the ranks. 'Fellow-soldiers, the traitors who defy you are old men, women, and children. They know nothing of war. They have made no preparations. They have no discipline. When the walls are breached, they will not stand.'

The brutal but honest faces of the veterans gazed up at him.

'When the rams have done their work, I give you this town, and everything and everyone in it. Take all by the right of conquest. The rams have touched the walls, they can expect no mercy. Aquileia will be demolished, the whole region turned into grazing land.'

Maximinus Imperator! The prospect of plunder and rape put them in good voice. They cheered him to the echo. *Maximinus Imperator!*

Maximinus swung down to take the weight from Borysthenes' back. Those around him also dismounted.

171

'Emperor.' It was Vopiscus. 'Two tribunes, and six troopers did not return.'

Maximinus gripped the Senator's shoulders with his great hands, pulled him close to his great, white face. 'Vopiscus,' he spoke gently, as if to a child, 'this is war.'

Vopiscus looked past Maximinus towards the town. His eyes went very wide.

'Men die in war.' Maximinus touched the thong of the amulet Vopiscus wore around his neck, hooked a finger under it. 'You should know that. Did none of your oracles, your soothsayers, your random lines of Virgil warn you?'

'Emperor . . .' Vopiscus pointed.

Maximinus turned.

A tracery of beams had risen above the walls where the three siege engines pounded. As Maximinus watched, the arm of the crane behind the gate swung out. It stopped over the ram. Men were scrambling out of the rear of the penthouse. The crane released its load. The massive piece of masonry smashed through the hides and wood below. Dust billowed up. A moment's pause, and the penthouse imploded.

Maximinus looked along the wall. One of the other penthouses was still intact, but abandoned by its crew. The crane above it was swinging back for another rock. In moments this third structure too would be destroyed.

Across the plain, his soldiers were being shot down as they ran.

Maximinus stood, clenching and unclenching his fists.

'Augustus—'

Maximinus punched Vopiscus to the ground.

No one else moved.

In the unnatural stillness, Maximinus gazed back at the rout.

'Sound the retreat,' Maximinus said.

172

Vopiscus was trying to get to his feet. There was blood on his face. No one went to help him.

Maximinus thought of Paulina. She had been the only one who could make him control his temper. He felt guilty, but an Emperor did not apologize. He reached down, and pulled Vopiscus up, patted him on the shoulder. That would have to do by way of apology.

'Capitolinus, form the 2nd Legion into line, cover the retreat in case the defenders come out.' Maximinus put Vopiscus out of his mind.

This was a setback, not a disaster. Not that many men had been lost. The three penthouses were ruined, but they might yet salvage the rams. He would send men out to drag them back under cover of darkness. If he brought up all the siege train the town would fall in a few days. It needed to, supplies were very low. An unwanted memory insinuated itself into his thoughts: the army of Severus had sat before Byzantium for months. Worse yet, it had twice failed before the desert city of Hatra. Aquileia was different, Maximinus told himself, it would be his in days.

PART V:
ROME

CHAPTER 18

Rome

The Senate House,
Four Days after the Ides of April, AD238

Timesitheus stood by the statue of *Libertas,* and watched through the open door as the Senators took their seats. As an equestrian he was forbidden to enter the Curia, but as Prefect of the Grain Supply it was degrading to have to wait on the threshold, jostled by the elbows of the masses; by off-duty soldiers, scum who followed the Circus factions, dyers, tavern-keepers, and worse.

There was a dangerous edge to this crowd. There were many more of them than would be expected. They were all around the building, wedged tight in all the doorways, the one here at the front and the two at the rear. There was an unusual air of anticipation. Timesitheus had thought it best to send his two retained gladiators to attend his wife. Even a small entourage of hired killers in the Forum made a bad impression. But he was glad that he was flanked by a couple of tough young members of the equestrian order. They had knives hidden under their tunics, as he did himself. Almost everyone carried a concealed weapon these days.

Timesitheus arranged his face, ignored his surroundings. It was a measure of his political isolation that he was reduced to waiting on the doorstep for news. He was excluded from the private deliberations of any of the senatorial factions. Menophilus was off defending Aquileia. Latronianus, the last surviving patron of his early career, was in the East as an envoy. Anyway, before leaving, Latronianus had married his daughter off to Armenius Peregrinus, Timesitheus' avowed enemy. Catius Celer, the sole remaining confidant Timesitheus had among the Conscript Fathers in Rome, was tainted by his brother's closeness to Maximinus. It was best to keep clear of Celer in the present climate.

Access to the imperial households also was exiguous at best. Balbinus, who seldom left the Palatine, only admitted Timesitheus with the general herd at his morning salutations. On the one occasion he had received an individual summons, Balbinus curtly told him to increase the amount of free grain distributed to the populace; it would add to the *hilaritas* of his reign. When Timesitheus had pointed out that the granaries would be severely depleted, Balbinus dismissed him without another word, and turned back to petting some painted catamite. The *Domus Rostrata*, of course, was barred to Timesitheus. Maecia Faustina had issued strict instructions that 'the treacherous little Greek' was not to be allowed anywhere near the young Caesar Gordian, as her son was now styled. As for Pupienus, it was probably as well that he had left to organize the defence of Ravenna. He had interpreted the elevation of Gordian as a bid for power on the part of Timesitheus. Of course Pupienus was right. And Timesitheus had to admit, by sending the boy back to his mother, and having him guarded by Praetorians officered by Felicio, a loyal client of the Gordiani, old Pupienus had

178

outmanoeuvred him brilliantly. For all his ponderous *dignitas*, there was an astuteness behind Pupienus' long beard.

Every politician was bound like Ixion to the wheel of fortune. Timesitheus knew he was no exception. Sometimes, on the downward turn, there was nothing to do but endure.

Inside, the presiding magistrate, Licinius Rufinus the Consul, had concluded the religious observances. As usual, the Emperor Balbinus had not roused himself to attend. Licinius called for one of the Quaestors to read the despatch from Aquileia.

'Rutilius Pudens Crispinus, and Tullius Menophilus, Members of the Board of Twenty, to the Consuls and Senate. If you are well, it is well. We and the army are well.'

The tight-packed throng around Timesitheus eddied forward. At the far end of the hall, some of the onlookers, soldiers by the look of them, were actually inside the doors, level with the statue of Victory.

The letter started well. Four days previously the detachments of the Pannonian Legions, under the command of Flavius Vopiscus, had assaulted the walls of Aquileia, and been thrown back in disarray.

In the chamber the Senators shook back the folds of their togas, expressed their delight, waved spotless handkerchiefs.

Outside, around Timesitheus, the response was muted, as if the news was somehow incidental. Some of the crowd appeared to be waiting for something else.

The communication took a more sombre turn. At the time of writing, the outriders of Maximinus' main army had been sighted. Further attempts on the town were expected. The despatch ended with sonorous defiance: Aquileia was ready to stand siege, every man would do his duty, *libertas* would be defended, the gods would confound the tyrant.

The Senators sat in silent dignity. The crowd shifted with excitement, as if waiting for the start of a horse race or gladiatorial combat. Timesitheus felt a growing unease. There was something unnatural about the plebs today. Were they aware of something that was hidden both from him and the body of Senators?

Gallicanus, shaggy in his rough toga, took the floor. His inseparable companion Maecenas was at his elbow.

'Conscript Fathers, you are distracted with petty things.'

Gallicanus paced up and down, working himself up. Even the more urbane Maecenas was agitated.

'While the world blazes, here in the Senate House you are busied with an old woman's cares.'

At the far end, two of the soldiers had advanced beyond the statue of Victory into the chamber itself, the better to hear. They stood modestly enough, arms in their cloaks, by the altar. They laughed at the disrespect Gallicanus showed the Senate.

'Day after day you discuss the embellishment of a basilica and the Baths of Titus, or the repairs to the amphitheatre. While Crispinus and Menophilus fight for their lives, for all your lives, for the freedom of Rome, you debate roads and sewers and drains. Make no mistake, open your eyes, Maximinus is on his way. In battle-order, with camps pitched everywhere, he is coming with fire and sword. He is at Aquileia already. His hired killers are in this very chamber. They are intent on massacre.'

With a flourish, Gallicanus pointed at the two soldiers by the altar.

They were not young, probably Praetorian veterans awaiting their discharge. One looked around, smiling uncertainly. There was alarm on the face of the other.

The toga was a voluminous garment, deliberately ill-fitted to violent action, but anything could be hidden in its folds. The knives appeared in the hands of Gallicanus and Maecenas as if by magic. Arms tangled in their cloaks, the soldiers were defenceless. They went down under a flurry of blows.

It was done in seconds. The two corpses lay on the floor, blood pooling out across the inlaid marble.

Gallicanus and Maecenas were incarnadine, arms red to the shoulder, gore spattered across the snowy fronts of their togas.

White-faced, the Senators sat immobile, making no sound, barely breathing.

Those soldiers by the doors turned to flee. Some of the crowd punched and pulled at them as they pushed through.

Gallicanus lifted his bloody dagger high. 'Death to the enemies of the Senate and people! Death to the agents of the tyrant!'

He and Maecenas walked the length of the Curia. At the door, the throng parted for them. Timesitheus was shoved aside.

The assassins processed down the steps and across to the Rostra. The crowd surged after them.

Now there was room to move, Timesitheus scuttled to one end of the portico, and peeped out from behind a pillar.

Gallicanus mounted the Rostra. As ever, Maecenas was behind him.

'*Quirites*.' The crowd was quiet, tensed like a greyhound in the slips. 'Citizens of Rome.' All hung on Gallicanus' words. 'The time for talking is past. It is time for action. War has come to the eternal city. Today we have struck the first blow for freedom.'

Libertas, libertas: sections of the audience began to chant.

Timesitheus scanned the crowd, saw the pattern emerge. There was a theatre claque and its leader, nearby a *Collegium* of bargemen headed by its elected officials, over there another guild, the fullers stinking of urine, beyond them toughs from the Circus faction of the Greens. Gallicanus had summoned the lowest of the low. The respectable representatives of the plebs – the magistrates of the districts of the

181

city, the neighbourhood priests of the Emperors – were nowhere to be seen.

'People of Rome, rise up, and save the *Res Publica*. Hunt down the enemies of the state. Burn them. Drag them with the hook. Throw them in the Tiber.'

To the Tiber! To the Tiber!

Behind Timesitheus Senators emerged from the Curia. They slid along the portico, then, gathering up the skirts of their togas, vanished down the Argiletum which ran by the side of the House or under the arches which fronted the Basilica Aemilia. Timesitheus did not think that he was in any imminent danger. His mutilated left hand was proof of his commitment to the cause against Maximinus, the grain he had distributed should act as a safe conduct. He became aware that the two young equestrians were still with him.

'Hunt down the Praetorians!' Gallicanus was in his element, a demagogue inciting his audience. 'Hunt down the friends of Maximinus!'

Over by the Lake of Curtius a space opened around one man. His dress proclaimed him an off-duty soldier. He turned this way and that, searching for an avenue of escape. He stretched out in supplication. The crowd closed on him. They beat and kicked him. A flash of steel in the sunshine, and he was lost to sight, trampled underfoot.

'Hunt down the traitors in our midst. Those who are not with you are against you. Do not spare the enemies of the state. Retribution is at hand. To the Praetorian camp.'

The crowd seethed; some moved one way, others another. Cries and oaths and terrible threats echoed off marble façades. *To the camp. To the camp.* Before Timesitheus' eyes men cast off all conscience and pity, subsumed their individuality into the mob. The people of Rome were transformed into a single beast baying for blood.

It was time to leave.

182

Timesitheus took off the ring that bore his seal. 'Aelius, get down to Ostia. Tell Masculus who commands the Watch there to set armed guards around the granaries. Give him this ring as proof of my authority. Gnaeus, go to my house. Arm the slaves, get them to barricade the doors and windows. Have water ready on the roof in case they try to burn us out.'

'What are you going to do?' Aelius asked.

'Fetch my wife.'

Tranquillina was in the Temple of Peace. When the two equestrians had gone, Timesitheus considered the safest route to her. Already elements of the mob were entering the portico in front of the Basilica Aemilia. It would have to be down the Argiletum, through the Forum Transitorm, and along the Street of the Sandal-makers to the northern gates. He left the shelter of the column and ran.

Behind him the beast was in full voice. *To the camp! To the camp!*

Winged rumour travelled faster than a man. By the time that Timesitheus – chest burning – reached the Street of the Sandal-makers a group of innkeepers and other brutes had cornered a Praetorian. The soldier cowered at the foot of the statue of Apollo Sandaliarius. 'Balbinus Augustus,' he shouted. 'Gordian Caes—' The first stone struck him full in the face. Timesitheus did not wait to see where the others landed.

Tranquillina was just inside the gate. The two gladiators and her *custos* were grim-faced, blades in hand. Her maid was sobbing.

'Quiet.' Tranquillina slapped the girl hard.

'We must go,' Timesitheus said.

'What is happening?'

'Gallicanus has got the mob out. They are lynching the soldiers, anyone they think is a friend of Maximinus. They

183

are going to storm the Praetorian camp. We must get home.' He put his good hand on Tranquillina's arm.

She put her hand on his. 'Wait.' Her dark eyes were alive with calculation. 'Where are the Prefects of the Praetorians?'

'Felicio is in the *Domus Rostrata* with Gordian, Pinarius is in the camp. We must go now. There is no time.'

Tranquillina smiled. 'You have never been a cat that was afraid to get its paws wet. Pinarius is a civilian. He cannot defend the camp. This is your opportunity to be the saviour of Rome.'

'Leave you?'

'The gladiators will see me to our house. Go and save the camp. With the Praetorians at your back, you can command Rome.'

'Will you be safe?'

'I will get Maecius Gordianus to send a detachment of his *vigiles* to the house.'

'Maecius Gordianus?'

'There is no time for your petty jealousy. We all do what we have to do.' Tranquillina kissed him. 'Go now.'

CHAPTER 19

Rome

The Praetorian Camp,
Four Days after the Ides of April, AD238

'Thank the gods you are here.'

Praetorians running for their lives had brought the news, outstripping the mob. Pinarius, the aged Prefect, had told the troops to stand to, some on the walls, most drawn up outside on the parade ground. The gates of the camp were still open. Pinarius was no soldier, and had been more than happy to hand effective command to Timesitheus. Yet in regard to official rank, he had expressed a certain reluctance.

'Only an Emperor can appoint another Praetorian Prefect. They say Balbinus is trapped in the Palace and Pupienus is in Ravenna.'

'Your adoptive son is my friend,' Timesitheus had said. 'He will give retrospective approval.'

'I do not know.' Pinarius had shaken his head in rustic doubt. 'He did not speak highly of you, last time we talked.'

Timesitheus had arranged his expression into something dutiful and serious. 'Pupienus chose me to go to the North.

185

On my return our disagreement over making young Gordian Caesar was a passing squall. Friends can differ, but friendship remains.'

'I suppose you are right.' Pinarius had looked far from convinced.

'Excellent, let us call me an *acting* Prefect.'

'If you are sure it is necessary.'

'It is essential.'

'Then let it be so.' Pinarius had adopted a thoughtful demeanour. 'A true friendship endures. It is similar to the way plants with the deepest roots survive a drought.'

'Quite so.' Timesitheus had had no desire to endure another ponderous analogy drawn from botanical endeavour. 'Perhaps it would be best if we got to work.'

As acting Prefect, Timesitheus had taken stock. Of the thousand or so Praetorians in Rome, a detachment was with Balbinus on the Palatine, another guarding Gordian in the *Domus Rostrata*, yet others were on leave or unaccounted for, quite possibly already dead. Only four hundred remained in the camp. Fortunately it was the usual arrangement for a proportion of the Urban Cohorts to share their barracks. They were accustomed to following the orders of the Praetorian Prefects in the camp, and added no less than three thousand swords to the defence.

The camp had high, battlemented walls and heavy gates. Timesitheus had marched everyone inside, and broken out the weapons from the armoury. All those of the garrison who claimed any proficiency as archers – a couple of hundred – had been issued with bows and stationed on the wallwalks. They had been joined by two thousand equipped with long pikes to stab down at any attackers. It had left a reserve of twelve hundred.

The gates had been shut and barred, heavy beams propped against them inside, and secured in place by wedges. Just the wicket gates were still open to admit any stragglers. The camp had a plentiful supply of water from the Tepula aqueduct, and there was food for seven or eight days, more if the men were put on reduced rations. All in all, given the lack of warning, they were well prepared for a siege. Wider issues addressed, Timesitheus borrowed a helmet, armour, and sword, then called for a trumpeter, and told him not to leave his side.

Timesitheus had taken charge of the battlements, and given Pinarius the reserve. He had suggested that Pinarius employ the latter in breaking up some of the numerous statues and inscriptions, memorials to deceased Praetorians and the like, that crowded the camp. The fragments would be used as missiles. The task was within the competence of the old gardener, and would allow him to feel that he was making a contribution. Sensitivity has always been one of my failings, Timesitheus had thought.

Leaning on the parapet, he gazed out across the parade ground at the city and the deserted streets. Why was the mob taking so long to get here – the afternoon was wearing on – and what would happen when it arrived?

Of course he would try to negotiate. He would wave his mutilated hand at them, remind them that he was no friend of Maximinus, but had suffered for the resistance. He doubted it would be enough. They might hold a certain regard for him as the *Praefectus Annonae*. But those on the official lists regarded free grain as their due, and those who were not would be resentful. It was as well this riot had not erupted later in the year. With the extra distributions ordered by that fat fool Balbinus, the public granaries were likely to be empty by late May or June when the Alexandrian grain fleet was to be expected. If it arrived at all. The Prefect of Egypt had been appointed by Maximinus; quite likely he would remain loyal to the Thracian. And, since Capelianus had killed the elder Gordiani, nothing would come from Africa.

187

It would be unwise to hope for outside military intervention. There were another three thousand men of the Urban Cohorts, mainly stationed across the river. But Rufinianus, the Prefect of the City, would be barricaded in the Palatine with Balbinus. Anyway, Rufinianus was nearly as corpulent and lethargic as his friend the Emperor. The *vigiles* were seven thousand strong. Maecius Gordianus might send help. *What had Tranquillina done to secure his support?* Yet the men of the Watch were scattered at their posts across the city, and were no more than armed firemen.

The soldiers in the camp would have to secure their own victory. A sudden sally, cut down a few hundred, make sure Gallicanus was among them, scatter the mob, at least for a time. Use that respite to send men to persuade the more respectable leaders of the plebeians to use their influence to get the rioters off the streets. The magistrates of the districts of the city and the priests of the local imperial cult mostly were freedmen. Ex-slaves who had come up in the world, they were now property owners, and would have no sympathy for revolution. They had too much to lose, too deep an investment in the status quo.

'They are coming.' A noise like surf on a distant shore. Then across the parade ground dark figures flitted from cover to cover, peered around doorjambs and street corners.

The main body of the mob would not be far behind.

What madness was this of Gallicanus? No one, not even the most rabid and ignorant Cynic preaching on a street corner, could believe that the free Republic might live again. If not bent on creating utopia, what was his intent? Gallicanus was keen enough for his own advancement; avidly grasping at the Consulship and membership of the Board of Twenty. Did he imagine the mob might sweep him into power as some philosopher–Emperor, a latter-day Marcus Aurelius? It took more than a ragged cloak and a scowl to make a wise man.

Now the noise sounded like the crowd at a distant amphitheatre. It rolled up to the camp.

Timesitheus remembered a line from his schooling. *What is born must also die, it makes no difference whether a fever shall bring that about, or a roof tile, or a soldier.*

'They are here.'

A black phalanx of men filling the old Via Tiburtina, debouching into the parade ground. There was something wrong about this mob; it moved too steadily, those at the front wore outlandish armour. Gladiators. That explained the delay. Gallicanus had recruited the fighters from the *Ludus Magnus*. Alcimus Felicianus had charge of the gladiatorial school. Timesitheus hoped his friend was unhurt, hoped even more fervently Alcimus had not joined Gallicanus. He had no desire to have to kill his friend.

'No one is to shoot, until the word of command.'

The phalanx stopped just beyond the cast of a javelin.

In the unnerving silence, little dust devils spun across the no man's land between the mob and the walls.

Gallicanus – ragged and barefoot, carrying a wooden staff – stepped forth. Maecenas was a pace behind.

'Praetorians, we have come to accept your oath of allegiance to the Senate and people of Rome. Open the gates, lay down your arms, give us the weapons in the armoury, and you will not be harmed.'

Timesitheus leant out between two of the merlons. 'Kiss my arse.'

Gallicanus ignored the abuse. 'Where is Pinarius?'

'Preparing your cross.'

Gallicanus laughed. 'You of all people.' He turned to those who followed him. 'Timesitheus, the little Greek, blown into our city with the figs and damsons and eunuch priests, and all the other decadent luxuries of the East. What do you take this fellow's profession to be? He has a whole bundle of

189

personalities – rhetorician, diviner, masseur, tightrope-walker, magician – your versatile *Graeculus* is all by turns. Tell him to fly, and he is airborne. Now he wants to play the role of Praetorian Prefect.'

Timesitheus raised his damaged hand. 'Unlike you, Gallicanus, I have commanded troops in the field. While you posture and make speeches in safety, I have fought Maximinus.' He raised his voice. 'All of you, disperse now. If you return to your homes, before further blood is shed, our Emperors will be merciful.'

Gallicanus spat. 'Citizens of Rome, this little Greek offers you *clemency*. This *Graeculus* has the audacity to tell *you* what to do – *you* who drew your first breath on these Roman hills, *you* who were raised on Sabine olives.'

Timesitheus leant back, and spoke to the soldier at his side. 'Shoot him.'

The archer drew, aimed, and loosed. The arrow missed its target.

'Loose!'

The trumpeter sounded the order.

Gallicanus turned to run. Shafts whistled around him. He had made three or four steps before one took him in the thigh. Gallicanus fell. Gladiators ran forward, covered the prone figure. Arrowheads pinged off their shields and armour as they dragged him back into the safety of the crowd.

'That could have gone better,' Timesitheus said to no one in particular.

The bowmen continued to shoot. Rioters were being hit, and there was plenty of ammunition. Timesitheus saw no reason to order the archers to desist. Killing men who have no way of hitting back gets the blood up.

The mob eddied and shifted: men at the front trying to shove their way backwards, those to the rear pushing forward. All was balanced until an aisle opened in the sea of humanity, and a group burdened with a massive beam started towards the gate. *Maecenas*, they were urged on by Maecenas. With a roar the whole mob surged against the camp.

'Shoot the men with the ram.'

The archers bent their bows with a will. As soon as one man dropped, another took his place. The ram lumbered onward. The rest of the mob, like a beast with too many legs, raced past the ram. Shovels and pitchforks, scythes and flails, bobbed above the heads of the onrushing mass.

'The men with the ram, keep shooting the men with the ram.'

Stones rattled like gigantic hailstones against the battlements, too many to dodge. The first soldiers reeled back, clutching their scalps and faces, blood running through their fingers.

The crowd broke against the foot of the wall. Ladders reared skywards. Grunting with effort, soldiers hefted chunks of broken masonry, and hurled them down. Shouts and screams from below; warnings yelled too late. Men crushed like insects, rungs snapped like kindling.

Some ladders rattled home against the brickwork. Soldiers with long pikes jabbed down at the heads and shoulders who dared to try and mount. Others dragged the ladders off balance, hurled more masonry.

Timesitheus walked behind the fighting line, the trumpeter at his heel. A word of encouragement here, a pat on the shoulder there. He heard the first strike of the ram against the gate.

A commotion further along the wallwalk. A gladiator – a *Myrmillo* by his helmet, but all encased in armour – heaved over the merlons. He stood, like some brazen warrior of myth, impervious to blows. Timesitheus ran, pushed the soldiers aside, and confronted him.

191

'Those about to die,' Timesitheus said.

'You not me,' grunted the gladiator.

Wild, savage eyes peering through the narrow grille. A moment of stillness at the heart of the chaos. Then the *Myrmillo* lunged. Timesitheus parried, stepped back. The gladiator pressed forward, cutting and thrusting. Timesitheus gave ground, until he felt the edge of the wallwalk under his rear boot. He was oddly calm, aware what he had to do. The *Myrmillo* was near invulnerable in steel and bronze; this was the only way.

The gladiator lunged, his weight behind the blow. Deflecting the tip of the sword from his stomach, Timesitheus side-stepped. The momentum of the *Myrmillo* took him past. Vision restricted by his helmet, he could not have seen the drop. His fingers clutched at Timesitheus, failed to get a grip, and he was gone. Timesitheus heard the clangour of his fall.

Only a couple of ladders remained against the battlements, but the ram still pounded at the gate.

Shouting for his trumpeter to follow, Timesitheus took the nearest steps two at a time.

Pinarius stood, wringing his hands. The reserves, shields grounded, leant against their legs, all looked at Timesitheus.

The boards of the gate leapt under the next strike of the ram. A impact dislodged one of the long iron bolts of a hinge. The gate would not stand much more.

'Reserve, form column.'

Eager to do anything rather than wait, the soldiers jostled into formation.

'Knock out the wedges, remove the beams. Unbolt the gate. Prepare to lift the bar.'

Soldiers wielded mallets, hauled away the heavy timbers.

Timesitheus took his place at the head of the column, the trumpeter tucked in behind him. 'No shouting. Take them by surprise. Kill everyone you can reach. No mercy. Listen for the recall.'

192

Habit made one or two shout: *Ready! Ready!* It was lost in the din of battle.

'On three, lift the bar. One, two, three!'

The next blow of the ram spread the leaves of the gate wide. Those bearing it stumbled forward, tripping, falling. The ram thumped to the earth.

'Charge!'

Timesitheus drove his blade down between the shoulder blades of a man on his hands and knees. Withdrawing the sword, he jumped up onto the fallen ram. Soldiers poured past on either side.

Broken by the shock, the rioters fought each other as they scrambled to get away.

The soldiers fanned out after them, arms rising and falling.

Timesitheus checked the trumpeter was still with him, and walked out to where the bodies littered the parade ground. Calmly he put one or two of the wounded out of their agony, as he would an animal.

Gallicanus really was a fool. Gladiators were all very well in the arena, but they could never face troops in the field, and the frenzy of a mob was cooled when it came close to the steel.

The soldiers were about a hundred paces from the gate. Timesitheus turned to the trumpeter.

'Sound the recall.'

The mob would be back, but not for some hours. Timesitheus would put that time to good use.

CHAPTER 20

The Palatine,
Four Days after the Ides of April, AD238

The Emperor Balbinus clapped his hands with delight to see the monkeys.

He had enjoyed a light lunch – turbot and lamprey and pheasant, washed down with some excellent Falernian and Caecuban. Now for some entertainment. The Sicilia was one of his favourite places in the Palace. He loved both the sound of the fountain playing over the representation of the island which gave the courtyard its name, and the way the sunlight shone off the polished stone cladding of the walls. Long ago Domitian had ordered the reflective stone brought from distant Cappadocia. It was odd to think how an Emperor's paranoia – Domitian had wanted to see what was happening behind his back – inadvertently had created such beauty.

Balbinus ruffled the hair of the boy that sat at his feet.

'Let the games begin.'

The two monkeys wore miniature helmets, and each

clutched a small spear. At a command from their trainers, they scrambled up on the backs of the shaggy she-goats.

Balbinus laughed out loud. Life in the Palace was infinitely more agreeable now Pupienus was in Ravenna. There was something about his co-Emperor's gloomy features, and long philosophic beard, that sucked joy from the air as a weasel sucked eggs. A well-ordered life was a balance of public service and civilized ease. Pupienus was all dour *negotium*; the man had no concept of *otium* at all. But then he was very ill-bred.

As a weasel sucked eggs . . . Balbinus turned the image in his mind. Perhaps later there would be time to compose some verse. All his life Balbinus had been a devotee of the poetic muses: Erato, Terpsichore, and Thalia. He had a facility for most modes, lyric, choral, and comedy, although he had less affinity with epic or tragedy.

The trainers cracked their whips, and the she-goats jumped forward. The first monkey made its throw. Nimbly, its opponent dodged. Gibbering with rage, bearing its long, yellow teeth, the second hurled its spear. The throw was good. The sharp steel took the first beast in the chest. It fell backwards off its mount, writhed on the ground, its almost human hands clutching at the shaft.

The courtiers applauded, but the Emperor's catamite had covered his eyes.

Balbinus pushed the boy's hands away, tipped up his chin. 'Look at the blood.'

The boy snivelled.

'You Greeks taught monkeys to dance, play musical instruments, drive little chariots. But we Romans are made of sterner stuff. We are Ausonian beasts, suckled by the wolf. Blood is our heritage.'

Rufinianus burst into the courtyard, trailed by half a dozen armed men of his Urban Cohorts.

The Praetorians behind Balbinus stiffened. It was their duty to protect the Emperor, and there was no love lost between the two bodies of troops. Rufinianus was an old friend, but this lack of respect was insolent.

The Prefect of the City did not glance at the monkeys, but hurried across to Balbinus. He made a sketchy salute, and did not wait to be asked to speak.

'Augustus, the mob is out on the streets.'

'What?' Balbinus felt his lunch congealing in his stomach.

'Gallicanus and Maecenas killed two Praetorians in the Senate House. They have broken into the *Ludus Magnus*, freed the gladiators from their cells, armed the people. The plebs are lynching every soldier they can find.'

'Are we safe here in the Palace? Are the doors bolted, guards set?'

'It has been done, Augustus. Gallicanus and Maecenas have led the mob against the Praetorian camp.'

'What do they want?'

'No one knows, but we must take action.'

'Yes, of course. Action, we must take action.'

Everyone was silent, gazing at Balbinus. His thoughts were in turmoil. From far away, he heard the chattering of a monkey, the rill of the water. Action, an Emperor must take decisive action.

'We will issue an edict, commanding them to cease and desist. If they do not comply, Rufinianus, you will use the troops to clear them from the streets.' There, that was decisive, the firm measures of a stern Emperor.

'That may not be possible, Augustus. The majority of the Urban Cohorts are over the river, or in the Praetorian camp itself. There are no more than two hundred swords here in the Palace, about the same number of Praetorians.'

Damn the man to Hades. Balbinus felt a wave of nausea; the lamprey might have been a mistake. Concentrate, he had to concentrate. If force was impossible, he must employ cunning.

'Rufinianus, you will go to them, and discover their grievances. Promise them, if they are justified, their Emperor will address them. If they disperse, and return to their homes, without further violence, my magnanimity will ensure that there are no reprisals.'

The Prefect of the City looked unimpressed.

Rufinianus was a dear friend, but friendship had its limits.

An imperial secretary appeared, writing materials in hand.

Balbinus kicked the boy out from under his feet. This was no time to be distracted.

'Imperator Caesar Decimus Caelius Calvinus Balbinus Pius Felix Augustus to his loyal subjects . . .'

After a lifetime of high office, words came easily. The act of dictation itself was calming. As he spoke, Balbinus scouted possibilities. Not everything brought about by this uprising might prove deleterious. Indeed, haste in its suppression might be ill-advised. Pinarius had been appointed by Pupienus. It would not be a bad thing should the Prefect be struck down heroically defending the camp. The other Praetorian Prefect was with the Caesar Gordian. Felicio had few men in the *Domus Rostrata*. Inexplicably the plebs seemed to favour the youth, but a mob was unpredictable, savage by its nature. Whatever sympathy the plebs felt towards young Gordian was unlikely to extend to Felicio. In any event, accidents happened – or could be arranged.

'And so return to the peace and security which is fitting to our reign.'

The secretary finished writing.

'Have it painted in red on a whitened board.'

Another patrician, Acilius Aviola, came out into the courtyard. What of imperial dignity, Balbinus thought, will anyone just wander in as if this was some public tavern?

'Augustus.'

What, by all the gods below, did Rufinianus want now?

'Excellent as your edict is, Augustus, it may not be quite enough.'

Balbinus' stomach was unsettled. 'Give me your advice.'

Rufinianus nodded. Only generations of high birth could endow a man with such weighty dignity. 'You should appear before your people.'

Balbinus had an urgent need to ease his bowels. 'Very well. Have the heralds go out into the city and proclaim that the Emperor will address the people from the balcony of the Palace in, let us say, one hour.'

'The imperial edict must be posted in the Forum. It would be best if the Emperor was present when it was set up.'

Balbinus' stomach gurgled unhappily. 'As you tell me that the mob are attacking the Praetorians, might that not be seen as something of a provocation?'

'Given the circumstances, Augustus, possibly you should dispense with a military escort.'

An icy sliver of suspicion lodged in Balbinus' mind. Not Rufinianus, not his childhood friend? Each Emperor lived with a sword over his head suspended by a thread.

'You have twenty-four Lictors.' Rufinianus was still talking, his tone bland and helpful. 'Apart from your attendants, we could arm some of the Palace staff. You could wear a breastplate under your toga.'

Balbinus shifted in his seat. He badly needed to move his bowels. Yet he could not leave now, not without accepting Rufinianus' advice. Word of the cowardice of the Emperor would spread through the corridors of the Palace, be all over the city by nightfall.

'Very well. We will go to the Forum in an hour.'

'Time is of the essence.'

'Half an hour then. Make everything ready.' Balbinus got up, and, gathering his robes around him, scurried towards the nearest latrine.

'Whatever pleases you, Emperor.'

Apart from the guards, the entrance hall to the Palace was deserted. No throng of petitioners and clients waited between the tall columns. Balbinus heard his footfalls echo in the desolate space. Had it been like this when Didius Julianus, abandoned by all, roamed the empty Palace? That Emperor had been found cowering in the kennels. They had dragged him out, and butchered him.

The soldiers opened the doors, and Balbinus walked outside. The forecourt was empty as well.

Balbinus waited. The heavy armour concealed by his toga weighed uncomfortably on his bruised shoulder. Rufinianus and Acilius Aviola came to stand on either side, as the Lictors carrying the fasces formed up around them, and the imperial slaves fell in behind. Ceremonial axes bound with rods might symbolize the authority to beat and to execute, but Balbinus would have felt safer surrounded by the swords of soldiers.

They went down the path towards the Forum.

As they emerged from under the arch, they saw the first of the plebs. Knots of ill-kempt men lined the path. They made no sound as the procession passed.

A solid, silent mass of humanity blocked the Sacred Way by the Arch of Titus.

'Make way for the Emperor.'

The plebeians did not move.

'Make way for the noble Augustus Balbinus.'

Wielding the fasces in both hands, the Lictors began to push men aside.

'Cancel all debts,' someone shouted.

Here and there plebeians shoved back at the Lictors.

'An end to oppression. Restore *libertas.*'

Scuffles were breaking out.

Balbinus' bowels turned liquid. He needed to relieve himself again.

'*Libertas. Libertas.*'

This was no time for physical weakness. Balbinus spread his hands, reached out towards his subjects.

'Citizens of Rome, your Emperor hears you. He feels your distress.'

The crowd quietened. The pushing and shoving died down.

'Your Emperor cares for you as a father cares for his children.'

The crowd was silent, unnaturally still.

'The registers of debts owed to the *fiscus* will be burned in the Forum.'

No one cheered.

'Those who have oppressed you will be brought to justice.'

'Then hand yourself over,' a voice cried from the back of the crowd. 'Hand yourself over, you fat sack of lard.'

'Citizens,' Balbinus spread his hands wide, 'listen to your Emperor.'

Jupiter is our only ruler! Quickly the chant spread through the multitude.

'Citizens—'

Jupiter is our only ruler!

The first stone flew.

Gathering up the skirts of his toga, Balbinus turned to run. The imperial slaves closed around him, swords in hand. Those citizens who tried to block the way were cut down. Panting and lathered in sweat, Balbinus fled with shambling steps back up towards the Palace.

Looking back from beyond the arch – almost to safety – he saw the mob overwhelm the Lictors, beat them to the ground, trample and kick them. Rough, uncouth hands seized the sacred fasces, and broke them to kindling.

Drag Balbinus with the hook! To the Tiber! Drag him with the hook!

CHAPTER 21

Rome

The Subura,
Six Days after the Ides of April, AD238

'There was nothing I could do.'

Caenis ignored the die-cutter, pushed past him, and ran up the stairs of the tenement. All the way from Ascyltos' bar, she had feared the worst.

'How could I have stopped them?' The die-cutter was limping up after her.

The door of her room was open. The bowl and jug were smashed, the lid off the chest, its contents strewn about. In two places the floorboards had been ripped up. She went over to the corner where the brick was loose. With a sinking heart, she worked it free. The space behind was empty.

The die-cutter was in the doorway, breathing hard.

All gone. They had taken everything. The bags of coins, the trinkets and cheap jewellery, all her carefully hoarded savings. They had left nothing, nothing at all.

'Who did this?'

The die-cutter shrugged. 'Some of the rioters. Five or six men, I did not recognize any of them.'

Caenis stood, her eyes roaming over the room, taking in none of it.

'We should go,' the die-cutter said. 'The Praetorians are coming. We may be safe if we take sanctuary in a *temple*.' He pronounced the word with bitterness.

All her hard-earned savings were gone. They had not been enough, but they had been a start. Every coin, every ring and bracelet, had been a small down payment on a new life, a life on an island far from here, a life of respectability.

'You go,' she said.

'The Praetorians . . .'

She knew that he had been about to say that the Praetorians will rape you, before he remembered she was a whore. Men thought that sort of thing did no great harm to those of her profession.

'Just go.'

The die-cutter left.

She listened to his lame footsteps on the rickety stairs, heard the noise of rioting outside on the streets.

Now she had nothing, she might as well gamble everything. She had nothing to lose but her life, and she hated her life. If it did not pay off, she was better off dead.

She picked up her cloak from where it had been trampled on the floor, wrapped it around herself. Out of habit, she went to lock the door as she left. The latch was broken. She pulled the door shut anyway, and went down.

She peered out into the street. Gangs of men and youths roamed about, drinking and shouting. All had makeshift weapons, some carried sacks. She wished she was a man, had a sharp sword, knew how to fight like the knife-boy Castricius. Rioters, Praetorians, she would like to kill them, every one of them – kill them slowly, carve them into pieces, hear them howl.

The city was in chaos, and it was all the fault of Gallicanus. The Senator must have thought he was so clever yesterday when he cut the aqueduct carrying water to the Praetorian camp. Had it not occurred to Gallicanus or his dear friend Maecenas that the soldiers might not meekly wait until thirst forced them to surrender? No matter their numbers, Gallicanus' gladiators and street toughs would not face soldiers in open combat. Timesitheus the Prefect had led the sally from the camp. One charge had broken any organized resistance. Now the troops had slipped their leash, and were killing and raping at their pleasure. Where there were no soldiers, the scum of the Subura were plundering those who could not fight back.

For a moment her resolution deserted her. If she went back to the bar nothing too bad would happen. Ascyltos was a good talker. He would give the soldiers drink, let them have the girls for nothing. The place would not be ransacked, there would be no bloodshed. If a gang of rioters appeared, Ascyltos would do the same. An innkeeper in the Subura had to be adaptable.

No, if she took that course, she would never escape, never get another life. The gods had given her this one opportunity. All she prayed was that Gallicanus would not be hunted down before she got to Timesitheus.

She waited until the street was near empty. Pulling her hood over her head, she hurried out.

The Praetorians were advancing down the Via Tiburtina, and she went to meet them.

'Not that way. The soldiers are coming.' A man caught her arm.

She shook it off.

'Stupid bitch.'

Not all the mob had turned to looting. As she got nearer

to the troops, gangs of plebeians lurked in alleyways, ran into tenements carrying stones. The leaders of theatre claques and *Collegia* shouted orders. She slunk past, close to the walls, hood up.

The soldiers moved down the road in loose formation. Shields up, swords ready, their eyes darted from building to building. Discipline had not been completely abandoned. In their midst a Centurion, distinctive with the traverse crest on his bronze helmet, called out commands.

Caenis pulled back her hood, and walked steadily towards them.

There was no one else in sight.

'We are in luck, boys. A volunteer, this one must be desperate for it.'

A soldier grabbed her arm.

'I must talk to your officer.' Years of dealing with rough men helped Caenis keep her nerve.

'Never mind him, my little she-wolf. On the whole he prefers boys.' He ran a hand over her buttocks.

'Centurion!' she shouted.

'Bring her over here.'

The soldier obeyed.

'Well?'

'I have information your Prefect Timesitheus needs to hear.'

The Centurion stopped scanning the surrounding balconies and rooftops, looked down at her with disbelief. 'What might *someone like you* possibly know that the Prefect needs to hear?'

She had to say something to convince him to take her to Timesitheus. 'I know where Gallicanus is hiding.'

'Tell me.'

'And get no reward? No, I will tell the Prefect.'

A rock hit a soldier in the face. He doubled up, pressing his fingers to his eyes.

'A trap! There are hundreds of them up on the roofs.'

More rocks shattered on the road, on helmets, shields and armour. Jagged splinters were flying everywhere, slicing through exposed flesh.

'Get to the sides, under the balconies.'

The Centurion hauled Caenis with him as he ran. A sting of pain in her leg. The Centurion shoved her against the wall, covered them both with his shield.

The hail of missiles slackened, but did not cease. The wounded soldier, dragged to comparative shelter, was sobbing. *My eyes, my eyes. I cannot see.*

Caenis' thigh was bleeding. She peered out from behind the Centurion.

On the other side of the street a soldier was trying to kick open a door.

'Marcus,' the Centurion roared, 'do not get drawn into the houses. Hold your position.'

'Fucking cunts, arseholes.' A soldier somewhere was swearing mechanically, without thought.

'Silence! Listen for the words of command.'

The Centurion was admirably calm. He spoke to two soldiers. 'Aulus, Gnaeus, break down this door. Kill anyone on the ground floor, then bring me a lamp, some oil, and plenty of cloth.'

Another volley of roof tiles smashed on the pavement.

The soldiers returned, and handed the things over.

The Centurion poured some of the oil on the rags. He reached up – high on tiptoes – and stuffed the cloth under the joists of the balcony. Then he lit the inflammable material. It caught with a whoosh.

'Smoke the bastards out.' He handed the lamp to a soldier. 'Set it on fire in a couple more places.'

The soldier laughed. 'See how brave the fuckers are then.'

As the smoke rose, there were shouts of consternation from the rooftops.

'Right, boys, get ready. On the count of three, form *testudo* out in the street.'

'Ready,' they shouted.

'One, two, three.'

Caenis was propelled from the protection of the balcony. Again the air was full of the explosion of rocks, of hissing sharp splinters. Then she was in the gloom under a roof of shields. Missiles hit on the carapace like hammer blows.

'Steady, boys. Leave the fuckers to fry. Let us get out of here. By the left, slow march.'

The Centurion looked down at Caenis. 'Seems you will get your wish. It is a lot safer back where the Prefect is stationed.'

The smoke was catching in her throat, and she could not reply.

'So you know where Gallicanus is holed up?'

'No.'

A Centurion pushed past her. 'Prefect, can I order the men to pull back into the camp?'

Timesitheus looked out across the parade ground at the smoke-shrouded city.

He was good-looking, Caenis thought; dark hair, white skin, now smudged with soot, nice, strong arms.

'Tell them to hold their positions. They are safe enough. The fire cannot jump the open space of the *Campus Praetoria*. Some of the roads are still open. I will not shut the gates while some of our men are still out there.'

He turned back to Caenis. 'Did you just say *no*?'

Before she could reply, another man in the uniform of a senior officer bustled up.

'It is a tragedy. The city is burning.' He was wringing his hands, looked distraught.

A flash of irritation crossed Timesitheus' face, before he

arranged it into a more amiable expression. 'A tragedy indeed. Now, Pinarius, it would be good if you could have the men bring what water there is in the camp to the battlements.'

When the officer called Pinarius had left, Timesitheus laughed.

'Do you know how to play a musical instrument?' he asked Caenis. 'No, never mind.'

Baffled, she starred at him.

'Now, if you do not know where my philosophic friend is lurking, I take it that you have not braved the streets solely for the pleasure of my company?'

This was her chance. She might never get another. Desperately she tried to choose her words.

'Charming though you are' – Timesitheus touched her cheek – 'I am rather occupied.'

'I know something about Gallicanus, something you can use to destroy him. Send soldiers to his house. There is a slave called Davus. You will need him as a witness.'

CHAPTER 22

Rome

The Praetorian Camp,
Eight Days after the Ides of April, AD238

On the battlements above the gate Timesitheus watched and
waited.

Smuts of soot drifted on the breeze, settled like thin, black
snow across the parade ground.

Would Gallicanus come?

Yesterday, after the fires in this area had been contained
or burned out, the mob had returned to their blockade of
the camp. Timesitheus had sent Pinarius out with a herald.
Given everyone knew that the soldiers had started the conflagration, the old man might have expected a hostile reception.
Better Pinarius was torn limb from limb than Timesitheus
himself. In the event there had been nothing but threats and
vulgar abuse. The plebs perhaps were somewhat sobered by
the scale of the disaster.

Gallicanus had left Pinarius to wait for an hour before
appearing. The Senator had been suspicious. Was this some
trap? All Greeks were cunning. And why did Timesitheus

wish to talk to him alone? Greeks were untrustworthy. What was there that could not be discussed openly, with the people of Rome as witness?

Eventually, using words given to him by Timesitheus, the gardener-turned-Prefect had secured a grudging agreement to meet the next day. If it concerned the very safety of the *Res Publica*, Gallicanus had announced with all his customary pomposity, it was his duty to meet Timesitheus. He had taken an oath: just the two of them, no weapons and no violence, in the middle of the deserted *Campus Praetoria*. The health of the *Res Publica* must count above personal mistrust or animosity.

Timesitheus trusted Gallicanus no more than the Senator trusted him. Wilful and vain, an overeducated man like Gallicanus was capable of using his much vaunted philosophy to underpin and justify the most appalling acts of treachery and cruelty. For men like him an appeal to the greater good always could negate mere trifles like temporal laws or a sworn vow. Brutus had struck down Caesar. Timesitheus would not forget that Gallicanus and his *friend* Maecenas had murdered two unsuspecting men in the Senate House itself.

The fires were still burning in other parts of the city. No sooner were they extinguished in one place than they flared up somewhere else. It was as if they ran underground, or malcontents were kindling them afresh. Great swathes of the city were devastated. In some streets and alleys the *vigiles* had been stoned by looters when they turned out to fight the blaze. While many lost everything in such a disaster, there were those without principle or compassion who would turn it to their profit.

Gallicanus had better appear. A note had got through from Maecius Gordianus saying that his *vigiles* were fully occupied with the conflagration. Much to his regret the *vigiles* were unable to come to the relief of the Praetorian camp. But

Timesitheus was to have no fears for his wife. Maecius Gordianus had made the safety of Tranquillina his especial concern.

Maecius Gordianus was an unwelcome presence in Timesitheus' thoughts. What *exactly* had Tranquillina done to make him so well disposed? She was not wanton in the usual way of things, but Timesitheus knew that his wife would not let conventional morality stand in the way of ambition or advantage. If he survived this siege, there would be an uncomfortable conversation.

If he survived this siege. There had been no message, but nothing was to be expected from the main body of the Urban Cohorts. Their commander, the sluggish patrician Rufinianus, lacked the courage to venture out from the security of the Palatine.

The camp must stand or fall on its own. Those who had returned from talking to the district magistrates and the priests of the neighbourhood cults of the Emperors had brought no good news. The local worthies deplored the situation, prayed for the return of peace, but the influence of Gallicanus was too strong to allow them to prevail on the plebs. They were unable to get the mob off the streets.

Gallicanus was the key. He had to be removed.

'Something is happening.'

Timesitheus looked across to where the crowd was stirring. The sunlight was weak through the pall of smoke that hung over the seven hills. Almost midday, and it was as dark as Hades.

Gallicanus had come. For now he stood ringed by others like himself clad in the rough cloaks of philosophers. Did he imagine Plato's Academy could be translated to the dung heap of Romulus? He would do well to think on the end of Socrates.

Timesitheus checked everyone was in their place on the

walls: Pinarius, the prostitute and the slave, the guards. He caught the eye of Caenis, and smiled. He had enjoyed her in his quarters these past two nights. With the aqueduct still cut, and water rationed, there had been no chance for them to bathe, but sometimes sex was better dirty and rough. She was a scheming, mercenary little bitch. Not content with the generous reward he had already promised her, she had angled to get more by denouncing two other men. One was some die-cutter who turned out to be a Christian. Of course he deserved death or the mines, but the gods knew there were enough of the atheists in Rome. At first her other tale held little more interest – a backstreet murder of someone of no account – until she named the killer: Castricius. Menophilus had sent him as an assassin against Maximinus. Obviously the knife-boy had thought better of the suicidal task. Like a dog to its own vomit, he had returned to Rome. When normality was restored, Timesitheus would hunt Castricius down. He had employed the youth before, and could do so again. These revelations put the knife-boy's life in his hands.

'Here he comes.'

Timesitheus walked down the steps, under the arch of the gate, and out onto the bare field.

Leaning on a staff and limping, ashes blowing about his bare feet, Gallicanus resembled the prophet of some apocalypse.

'You are looking very pale,' Timesitheus said. 'Is your leg troubling you?'

'I did not come here to exchange small talk.'

Timesitheus arranged his face. 'The *Res Publica* is lucky to have men like you in this debased age. No artful pleasantries, straight to duty and the public good. No tunic, just a cloak whatever the weather. The shaggy beard and the bristling hair of our ancestors. You might be taken for the embodiment of the *mos maiorum*.'

Gallicanus scowled. 'Do not imagine that you can flatter or charm me.'

'Oh, I would never imagine anything of the sort.' Timesitheus looked Gallicanus up and down. 'Gait and costume, gestures and expression; they form a kind of language, do you not think?'

'What do you want?'

'Yet sometimes language can be so deceiving.' Timesitheus was enjoying this. 'A eunuch priest of the Mother Goddess; now at least he is open. The ribbons and robes and necklaces, all proclaim his twisted nature. He is sick, a freak of fate, not to be blamed. Indeed, his wretched self-exposure, the very strength of his passion, beg pity and forgiveness.'

'I did not come here for a lecture on eastern religions,' Gallicanus snapped. 'Piss on the mark, or be silent.'

'Stern old Gallicanus, friend of the people, earthy and direct.' Timesitheus turned, and pointed up to the gatehouse. 'You recognize that slave up there?'

Gallicanus could not help but stare.

'Of course you do. Until I had him abducted yesterday, he served in your bed chamber.'

Gallicanus said nothing.

'It took only a gentle persuasion to make him talk; turns out he never cared for you much as a master. Is it true that when your friend Maecenas climbs on board you squawk like a hen when the cock gets at her?'

Gallicanus hefted his staff.

'Now, now,' Timesitheus said. 'No weapons, no violence.'

'No one will believe a slave you have tortured.'

'Actually, I think they will. If you remember in law slaves have to be tortured to make them tell the truth.'

'You piece of shit.'

'Please, no Cynic diatribe. I do not judge you.'

Gallicanus' knuckles were white around the staff.

'You know they say that in distant Bactria women mount their husbands, and in the dank forests of Germania warriors take young boys to wife. Everywhere custom is King. It is odd that here in Rome a man can stick it into anyone he wants, and no one thinks any the worse of him. But let there be so much as a whisper that he plays the woman's part, and he is tainted, unclean for the rest of his days, a laughing stock.'

'No one will believe it.' The defiance was draining out of Gallicanus.

'It should be a consolation to you that the reputation of Maecenas will not be much harmed; although, of course, you are not exactly an attractive youth. But yours . . .'

'What do you want?'

Timesitheus smiled. 'To be friends. My attitude to what people do in their bedrooms is broadminded.'

'Friends?'

'Call off the mob.'

'How? What reason could I give?'

'Love of Rome. In the face of civil war and catastrophe – Maximinus marching against us, a conflagration destroying our homes and temples – the good of the *Res Publica* demands concord. In fact, I think, the gods demand *Concordia*.'

Gallicanus muttered. 'It will be the end of everything for me.'

'Not at all. Far from betraying your principles, you can announce to your motley followers that you will be putting your philosophy into practice by schooling the young Caesar Gordian in the ways of righteousness.'

'But I am not his tutor.'

'Call off the mob, and I will see that you are appointed. Not many philosophers get the chance to mould an Emperor. Forget the idle dream of a restored Republic, and serve the *Res Publica* by embracing future offices.'

214

Gallicanus stood defeated, like an ape in a cage.

'Come,' Timesitheus said, 'let us shake hands, and show those watching that we are reconciled.'

PART VI:
THE PROVINCES

CHAPTER 23

Dalmatia

*The Mountains East of Bistua Nova,
Eight Days after the Ides of April,* AD238

Iunia Fadilla had tried her hardest to keep running. A young matron had no more practice at the activity than a town councillor. They were not far clear of Bistua Nova before she had had to stop. Her cousin had dragged her up a dark slope into cover.

As she had sat gasping, she remembered Gordian telling her of a philosopher who had praised the men of Rhodes for always walking with a seemly slowness. The Rhodians might regret that should they ever have to flee for their lives on foot in the dead of night.

She had barely got her breath back, her heart was still racing, when Fadillus had said they must continue. The night wore on, and they had to put some distance between them and the pursuit. The cavalry would have caught Vertiscus and her maid soon enough. Horsemen would always overtake a cart. Even if the servants did not talk, the troopers would realize they had followed a wild goose chase. Returning to

Bistua Nova, by morning they would be fanning out, searching the other routes from the town.

Fadillus had shouldered her bundle of possessions along with his own, and led her back down to where the road was a pale ribbon in the darkness.

They had walked the rest of the night, frequently stopping to listen. Once they had disturbed a mountain goat, which had clattered away with heart-stopping noise up the rocky hillside.

When the eastern sky showed the merest hint of lightening, Fadillus again had led them off the path. After a short climb, he had found a fallen pine, which he had thought should shelter them from view from the road.

Iunia Fadilla had lain awake. Was this worth it? She knew it was. Anything to escape from Maximus. Anything rather than return to her husband. Eventually, exhaustion had triumphed over fear, and Iunia Fadilla had fallen into a deep sleep.

She had woken, chilled and stiff, enveloped in a cold mist. Her shoulder and hip ached from the unforgiving ground. Fadillus passed her a flask of watered wine. It was thin and sour in her stomach. She declined a piece of yesterday's bread.

Through the fronds of the fallen tree was a grey, shadowed landscape such as she had never seen before. The opposite slopes were bare, littered with mounds of shattered rocks, and pocked with the entrances to tunnels and shafts. Above many of the latter were elaborate structures of wooden beams supporting great wheels. Here and there stood conical chimneys of mud-masonry and field stones. Odd ceramic pipes emerged low down from them, and each had a circular stone trough at its foot. A stream ran down from the workings. As the mist lifted, she had seen that it was an unnatural yellow-brown, the rocks on its banks somehow stained and corroded.

220

At the foot of the hillside was a settlement. Amid a jumble of stables, sheds and barns were two stone-built barracks. The larger had bars on the windows. At either end stood a wooden watchtower.

Iunia Fadilla had gone to stand, so she could find a place to relieve herself in privacy. Her cousin had gestured for her to remain hidden. He had pointed to the guard towers. When she had looked closely, she had seen the lookouts huddled in their cloaks.

She had retreated to the extremity of the cover, and Fadillus had turned his back as she hauled up her tunic and eased her bladder. She remembered pissing in an alley in Sirmium. From beginning to end this journey was a continuous humiliation. Anything not to be returned to Maximus.

Before the sun had crested the hilltops, figures were moving through the settlement. Kitchen fires were lit, and the tang of wood smoke drifted across. Soldiers had emerged from the smaller barracks, and ambled to the cookhouse. They reappeared carrying bowls of steaming food. A few had sat outside to eat, most went back indoors. When the troops had fed, they unbolted the gate of the larger barracks, and led out the slaves. The latter ate more hurriedly, and soon were assembled in groups, handed picks and hammers, baskets and lamps, and led off to the mines. One by one the filthy, miserable men and women, and even children, had climbed down beneath the earth.

'A drawn-out death sentence,' Fadillus muttered. 'No one comes back from the mines.'

With the day, traffic had appeared on the road. Most went to the camp. Wagons brought timber, strings of pack animals delivered food and fodder. Twice a line of chained slaves was driven along and secured in the big barracks. Only one convoy had left the camp: four wagons with military drivers, and eight mounted outriders. By the second hour there were others, not necessarily connected to the mines about. Peasants had plodded past in both directions; those with laden donkeys and mules on their way to sell their produce at market, the unburdened presumably returning home having spent the night in some village or hamlet.

'Follow me,' Fadillus had said. 'We will join that peasant couple coming from the West.'

'The watchtowers?' Iunia Fadilla had felt an extraordinary reluctance to risk leaving their inadequate shelter.

'I have been watching them. The guards are looking to keep the miners from escaping. They take little interest in the road. With luck, they will not even notice us.'

'What if the cavalry arrive from town?'

'We cannot stay here.'

They had clambered down, joints complaining after their night of hard lying. Iunia Fadilla could not take her eyes off the watchtowers. There was no outcry. As far as she could tell, none of the guards gave them so much as a glance.

They had stood waiting, dishevelled and dirty, bundles at their feet, like vagabonds habituated to the road.

'Health and great joy.' Fadillus had blocked the way.

The peasants halted. Neither spoke. They exhibited less curiosity than the donkeys they led.

'They say there are bandits in the hills. For safety we would travel with you.'

The man spat at his feet. 'And how do I know you are not intent on robbery? You wear a sword under that cloak, and the well-spoken are often the worst thieves.'

Fadillus took a coin from his purse. 'We mean no harm.'

The peasant accepted the coin. 'What would a couple with money be doing all alone; no horses or carriage, no servants?'

Fadillus fished out another coin. 'Can you keep a secret?'

'Depends.'

'Our families did not wish us to wed. We ran away, but

they nearly caught us in Bistua Nova. We had to abandon our carriage and servants.'

Fadillus handed over yet another coin.

'We need somewhere to hide. Not for long. A few days and we will be on our way to the coast.'

The peasant grunted. 'For sure you are on the run from something.'

His wife whispered in his ear.

'Silence, old woman.' He raised his hand, and she stepped back.

'Another coin for our food every day we stay,' Fadillus said.

'Most likely there is a reward on your heads. A coin every day, another six at the end, and you leave when I say.'

The peasant spat on the palm of his hand, held it out.

Fadillus took it, relief overcoming any reluctance.

Neither the *Eclogues* of Virgil and other bucolic poetry, nor her journey so far, had prepared Iunia Fadilla for the realities of peasant life. No rustic swains sighed or tossed apples at virginal milkmaids. Antique virtue was notably absent, and it seemed unlikely that one would find a rustic god strolling in the cool of the evening.

The hut was half sunk into one of the remote heights. One end was occupied by a heterogeneous herd of animals. In the other dwelt the peasant couple, and his brother and wife. The filth was indescribable, and the stench choking. The smoke from an ill-drawing fire made eyes stream. Far from rustic feasts of suckling pig, the food consisted of a thin gruel of dried beans and barley, and the flour of the bread was eked out with ground acorns.

Worse still was the enforced intimacy of the living arrangements. Of course Iunia Fadilla was accustomed to the presence of servants. But they were trained to avert their eyes, and tactfully remain in the background. Here she and Fadillus had to bed down next to the peasants and their wives. She could not shut her ears to their snoring, thunderous farting, and the bestial grunts of their occasional rutting.

Although they accepted the money readily enough, none of the peasants was prepared to put any warmth into their hospitality. Most nights they held earnest discussions in incomprehensible dialect. These conclaves were punctuated by meaningful, and calculating looks at the interlopers. Did they intend to inform against them, hoping for some reward? If they murdered them, and took their possessions, who would know?

Just a few more days, Fadillus kept saying. Let the search die down, and we can be on our way to the coast. It is not far now.

One afternoon, to escape the prurient attention of the peasants, Iunia Fadilla followed the stream which ran by the hut. Far up in the mountains, where it tumbled over an outcrop, it formed a clear pool. Nothing moved on the wooded slopes as far as the eye could see. She pulled off her tunic, and – gasping with the cold – stepped into the water.

Some sense warned her that she was not alone.

The peasant was standing watching, openly fondling his prick through his clothes.

She scrambled out of the pool, and, still wet, tugged her tunic over her head.

The peasant was in front of her, the water behind. His stale breath in her face.

'You are no newlyweds,' he said. 'Days you been here, and he has not fucked you once. Seems a shame to let that trim little delta go unploughed.'

'Touch me, and Fadillus will kill you.'

'Maybe, maybe not both me and my brother.'

He reached out to put his hand up between her thighs.

She slapped his hand away. She had not come this far to be raped by some peasant. 'If he does not, I swear I will kill you. Wait until you are sleeping, cut your prick off, and ram it down your throat.'

Her vehemence made him pause.

She pushed past him.

Recovering, he called after her. 'If that man of yours had any balls, he would put his belt across your arse, teach you how to behave.'

They trudged down the road.

Gathering their things, before the peasant had got back, Fadillus had told the brother that if they denounced them, he would return with armed men, and kill everyone. The threat had seemed improbable.

'Not far to Salona now.' Fadillus repeated it every so often, like the refrain of some obscure ritual.

They had been walking through the mountains for four days. They had passed through an upland market town called Bariduum with no alarms. They had stayed at an inn, visited the baths, bought new clothes, all without seemingly attracting undue attention. Saving money to buy passage on a ship, they had not hired a carriage. Anyway, now they were nearer the coast, there were more travellers on the road. There seemed less likelihood of a couple on foot being noticed.

At midday, they stopped by a wayside shrine. They had some bread, olives and cheese. Eating it in the sunshine, Iunia Fadilla felt some of the apprehension she had carried so long begin to lift.

'Not far to Salona now.'

She wished Fadillus would stop saying that. It tempted fate.

'We have enough left for a passage to Africa?'

225

'Most likely we will need to take a boat sailing to Corcyra, then pick up a ship bound to Africa there, but, yes, we should have enough.'

'Gods below . . .'

The stamp of hooves, the jingle of harness – the unmistakable sounds of a troop of cavalry – they would be around the corner in moments.

Without words, they scooped up their bundles, and ran up the slope.

They reached the treeline, but a shout from below told them they had been seen.

They hurled themselves up the incline, deeper into the timber.

Iunia Fadilla glanced back. At least twenty troopers, dismounted now. Some were holding the horses, the majority setting themselves at the slope.

The hillside was steeper, and Iunia Fadilla and her cousin had to grab branches to haul themselves up.

'Stop,' Fadillus said. 'We are out of sight. You carry on up. I will lead them off.'

'No.' She was panting like a dog.

'Here.' He thrust the purse at her. 'Go.'

'No.'

He managed to grin. 'The peasant was right; you need a belt across your arse. Do not argue, just go.'

Before she could gather herself to argue, he had turned, and was crashing away through the trees.

Drawing as deep a breath as she could, she climbed on.

'Over there!' The soldiers had seen Fadillus. She heard the noise of their pursuit.

Doggedly, she went on.

Just when safety had been almost within grasp. Gordian was right; there were no gods, and if they existed, they did not care.

Sandals slipping, branches whipping at her, head swimming, she went higher and higher. The wood cut off any sound from below.

Suddenly she was out of the trees. Ahead a sheer cliff fell away.

She stood for a moment, trying to think. Gods, just think clearly, make a plan.

A rest, she had to rest.

She slumped down, back against the nearest tree.

They would have caught Fadillus by now. She could not rest long. She must track along the top of the wood – north or south? – then work back down.

Fadillus – what would Maximus do to her cousin? The cruelty of her husband was infinite. Poor, poor, gentle Fadillus.

'Iunia Fadilla, my lady, Iunia Fadilla.' The calls were muffled by the trees, no way of telling how near.

She staggered to her feet. There were scratches on her legs, her arms. She felt blood trickling down her forehead.

'My lady, Iunia Fadilla.' They were closer now.

She had done all she could. Slowly she went to the edge of the precipice. The drop was forty, fifty paces; more than enough. She would not be dragged back to Maximus.

'Iunia Fadilla.'

Philosophers always said the road to freedom could be found at any cliff.

'My lady.'

The wind was singing in her ears. If she looked down again, she might lose her nerve. She had done so before; the dagger at Maximus' sleeping throat. She would not do so again.

'Cousin!'

She turned, looked at Fadillus with the soldiers.

'Step back from the cliff. We are safe.'

She swayed, unable to comprehend his meaning. A stone skittered from under her foot out into the abyss.

'Iunia, they are not Maximinus' men. Claudius Julianus has pledged Dalmatia to the revolt. We are saved.'

Dumbly, she walked towards him.

'He thought the first messenger was a trap set by Maximinus, but when Egnatius Marinianus told him the Senate had declared Maximinus an enemy of Rome . . .' Fadillus tailed off.

'Then we can go to Gordian,' Iunia Fadilla said.

'Gordian and his father are dead.'

'What?'

A look of awful sadness appeared on her cousin's face. 'I am so sorry. I had forgotten – Gordian and you.'

She started to cry. There were no gods, and if there were, they did not care.

CHAPTER 24

Moesia Inferior

The Town of Istria, South of the Mouths of the Danube,
The Day before the Kalends of May, AD238

Even here in the North, the winter was over, and the crops sown. It was the second day of the festival of Flora, with all the licence and feasting that entailed. They had reached the apples and nuts, and Honoratus was glad that this meal with the local dignitaries would soon be over. Conversation had been dominated by the alarming news from north of the river.

'But how dangerous is this development?' The town councillor certainly looked concerned.

'It is unwelcome,' Honoratus conceded. 'But we should not give way to undue alarm. We must remember that we are dealing with barbarians. They are inconstant by nature. The next report we receive may be that they are set on an entirely different path. Among them rulers come and go. They are incapable of political stability, or long-term planning. If they do make an attempt on the frontier, we will have good warning. Their warbands move slowly. In any event, the fleet patrols the river, and the army is stationed along the banks.'

The councillor did not seem reassured. 'But our forces have been depleted by drafts to the field army of the Emperor – *May the gods preserve Maximinus Augustus* – and those that remain cannot cover the entire length of the frontier. The river is so long, and the marshes of the delta are a wilderness. Apart from the fleet, there are no troops at all here in Istria.'

Honoratus deployed his most charming smile. 'Barbarians lack the vessels and the organization to ferry a horde across without our knowing. Even should they somehow sneak across, they would not attempt to take a walled city like Istria. They say that they have no quarrel with walls. Indeed they claim that we are like birds that have abandoned the nourishing earth, and rely for our defence on stones not our own strength. Anyway, it is our duty as members of the higher orders to set an example of calm resolution to the populace.'

That stopped the man's whining, but in truth Honoratus was deeply troubled. Five days after the meeting with Tharuaro, the Gothic King had been led into an ambush somewhere out on the trackless Steppe. Tharuaro was dead, and the Goths now acknowledged Cniva as their ruler. Tharuaro had been betrayed by his son Gunteric. There was no doubting the grim tidings brought by the Gothic priest who had been Tharuaro's companion. The *Gudja* had assured Honoratus, with much shaking of amulets, and rattling of the bones braided in his hair, that Cniva intended to descend on the province.

For all the talk of the Goths, there had been another spectre at the feast; something that could not be discussed. As soon as Maximinus had crossed the Alps, first Claudius Julianus of Dalmatia, then Fidus of Thrace had renounced their allegiance and declared for the rebels. It spoke of confidence or recklessness among the insurgents, for there were legions in neither province. Egnatius Marinianus, the man who had persuaded them, was variously said to have travelled on to Bithynia-Pontus, or south to Achaea. Another rumour put him on the Danube in neighbouring Moesia Superior. Wherever Egnatius had gone, Honoratus knew he could not long delay a decision. There were three realistic choices: throw in his lot with Pupienus and Balbinus, remain true to Maximinus, or make his own bid for the throne. Each was fraught with danger, and neutrality was not an option. Honoratus wished his wife was with him, not in Durostorum. There was no one else in the province to whom he could open his mind, not without the fear of betrayal to Maximinus. Unguarded words had led to the deaths of too many men in the last three years.

Honoratus drank a toast with his guests: *Long life*. That was a nice irony for a man in his position, a man with just three choices; none of them safe, none of them good. Inherited status had conspired with ambition to elevate him to a dangerous eminence that he felt more and more was beyond his capacity. *Know yourself*, as Apollo commanded. All he wanted was to leave the dismal lands of the Danube, collect his wife, and the ashes of his son, and retire to his estates in Italy. Lines of Homer moved through the wine fumes in his thoughts.

But Zeus drew Hector out from under the dust and missiles,
Out of the place where men were killed, the blood and
*   confusion.*

Perhaps he had owned more resolution before his son died.

A final libation, clasped hands and kisses, and the meal was over.

Honoratus retired to his study, and sat alone. Head light

231

from the wine, he brought the lamp nearer, and scrolled through the *Orations* of Dio Chrysostom, looking for the one set in Olbia. Like all men of his class, Honoratus constructed his identity in large part via literature, viewing his life through its prism. Merely unrolling the papyrus, smelling the cedar oil with which it was preserved, served to bring him a certain tranquillity. He liked to read texts that were relevant to his situation. Although outside Moesia Inferior, the town of Olbia on the northern shore of the Black Sea was his military responsibility. The *Providentia*, the trireme that had brought him downriver from Durostorum, had been due to take him to the settlement in a few days. The tidings from the Steppe had forestalled the voyage. Olbia might well be threatened, but his primary duty was to his province. Before such thoughts could dispel his nascent calm, he settled to read.

The *Oration* opened with Dio strolling outside the walls of Olbia. Although there had been a barbarian attack the day before, a great crowd of townsmen accompanied him, hanging on his words of wisdom. Honoratus smiled at the vanity of the philosopher; as if men under arms might not have more pressing things demanding their attention. Of course, it was an element in Dio's depiction of the Olbians as men of antique virtue. Hairy, like the heroes of the Trojan War, they possessed old-style courage. They loved the poetry of Homer, and their isolation had ensured that they remained uncorrupted by the meretricious sophistries of more recent writers.

It was an elegant piece of work, but, Honoratus thought, in some ways the reality of the North peeped through. In dress the Olbians were indistinguishable from the barbarians of the Steppe, and in speech they could hardly still be counted as Hellenes. Honoratus had greater sympathy with the more pessimistic outlook of Ovid on these shores and their inhabitants.

Wherever you look, the same flat uncultivated landscape,
Huge vistas of empty Steppe.
Turn right, turn left, a dangerous enemy threatens,
Encroaches: terror on either flank . . .

Scarcely men in the meaning of the word,
Show greater savagery than wolves, do not fear
The constraints of law: here might is right, and justice
Yields to the battling sword . . .

How much longer could he survive in this place?

Would he were not alive, might he die among them, could but
His spirit struggle free of this hated place!

The sound of running feet thudding down the corridor.
'The Goths! The Goths!'
A slave burst into the room.
'Master, the Goths are in the town.'
Honoratus dropped the papyrus roll.
'Bring me my boots.'
As the slave crouched at his feet, busy with straps and buckles, Honoratus pulled on his sword-belt.
'Your armour, master.'
'No time.'
Honoratus took the stairs two at a time.
It could be a false alarm. Honoratus had served in enough armies to know that a loose mule, or a drunk overturning a lamp, could cause a panic in the dead of night.
A motley crowd was assembled on the roof: some slaves, two marines, and, off to one side, the Gothic priest.
The *Gudja* walked across. 'I warned you, as the gods foretold, Cniva has come.'
Honoratus did not reply.

233

The slaves were wailing, imploring the intercession of their various deities.

Honoratus looked out over the dark town. There were fires burning in the temple district. By their light mobs of men could be seen surging through the streets.

'Soldier.' Honoratus called one of the marines to his side. 'The situation?'

'The Goths must have got in over the northern wall. The guards may have been drunk with the festival.'

Most likely the soldier was right. Somehow the Goths must have come down through the marshes of the Delta.

Now the first torches were flaring close by on the Acropolis. A roaring sound drifted up, like standing on a headland and listening to a storm at sea. It was too late for resistance, the town was lost.

'You two with me,' Honoratus ordered the marines. 'You as well,' he said to the *Gudja*.

The ships in the harbour at the south of the town offered the only hope. If they could get to the *Providentia* before she cast off . . .

'Master, what about us?'

'You slaves must see to your own safety.'

Honoratus pounded back down the stairs, the three men at his back.

Outside in the street civilians ran past, mad with fear.

Honoratus set off for the harbour. Their footfalls echoed back from the blank walls. High above, the moon shone behind scudding clouds. Selene was motionless and serene, remote from human suffering.

There was a tang of burning in the air. It caught in Honoratus' throat, as his breathing became ragged. Not far now, not far.

They ran around a corner, and the Goths were at the far end of the street, between them and the port.

Seeing them, the Goths gave voice to a guttural *hooming* sound. The majority were intent on looting, only a few gave chase.

Honoratus and his three companions turned, and fled.

Back around the corner, there was a door to the right. It was closed. Honoratus tried to kick it open. The door jumped on its hinges, but did not give. The soldiers threw their shoulders against the boards, and the lock splintered.

Down a black corridor, and out into the moonlit atrium.

A slave ran past. Honoratus grabbed him by the front of his tunic.

'The rear door?'

The slave was incoherent with terror.

'Take us to the backdoor.'

The slave nodded, went to move away.

Honoratus following, held him by the scruff of his neck.

The warren of the slave quarters reeked of unwashed humanity and stale food.

'Unbar the door.'

The slave squirmed with indecision. 'The master said to keep the doors shut.'

Honoratus pushed the slave aside, yanked back the bolts himself.

Another street, once again full of long-haired barbarians, of outlandish leather and furs.

The rear door slammed shut and rebolted, Honoratus doubled up, panting. *Zeus drew Hector out of the place where men were killed, the blood and confusion.* There had to be a way out.

'The south wall.'

They doubled back through the cells of the servants, across the atrium, and barged and blundered through stately chambers. Vases of ancient Corinthian workmanship tottered and smashed in their wake.

'Give me a leg up.'

One soldier linked his hands as a stirrup, and the other boosted Honoratus onto the wall. The alleyway beyond was empty. He reached down, and hauled the marines up after him.

The *Gudja* remained at the foot of the wall.

'Leave the bastard, sir. He is one of them.'

'No, we might need him.'

They dragged the Gothic priest up with them.

One by one, they dropped to the ground. As if by some unspoken command, all four men drew their swords.

'Keep running.'

Narrow lanes, twisting this way and that, muddy, choked with rubbish.

Screams and shouts rang down the alleyways, like noises off stage in the theatre.

Once Honoratus slipped and fell. He was up and running again in a moment; hands and knees skinned and smarting.

Clouds sailing across the moon. They ran through darkness and light, like initiates in some crazed mystery cult.

The harbour at last. A dense throng on the quayside. Men, women and children, all pushing and shoving, fighting to get to the remaining boats.

The water glittering, placid in the moonlight beyond.

'Make way for the governor! Make way!'

No one heeded the shouts of the soldiers, and they used the flats of their swords on defenceless heads and shoulders and backs.

Belabouring the civilians, they forced a passage to the lip of the dock.

There was the *Providentia*, already twenty paces out, backing away. Figures in the water were floundering after the slowly departing vessel.

Near at hand, Honoratus saw a fishing boat capsize under the weight of the people struggling to board.

'We swim.'

Honoratus dropped his blade, tore off his sword-belt.

'I do not know how to swim.' The *Gudja* stood still, a prophet deserted by his god.

Honoratus kicked off his boots.

'I do not swim.'

Honoratus shoved the *Gudja* off the quayside. Limbs flailing, the Goth splashed down, and vanished beneath the surface.

Honoratus dived. He landed poorly, his breath half knocked out. There were figures thrashing all around. No sign of the Goth. The two marines were ploughing off after the trireme.

Like some aquatic beast from myth, the *Gudja* erupted from the deep, then sank again.

Honoratus caught his bone-embroidered hair, went to pull the barbarian back up.

The *Gudja* grabbed Honoratus around the neck.

They sank, locked in a lashing, doomed embrace.

To die like this, so near safety, drowned by a barbarian's lack of self-control.

They broke the surface.

'Stop fighting!'

Down they went again, deeper this time. Honoratus' chest hurt. This time there would be no surfacing.

Honoratus raked his fingernails down the barbarian's face, hoping to catch an eye.

The *Gudja* released him.

Bobbing up to the surface, Honoratus sucked in air, and swam strongly away. The *Providentia* was thirty or more paces off. The trireme looked huge from this angle. She was turning, getting ready to depart. Honoratus did not look back.

Strong in the water, Honoratus closed the distance before the great banks of oars got the warship under way.

'Lend a hand for your governor!' Honoratus yelled.

He was closing with the stern, near the left-hand steering oar.

'A hand for your governor!'

A flash of movement in the darkness.

'Wait!' Someone was shouting.

The boathook was the last thing Honoratus saw. It hit him square on the head. As he sank, a line of poetry drifted through his thoughts. *His spirit struggles free of this hated place.*

PART VII:
RAVENNA AND AQUILEIA

CHAPTER 25

Ravenna,
The Kalends of May, AD238

Up on the tribunal the wind fretted at Pupienus' purple cloak. Behind him it tugged at the assembled standards. It was a small price to pay. Ravenna was surrounded by marshes, ringed with lagoons. Without the ceaseless breeze, and the tides which washed the filth of the settlement down to the sea, Ravenna would be uninhabitable with fever.

Waiting for the next unit to begin its demonstration, Pupienus looked beyond the parade ground, and let his gaze follow the line of poplars that fringed the canal which ran past the amphitheatre and back towards the walls of the town. It was a beautiful spring morning. In the sunshine the grass was very green, and the flowers in the fields a vibrant yellow. Yet there was always something ineffably melancholy about tall, dark poplars.

The 4th Cohort Alpinorum Sagittarorum, four-hundred strong, marched out by Centuries in columns of five. They wheeled and counter-marched creditably, before coming to a halt before the tribunal.

'Hail, Pupienus Augustus.'

Pupienus gave the word of command, and they about-turned as one. The targets, nailed-together planks about the size and shape of a man, were a hundred and fifty paces distant.

'Draw.'

Left hands steady, right well back, eyes and minds concentrated, the archers bent their bows.

'Loose.'

The untipped practice shafts hissed away. Moments later they clattered against and around the targets.

'Loose.'

Four squalls of arrows darkened the sky in rapid succession.

With advancing years, Pupienus' eyesight was not what it had once been. Yet he had spent much of his earlier life in army camps, all those long years on the German frontier. He did not need perfect vision to tell that the grouping had been good.

Pupienus had expected the proficiency of these auxiliary bowmen shipped across the Adriatic by Claudius Julianus, the governor of Dalmatia. The same had been true of the two units earlier in the day. Admittedly the thousand legionary veterans tempted by a large donative to come out of retirement and form a temporary Praetorian Cohort had moved rather slowly, but they had done their arms drill with the shrewdness of long experience. If they were not asked to march too far or too fast, the old soldiers had one more campaign in them. The three thousand marines and sailors seconded from the Ravenna fleet to serve on land had stepped out smartly, and wielded their wooden swords on the wicker shields and any exposed part of their companions' anatomy with a will. The men of the fleet were always eager to dispel the disdain in which they were held by the rest of the army. After such expertise and enthusiasm, the formations that were to follow might seem less than acceptable.

Pupienus had done what he could in a short space of time with unsatisfactory materials. He was not Prometheus, able to fashion men out of clay. The thousand gladiators in the imperial school here in Ravenna had been recruited. Levies had been conducted to conscript five thousand townsmen to the standards. In total he had cobbled together over ten thousand swords, approaching half of them real soldiers. Of course, it was not an army that could take the field, let alone challenge the forces of Maximinus in open battle. But, when Aquileia fell – he corrected himself, *if* Aquileia fell – it might be enough to hold Ravenna. The walls of the town were being repaired, and the endless waterways and swamps made it hard to approach.

As the 4th Cohort moved off to take its place on the edge of the parade ground, Pupienus thought about Rome. Macrianus, the new commander of the *frumentarii*, kept Pupienus well informed about all that happened in the eternal city. The lame veteran had a talent for prying into the affairs of others; his spies were everywhere – eavesdropping and opening letters – and his reports detailed and prompt. Yet it had come as little surprise, and perhaps had needed no arcane knowledge to foretell, that Balbinus, within days of being left alone, had allowed the city to slide into an anarchy of riot and street fighting. After one ineffectual foray, the corpulent fool had abnegated all responsibility, and barricaded himself on the Palatine. Rufinianus, the Prefect of the City, had been no better.

It had been left to Timesitheus to defend the Praetorian camp and end the violence. Somehow the little Greek had persuaded Gallicanus to get the mob off the streets. The responses of Balbinus to the return of order had been typically ill-judged. Timesitheus had been stripped of the Prefecture of the Praetorians which he had assumed during the crisis. Balbinus, one had to suppose, thus had further alienated the *Graeculus* from the regime. With the elevation of Gordian, Timesitheus had shown himself active and unscrupulous, ready to play for the highest stakes, and he controlled the grain supply of Rome. The little Greek would make a dangerous enemy. He should have been requited for his endeavour or, better still, eliminated. Conversely, Gallicanus, the instigator of the unrest, in effect had been rewarded by being appointed tutor to the young Caesar. It baffled belief that even the mean comprehension of Balbinus could consider it a good idea to put such a lever of potential power into the hands of a murderous hothead like Gallicanus. There was no doubt in Pupienus' mind, on his return to Rome, one way or another, his co-Emperor must be removed from the throne. It was for the good of the *Res Publica*. Philosophy agreed; kingly power was indivisible.

The gladiators processed across the parade ground to the tribunal. Rather than march, each man swaggered. Seeing them armed and clad in their peculiar equipment outside the confines of the amphitheatre was an all too visible reminder of the instability of the times. Tridents and nets, grilled helmets crowned with fishes, *Retiarius* and *Myrmillo*, Samnite and Thracian; their very names and accoutrements proclaimed them the antithesis of *Romanitas*. The world was turned upside down.

'Those who are about to die salute you.'

'Carry on.' Needs must, however, Pupienus' voice contained nothing but disdain.

The gladiators paired off. They circled and posed, with much twirling of weapons and stamping of boots. Eventually, when the mood took him, each bounded forward, and sparred with exaggerated cuts and thrusts and ostentatious parries.

The throng of watching civilians exclaimed and called out the odds, as if at the spectacles.

The plebs were fools, Pupienus thought. Gladiators were the dregs of the earth, slaves and barbarians, barely human. Fat and overfed, they had no stamina or discipline. Battles were not won by fancy strokes and posturing, by individuals leaping and jumping. Soldiers won battles by getting close to the steel, thrusting with the point, by holding the line, gritting their teeth and enduring. No troop of gladiators would ever beat soldiers in a set-piece battle. Pupienus was uncertain if they had the fortitude to defend the city walls.

The dust shifted up, and the crowd roared.

Pupienus removed his thoughts from the unseemly pleasures of the plebs, set them to matters of importance.

At last good news had come from the provinces. In the West, Aedinius Julianus had brought over Gallia Narbonnensis and neighbouring Lugdunensis. He had written of his confidence that Aquitania would soon join them. Control of all three Gallic provinces would isolate Maximinus from two of his loyalists, Decius in Spain, and Capelianus in Africa. Yet it had to be remembered that the provinces of Gaul were unarmed.

Events across the Adriatic might prove more telling. The Procurator Axius had deposed the governor and seized control of Dacia. Unlike Dalmatia and Thrace, the only other provinces in the region so far to acknowledge Pupienus and his imperial colleagues, Dacia was garrisoned by two legions and numerous auxiliaries. At last the Emperors chosen by the Senate had a regular provincial army at their disposal, and the example of Dacia might ease another armed province into the revolt. The two senatorial envoys, Egnatius Marinianus and Celsinus, were both in negotiations with Tacitus in Moesia Superior. Whatever the outcome of their diplomacy – and failure would bring their deaths – the allegiance of the armies along the Danube ultimately depended on the urbane Honoratus in distant Moesia Inferior.

There were grounds for guarded optimism, but no more. Apart from a merchant telling that Carrhae had fallen to the Persians more than a month before, Pupienus had heard nothing from the provinces bordering the Euphrates. Recently, sleepless in the long watches of the night, he had found himself praying that the inducements that he had offered his brother would prove enough to sway Catius Clemens in Cappadocia. If he deserted Maximinus the other governors most likely would follow, and finally the rebellion would rest on a significant base of military force. The armies of the East had put men on the throne before – the worthy Vespasian, and the perverted Heliogabalus – and they could do so again. Once that had been accomplished, the loss of Carrhae showed that they would get no rest. There could be no doubt but that one of their new rulers must lead them against the Persians.

Finally the gladiators drew to a close their inaccurate simulacrum of battle.

If the spectators had cheered the gladiators, it was as nothing to their enthusiasm for the final unit. The militia were their own, their sons, brothers, husbands.

The two long columns, both twenty men wide, attempted nothing beyond forming up opposite each other. It did not go well. Individuals lost their place, bumped into and impeded their companions; Century collided with Century. Eventually they shuffled into their lines.

'*Testudo.*'

The shields of those on one side clattered together, forming ramshackle walls and roof.

'Throw.'

The men of the other line took a few faltering paces, and

threw the wooden staves that served as javelins. The distance was not above twenty paces, but many fell short. Most of those that hit the target rattled off the leather-clad shields. Yet, some found the inadvertent gaps. The screams and yells of consternation of the shocked and wounded were muffled by the *testudo*.

'Reverse.'

The manoeuvre was repeated, with an identical result.

'Enough.' The militia had been scheduled to indulge in a mock hand-to-hand combat, but Pupienus considered that they would do each other too much unintended damage.

When regular soldiers had chivvied the armed citizens to their allotted station, the ground was littered with the fallen. Some moved gingerly, holding heads and limbs, some lay stretched in the dust.

A great wailing rose from the audience. Servants ran out to tend the wounded and remove any who were dead.

Pupienus looked away from the debacle, studied the line of poplars. He would make his speech when calm had returned.

The lamentations rang in his ears. He did not blame those who grieved. Had not the Heliades, changed into the poplars on which he gazed, shed bitter tears for their dead brother Phaethon? Had not Phaethon's father, the immortal Helios, clad himself in sordid mourning, abandoned his duty, and given himself up to grief, having sent his son to his death? And what of a man who had encompassed the death of his own father? Only iron self-control could prevent him weeping, even if he wore the purple. *Such is the fate the gods have spun for poor mortal men, that we should live in misery.*

CHAPTER 26

Aquileia,
The Nones of May, AD238

It was another foul night. Statius, the local magistrate, had said he could not remember such weather, not at this time of year, not since his childhood. Every evening the thunderheads built out in the Gulf of Tergeste. Nightfall came early as the storm swept inland to Aquileia. The heavens opened, and the gutters and streets sluiced with water.

Menophilus left his dripping cloak at the door. The warehouse was lit only by the flashes of lightning. Lamps or torches were too much of a risk. The ranks of amphorae looked deceptively innocuous, but the smell betrayed them: a compound of pitch and oil mixed with sulphur and bitumen.

'You did well,' Menophilus said to the *Trierarch*.

The previous night the commander of the small galley had run the blockade. Although the besiegers had no ships, the Natiso was no more than fifty paces wide. Even keeping to the centre of the channel, a vessel was in javelin-cast of both banks. Most likely it would not have made it but for the darkness of the wild night. As it was, the ship had almost reached the south wall of the town before the alarm was raised.

'Fifty jars of naptha. No matter how well sealed, the stench seeps out. One fire arrow, one broken pot, and it would have been the end of us,' the *Trierarch* said.

'Your men did their duty. They will be rewarded.'

'I am sure they would appreciate a few coins for a drink, as they are not going home.'

With the enemy alerted, it would be near suicidal for the galley to attempt to leave. It was moored close under the southern wall. The sixty men of the crew – oarsmen, sailors, and marines – had been armed, and stationed as a reserve in the Basilica that opened onto the Forum.

A flicker of lightning illuminated the rows of amphorae. They looked smooth, and ominously delicate.

'Tomorrow, we will move twenty each to the northern and western walls. We must find somewhere safe to store them. The rest can remain here.'

With the arrival of the main body of the imperial field army, the besiegers had surrounded the town. Two large camps faced the exposed northern and western walls, two smaller ones where the Natiso flowed around Aquileia to the east and south. The encampments had been protected by ditch and rampart, but no field works connected the fortifications one to another. Evidently circumvallation had not been thought necessary. Maximinus would know how few regular troops were in the town.

Responding to these dispositions, Crispinus had shifted the three hundred and forty men of the Ravenna fleet under his direct command to the western defences. Apart from the crew of the blockade runner, the rest of the garrison remained as before: two thousand militia on each wall, another two thousand in the porticos of the Forum, the five hundred auxiliaries of the 1st Cohort on the north wall. The fighting men were supported by twenty-four pieces of torsion artillery, two thirds of them concentrated on the northern and western walls, behind which stood the dozen cranes for dropping boulders on the heads of attackers.

The night after the assault there had been a sharp action. The besiegers had managed to recover the rams, but at a heavy cost in casualties. In the seventeen days since, there had been no further attempt on the walls. The reasons for the respite stood in front of the northern camp. Day by day the defenders had watched the construction of the three enormous siege towers. Progress had been slow. On arrival, with wanton destructiveness, Maximinus' men had torched all the buildings in the vicinity which Menophilus had not had demolished before the siege. The troops' lack of foresight had made labour for themselves. Timber for the towers had had to be hauled from far away.

The delay had been welcome. Aquileia was well stocked with munitions and food, and thanks to the river, wells in the town, and the nightly downpours, would never run short of water. Treachery was unlikely, given the inhabitants could expect no quarter. Menophilus had used the time to train the militia, although he still had doubts about their ability to stand close to the steel if the defences were breached. The gods willing, it would not come to that. The walls were sound. The river made a barrier on two sides, there was no cover on the approaches to the other two sides. The water table was too high to permit undermining. It was the siege towers that posed the greatest threat. Somehow they must be destroyed.

It was late. *Intempesta*, the dead of night, when it was ill-omened to be abroad. It made no odds. Sleep shunned Menophilus. No point in taking off his armour, only to struggle back into it after lying awake for an hour or two.

250

'Make sure the guards are watchful.'

Collecting his cloak, he walked back to the door, the *Trierarch* at his heels.

The storm had not eased. Standing under the lintel, he held out his hand. In the lightning, he watched the rain beating on his palm, running up his forearm. The life of man was but a moment, his body no more than water, his soul vapours and dreams.

'Earth is in love with the showers from above, and the all-holy heaven itself is in love.'

'Sir?'

'Euripides.'

'A great consolation is culture.'

'Sometimes.'

Between the roar of the thunder, came the sound of someone running down the street.

'No one brings good tidings on a night like this,' the *Trierarch* said.

One moment vivid in the lightning, the next plunged in darkness, the messenger seemed to advance in bounds towards them.

'Sir, the enemy are across the river. They are at the east wall, breaking through the port.'

Menophilus stepped out into the downpour, pushed back the hood of his cloak, listened. Nothing to be heard but the thunder, the rain, and the rushing water. Rain streaming down his face, into his eyes, down his neck. His thoughts were splintered, crowding him in no order. Could this be true, not some false alarm? The east, the harbour – the only soldiers on the wall there were the crews of four ballistae, apart from them there were just the civilians under Servilianus. How in Hades had Maximinus' troops got across the river? If they were through the docks it was all over.

The messenger and the *Trierarch* were waiting for orders.

251

Menophilus could not let this ill-fortune unman him. He had to think clearly, take control. The reserve in the Forum, get the crew to the galley, send it upriver – no, there was no time for that – get them all to the walls. There was nothing else for it – stake everything on a desperate rush in the dark. One last throw of the dice.

'Follow me.'

He ran north up the main street, his boots splashing through the puddles. One block, two. The blank walls searing white at the crack of the lightning, then disappearing in the gloom. His heart was knocking in his chest, his laboured breathing drowned out the din of the storm. Three blocks, four.

The rain-lashed Forum was empty.

Shoving open the doors, Menophilus burst into the Basilica.

Two drowsy sentries stumbled to attention.

'Sound the alarm. Get the men formed up in the square.'

'Sir, it is a tempest out there.'

'Do it now.'

'We will do what is ordered—'

'Now!'

Menophilus shrugged off his cloak; being soaked was the least of his problems. He doubled up, hands on knees, dragging air into his lungs.

Troops clattered and banged out into the Forum.

No time to waste. Menophilus straightened up, pushed his sodden hair out of his face. Play the role Fate had assigned. Act like a man. He squared his shoulders, and marched outside.

The crew of the warship were drawn up to one side. The militia stood in an amorphous mass out in the middle. Menophilus looked down from the steps at their white, scared faces.

'Soldiers, the tyrant's men are down on the quayside. We will go and support Servilianus' defence. Are you ready for war?'

Ready! The men of the warship shouted the traditional response.

Ready! The armed civilians sounded anything but prepared to hazard their lives.

'*Trierarch*, your men will go in the vanguard.'

'Quick march.' The officer led his men from the Forum, and out of sight.

The militiamen stood as if rooted into the wet paving slabs. Menophilus knew if he did not put some heart into them, they would be too frightened to obey. No time for a long speech. He had to summon the right words. If only he was not so tired, so shaken and afraid himself.

Above veins of lightning pulsed in the dark of the sky.

'Citizens of Rome . . .'

A bad start. Rome was far away, men there were safely abed. In this terrible, storm-wracked night, patriotism and honour were no more than words.

'Men of Aquileia, the enemy are at the gates. If we let them pass through, we will die, every one of us. If we let them enter, your wives and children will be raped and enslaved, your aged parents butchered. Only you can save your loved ones. Let us be men.'

As his words were torn away by the wind, he could not judge their effect.

'Stand against those who serve the tyrant, and they will run. They have nothing to fight for, you have everything. You fight for your families, your homes, the tombs of your forefathers, the temples of your gods. Do not let them down. Do not let your companions down.'

Like an actor, he needed some rousing line to finish the play.

'The great god Belenus watches over Aquileia. He saved your ancestors from the Marcomannic hordes. Now he promises you victory. His sacred birds have not left the temple. The oracles are good. The shining one himself will stand beside you on the walls. Gather your courage. Prove yourselves worthy. Let us be men!'

Belenus, Belenus. The chant rose up, weak at first, growing stronger. It was now or never.

'Let us go. With me.'

Menophilus drew his sword, and jumped down from the steps.

The men of Aquileia followed him out of the Forum, and down the rain-swept street. Less a military unit, more of an armed mob. They were filled with a fragile resolve. Menophilus prayed it might hold long enough.

It was no distance to the docks. Beyond the roofs of the warehouses, the battlements were very distinct in the lightning; every stone, the mortar between, clearer than daylight. There were men on the wallwalk, but no fighting.

'Stay here. Do not move. Call on your god.'

Menophilus ran between two warehouses, took the steps up to the wall two at a time.

'Where is the attack?'

The militiaman, too shocked to reply, pointed out into the night.

Menophilus leant out over the machicolations. There was the river. Rough pontoons built of big, round wine barrels bridged the Natiso in three places. Troops milled at the foot of the wall. Four or five ladders reared up against the battlements. As he watched, one was sent crashing sideways and down. Rocks and missiles rained down on those below. His spirits lifted. The wall was not breached.

Some movement below, an eddy in the dim shapes down by the river off to his right, caught his eye. His vain hopes were dashed. Troops were funnelling towards a tiny postern gate. They must have broken down the brickwork. The soldiers pushed and shoved, getting in each other's way. Yet one at a time, they were squeezing their way inside.

Menophilus ran back down the steps.

Belenus, bringer of light, hold your hands over your worshippers.

The chant was thin, insubstantial against the howling rainstorm. There were fewer men than there had been. Fools. Slinking off to cower at home would not save them.

'The walls are secure. Only a handful are entering by one door. Drive them out, and we are safe. Drive them out, and Aquileia is safe. Do not desert me. Do not desert your families. Follow me.'

Menophilus had taken no more than two or three paces when a muscle in his left calf snapped. The pain white-hot, he hobbled to a halt, bent over. Militiamen jostled into his back, nearly knocking him to the ground. How could the gods be so cruel? Not now. Safety almost in his grasp.

He took a step, his leg almost gave under him. The agony made him gasp. He grabbed someone's shoulder. All resolution was draining out of the man's face.

Something so trivial; a heartless joke of a malevolent deity.

Without him, these civilians would not fight.

The body was nothing. A corpse a man dragged around. Nothing that was external was of any consequence. Pain was to be despised. Pain could not touch the inner man, not deflect his purpose.

'With me.'

He hobbled forward. Pain was nothing. It had no consequence.

The alley was for men on foot, not goods, so narrow that two men would find it hard to pass through at once. As Menophilus limped around the corner, the last defender elbowed him aside, and fled into the town.

A cheer from the attackers.

Menophilus set himself in the opening.

Seeing this unexpected resistance, the advancing wedge of armoured men halted. A young officer was forcing his way to the front.

Menophilus spoke over his shoulder to the militiamen. 'You at the back, get up on the roofs on either side. Throw the tiles down on their heads.'

There was no chance to see if his command was obeyed. The officer had reached the first rank. He was tall, wore chased armour. There was something familiar about him. The tribune began to harangue his men.

'Legionaries of the 4th Flavia Felix, where is your courage? A lame soldier, and a few civilians stand between you and victory.'

Menophilus knew him now: young Barbius, the son of the Aquileian magistrate, Maximinus' failed envoy.

'Barbius, do not do this. Your father has lost one son, do not make him grieve for another.'

The tribune stared, as if unable to believe the evidence of his senses. 'You, the coward who abandoned my brother.'

'Barbius, you know Maximinus has promised the town to the soldiers. What will happen to your family; your father, your mother, your own wife and children? Do you want to be responsible for their deaths?'

'I will protect them.'

'How? Your father fights on the north wall, your wife and children wait at home with your mother. Which will you try and save?'

'I have no choice,' Barbius said.

'Leave the tyrant. Join us. Fight for liberty and your family. It is your duty.'

'A man like you – an oath-breaker, a murderer – and you tell me about liberty and duty.'

'Barbius, you serve in the army, you know what the soldiers do when they sack a town. No one man can stop them.'

The first tile caught a legionary behind Barbius. It shattered on his helmet, but he went down like a felled ox. Then the air was filled with missiles. The men on the roofs were like daemons, flickering in and out of sight, hurling everything that came to hand. Trapped in the alley, the soldiers hefted their shields, cowered beneath them, but men were falling, battered down, sharp shards scything through their flesh. A legionary shoved Barbius aside, rushed at Menophilus. The legionary went down under a hail of tiles and bricks.

Panic seized the legionaries. Huddled under reverberating shields, they blundered over their own fallen, back towards the postern.

'Stop,' Menophilus shouted at the rooftops.

If they heard, the men up on the eaves paid no attention.

'They are Romans, like you. For the love of the gods, stop.'

Missiles crashed down. Barbius was at the rear of the stampede.

'Do not kill them. Not him.'

CHAPTER 27

Aquileia,
Two Days after the Ides of May, AD238

Ten days after the failed attempt on the docks, and at long last the siege towers were ready. In the bright sunshine Maximinus walked to inspect the third, and final *City Taker*. From a base twenty feet across, the structure gently tapered to a height of almost fifty feet. The rear was open, but the interior was gloomy.

'Wait here.'

The senior commanders of the imperial entourage did as they were told.

'Javolenus and Apsines with me.'

Clambering inside Maximinus was struck by the smell; a compound of freshly cut, unseasoned timber, damp clay and leather, the sharp tang of vinegar, and the underlying sourness of human sweat. When his eyes adjusted, he took in the square frame, and the three axles that would turn the six solid wheels. These were all cut from hardwood; oak and ash. Obtaining them had constituted the principal delay.

Between the preparations of the defenders and the thoughtless destruction of his own soldiery no buildings had remained in the vicinity from which to scavenge construction materials. Mature trees had had to be felled miles away. As almost all the baggage animals had been slaughtered for food, it had been necessary to manhandle the massive baulks of timber on rollers the entire distance. The backbreaking labour had been unpopular with the men.

Maximinus ran his hand over the smooth surface of the ram, which for now was lashed down in the middle of the space. It had been well worth a couple of hundred casualties to recover the three rams from the wreckage of their shelters at the base of the town walls. He squinted out to where its metal head projected, already relishing the awesome destructive power it would unleash. Under his hand, the ram felt almost alive.

Satisfied, Maximinus took the ladder up to the higher levels. Above the ground there were three floors. The first was where the second wave of assault troops would assemble. The front of the next comprised the boarding bridge, which would be let down to release the forlorn hope onto the wall. Few of those initial attackers would expect to survive. If they did, they would be rich for life. If not, their dependents would never want. The top level was open to the sky. This would be filled with archers, shooting down to clear the defenders from the wallwalk.

The upright timbers and the planking of the floors were fir and pine; lighter than the base, but still solid. All military precedents argued that the walls should have been constructed of the same materials. The shortage of wood – the willows that lined the Natiso were deemed unsuitable – and the pressure of time, had prompted the engineers into ingenuity. Apart from the bracing beams, the sides of the towers were wattles of reeds coated in wet clay from the river. On the

259

outside were hung sacks of hide, stuffed with more reeds and grass. The latter had been soaked in vinegar and water to retard fire. The relatively flimsy walls did not perturb Maximinus. There were no stone-throwing engines inside Aquileia, and the lightness of the sides would allow the *City Takers* to advance faster than the normal glacial pace. It was a pity that some of the troops had had to give up their tents to make enough sacks, but the weather had improved, and serving under the standards had always been hard.

From the god-like height of the machine, Maximinus surveyed the field. The siege towers were aimed at the same places that the rams had attacked. The one on which Maximinus stood would advance down the road against the northern gate. To the left, beyond the aqueduct, the other two would make for the two sections of hastily repaired wall.

Time was of the essence. There was no reason for further delay.

'To your positions,' Maximinus called down over the side of the tower.

It amused him to see the imperial entourage have to move out of the way. The great officers and dignitaries – Flavius Vopiscus, Julius Capitolinus, Marius Perpetuus, Consul Ordinarius the previous year, even the unnaturally calm Praetorian Prefect Anullinus – all had to step sharp to avoid the legionaries rushing to their places under the gaze of their Emperor.

While some men would push directly against the axles and the base, more took up station behind the tower. Anchors had been thrown out in front, and great cables ran back through the structure to winches and pulleys at the rear. The soldiers operating them would be sheltered by mobile screens when the *City Takers* finally edged into bowshot of the walls.

'Advance.'

A deep groan issued from the tower as the pressure built. A tremor ran through it, like a mild earthquake. For a moment Maximinus wondered if the entire thing would collapse. It would be a strange way to die. Like everything, it was in the lap of the gods.

Squealing and complaining, the tower shifted slightly. Of course it was sound.

Maximinus looked beyond the aqueduct at the other two towers. Surely nothing on earth could withstand such power. This sight would bring any rebel back to heel. Only an occasional messenger now reached the imperial headquarters, but what news had come from the provinces was not good. In the west, both Gallia Narbonnensis and Lugdunensis had renounced their allegiance. Across the Alps to the east, Dalmatia, Thrace, and Dacia had also turned traitor. They posed no significant military threat. Only Dacia contained any legions. Maximinus could order expeditions from the forces along the Rhine and Danube to crush them. Yet to do so would leave the frontiers dangerously exposed to barbarian incursions. Unconfirmed rumours claimed that the Goths had sacked Istria in Moesia Inferior. There lay the difference between Maximinus and those who opposed him. Unlike the insurgents, Maximinus would never countenance inviting a barbarian like Cniva into the empire. To act thus would be a betrayal of everything for which he fought. No true Emperor, no true Roman, would put personal advantage above the good of the *Res Publica*.

The provinces could be dealt with swiftly enough when Aquileia fell. It was four hundred paces to the walls. The towers would advance at some fifty paces a day. Eight days until the boarding bridges crashed down and the storming parties went in. If they were repulsed, the rams should breach the walls in another two or three days. Eleven days at most until the town was taken. With the fall of Aquileia, even the

261

most stubborn revolutionary must realize that their cause had no hope. The rebellion would collapse.

The sun was warm on Maximinus' face. Thank the gods the rain had stopped days ago. The ground had dried out, and now there was no danger that their wheels would sink into the earth under the weight of the towers. The only worry in Maximinus' mind was the commissariat.

The ration of sour wine had been halved to one pint a day to provide enough vinegar to soak the coverings of the towers, and there had been no fresh bread or meat for days. Veterans did not mind hard tack and bacon, but they would have missed the wine. With grain unobtainable, now the amount of biscuit issued must be cut to just two pounds a day. The men would go hungry, but it would not be for long. Eleven days, and they could all feast on the plunder of Aquileia.

The supplies brought an unpleasant duty to mind. Maximinus climbed down, the rungs of the ladders creaking under his bulk. The tower had stopped moving. To avoid exhaustion, the men hauling on the ropes had to be relieved regularly.

'Barbius.'

The young tribune saluted.

'Double the night guard; twenty men at each siege tower. Have them keep a good watch on the walls of the town. There are only civilians in there, they would not dare try anything in daylight, but they might attempt a sally in the dark.'

'We will do what is ordered, and at every command we will be ready.'

Against all the odds, Barbius had survived the failed attack on the docks. Maximinus thought that he might be favoured by the gods.

'Is the punishment parade drawn up?'

Julius Capitolinus stepped forward. 'Emperor, may I appeal to your clemency? In military law only desertion, mutiny, or insubordination make a soldier liable for the death penalty. Even then consideration is given to length of service, previous conduct, and conditions in the field. The soldier is guilty of theft, but he has been with the standards for ten years, and food is scarce. May I request that you commute the sentence to a flogging?'

Of course an officer should intercede for his men – the soldier was from Capitolinus' 2nd Legion – but Maximinus did not care to be lectured on the ways of the army.

'Times are hard, *disciplina* must not be compromised.'

'Emperor, the man fought under you in Germania and out on the Steppe.'

Maximinus took his time – Paulina would have been proud – and considered what he knew of the commander of 2nd legion Parthica

'Capitolinus, is it true that you are writing my biography?'

The Prefect looked taken aback, but rallied quickly. 'Emperor, that would be presumptuous, beyond my limited powers. It is true I have been collecting material for lives of the Caesars, but had thought it best to end with the reign of the divine Caracalla.'

Capitolinus was no fool; safer by far to stick to earlier reigns. Maximinus knew the Prefect was lying. Volo's *frumentarii* provided thorough reports. Anyway, it mattered little what people would say after his death. Maximinus had always acted in the interests of Rome. The gods willing, posterity would judge him correctly.

'Emperor, may I urge you to accede to the request of Julius Capitolinus? The troops may take it badly.'

Maximinus turned to Flavius Vopiscus. Had the Roman army degenerated into some sort of martial democracy? Before he could frame a reply, the Praetorian Prefect intervened.

'The Emperor acts on my recommendation.' Anullinus made no attempt to disguise the implicit threat. 'Are you questioning an imperial order?'

'Never. We will do what is ordered, and at every command we will be ready.' Vopiscus' hand went to where an amulet hung under his cuirass. 'It is our duty to say what we believe is best for the *Res Publica*, and give our open and honest opinion to the Emperor. Not all of us have sunk into sycophancy.'

Evidently there was no love lost between Vopiscus and Anullinus. Some intervention was necessary to defuse the imminent confrontation.

'No need for harsh words.' The role of mediator did not come naturally to Maximinus. He searched for something to say. 'For many years I served in the ranks. No Senator or equestrian could know the mood of the troops as I do.'

'You are right, Emperor,' Vopiscus said.

Anullinus saluted, but his baleful eyes remained fixed on Vopiscus.

Tiberius had been wrong. Being Emperor was not to hold a wolf by the ears, but to keep a pack of the beasts from each other's throats. Maximinus thought of the wolf in Emona. One by one he had broken her legs, then cut her throat.

'To the parade ground.'

Maximinus ascended the tribunal, and settled himself on one ivory throne. His son took the other. The senior commanders stood at their backs, the standards were arrayed above.

The prisoner was brought out into the square formed by the troops. His tunic was unbelted, and his feet bare. Yet he bore himself like a soldier.

Sometimes, Maximinus thought, an individual has to suffer for the good of all.

'Behold a thief who would steal food from his brothers.' The herald had a powerful voice. 'Let no man think to do the same. By order of the most noble Imperator Gaius Iulius

Verus Maximinus Augustus, and the most noble Caesar Gaius Iulius Verus Maximus, let the sentence be enacted.'

When the executioners seized him, the soldier's resolution gave. He struggled as they dragged him to the cross, forced him down. When the nails were hammered through his flesh, he screamed.

Maximinus regarded the victim without emotion. Beside him, Verus Maximus was smiling. His son was developing a taste for executions.

The cross was raised, dropped into its base, made fast. The soldier was beyond making much noise.

Maximinus had been merciful. The executioners knew their craft. A man could survive for hours, or even days, on the cross. Maximinus had told them to place the nails so the end would not be too prolonged.

There was no interest in watching a man die.

Maximinus took a coin from the wallet on his belt. DIVA PAULINA. The hooked nose, the jutting chin; more and more looking at his dead wife was like looking at himself.

CHAPTER 28

Aquileia,
Five Days after the Ides of May, AD238

'You do not have to do this,' Crispinus said.

'It was my idea. It is my duty.' All true enough, but Menophilus wished it was not.

'May the gods hold their hands over you.' Crispinus' prayer was sincere.

Menophilus embraced Crispinus – for the last time? – and nodded for them to open the little postern gate that led down to the river.

Crispinus raised a hand in blessing or valediction.

Outside the night was horribly bright. There was cloud cover, but the moon was near full. It backlit the big, high clouds silver. When there was a gap, it cast a white light on the landscape, near as bright as day. There could be no postponement. By the time the moon was waning, the fate of Aquileia would be decided.

Menophilus led the men down to the water.

The bank of the Natiso was a little higher than a man,

sloping at some thirty degrees. It was bare of trees, but provided a modicum of concealment.

There was no outcry.

Menophilus waited. The smell of the river was strong in his nostrils: mud, the mulch of last year's fallen leaves, rubbish carried down from the northern camp of the enemy.

Soon the twelve men in the party were in position. They were all soldiers, every one a volunteer. Mindful of how soldiers talked, of the dangers of betrayal, Menophilus had not told them the nature of the hazardous duty until a few moments earlier. The 1st Cohort Ulpia Galatarum had a proud record. They had taken the news well. It was quite likely that none of them would return.

Six men, including Menophilus himself, carried nothing but their swords and a shuttered lantern. The other six had the amphorae in packs strapped to their backs. There was no doubt which group thought they had the more dangerous task. All had blackened their mailcoats, and wore dark clothes. They had tied black rags around their helmets and boots, and rubbed mud into their faces, forearms and hands. Menophilus had personally inspected that everyone had removed every ornament from their sword-belts.

The breeze was picking up. It soughed through the grass and reeds.

Menophilus peered north, up the river. Before the siege, he had had the poplars and willows cut down for almost two hundred paces to prevent the attackers using them as cover. The irony was not lost on him. His old tutor had insisted that a man with a philosophical education had an advantage over the majority of mankind. While the philosopher had considered all circumstances beforehand, everything came as a surprise to others. That might hold true in the lecture theatre, less so in a hard-pressed siege.

267

Menophilus touched the man behind him on the shoulder, and set off.

Lantern in his right hand, Menophilus used his left to grasp the vegetation and the roots and stumps of trees along the bank. His feet kept sliding in the mud. The muscle in his left calf was still tight; with luck it would last the night.

The gurgle and lap of the river, and the sigh of the wind, were overlaid by squelching, skidding footsteps, laboured breathing, and sudden grunts when a man's boot slipped. Noise carried at night. It seemed enough to wake the dead.

No choice but to see this to the end.

A clatter of wings, right under Menophilus' boots, as a duck took flight.

'Steady.' Menophilus just stopped himself speaking out loud.

The duck whirred away across the dark land.

Heart thumping in his chest, Menophilus slithered along the greasy incline.

The world narrowed; three paces of muddy bank, the black water, the silver clouds overhead. On and on, painfully slow, like the souls of the damned condemned to some punishment with no hope of release.

A clink of metal on metal.

Menophilus froze. The men behind bumped to a halt.

There it was again.

Menophilus held his breath.

The silhouette of a figure walking towards them down the opposite bank.

Who in Hades would be abroad in the dead of night?

Unhurriedly, looking neither left nor right, but at his feet, the man passed by downriver.

A man, a daemon, the unquiet soul of one of the unburied?

Whatever the nature of the nocturnal walker, he was gone.

Menophilus pulled himself together. Distances were hard

to judge at night. Perhaps they were more than halfway to the inviting, if illusory, safety of the black tunnel where the willows still bent down over the stream. Again, he tapped the man next in line on the shoulder, and moved on.

He had gone no great distance when something snagged his foot. He stumbled, and half fell. Better spaced than before, the men behind came to a halt this time with no fuss. Putting down the lantern, Menophilus sought with both hands along the ground to find what had tripped him. A line, another, both tied to pegs, and leading off into the water: a fishing trap. That might explain the solitary figure walking the other bank.

Pulling the pegs out of the earth, he let the lines disappear into the water. He set off again, now even more slowly, trying to detect further obstructions.

Perhaps the scouring of the land before the besieging army arrived was paying dividends. If soldiers were reduced to fishing between the siege lines, it could be that Maximinus was running short of supplies. Whether that was the case or not, this was evidence of poor discipline. The river downstream of the camp was foul with the filth and excreta of several thousand men. It was no place to let men draw water or catch fish. Since Troy, disease had haunted armies camped for any time before the walls of a town.

There were half a dozen more fish traps before they reached the trees. Dismantling them took a little time, but was quieter than warning those following of the obstructions.

It was gratifyingly dark under the hanging branches of the willows. In the enclosed space the quality of the sound changed: the river louder, their own passage quieter. Menophilus somehow felt safer, as if the deity of that sylvan place stood beside them.

By his earlier, careful calculations, they needed to creep another fifty paces upstream. Lips moving, but silent, he began to count: ten, twenty. His paces were shorter than walking on good going. Fifty, sixty.

At seventy, he raised his arm to halt the column.

Not a word had been spoken since they had left the town. The men were well briefed. Now they sank down, and arranged themselves in what cover was available. Like the duck downstream, you would almost have to tread on them before you knew they were there.

Paccius, the *Optio*, came up from the rear to join Menophilus. Together they wormed their way to the top of the bank, and parted the grass to take their bearings.

The clouds had thickened while they were under the trees. Perhaps the gods really were with them.

Off to the right, all too close across the darkling plain, stretched the low, black mass of Maximinus' northern camp. There would be sentries on the rampart, but repeated nights of observation had revealed that they never carried torches.

Ahead, and a little to the left, the tall shapes of the two siege towers could be made out. The nearest was no more than a hundred paces. The third was obscured by the arches of the aqueduct. Here too no lights showed, but for the last three mornings, at the dawn changing of their guard, Menophilus had counted the twenty guards stationed to the front of each tower.

Away to the left moving halos of yellow light showed where the guards on the walls of Aquileia made their rounds. It was hard not to think of the men snug behind those defences. It had taken so long to get here; best not to dwell that safety lay a few moments' hard running to the south.

The moon was hidden by thick banks of cloud. Menophilus could not reckon how much time had elapsed. It made no odds; there was nothing to do but wait.

A bird was singing nearby in the covert: a long drawn-out note, modulated into short, fast phrases, soaring high and low. Another nightingale answered from further upstream. Was it true that they competed with each other, and the defeated bird died, her breath failing with her song?

Paccius lay next to him. Menophilus wondered if he was listening to the birdsong. He had not wanted to bring the young officer. The *Optio* had done well at the Aesontius. It had seemed a shame to curtail such a promising career. But if Menophilus himself was struck down at the start, someone reliable must take command.

Menophilus did not think he was afraid to face his own death. A release from the twitching of appetite, from service to the flesh, a release from guilt and fatigue. In death you feel nothing at all, and therefore nothing evil.

Unearthly music – flutes and pipes – floated on the air. The nightingales fell silent. The distant sound of a choir singing a hymn. A flare of light on the north-east corner of the walls of Aquileia. For the fifth night running the god Belenus, the shining one, would patrol the battlements of his beleaguered city.

Even at this distance the cult statue of the god was awe-inspiring, twice the size of a man. The gold and silver of its robes glittered in the light of the many torches in the procession. The money Menophilus had given to the temple when he arrived in the city had proved its worth. The priests and the deity had pledged their support to the Gordiani, then seamlessly transferred their allegiance to Pupienus and Balbinus. The devotees believed that the nocturnal peregrination of Belenus raised the morale of the townsfolk. Menophilus was satisfied that it drew the eyes of the besiegers, and might mask other noises in the darkness.

'It is time,' Menophilus whispered to Paccius.

They slid back down the bank, made their way along the line of dark shapes.

'Get ready, boys. Light the lanterns.'

271

The chink and flash of steel on stone. Brief flares of light, before the lanterns were shuttered.

'To your places.'

They crawled up to the lip of the bank.

Menophilus had the right of the line, Paccius the left. Each man with a lantern was paired with one with an amphora. The soldier with Menophilus was called Massa.

'Let us go.'

There was something theatrical, vaguely unreal about the men getting to their feet in the darkness.

'Run.'

The ground was flat, except for the occasional shadowed dip or hollow where buildings had been demolished, trees grubbed out.

The pulled muscle in his left calf gave Menophilus no trouble.

It was as if their feet had wings. They were at the first siege tower in no time. There were no guards stationed out to the rear. What was to fear from the direction of their own camp?

Paccius led seven men to the tower.

Menophilus and the other three did not deviate.

Running past, Menophilus glimpsed four or five soldiers sitting on the axles inside the construction. They were throwing dice, their faces lit from below by a tiny lamp. They looked up at the sound of running feet.

A moment of stupefaction. What were these black figures emerging from the night? Then cries of alarm. The guards scrambling to their feet, grabbing for their weapons. Menophilus saw two cut down by Paccius before they were all lost to sight.

Dark figures moved around the base of the second tower. Menophilus saw the shape of an officer standing on the top outlined against the sky. He was shouting orders.

Fidus!

The challenge came from the darkness. It went unanswered. Menophilus' party ran straight past. When the first *City Taker* was burning, it was Paccius' task to attempt to fire the second.

Uproar behind. Torches flaring off to the right along the rampart of the camp. The arches of the aqueduct ahead.

Sleepless nights and the weight of his mailcoat dragged at Menophilus. His chest was tight, each breath searing. *Petty breaths supporting a corpse.* The body was of no account. Suffering could not touch the inner man.

Sword in one hand, lantern the other, he ran through the darker shadows under the aqueduct, and out again onto the blue plain. The tall bulk of the last tower, not far now. Movement to the right, the gates of the camp were thrown open, men on horseback issuing out.

'*Fidus!*' Menophilus yelled at the guards.

The nearest hesitated. Menophilus knocked his blade aside, buried his own in his guts.

A wild, slashing blow from the right. Menophilus turned it with the edge of his sword. Another from the left, Menophilus swayed back, the steel sang past his face. Massa was beside him. They were surrounded, the other two lost in the night. There were too many to fight.

The sound of horses.

'Throw the amphora.'

The enemy were pressing Massa too close. Menophilus had to buy him time.

With an inarticulate yell, Menophilus attacked. Thrust to the face – always the face – make them flinch – thrust after thrust. Keep moving, keep your balance, boots together. Drive them back like cattle. Agony in his right arm – ignore it. The body was nothing. The sword an extension of the body. The memory in the muscle from a lifetime of training.

In the corner of his eye, the amphora, bone white, cartwheeling through the darkness, smashing against the side of the tower.

Thrust and thrust again. Now, it had to be now. Menophilus jumped backwards, dropped his sword, wrenched open the lantern. No time to transfer his grip. A left-handed throw, underarm and weak. The light spinning feebly through the night. Just, just reaching, hitting the side, dropping to the ground.

A moment of stillness in the eye of the storm. Everyone turning to watch. Nothing, then as if summoned by a god, shining Belenus himself, the first lick of flame. Then the fire was rushing up the covering of hides; vinegar and water no match for the naptha.

'Run!'

Menophilus ducked and weaved. Men cut at him as he fled. Belenus was with him. Nothing tore his flesh.

Massa was beside him. They were clear. Together they pounded south.

The walls of Aquileia were in near darkness. The extravagant torches of the procession had vanished, replaced by just three pinpricks of light. Menophilus ran towards the nearest.

The rattle of hooves closing from behind.

Not slackening his stride, Menophilus glanced over his shoulder.

Two horsemen – one a huge figure – bearing down on them.

A spider was proud to catch a fly, one man a hare or a boar, another a Sarmatian: robbers one and all. Like hunted beasts they ran through the night. The thunder of the horsemen almost on top of them.

At the last moment, Menophilus turned, leapt in the air, shrieking like a Bacchant. The horse swerved, its rider losing his seat, half up its neck. Menophilus caught a boot, momentum did the rest. They crashed to the ground close together. Menophilus rolled to his feet. The rider was winded, on all fours. Menophilus jerked the dagger from his hip, plunged it into the back of the man's neck; once, twice, three times. Blood hot on his arms, stinging his eyes.

Massa was still running. As Menophilus watched, the big rider's blade arced down. Massa tumbled to the dirt. The horseman slowed to a canter, started to rein his mount around.

Menophilus was off like a hare. A wide dark depression at no great distance. Menophilus hurled himself down into the ruined foundations. He lay very still among the broken bricks and tiles, the shattered remains of a hypocaust.

The remaining horseman was coming back.

'Javolenus?'

A huge black figure on a huge black horse. A great white face turning this way and that, scanning the ground.

'Javolenus!' The cry turned to despair.

Menophilus peered out as the rider spurred to where the humped shape lay in the moonlight.

Of all times for a break in the clouds.

The rider dismounted in a flurry, knelt, and cradled the dead man. The horse, scenting the blood, backed a pace or two, reins hanging down.

'Borysthenes.'

At his master's command, the charger stood.

'Javolenus.' The big man was sobbing. 'Javolenus, not you too. Micca, Tynchanius, Paulina – everyone, everyone – oh Paulina!'

The walls were not far. The solitary torch on the battlements, not more than a hundred paces.

The empty plain blue-white in the moonlight. No point in stealth.

Menophilus launched himself to his feet, scrabbled out of the ruins, and ran.

'Borysthenes.'

Legs and arms pumping, Menophilus ran as never before.

The jingle of harness and stamp of hooves as the man mounted.

Sixty, fifty paces to the wall.

The thud of hooves, picking up speed.

A stone turned under Menophilus' boot, he fought for balance, kept running.

The horse pounding up behind.

The torch on the battlements, the black spider web of lines on the wall underneath. Too far, he would be run down.

The hiss of arrows shot from the walls, a terrifying black rain.

'Stop. It is me. Stop shooting.' Menophilus wanted to shout, but he had no breath.

The arrows were whistling above his head.

A terrible cry of frustration ringing through the night. The sound of hooves retreating.

Menophilus grabbed the fishing net hanging down from the wall, hauled himself up hand over hand. Arms reached down, and pulled him over the crenulations.

'Welcome home.' Crispinus was smiling down at him.

'How many got back?'

A look of embarrassment crossed Crispinus' face. 'They did their duty. You all did your duty.'

The Senator pointed out into the night.

Three tall pillars of flame that human endeavour could not extinguish, no more than raise the dead.

CHAPTER 29

Aquileia,
Sixteen Days after the Ides of May, AD238

Maximinus could not remember Paulina wearing her hair in that style: the tight waves, the bun at the neck. He studied her strong jaw and chin. Without the anchor of the image on the coin in his hand would her face slip away from him altogether?

'Imperator.'

What new problem would be raised now? Maximinus glanced across the pavilion, and gave Flavius Vopiscus permission to address the *consilium*.

Maximinus was careful not to turn the coin over. He did not want to see the peacock that had carried his wife to the heavens.

'Imperator, many do not think Barbius should be executed.'

Maximinus got nothing but wilful obstruction from his council. He kept his temper. 'Barbius commanded the guard on the siege towers, and the towers were burnt. He was negligent.'

'An accident of war, Imperator.'

'Perhaps.' Maximinus was weary of these continual objections. Punishment was already too long delayed. 'There are reports that the enemy allowed Barbius to escape from the docks. It is said that Menophilus himself ordered him not to be slain.'

'No one can be certain in the chaos of a failed assault.'

'Sometimes exemplary severity is necessary to maintain discipline.'

Maximinus glowered at his son. Any intervention by Verus Maximus was unwelcome.

'The execution will proceed,' Maximinus said.

'*Quantum libet*, Imperator.'

'The sword, tomorrow at dawn.'

'Whatever pleases you, Emperor,' Vopiscus repeated.

'Imperator.' Now it was Anullinus. These meetings were an endless litany of complaints and importuning requests.

'The rumours of fighting in Rome are troubling my Praetorians. Their wives and children are there.'

'And we are not.' Maximinus laughed; a rare, grating sound. 'The divine Septimius Severus made a mistake letting the troops take wives. A soldier should be married to the army.'

'Imperator, it might be best if you addressed the Praetorians; allayed their fears, or promised them vengeance.'

Maximinus had always found something unsettling about Anullinus' eyes. 'An education under the standards did not equip me for oratory. You talk to them.'

'*Quantum libet*, Imperator.'

The Consular Marius Perpetuus asked permission to speak.

'More men are leaving the standards, slipping away into the countryside. The regular cavalry patrols cannot intercept them all.'

'There are a few cowards in every army,' Maximinus said.

'Double the patrols. Send out the Persian and Parthian horse archers, order them to kill the deserters on sight.'

Maximinus had had enough of these footling issues. The siege dragged on.

'How are our supplies?'

'Dwindling fast,' Julius Capitolinus said. 'There is no more olive oil, and the ration of bacon has been reduced to half a pound a day. Even so, the meat and hard tack will run out in eight or nine days.'

Maximinus was sure none of this would have happened if Domitius had not disappeared. Where was the Prefect of the Camp? There were no reports that Domitius had deserted. But there again, there were no reliable reports of anything beyond a mile or two from the army. It was almost as if they were under siege, not Aquileia.

'Is there still sour wine?'

'Enough for ten days at the current ration.'

'Vegetables and cheese?'

'All gone.'

'Two pounds of hard tack, half a pound of bacon, and a pint of wine will keep body and soul together. Issue bacon fat instead of oil.'

'Imperator, the men are hungry. They are eating roots, strange foods. Already there is sickness in the southern camp.'

Maximinus pondered. 'We have gone hungry before; last winter, out on the Steppe, before we defeated the Sarmatians. We will do as we did then. All officers will surrender two thirds of their private provisions to the commissariat.'

'Father, that would reduce us in the eyes of the men. It is bad for discipline.'

Maximinus turned on his son. 'You think to lecture me on the troops? We must set an example in endurance. The imperial household will give up all its supplies.'

'Imperator.' Vopiscus was nervous, fiddling with some lucky charm.

'Let the words escape the cage of your teeth.'

'Imperator, there are a few hundred officers, thirty thousand men – it will make little difference. In eight days the army will begin to starve.'

Maximinus nodded heavily. Vopiscus spoke the truth. Yet, thank the gods, only two more days were needed.

It was odd that, surrounded by experienced officers, it had been the unmilitary Syrian Apsines that had shown Maximinus the way. Of course, with Javolenus dead, there was no one else to whom Maximinus talked in his tent, no one else to whom he could open his heart.

Like someone attacking a towering city with siegeworks,
Someone with troops under arms who surrounds a moun-
taintop fortress,
Tests this approach, that approach, and explores every inch of
the defences,
Cannily varies his tactics in mounting assaults . . .

The lines of Virgil were more true than the Sophist who had recited them could know. A siege was like a wrestling match. Maximinus was a wrestler. In his youth he had overthrown seven men at one sweat. He had not employed cunning moves and subterfuge. One hard blow to the chest had stretched them out in the dust.

Since the burning of the towers, the siege had languished. There had been probes and feints, letters thrown over the walls promising rewards to anyone who opened a gate. Nothing had been accomplished. What was needed was one hard blow to the chest.

'The day after tomorrow, at dawn, we will take Aquileia. To distract the besieged, demonstrations will be made against the other defences, but we will storm the northern wall.'

The members of the *consilium* looked sidelong at each other. The silence expressed their dismay.

Anullinus broke the silence. 'Imperator, the troops may be reluctant. Volunteers for the forlorn hope may not be forthcoming.'

'We will not call for volunteers. There is no need to risk the lives of Roman soldiers. There are four thousand northern barbarians with the army; two thousand Sarmatians and two thousand German tribesmen. They will lead the assault.'

'Imperator, they will not succeed. The Sarmatians are unused to fighting on foot, and most of the Germans have no armour. They will die in droves.' Failure obviously concerned Anullinus more than the fate of the barbarians.

'So much the better,' Maximinus said. 'Let the defenders expend their missiles, exhaust themselves slaughtering the barbarians, then the men of Capitolinus' 2nd Legion will have the honour of taking the wall.'

'Will the Germans fight?' Capitolinus looked dubious.

'They will follow the son of Isangrim, ruler of the Angles.'

Vopiscus spoke. 'Imperator, Dernhelm is a hostage for the good behaviour of his father. To throw away his life defeats the object.'

'I do not think the boy will die. There is something about him.'

It was past midday, time for food, then a siesta.

'Friends, I will detain you no longer.'

The good and the great filed out. Only Anullinus and Apsines remained.

'Imperator, may I speak to you alone?'

'I have no secrets from Apsines.'

Anullinus' face betrayed nothing. 'Imperator, some of the senior officers have been meeting, in twos and threes, in their tents at the dead of night.'

'The *frumentarii* of Volo have reported nothing.'

'Your trust might be misplaced.'

Anullinus' eyes were like blank pebbles underwater. Was it true he had outraged the corpse of Alexander's mother? The corpses of the Emperor and his mother had been naked.

'Imperator?'

'Your concern is noted. Now return to your duties. Both of you.'

Maximinus sat alone in the cavernous room. Very gently, he picked up the alabaster vase from where it stood next to the throne, and turned it in his big, scarred hands. A precious thing that contained her ashes. Not long now. Take Aquileia and seize Rome. Crush this revolt, then one more campaign in Germania. Decide the succession and leave the empire safe. Just one more year. Not long at all. Soon he would be reunited with Paulina.

CHAPTER 30

Aquileia,
Eighteen Days after the Ides of May, AD238

'Men of Aquileia, soldiers of Rome, do not be afraid.'

Menophilus stood on a ballista. In the eerie half-light of the false dawn, he looked down on the upturned faces. The militiamen and soldiers of the 1st Cohort were packed together on the gatehouse. More stretched off into the gloom along both wallwalks: two thousand five hundred armed men, bound together by adversity, hardened by suffering.

'Time after time we have flung them back from the walls. This is the last throw of Maximinus. Hurl them back again, and victory is ours.'

A low murmur of *victory, victory* rose from the massed ranks.

'All their secrets are revealed, their sly plans laid bare. Last night, putting the freedom of Rome above his own life, the patriot Marius Perpetuus escaped from the camp of the tyrant, and came over to the cause of liberty.'

Menophilus reached down, and helped Perpetuus climb up to stand beside him.

Perpetuus, Perpetuus.

The man who had been appointed Consul by Maximinus waved; a mixture of pride and perhaps embarrassment at his tardy crossing of the lines.

'The news is all good for us, dire for our oppressors. The soldiers of Maximinus are starving. They are eating strange roots and herbs, noxious things the beasts of the field leave untouched. They are reduced to boiling the leather of their boots and equipment to stave off the pangs of hunger. Their tents burned with their siege towers, they lie on the bare earth, cold and exposed to the elements. Disease stalks through their encampments. Lacking wood for pyres and the energy to dig, they pollute the river with their dead.'

A pre-battle exhortation should not shy from exaggeration. Although much of what Menophilus said was true. Everyone had seen the bodies carried down by the Natiso.

'No wonder that hundreds of soldiers, driven by desperation, desert the standards. On those poor souls Maximinus has unleashed Persian and Parthian horsemen. The Thracian reveals his true nature, and orders citizens of Rome hunted down and massacred by cruel eastern barbarians.'

Drag him, burn him.

'No one is safe from the savage. You all know Barbius.'

Menophilus gestured to the Aquileian magistrate.

'No one has shown greater courage in defence of the town. No one has suffered more. Barbius' younger son fell like a hero, fighting against overwhelming odds at the Aesontius. Now Barbius' elder son, his only remaining son, has been murdered by the tyrant. Young Barbius leaves a wife and children here in Aquileia. Maximinus has made widows and orphans of your fellow townsfolk. There will be no safety – not for the highest or the lowest – not until the tyrant is dead.'

In the east the sky was lightening. True dawn was approaching.

'Those Romans who are forced to grovel before Maximinus do not want to fight. They will not fight. With daylight you will see who comes against you. The legions will not fight. Instead the tyrant herds to destruction before your walls a motley pack of barbarians. Sarmatian nomads so unaccustomed to walking that off their horses they can barely waddle a few steps. Germans whose huge, unprotected bodies offer easy targets for your missiles. Barbarians whose ferocity turns to abject panic at the first setback. These are the savages lashed forward to their deaths. And have we not prepared the warmest of welcomes?'

Burn them, burn them.

'Men of Aquileia, this is our final trial. Do not fear to be taken in the flank or the rear. We know that the enemy will not press the attack elsewhere. It is here on the northern wall that the fate of Aquileia will be decided.'

A few last words, and it would be time.

'Our courage will not fail us. The god Belenus will fight by our side. Now go to your posts. Light the torches. The watchword is *Victory*!'

The cheers rippled along the battlements.

A band of pink had appeared along the eastern horizon. Below it, misted with distance, the mountains looked like clouds. Above the sky was clear, turning from grey to a porcelain blue. Spring was moving to summer, and it would be a beautiful day.

In the gathering light, Menophilus could see the enemy array. Thirty-five wooden screens, some two hundred paces from the wall, sheltered the ballistae. It was a greater number than had been deployed so far against any one wall. Further out, beyond the range of the artillery of the defenders, stood two solid blocks of men. To the right, between the aqueduct and the river, would be the Sarmatians. Directly ahead, down the road, were the Germans. Behind them, indistinct at this hour, must be the archers who would support the barbarians, and the 2nd Legion which was intended to make the final assault.

Surely the gods would not let it come to that. No matter how polluted Menophilus was himself, the morality of the conflict was clear. One side fought for freedom and their homes, the other for tyranny. There had to be justice in the world, or there was no order in the cosmos.

No sign yet of the imperial standard. Menophilus walked the battlements.

'Coin for a shave?'

Menophilus pulled a coin from the wallet on his belt, tossed it over.

'May the gods hold their hands over you, general.'

'And over you.'

The man to whom he spoke was one of the levy. War was a hard teacher. After over a month of tough service on the walls, they were no longer a frightened mob of civilians. Now they talked and fought as soldiers. Most had acquired good weapons, leather or linen armour.

Little of which was true of the reserve waiting in the Forum. Menophilus wondered if he should have organized some form of reliefs, where they too would have served their turn on the battlements. Yet that might have taken the edge of those in the front line. There were so many decisions to make in a siege. Not all of them could be correct.

'A coin for boot leather?'

Menophilus threw another. 'Remember, a year's military pay to every man who fights today.'

It had been an easy promise to make. Either they would all be dead, and it would not need to be honoured, or Pupienus and Balbinus would owe them their thrones, and should be happy to pay.

There was no breeze, and smoke from the torches hung

over the battlements. As Menophilus walked back to the fighting top on the main gate, he reflected on the gratitude of Emperors. It was not an encouraging subject.

A long drawn-out wail of a distant trumpet.

'They are moving, sir.'

As he looked, the sun showed over the distant mountains. It struck glints of light off helmet and blade in the dark masses creeping forward.

The besiegers had grubbed up the range markers. Yet they must be almost within four hundred paces, extreme range of the eight ballistae on the wall. The enemy artillery were not shooting. Were they short of ammunition? At least there was plenty within the town.

'Ballistae, shoot.'

Menophilus followed the bolt from the nearest engine. It fell between two clumps of Germans, harmless but in range.

'Shoot at will!' Menophilus shouted.

Pockets of disciplined activity amid the motionless waiting men on the wall. The click, click of ratchets.

The enemy artillery were goaded into life. Screens were hauled aside. Menophilus focused on one ballista; saw it jump with the recoil as it shot. He just managed to pick up its bolt in flight, watched it fly over the crenulations, vanish into the town.

With a terrible hiss, an unseen bolt whipped past his head. Instinctively he ducked. The men around grinned, not unsympathetically.

Menophilus straightened up. 'Took me by surprise,' he muttered.

The men laughed.

A sudden crash along the battlements. Screams as a shower of jagged splinters of stone sliced men down. Blood on the walkway.

A stone-thrower. None had been used before. The besiegers must have improvised the machine.

Another shatter of slivers of rock, in a different place. Hades, they had more than one of the infernal things.

Menophilus leant out beyond the crenulations. One over there, another there. In all five of them. Not big machines designed to bring down a wall, but smaller pieces intended to strip away the battlements, kill and maim their defenders.

Hercules' hairy arse, another hard decision. No, there was nothing for it. They had to endure.

'Ignore the ballistae. We will burn them later. Keep shooting at the assault parties. Only they can threaten the wall.'

The Germans had passed their artillery. Less than two hundred paces.

'Archers, slingers, loose!'

A cloud of missiles darkened the sky, fell down into the oncoming ranks. Small figures twisted and spun to the ground.

'Incoming.'

Menophilus raised his shield above his head, peered out between its rim and the parapet. Through the arches of the aqueduct, he watched the Sarmatians lumbering towards the wall. They were bulky with scales and plate and mail, like exotic armoured animals you might see in the arena.

Less encumbered, the Germans were pulling ahead. They were big men – as big as wrestlers – with long fair hair and very pale faces. There was no order among them, except the close-packed groups who bore the long siege ladders on their shoulders.

'Shoot at the ladder-bearers.'

An auxiliary reeled back. Menophilus caught him before he toppled off the inner wall. There was an arrow in his throat. Menophilus lowered him to the wallwalk, cradled his head.

The soldier tried to speak. Blood pumped around the shaft of the arrow.

'The end is to the beginning, as the beginning is to the end. Nothing to fear.'

Blood welled from the soldier's mouth. He started to choke.

'Nothing to fear.'

A spasm wracked the man. A final twitch, and he lay still.

He is hit!

Men were shouting.

The general is down!

Menophilus struggled to understand.

Menophilus is dead!

By all the gods, no.

We are lost!

How many armies had been lost to such a false rumour. Menophilus scrabbled to his feet, ran to the ballista.

'Cease shooting.'

Again he clambered onto the machine.

Men were moving back from the parapet, some making for the stairs.

'Stop! Back to the wall.'

Faces gazed up in doubt.

'I am alive.' Face and arms and chest wet with blood; if he could be recognized at all, it would not be reassuring.

Desperately he fumbled one-handed with the strap of his helmet. The thing would not untie. He dropped his shield, used two hands, flung the helmet away.

An arrow whisked close by his head.

'See, it is me, Menophilus. I am alive. I am unhurt. Back to your places.'

Menophilus! Menophilus!

'Back to the wall. This will decide the war.'

As the soldiers rushed back to the battlements, Menophilus jumped down. He felt the muscle in his calf twang. It had not troubled him at all on the night the siege towers were burned. How the gods toy with mankind.

Menophilus hobbled to the wall, leant against the parapet, fought to master himself. Nothing external affects the inner man. Nothing. He started to laugh, high and slightly unhinged.

'Ladders!' The shout broke out along the defences.

The first ladder bounced against the crenulations.

'Light the naptha,' Menophilus yelled. 'One amphora to each escalade.'

The men with the long poles came crabwise, crouching below the line of the parapet, exaggeratedly careful with their deadly cargo.

Menophilus watched as a crew pushed a pole out beyond the wall over the nearest ladder. Slowly they turned the shaft, the amphora at its end tipped, and the flaming mixture poured down onto the ascending men.

The Germans screamed. Their clothes were burning and shrinking, clinging to them, their flesh roasting. One after another they fell from the ladder. The naptha rained down on those at the foot of the ladder, splashed those who stood nearby. Ineffectually, the barbarians beat at themselves, rolled on the ground, blundered into each other. Nothing could put out the flames.

Another pole was run out above the next ladder along. A tall German with shoulder-length fair hair and golden arm rings – some tribal leader – was halfway up. Menophilus saw his face clearly. He was very young. The youth spotted the amphora, and, without hesitation, threw himself to the ground. Menophilus watched him land heavily, doubted he would get up.

Self-preservation can overcome pain. The German youth was on his feet, running, bellowing something in his savage tongue to those around him. All but the slow turned and fled before the naptha cascaded down.

Menophilus! Victory! Victory!

Chanting did not stay the hands of the defenders. They plied their bows, hurled javelins, rocks, anything that came to hand. The defenceless backs of the barbarians made good targets. They were struck down by the dozens. Bodies lay with arrows sticking out, like wax effigies pricked with pins.

Menophilus' eyes followed the young barbarian. He led a charmed life. Missiles rained around him, tribesmen fell on either hand. Nothing touched the youth. Once, when an older warrior stumbled, he actually stopped, doubled back, and supported the other man to safety.

There was a spark of the divine *Logos* in every man, even in barbarians. But there was nothing Menophilus could do to stop the slaughter. *Menophilus! Menophilus!* A terrible, unstoppable killing, in his name.

Menophilus did not see it coming. He fell backwards. His head cracked on the stone. The arrow was embedded between his left shoulder and nipple. The dark blood was pooling up through his armour.

In the moment of victory. The gods were cruel.

A soldier was bending over him, saying something.

The pain in his head was worse than his chest.

The soldier was holding his hand.

The darkness was descending.

CHAPTER 31

Aquileia,
Eighteen Days after the Ides of May, AD238

'A creaking bow, a yawning wolf, a croaking raven . . .'

Dernhelm let the old man keep talking.

'The tide on the ebb, new ice, a coiled snake, a bride's pillow talk.'

Enough was enough. 'Calgacus, I know the words of the Allfather. I know the things not to trust. You have repeated them to me all my life.'

'Just keep your mouth shut in the tent of Flavius Vopiscus.' The old Caledonian's face assumed a look more peevish than usual. 'Say nothing and watch.'

'That is one thing that I have learnt among the Romans,' Dernhelm said. 'I am old enough to realize this summons will not bring me any joy.'

'You have sixteen winters, you know fuck all.'

'I never asked to come here.'

Calgacus stopped sorting through their weapons. 'Your

father had no choice. Maximinus demanded one of his sons as a hostage. You are the youngest.'

Most nights Dernhelm dreamed of the day the Centurion had ridden up to the hall of his father. When he awoke he wanted to cry. The sons of Isangrim, war-leader of the Angles, did not cry; not after they had been sent away for fostering, not after they had stood in the shieldwall, and killed their man in battle.

'Your father is not to blame. He loves you.'

Not enough to send one of his other sons to the Romans.

'One day we will go back,' Calgacus said.

Dernhelm wanted nothing more. But his return to Angeln would not be easy. There was the resentment in his heart. How *could* his father have sent him away? It was easy for Calgacus to prattle on about the hard choices a King must make. Calgacus was a slave. He would never have to make any decisions. And then there were Dernhelm's three remaining half-brothers. They had no desire to see him again. The succession to any throne was divisive.

But, to set against all that, it was his home. He knew every inch of Hedinsey, its fields and meadows, the streams and woods. His friends were there, his mother. And, above all, there was Kadlin. A wild girl, she had not tried to conceal what they did. Most had turned a blind eye, as it had been understood that she would become Dernhelm's wife. It was too painful to think that he might never see her again.

'Here.' Calgacus handed him the heavy gold and garnet brooch, the sign of the House of Himling. 'Wear that. You might be filthy, and stink of burning, but you are an Atheling of the Angles. I will not have you going before these south-erners dressed like a serf.'

They walked through the bedraggled camp. The soldiers were too disheartened to pay any attention to the tall, young barbarian decked in gold, and the shorter, ill-favoured servant who walked by his side.

'Halt.' The guards were from the 2nd Legion.

'I am Dernhelm, son of Isangrim of the Angles.' Now he spoke in correct, but accented Latin. 'Flavius Vopiscus has *asked* to see me.'

Calgacus shot him a look.

'You are expected. The ugly one stays outside.'

Calgacus scowled. 'I swore an oath to his father not to leave his side.'

'I could not care if you offered a hecatomb to every one of the gods of the underworld, sacrificed a small boy, and drank his blood to sanctify your oath; you stay outside. My orders are to admit just the youth. Anyway, an ugly bastard like you would upset the officers.'

'I do not think he has taken to you.' Dernhelm reverted to the language of Germania.

'Insensitive cunt.'

The guard glowered.

'He might know that word,' Dernhelm said.

'Remember—'

'A sword with a hairline, a playful bear, the sons of Kings; I remember them all.'

'Little prick.' Concern was written all over Calgacus' face.

The guard did not disarm Dernhelm. The whole encounter typified the mixture of contempt and deference with which a barbarian hostage was treated.

As the hanging was pulled back, Dernhelm was overwhelmed by the wonderful smell of food; roast meat, fresh baked bread. Allfather, he was hungry. The meal was set on a table off to one side. Evidently Maximinus' latest command that officers hand over all that remained of their private supplies to the army commissariat had been ignored.

Dernhelm forced himself to take in the men who stood in the centre of the big tent. There were eleven of them: Flavius Vopiscus the King-maker, Julius Capitolinus the leader of the 2nd Legion, a tribune called Aelius Lampridius, and three more tribunes and five Centurions of the legion, whose names he did not know. Then he noticed there was another man, sitting apart, behind the table. It was Volo, the head of the Emperor's assassins.

Every royal court had its factions and secrets. That of Rome was no exception. Dernhelm did not yet know his way through its shadowed corridors.

'You are Dernhelm, son of Isangrim, the one they call Ballista?' Flavius Vopiscus spoke.

'Yes.'

'You speak Latin?'

'Yes.'

'Are you hungry?'

'Very.'

'Eat.'

Dernhelm thanked him. There was a joint of beef. Dernhelm drew his knife, carved a slice, wrapped it in some bread. Volo was watching him. He tried not to eat like a wolf. He took another slice. He ignored the pitcher of wine. He needed his wits about him.

Volo was still watching him. A quiet, composed man, Volo struck Dernhelm as the most dangerous in the tent.

'He is big, but little more than a child,' Julius Capitolinus said. 'We should use one of the Sarmatian chiefs instead.'

'We have been through this,' Flavius Vopiscus said. 'His youth will allay any suspicions.'

This was typical of Roman arrogance. They had established that he knew Latin, yet they spoke in front of him as if he was not there, was of no more account than a slave.

'This is a terrible undertaking. We would risk everything.'

The tribune Aelius Lampridius was young, no more than twenty winters. He looked very frightened.

Volo spoke, very quietly. 'We already risk everything, just by being here.'

Dernhelm was unsurprised. Impressive as Roman discipline was, no body of fighting men would put up with the condition of this siege for long.

'Volo is right.' It was Vopiscus. 'We cannot draw back. There is nothing now between the summit and the abyss.'

'Will the soldiers follow you?' Dernhelm said.

All the officers except Volo looked surprised when he spoke.

'The wives and children of the men of the 2nd Legion are at their camp on the Alban Hills. The families of the Praetorians are in Rome. They are at the mercy of the Senate.' Volo spoke dispassionately.

'When?'

'Tomorrow,' Volo said. 'After midday, when the army is resting.'

'And what would you have me do?'

'You will go to the imperial pavilion, and tell the guards that you have been approached to join a conspiracy. That will gain you admittance. Maximinus takes his rest alone. While you distract him, the men of Capitolinus' legion will deal with the Praetorians; at that time there will not be many on duty. We will kill Maximinus.'

Dernhelm turned this over in his mind. The ways of Rome might still be strange, but it was clear that if he did not accept, he would not leave this tent alive.

'Maximinus will not believe me without written proof.'

'That is putting our heads on the block.' Aelius Lampridius was losing his nerve.

'Our heads are already on the block,' Volo said. 'Dernhelm is right. Vopiscus, get some papyrus. We will all sign and seal documents offering rewards for Dernhelm joining the conspiracy.'

'What rewards?'

Capitolinus snorted. 'Barbarian avarice.'

Volo ignored him. 'Roman citizenship, four hundred thousand sesterces, enrolment in the imperial school on the Palatine. What is offered has to match the risk.'

'Make this hairy, dirty barbarian a man of standing in Rome?' The danger of the undertaking, playing for the highest stakes, had done nothing to ameliorate the prejudices of Capitolinus.

Volo permitted himself a smile. 'If he was not already a figure of importance, he would hardly be a diplomatic hostage. His father rules many peoples around the Suebian Sea. The divine Marcus Aurelius extended friendship to his ancestor Hjar. The Himling dynasty have long been loyal to Rome.'

Volo was better informed than most Romans. Dernhelm's first impression was confirmed: the head of the *frumentarii* was very dangerous.

Papyrus and ink, wax and lamps, all the paraphernalia of writing was produced. As the styluses scratched, Dernhelm suspected he was entertaining the same suspicion as some of the others. Was this a trap constructed by Volo to hand them over to the non-existent mercy of Maximinus?

CHAPTER 32

Aquileia,
The Kalends of June, AD238

Maximinus walked down the village street. He tried to walk faster, but the thick, clay mud sucked at his feet. Although he knew what he would find, perhaps it would be different if he could get to the hut now. It was not far – only a few paces. He tried to run, it was impossible in this mud.

The door of the hut was open. He went inside. It was the same. They were all dead. Maximinus' father and mother, his brother and his sisters. All dead, the females naked.

'That is what you get with northern barbarians,' Paulina said.

He looked at her pale eyes, her strong mouth and jutting chin.

'You must lead the final assault yourself,' she said.

The Druidess Ababa stood where his wife had been.

He would not let Paulina go as if she had never existed.

'*Succurrite,*' she murmured, 'help me.'

Maximinus knelt by her in the mud.

She said his name.

'Imperator.'

The breath of life was leaving her.

'Imperator.'

Maximinus saw a fox jumping, chasing a beetle. It shrugged off the trappings of royalty, revealing its true nature.

As he woke, the image was gone beyond recall.

A Praetorian was standing over him.

'What do you want?'

'There is a barbarian outside, one of the hostages. He says he has evidence of a conspiracy.'

'Take his weapons. Search him. Bring him in.'

A slight movement in the far corner of the cavernous pavilion, a mere disturbance in the air. Maximinus reached for his sword.

'Father.'

'What are you doing here?'

'You were sleeping.' Verus Maximus was wearing an elaborately ornamented breastplate, a silver-chased sword on his hip, its handle shaped like the head of an eagle.

The stories of Apsines were full of Princes who could not wait for nature to run its course. His son was selfish and vicious enough. Maximinus remembered some lines from a mime. *The lion is brave, and he is slain. He who cannot be slain by one, is slain by many.* He remembered his son applauding, a sly expression on the face. Verus Maximus had commissioned the mime.

Maximinus put down the sword, lay back on the couch. His son was alone. Even with numbers, Verus Maximus would lack the courage for parricide.

'Father, I need to speak to you.'

'After the barbarian.'

'Father, it is important.'

Another outraged husband, another beaten woman, perhaps a dead hunting dog. 'After I have seen the barbarian.'

The sacred fire on the small, portable altar burned low, but the air was close.

'Father—'

'I have spoken.' He should have not have heeded a woman, not even Paulina. He should have beaten Verus Maximus more when he was a child, whipped some virtue into him.

A flood of light as the Praetorian brought in the barbarian.

Maximinus propped himself on one elbow. His dreams had left a vague feeling of disquiet. The white tunic in which he had slept was damp with sweat.

'Perform *proskynesis*.' As ever, Verus Maximus sounded petulant.

The Praetorian pushed the young barbarian to his knees.

It was the son of Isangrim of the Angles.

Maximinus sat up, swung his legs off the couch, sat on its edge.

The youth prostrated himself on the carpet, his reluctance to perform adoration evident.

Maximinus held out his hand. The youth kissed the heavy gold ring set with a gemstone cut with the image of the imperial eagle. Maximinus did not give him permission to get off his knees.

'Gods, he stinks.' Verus Maximus put a perfumed cloth to his nose.

Maximinus waved a hand to silence him.

'You know of a plot on my life. Who are the traitors?'

'The officers of the 2nd Legion Parthica, *dominus*.' The barbarian spoke up promptly. His Latin was good. 'Most of the tribunes and a few of the Centurions. And there are others.'

'Name them.'

Now the boy looked reluctant.

'Do not keep my father waiting. Name them.'

Maximinus suppressed a flash of irritation. Everything Verus Maximus touched was spoilt.

'They are powerful men.' The barbarian continued to address Maximinus, as if his son was not there. 'They have many friends, much influence. If they hear that I have denounced them, they will do me harm.'

Maximinus laughed. 'If what you say is true, they will be in no position to harm you or anyone else. If what you say is not true, what they might want to do to you will be the least of your concerns.'

Slowly the youth said the names – 'Flavius Vopiscus, Julius Capitolinus, Aelius Lampridius . . .' – twelve in all. Only that of Volo was a surprise.

'How do you know these men want to kill me? What proof do you have?'

'They asked me to join them.' The boy spoke loudly. Outside there was some sort of commotion. 'I asked them for written instructions. I have them here.'

'What is that row? Praetorian, tell them to be quiet.' Maximinus held out his hand for the documents.

'As you can see—'

'Silence.'

Rather than abating, the noise outside the pavilion grew. It was disgraceful so near the imperial presence. Maximinus turned to his son. 'Get out there and tell them to shut the fuck up.' In his anger, he reverted to expressions from the barracks.

The hangings closed behind Verus Maximus, and Maximinus continued reading, lips silently mouthing the words. The treacherous bastards! Honour and good faith were things of the past. The Senators and equestrians of Rome were corrupt beyond redemption, and now these Centurions as well.

A surge of noise made him lift his head. That sounded like a riot.

The youth leapt to his feet, grabbed the portable altar, swung the sacred fire at Maximinus' head.

Too slow. Maximinus caught the boy's wrist. With his free hand he punched him in the face, then the stomach. The boy dropped the altar, collapsed. Maximinus yanked him back to his feet.

'You will die slowly, you little fucker.'

Maximinus threw him across the chamber. He crashed through some chairs and overturned a camp table.

Whatever was happening outside – a sally from the town, some mutiny – Maximinus would quell it. He took up his sword, and strode through the curtain.

Looking into the bright sunshine was like surfacing from deep water. Maximinus stood in the entrance to the ante-chamber, letting his eyes adjust. Some Praetorians were running, others had joined soldiers from the 2nd Legion and were tearing the imperial portraits from the standards. Closer was a thrashing tumult of bodies.

Sword in hand, Maximinus turned from side to side, deciding where to intervene. This was the doing of Vopiscus. The Senator would discover that Maximinus was harder to kill than that weakling Alexander.

The tumult ceased. Something was hoist on a spear above the crowd. The severed head of Verus Maximus, muddy and bloodied. They had killed his son.

A weight landed on his shoulders. A sharp pain stabbed into his neck.

Maximinus roared, an inhuman sound.

With a sweep of his arm, Maximinus smashed the barbarian youth across the antechamber. He pulled the stylus from his neck, hurled it at the boy.

Blood was running hot down his neck. Sword raised, he advanced on the youth.

'You treacherous little fucker, you gave me your oath – you took the military oath.'

Desperately, the boy tried to fend him off with a chair.

With two strokes, Maximinus smashed it to pieces.

The youth twisted from Maximinus' thrust. The blade scraped across his ribs.

The barbarian was on the floor, on his arse, shuffling backwards.

Maximinus followed, shrugging off the pain, readying himself to deliver the killing blow.

A spear punched into Maximinus' back. He staggered a step forward. Another spear slammed into his back. He took another step, and toppled forward.

He landed on top of the boy. Maximinus brought up his hand to gouge out his eyes.

Somehow the stylus was back in the youth's hand. A flash in the sunlight, and Maximinus felt it drive deep into his throat. His fingers jerked back. He was choking on his own blood.

The light was dying. His fingers, now weak and clumsy, could not pry the stylus out.

He tried to speak. Hard to force the words out.

'I will see you again.'

The light was gone.

PART VIII:
AQUILEIA AND ROME

CHAPTER 33

Aquileia,
The Nones of June, AD238

Hail, Imperator Marcus Clodius Pupienus Maximus Augustus.

When the horsemen had brought the heads of Maximinus and his son to Ravenna the celebrations had been unconfined: sacrifices on the altars, and everyone joining in singing hymns for a victory that had been won without any effort on their part. Doubtless it would be the same in all the communities in which the grisly trophies were displayed on their way to Rome.

Hail, Imperator Marcus Clodius Pupienus Maximus Augustus.

Pupienus noted that here on the windswept plain outside Aquileia the joy was more restrained. Not all the troops chanted wholeheartedly. In part it might be due to Pupienus' reputation as a disciplinarian, yet the Praetorians seemed particularly reticent. It could be that they regretted that some of their number had joined with the men of the 2nd Legion in the killing of Maximinus.

In sole command, after Menophilus had been struck down,

Crispinus had acted with commendable resolve. The besieging army had put aside their weapons, dressed as in peacetime, and approached the walls. They had requested the garrison to admit them to the town as friends. Instead of opening the gates, Crispinus had brought out onto the battlements pictures of Pupienus and Balbinus, and the Caesar Gordian, wreathed in crowns of laurel. He had demanded that the field army acclaim the rulers elected by the Senate and people of Rome.

Even when the soldiers had sworn the military oath, the gates had remained closed. Crispinus had established a market on the ramparts. The soldiers had been able to buy all the things a flourishing, prosperous city could offer. But all their purchases – food and drink, tents and clothes and shoes – had been lowered down to them by ropes. Only the chief conspirators had been admitted into the town, and only when they had produced the head of the Praetorian Prefect Anullinus.

Pupienus had always had faith in the abilities of Crispinus, and his old friend had not let him down. Now it was time to address the troops.

Pupienus stood at the front of the tribunal, Valerian at one shoulder, Valerius Priscillianus at the other. A fine display of unity among the factions in the Senate, although probably lost on the army.

Rank after rank of soldiers, in good order, clean and neat. There were few signs of the siege: the charred skeletons of three siege towers, the broken spans of the aqueduct. Time would soon heal the physical scars. Pupienus had the harder task of salving those in the minds of men.

'Soldiers of Rome, you were hungry, now you are fed. You were cold and wet, now you have shelter. In place of war you are at peace with your fellow citizens and the gods. Keep your oath to the Senate and people of Rome and to us your Emperors, and you will enjoy these benefits throughout your service. Do your duty in a disciplined and orderly way, show respect and honour to your rulers, and you will find a pleasant life that lacks nothing.'

Rank after rank of faces that betrayed neither enthusiasm or hostility, as if the rigours of the siege had drained them of all emotion.

'The long years of campaigning are over. You will return to your camps. There you will live in comfort in your own homes, no longer in foreign lands suffering privations.'

That struck a chord. A few of the soldiers grinned at each other. Of course Pupienus knew it was a lie. Even if the civil wars were over, Roman authority must be restored in the East; Nisibis and Carrhae recovered. Many soldiers would be needed to campaign against the Sassanids, many would suffer and die.

'None of you should imagine that there is any recrimination on our part – you were obeying orders – nor on the part of the Romans or the rest of the provinces that rebelled when they were unjustly treated. Let there be no recrimination on your part. There must be a complete amnesty, a firm treaty of friendship, and a pledge of loyalty and discipline for ever.'

This did not seem to go down so well. What had it come to when soldiers found even the mention of discipline a reproach?

'When you return to your camps, to celebrate your home-coming and our accession, every man will receive a donative of a year's pay. Eternal Rome! The fidelity of the army!'

Fides Militum! Romae Aeternae! Fides Militum!

They shouted warmly enough as the imperial entourage descended the tribunal, and mounted their horses.

When Pupienus was fifty paces from the walls the gates swung open. As he rode under the gatehouse somewhere above a choir started to sing. The porticos of the long, straight street down to the Forum were thronged. The people of

Aquileia called out words of good omen, threw flowers. This was appropriate. Pupienus relaxed his stern face into a dignified smile. He went as far as to wave, although he looked neither right nor left.

Yet even in this moment of triumph, concerns crowded his mind. What to do about Capelianus in Africa, and Decius in Spain? Both had been closely bound to Maximinus. And what of Honoratus and the Goths on the Danube, or Catius Clemens and the Persians in the East?

As rose petals were scattered before the hooves of his horse, Pupienus ordered his thoughts. Capelianus was an opportunist, a man of no great account. Most likely he would make submission. As he had killed the elder two Gordiani, further office was out of the question, but he could be allowed to retire into obscurity on his estates. Decius called for more careful handling. Something tangible must be offered to compensate his removal from his army in Spain. Crispinus could be sent to negotiate his integration into the new regime. As for the Danube, now it appeared Menophilus would live, and when he had recovered from his wounds, it would be fitting to send him to fight the war that he had created. No further news had come from the East. The gods willing, Clemens would accept the deal which Pupienus had hammered out with his youngest brother.

Pupienus Augustus, may the gods keep you!

More acclamations, more flowers. He waved, but his thoughts were elsewhere.

Across the empire other tidings were more certain and reassuring. Having secured the oath of three of the Gallic provinces – Narbonnensis, Lugdunensis, and Aquitania – Aedinius Julianus had returned to Rome. Pupienus had sent orders that Aedinius replace Felicio as Praetorian Prefect. Now the Praetorians would be jointly commanded by his foster father, old Pinarius, and another man who owed the position to Pupienus. On his return to Rome, Pupienus would remove Maecius Gordianus from the *vigiles* and Serapamum from the 2nd Legion. That would be an end to the officers of the Roman garrison appointed by the Gordiani.

The cavalcade clattered out into the wide space of the Forum. Pupienus rode to the far end and dismounted before the Basilica. At the top of the steps Crispinus was waiting. Slowly, mindful of the imperial majesty, Pupienus walked up, and let his friend bow and kiss the seal ring on his finger.

Menophilus struggled to rise from his chair. He was pale, obviously weak and in pain. He hobbled forward, and performed adoration. Pupienus did not give him permission to resume his seat. Subjects should remain on their feet in the presence of their Emperor.

Pupienus settled himself on the white ivory throne.

Apsines the Sophist, elaborately coiffured and elegant, was to make the speech of welcome. The Syrian was lucky to be alive. It was said he had been close to Maximinus. If Apsines hoped for further imperial patronage, the oration had to be good.

'The two greatest things in human life are piety towards the divine and honour to Emperors. Yet as it is impossible to take the measure of the sea with our eyes, so it is difficult to take in the fame of the Emperor in words.'

A measured and unremarkable start.

After the speech Pupienus would hand out rewards for loyalty and timely betrayal.

This was straightforward for the defenders of the city. Patrician rank would be bestowed on Crispinus and Menophilus, and senatorial status on Barbius and Statius, the two Aquileian councillors.

With the conspirators things were more delicate. The Centurions simply could be granted the gold ring of the equestrians, and the tribunes adlected into the Senate, with Julius Capitolinus honoured as if an ex-Consul. The young

311

barbarian hostage – was he called something like *Ballista*? – would receive the rewards promised, including Roman citizenship. Henceforth he would carry the imperial *prae-nomen* and *nomen*: Marcus Clodius Ballista.

Flavius Vopiscus and Volo were trickier. Ennoblement as a patrician, and the promise of a further great office – Africa or Asia? – might recompense Vopiscus for the loss of Pannonia Superior, which was promised to Egnatius Lollianus. The main problem was Volo, *Princeps Peregrinorum* under Maximinus. Pupienus had been more than pleased with the work of his replacement Macrianus as the acting head of the imperial spies in Rome. Two men could not handle the secrets of empire. By definition neither was trustworthy. Volo, however, had now been instrumental in the deaths of two Emperors. It was time that he was promoted to a post where he posed less threat. He could be made Prefect of Egypt, and later quietly removed.

'I should have spoken of his family, but since the Emperor's own achievements prevail over everything, let us make haste to speak of him. Our Emperor is by repute of human origin, but in reality he has his begetting from the heavens.'

Better if his origins had been avoided altogether. Pupienus' thoughts slid dangerously towards Volaterrae. He had sent Fortunatianus to make sure the old man was decently buried, his one slave sold abroad. This was no time to let his self-control slacken. Only Fortunatianus and Pinarius knew. They could be trusted. The secret would never be disclosed. His father had had a long life. Pupienus had not forced his hand. This was how one ate and drank at the court of a King. One must smile at the slaughter of one's kin.

'Through your wisdom, you discovered their traps and ambushes.'

Apsines had moved on to Pupienus' time as governor in Germania; safer ground for amplification.

312

'If the Rhine had been poetical, like the Scamander, it might have said, I fancy:

Away from me! Do deeds of horror on the plain.
My lovely streams are full of corpses,
And nowhere can I roll my waters down . . .'

This was poor stuff, reeking of the lamp and textbook.

The years in Germania would serve Pupienus well here in Aquileia in the aftermath of civil war. He knew the ways of the northern tribes, and would recruit all the Germans from the army of Maximinus into an imperial guard. Once they had taken their barbaric oaths, they would follow him to Rome with loyalty. Their existence would allow him to discharge the thousand veterans that in Ravenna he had formed into a makeshift unit of the Praetorian Guard. Two thousand German warriors sworn to his service, that could be more than useful in Rome.

Pupienus gazed up at the sun. The deeds of a commoner could be hidden, buried out of sight. But those of an Emperor, like the sun, were exposed to everyone. And just as only Helios could control the fiery chariot, so only one man could rule the empire. The reins could not be left long in the hands of a snivelling child like Gordian, let alone those of a perverse dotard such as Balbinus.

'Thus not only is the Emperor to be admired for his deeds in war, but even more so for his acts in peace.'

At last the interminable panegyric was nearing its conclusion.

'Just as fugitives obtain security in the inviolate precincts of divine power – for we make no attempt to drag anyone away – so also he who comes into the sight of the Emperor is freed from his perils.'

CHAPTER 34

Rome,
Four Days before the Nones of June, AD238

The Palatine

The heads of Maximinus and his son were exhibited on pikes in the Forum. Later they would be burnt and cast into the Tiber. The ghost of a man denied burial could not cross the Styx. Balbinus hoped that he never met the unquiet shade of Maximinus. By all accounts the Thracian had been frightening enough in life.

The day before, Balbinus had been with young Gordian when the heads were brought into the theatre. The performance abandoned, the Emperor and Caesar had gone to make sacrifice in the Forum, then attend a hastily summoned Senate. With the sycophancy customary to men of no ancestry, the friends of Pupienus had decreed that twenty Senators should travel to meet him bearing crowns and the offer of a statue of him on horseback to be made of gold. Balbinus had suppressed his irritation, merely remarking that throughout the war Pupienus had sat in tranquillity safe in Ravenna, while Balbinus himself had risked his life here on the streets of Rome.

Balbinus really had thought that he would die in the riot by the Arch of Titus. It had been much worse than the earlier disturbance on the Capitol. The plebs had been out for blood. They had torn six of his Lictors limb from limb. Once back in the Palace, Balbinus had acted with restraint. The plebs were by nature unstable, and he had known that they would soon change their course. It was just a question of waiting. When peace had returned, and the plebs were off the streets, the little Greek Timesitheus had appeared claiming the credit for the cessation of violence. Balbinus had dealt summarily with that affront. He had dismissed Timesitheus from his self-appointed office of deputy Praetorian Prefect. It would have been satisfying to strip him of the post of *Praefectus Annonae* as well, but someone had to ensure that the urban mob were fed, and the *Graeculus* handled the tiresome details of the grain supply with efficiency.

The close brush with death had made Balbinus reflect on his own mortality. Now, under the portico in the Sicilia courtyard of the Palace, he studied the sarcophagus. He had commissioned two groups of sculptors, and the work would soon be finished. There were three main scenes. On the lid Balbinus reclined with his late wife. They gazed at each other with fondness. In a gesture he remembered, her chin rested on her hand. On the right of the main panel, was their marriage. Hymen in attendance, she was veiled, and he looked serious in a toga. On the left they offered sacrifice. Mars stood behind, while Victory crowned him. She was backed by Virtue and Concordia. He was armoured, and her head was uncovered. She was very beautiful.

The sculptural programme conveyed the messages he intended. He would be remembered as a man possessing the virtues of both war and peace, a man blessed with a happy marriage. With a pang of regret, he examined where the folds of drapery, as if wet, clung to her breasts. It had been a good marriage in every way. They had been close in body

315

and soul. Their pleasures might have been curtailed if they had had children.

The two short sides of the sarcophagus were carved with the Three Graces and a group of dancers. It was all very fitting. The Graces were goddesses of beauty, grace and mirth, and his wife had loved to dance.

Standing on the banks of the Styx changed a man. Balbinus had no heirs, and he was damned if the arrogant sons of a jumped-up nonentity like Pupienus would inherit the throne. At least young Gordian came of decent stock; through the Sophist Herodes Atticus the Gordiani were distant kin of Balbinus himself. The uncle and grandfather of Gordian had been congenial enough. When the riots had died down, Balbinus had invested Gordian with the *toga virilis*. As a man, it was right that Gordian should move to the Palace. It was a pity that his ghastly mother had insisted on accompanying him. But the Palace was enormous. It was not too difficult to avoid Maecia Faustina and her coterie of sanctimonious matrons and freedmen. Felicio, the commander of the Praetorians on the Palatine, was a client of the Gordiani, but he was a man of tact, and did his best to keep the old woman out of sight.

'Imperator.' It was Rufinianus reminding him of yet another wearisome official engagement. Thank the gods Pupienus would soon be back in Rome. Life should be a balance of *otium* and *negotium*. Sour-faced Pupienus needed watching, but he thrived on the latter. Let him deal with the tedium of public duties, while Balbinus concentrated on the pleasures that constituted the better half of a civilized existence.

The Subura

The fastings, bendings of the knee, prayers and night-long vigils were at an end.

'Do you renounce the Devil, his retinue, and his works?'

'I renounce you, Satan, and all your service, and all your works,' the die-cutter said.

'Do you renounce the world and its pleasures?'

'I renounce the world and all its pleasures.'

Was he free from sin? Often enough he had been told if someone who was still sinning came to the water, he did not receive the forgiveness of his sins. He was free of the sins of the flesh. That had been easier after Caenis had disappeared. But other things troubled him.

Should he have given Castricius the money? The youth was a thief, knife-boy and murderer. Yet he had saved the die-cutter's life. Without Castricius' intervention, the die-cutter would have bled to death after the fight in the Street of the Sandal-makers. It could be true that high-placed men were hunting Castricius, and he needed the money to escape from Rome. Christian charity should extend beyond the faithful. And in the last resort, who was the die-cutter to judge others? Let he who was without sin cast the first stone.

His instructor Africanus led the way to the bath, where the new Bishop of Rome was waiting. The die-cutter limped after.

Steps led down into the bath. The water was not warm. The die-cutter stood with just his head and shoulders above the surface, his sodden tunic plastered to his body.

'Do you believe in God the Father omnipotent?' Bishop Antheros' voice was frail. He did not look well.

'I believe.'

Antheros placed his hand on the die-cutter's head, and gently pushed him under.

Having held his breath, the die-cutter came up with nothing worse than streaming eyes.

'Do you believe in Christ Jesus, the Son of God?'

'I believe.'

Again the die-cutter went under.

317

'Do you believe in the Holy Spirit and the Holy Church and the resurrection of the flesh?'

'I believe.'

After baptism for the third time, he climbed out.

Water poured down his legs, sluiced across the floor. He was shivering violently.

Antheros made the sign of the cross over him, laid his hands on his head.

'Let the soul be illuminated by the Spirit.'

Antheros tipped the oil on his forehead.

'The flesh is anointed that the soul may be consecrated.'

A huge step. After four years of waiting, the die-cutter was one of the Gathering, a full member of the Church. From now on his fate was bound to that of his brothers and sisters in Christ. Under Maximinus many of the brethren had died in Cappadocia, and Pontianus, the Bishop of Rome before Antheros, had won the crown of martyrdom in the mines in Sardinia. Now Maximinus was dead, but the future was uncertain. The new rulers might encourage persecution. The severity of old Pupienus did not bode well. Perhaps the indolence of Balbinus might ameliorate his perversity. The only hope was young Gordian. The boy appeared mild. His mother was virtuous in pagan terms. Better, three of his attendants – the freedmen Montanus, Reverendus, and Gaudianus – belonged to the Church.

A terrible risk. The die-cutter knew he was weak. He had played Judas when Pontianus was arrested; denied he knew him, chanted for his death. The claws and pincers of the imperial cellars haunted the die-cutter's dreams. Yet it was a risk worth running when you dwelt on Hell: the unquenchable and unending fire that awaited those who were not saved. No sleep would give them rest, no night soothe them, no death deliver them from punishment, no appeal of interceding friends profit them. Weeping would be useless.

They helped strip the clinging tunic from him, towelled him dry, clad him in white garments. They made him welcome, gave him milk and honey to eat and drink.

The Esquiline

'What do you want me to do?'

'Be a man.'

Many wives would suffer a beating for such words, even if they were spoken, as now, in the privacy of the bedroom. No one would condemn the husband. Perhaps, when her bruises had faded, the wife herself might accept its justice. Timesitheus had never raised his hand to Tranquillina.

'You saved the city, and, far from reward you, that fat degenerate Balbinus would not recognize you as Praetorian Prefect. Pupienus will never forgive you for the acclamation of Gordian as Caesar. When he returns, he will strip you of the office of *Praefectus Annonae*.'

'That might be no bad thing,' Timesitheus said. 'The Alexandrian grain fleet has not arrived. The granaries are nearly empty.'

Tranquillina frowned. For all her delicate looks, at times there was something mannish about her. 'Pupienus is no fool, unlike Balbinus. He will leave you in charge until the distributions begin to fail. You will be dismissed, and you will take the blame.'

Tranquillina prowled the room. She was short, but slender. Her neck looked like it had been sculpted from marble. She wore just a thin tunic, nothing underneath. It accentuated every movement of her body.

Timesitheus could not stop staring at his wife. He had thought the servants had been sent away for another reason.

Her eyes were very dark, and her hair very black, as it framed her white face, curled over her white shoulders.

'The boy Gordian likes you,' Tranquillina said. 'He would obey you like a father.'

'His mother does not care for me, let alone you.'

'Maecia Faustina is a dried-up old bitch. She can be dealt with when the other obstacles are removed.'

Timesitheus felt the stirring of fear, like a rat moving through his thoughts. It must have showed on his face.

'If you want to be someone today, you must nerve yourself for deeds that could earn you an island exile, or the executioner's block.'

Tranquillina had always been able to see through his carefully arranged face.

'Duty is praised, but dutiful men get nothing. Wealth springs from crime, power from daring.'

Only Tranquillina could be so honest.

'The Praetorians have no loyalty to Balbinus and Pupienus. They do not know this new Prefect Aedinius Julianus, and they have no respect for old Pinarius. How could an aged gardener hope to be accepted as a Prefect? You defended their camp, saved their families. They would follow you.'

The servants had been sent out of earshot. Timesitheus mastered the urge to check, make sure that no one was listening behind the door.

'Felicio did not take well to being replaced by Aedinius. He could be won over.'

Timesitheus smelt the fetid breath of fear, felt its sharp teeth seeking his throat.

'As Prefect of the Watch, Maecius Gordianus would ensure the *vigiles* were on our side.'

The scrabble of claws as fear was driven out by jealousy and anger.

'Why?' Timesitheus said.

'Valerius Valens, the Prefect of the Fleet at Misenum, is your friend.' Tranquillina ignored the question.

'What have you done to ensure Maecius Gordianus is so devoted to our cause?' This difficult conversation had been long coming.

Tranquillina stopped pacing.

'What *exactly* have you done?'

'What do you think?' She looked very angry. 'You may be ready to go back to herding goats on Corcyra, or some other dismal backwater. I am not prepared to be married to such a man.'

She walked around him, and sat on the bed.

'I would not let another man do what you do.'

She hitched up the tunic, spread her legs.

'Now come here,' she said.

Excited by his own degradation, he got down on his knees.

'Do *exactly* what I tell you.'

PART IX:
THE PROVINCES

CHAPTER 35

Cappadocia

The City of Samosata,
Five Days before the Ides of June, AD238

Over the river was Samosata. The walls of the sprawling lower city were dominated by the citadel on its long, unnatural-looking, flat-topped hill.

Priscus rode with just Sporakes his bodyguard, and an escort of twenty troopers commanded by a tribune called Caerellius. He had not wanted to risk his brother Philip, or any of his friends. If there had not been the threat of bands of Persian stragglers in the high country, he would have ridden alone apart from Sporakes. If he was fated to die, he would not drag others to their ruin.

After the victory over Hormizd, he had marched the army south to relieve the blockade of Edessa. The Persians had been long gone. Priscus had rested and refitted his men, before leaving them in the charge of Manu Bear-blinder, the heir to the abolished kingdom of Osrhoene. The wealth of Manu had underwritten much of the cost of the army. Before Priscus had left, Manu had revealed what he wanted in return. It was a huge thing to ask, but paled into insignificance beside the much more lethal questions that were the reason for this meeting in Samosata.

They rode down to the water, and the guards from the 16th Legion waved them onto the bridge over the Euphrates. The hooves of their horses rattled on the wooden boards as they crossed out of Mesopotamia.

Priscus loathed his province, the land between the two rivers. But he loathed all the East: its heat and dust, and stifling morality. The accident of birth did not mean you had to care for the place where you had drawn your first breath. Priscus was not burdened with the sentimentalism of his brother. Philip genuinely cared for their terrible old father, and the ghastly village of Shahba where they had been born. Priscus would be happy if he never saw parent or birthplace again.

He did not ask for much. To be in Athens or Rome, somewhere civilized. To sit under the shade of a tree in the gentle heat of summer, with a book of poetry and a flask of wine, a boy beside him. He had always preferred the grapes when they were green.

Might as well cry for the moon. He could not leave. For a governor to desert his province carried the death penalty. Even if it had not, his *dignitas* would not let him leave a task undone. When strongly garrisoned, Mesopotamia formed a bulwark protecting the empire from the Persians. When denuded of troops, as now, it offered the Sassanids easy plunder, and a route to the West. All his life, Priscus had done his duty, had served all over the empire. It was not the selfish hope of gain, or a womanish desire for leisure, that had led him to summon the governors of Cappadocia and Syria Coele to Samosata.

The Edessa Gate stood open. In these unsettled times, there were few merchants or peasants bringing goods to market. Priscus announced himself, and again the legionaries let him pass.

The streets were very quiet, until they came out into a square. They had to halt to let a religious procession pass. The barefooted worshippers drove asses, which were hung with loaves, and garlanded like themselves with violets. The ninth of June, the Festival of Vesta, the day the bakers honoured the hearth and the mistress of the hearth and the she-ass that turned the millstones of pumice. They would be celebrating the *Vestalia* in Rome. Priscus thought of the house he had bought on the Caelian, of his wife, and the son he had not seen in three years. The boy would be twelve now. Two years until he took the *toga virilis*. Priscus wondered if he would be alive to see that day.

It was necessary to dismount to climb the steep path to the citadel. Leaving Caerellius to see to the horses and find quarters for the men, Priscus walked up with Sporakes. There was no need for a guide. He had been here before.

Two years had passed since that gathering: Priscus; his brother-in-law Otacilius, governor of Palestina; his friends Serenianus of Cappadocia and Timesitheus of Bithynia; the Princes Chosroes of Armenia and Ma'na of Hatra; the King-in-waiting, old Manu of Edessa. A pleasant early autumn day. They had taken food and drink. Together Priscus and Serenianus had led them to the edge of treason. The others had stepped back from the precipice. And later Serenianus had died under the hands of the imperial torturers, and had not betrayed any of them to Maximinus.

At the door of the governor's residence, Priscus gave his name, and a chamberlain asked him to wait.

Idly, Priscus let his eyes run over the diamond pattern of the brickwork. Once this had been the Palace of the Kings of Cappadocia. They had lived and ruled and fought wars and were gone. Nothing lasts in this world. The cosmos itself was doomed to end in fiery destruction.

Sporakes hawked and spat. A typical easterner. It was three

327

years since Priscus had bought him out of a gladiatorial school. They had nothing in common, but they had fought side by side in a dozen desperate places: the ambush outside Singara, the bloody retreat from Nisibis, the flight from Carrhae. Priscus was glad that he had given Sporakes his freedom.

'This way, please. The governor is expecting you.'

The same south-facing garden as two years before. The same marble busts of philosophers. The stern, virtuous gaze of Aristotle to Zeno, still arranged alphabetically. As before, tables were spread with delicacies. Catius Clemens and Aradius reclined together on a couch.

Yet this time there were armed guards. Twenty or more of the 16th, a Centurion in command. Priscus felt his heart shrink.

'Health and great joy,' Clemens said.

'Health and great joy.'

Clemens made a sign, and the legionaries leapt forward. Some of them seized Sporakes, and disarmed him. Others ringed Priscus.

'Please, Priscus, do not draw your weapons,' Clemens said.

So this was how it ended. Priscus felt a resignation, almost like relief. Nothing could stop him killing himself before he was taken to Maximinus, even if he had to dash his brains out against the wall of a cell. With luck, his brother and friends could win a pardon by denouncing him. Even Maximinus would not risk alienating the rulers of Armenia and Hatra by executing their sons. Perhaps Philip and old Manu might make their escape to Persia. The Sassanid King was said to welcome Roman deserters.

The soldiers were binding Sporakes' arms.

'I am afraid that you have been betrayed,' Clemens said. 'Aradius' soldiers searched a man crossing the river at Zeugma. He was a *frumentarius* carrying a message to Volo.'

Clemens began to read from a small papyrus roll.

328

'The traitor Gaius Julius Priscus has called the governors of Syria Coele and Cappadocia to a meeting, intending to embroil them in a plot against our noble Augustus Maximinus. He hopes to induce Catius Clemens to make a bid for the throne.'

Clemens looked at Priscus. 'Who did you talk to on your staff or among your *familia*?'

'No one.' It was near the truth. No one except his brother. They had spoken in private, only one person could have overheard.

'Do not be alarmed,' Clemens said. 'You misread the situation. The man who betrayed you was foolish enough to sign his name.'

'Sporakes?'

The bodyguard stared back at Priscus.

'Why?'

Sporakes said nothing.

'You should not have put your trust in an ex-gladiator,' Clemens said. 'Such scum have no loyalty, and will do anything for money.'

'Yes, I took the money, but it was not that.' Sporakes glared at Priscus. 'You disgust me. All these years I have had to witness your revolting Greek practices. Corrupting children, using young boys to satisfy your perverse desires. Maximinus will know how to deal with you, and your sort.'

Priscus was amazed. 'All this over such a small thing?'

'Only a small thing to those who are blind to righteousness. You are a traitor to the ways of your people.'

'Take him away,' Clemens said.

'Maximinus will kill you all.'

'Guard him carefully. He must be questioned to see what other informants he can reveal.'

'The Thracian will crucify you, sew you alive in the carcasses of beasts, all of you.'

Sporakes was still shouting threats as he was hauled out.

'Ask the others to come in.' Clemens got up, walked over, and embraced Priscus. 'We have no need to ask for proofs of your loyalty to the cause.'

'You had already decided to take the purple?'

'Heavens forbid, not me. I have no wish to hold the wolf by the ears.' Clemens stepped back, indicated the newcomers. 'You know the Senators Latronianus and Cuspidius Flaminius.'

'Health and great joy.'

'And to you,' they said.

Clemens smiled. 'Aradius and I have sworn allegiance to the Emperors Pupienus and Balbinus and the Caesar Gordian. With you, and your brother-in-law, we hold four of the armed provinces in the East. Domitius Valerianus in Arabia has no love of Maximinus. Egypt and Syria Phoenice will have no choice but to join us.'

Priscus stood bewildered.

'Did you not know that the Gordiani were dead?'

'No.'

'I am afraid they have crossed the Styx.'

Priscus was trying to make sense of it all. He was not the monkey, but the cat's paw.

Clemens was still talking. 'Cuspidius will take command of Cappadocia, while I go ahead to order the defence of Rome. Aradius will organize an expeditionary force to march West.'

'But the Persians? The East is stripped of troops already. The reason Maximinus must be deposed . . .'

'When Maximinus is dead, we have the word of Cuspidius that an imperial army will campaign on the Euphrates, restore the frontiers, bring vengeance against the Sassanids.'

Priscus stood irresolute.

'What is troubling you?'

'To defend Mesopotamia, I have borrowed heavily from

Manu of Edessa. As the price of his aid, I have promised him restoration to his father's kingdom of Osrhoene.'

'A request to which I am sure our noble rulers will agree. His love of Rome must be rewarded, as should yours. What do you want?'

'To leave Mesopotamia.'

'For now you are needed here. No one has your experience of fighting the Persians. Perhaps in the future.'

CHAPTER 36

Moesia Inferior

South of the town of Durostorum,
The Day before the Ides of June, AD238

'The enemy are doing something, sir.'

'What?' The pain in Honoratus' head did not improve his patience.

'Dancing.'

'They often do that. We have some time. I will be there in a moment.'

Honoratus sat and rested his eyes in the gloom of the tent.

He was still suffering headaches from having been struck on the head by the boathook. They came and went, but even when the blinding pain made every slight noise agony, when he had to shut his eyes and lie down, he considered himself blessed. If the sailors had not hauled his unconscious form aboard the *Providentia*, no doubt he would have drowned in the harbour of Istria.

Honoratus had come round as the trireme pulled into the port of Tomis. The smells of tar and mutton fat and bilge water had made him throw up. The convulsions had made

332

the excruciating pain in his head yet worse, robbed him of the ability to think with any clarity, made him wonder if he would die.

Tomis of all places – Ovid's wretched place of exile. Like the poet, he really had not wanted to die in Tomis.

Four days later the news from Istria had forced him from his bed. After a night and a day of looting, Cniva and the Goths had stowed their plunder in native boats, and melted back into the marshes of the Danube estuary. Their allies, the Carpi, had remained. Perhaps their chiefs had been unable to drag them from the wealth of a civilized town, from the pleasures of rape and murder. Within three days Roman warships patrolled off Istria. With retreat across the river impossible, the Carpi had marched south towards Tomis.

Honoratus got to his feet. The tent reeled around him. He leant on a stick – a Centurion's vine staff – until the dizziness passed. He was in a bit better shape than that day in Tomis.

The initial stories brought by refugees had put the number of the Carpi at three hundred thousand. A military patrol had downgraded them to six thousand in the main horde, with smaller bands spreading out across the country. Even so it was a major threat to Moesia Inferior.

The town councillors of Tomis had not seen the need for the governor to leave to organize the defence of the province as a whole. They had stopped short of accusing him of cowardice, but their complaints and entreaties had been interminable. Honoratus had sat, head splitting and feeling sick, listening to their barbarous Greek for as long as he was able. When he could take no more, he had issued brusque instructions. The walls of Tomis were in good repair. They would be manned by the auxiliary cavalry stationed in the town and the militia. The Carpi had no siege engines, and they could not feed such numbers if they remained in one place. They could neither besiege nor blockade the town. Surprise

333

was not an option, so the only threat to Tomis was treachery. No one in the town could be such a fool as to open the gates to the barbarians. If the chieftains asked for a ransom to move on, the town councillors should pay. Honoratus would do his best to recoup their money when he had defeated the Carpi. The local worthies had not seemed much pleased.

Unable to ride, Honoratus had taken a light two-horse carriage, and an escort of thirty cavalry; the latter much begrudged by the citizens of Tomi. He had been driven west, past Tropaeum Traiani, to Durostorum. The jolting and lurching had made him continuously sick. Sometimes he had had to call a halt. The journey had taken two days.

At Durostorum he had been nursed by his wife. She would not lose a husband as well as a son to this accursed place. From his bed, he had issued orders to gather his forces, and sifted the news of the barbarians. Amid the garbled reports of atrocities – villages, villas and farms burnt, men, women and children outraged and enslaved – the progress of the main barbarian horde could be reconstructed. Bribed to leave Tomis, they had gone south-west to Marcianopolis. Likewise impotent before the walls of that place, and again paid to move on, they had set off north towards Durostorum and the Danube.

Honoratus had known they would come. There was nothing else they could do. It was hard to see what they had ever hoped to achieve. Barbarians were irrational. They were incapable of foresight or strategy. Now they must fight on ground of his choosing.

Taking a deep breath and squaring his shoulders, Honoratus left the tent.

'A lovely day, general.' Celsinus was in offensively good health. 'Those barbarians must be as apprehensive as a debtor on the *Kalends* of January when the rent is due as well as the interest.'

Estates mortgaged for twice their value, the ex-Praetor should know all about debt, Honoratus thought sourly. 'Are the omens good?'

'Could not be better. Not so much as a shadow on any of the organs.'

In his weakened, queasy state, Honoratus had known he would be unable to handle the bloody, slippery entrails.

'Our dispositions are as we decided last night?'

'We have extended our line to match the barbarians. The men are just five deep – the 11th Legion in the centre, the 4th Cohort of Gauls on the left, the 1st Lusitanians on the right. The cavalry are in reserve, out of sight with Egnatius Marinianus. Everyone is itching to get at them.'

That was good. The infantry were outnumbered two to one, and the Carpi would fight with the ferocity of their nature, and the desperation of their situation.

'Well done, Celsinus. You had best get to your post with the Lusitanians. The watchword is Revenge.'

'*Ultio*, it is.'

A legionary gave Honoratus a leg up. Even on the quiet hack, Honoratus felt vertiginous and unsteady. He walked his mount to the rear of the legion, close by the trumpeters and standard bearers.

Over the helmets of the legionaries, Honoratus could see the enemy some two hundred paces away. The mass of the Carpi stretched across the flat plain. Here and there individual warriors danced in front of the shieldwall. They lunged and twisted, tossed their spears in the air, howled and bayed like savage beasts. Behind them, the rest stamped their feet in time, clashed their weapons on their shields.

Every people had their rites to help men face the storm of steel. It was time for the Roman ritual.

'Soldiers of the 11th Legion, Claudian, Pius and Faithful, remember your heritage. The 11th was raised by the divine

335

Julius Caesar himself. You were the victors at Bedriacum. You crushed Civilis. Then you conquered real soldiers. Today you fight barbarians who you have beaten a hundred times. Remember how they ran at the Hierasos river. You know their nature. You have the measure of them. Hold their first rush, and they become despondent, their huge bodies tire. Unarmoured, they have no protection against our swords.'

All this shouting was making Honoratus feel worse.

'Think of those they have slain, and those they have enslaved. We will avenge the dead, and free the captives of their chains. The gods support our just cause. Revenge is our watchword. Are you ready for war?'

Ready!

Three times the men roared the traditional response. Celsinus was right. They seemed in good heart.

'Hold the line. Silence in the ranks. Listen for the words of command.'

Now there was nothing for it, but to wait. Honoratus' head throbbed. If only he had managed to eat more than a scrap of bacon. The lives of all these men in his hands. the safety of the whole province. The awful responsibility was crushing. Istria had fallen, and he had been healthy then. *Know yourself.* He was unworthy of command.

Honoratus gripped the horns of his saddle, forced himself to survey his chosen field. A broad, featureless plain with no cover except for the village of Palmatis, a mile or so to the rear. Egnatius Marinianus was an experienced commander, there was no sign of the thousand horsemen concealed among its huts and barns. The horses would be blown when they arrived. The gods willing, it should not matter. All depended on the timing, and that – oh, the cruelty of the joke – rested on no one but Honoratus himself.

'Sir.' The Centurion pointed ahead.

There was a stirring in the enemy ranks. New men were

being pushed to the front. They were unarmed. Their hands were bound. They were not barbarians.

'The bastards.' Horrified, the legionaries yelled at the sight of the human shield. 'Cowards!'

'Silence!'

The Centurions were obeyed.

Honoratus hunted for something to say.

The Carpi were moving forward, shoving their prisoners in front.

'Spare them, and we all die. Those civilians are dead men anyway. Ready your javelins. Wait until the command.'

Gods below, there were women among the hostages, even children. So this was the glory of war – to order the massacre of the defenceless.

The barbarians were almost within a hundred paces. No archers on either side. This would be at the point of the sword.

Honoratus half turned to the signallers. 'Ready.'

Fifty paces. The terrified faces of the stumbling prisoners. Fierce, bearded faces over their shoulders, roaring defiance.

'Make the signal.'

The trumpets rang out, and a huge red flag was hoisted.

No time to watch for a response.

Thirty paces.

Would the soldiers cut down fellow Romans?

'Throw!'

Hundreds of steel-tipped missiles whistled away.

Thank the gods the soldiers were a caste apart, shared little with those who did not live under the standards.

Figures – Roman and barbarian – plunged to the ground.

'Throw!'

The javelins of the rear ranks arced out. More fell.

The hostages were gone. The living and the dead trampled underfoot.

With the shock of an earthquake, the Carpi crashed into the legionaries. The line of shields buckled, in places shuddered back a few paces. Nowhere did it break. The legionaries, crouching, knees bent, thrust with shield boss and sword. The Carpi slashed and swung ungainly great blades. Some tore at the shields and the men behind with their bare hands.

An incoming javelin shot past Honoratus' face. He jerked up his shield, freed from the trance of the violent drama.

A Roman general did not fight, not unless almost all was lost. He managed the battle, set an example, encouraged the men. Honoratus put down his shield, and, feigning unconcern, walked his horse behind the line.

'Thrust to the face. Make them give ground.'

He called out above the din of battle.

'See they are tiring. Give me a step forward, boys. Drive them back.'

A bellowing like a thousand bullocks, away to the right.

Under Honoratus' horrified gaze, Celsinus toppled from his horse, a shaft embedded in his chest.

Their commander down, the Lusitanians began to give way. One or two at the back had already turned to run.

Without thought, Honoratus kicked his horse into a gallop.

By the time he reached the Cohort, the rout was near general.

Honoratus drove through the panic towards a retreating standard bearer.

Reining in hard, almost setting his mount back on its haunches, he jumped down.

'Give me that.' He snatched the standard, turned the pole horizontal, blocked those falling back.

'Turn and stand.'

Some pushed past. A few halted.

'Hold them here, and the day is ours.'

A barbarian burst through the melee. He chopped down

at Honoratus' head. Using the standard as a staff, Honoratus blocked. The impact jarred up through his arms. The barbarian pulled back to launch another attack, and a Centurion cut him down from behind.

'With your general!' the Centurion shouted.

A small knot of men clustered around Honoratus; twenty or thirty, no more. The Carpi lapped around them, pressed in from all sides. Shifting the standard to his left hand, Honoratus drew his sword. If ever a Roman general fought, it was now. Use the blade on the enemy or yourself. Do not be taken alive.

A huge barbarian chief chopped down an auxiliary in front of Honoratus, then another. Bright with gold, larger than a man, this was some great war-leader of the Carpi. He aimed a mighty overhead blow. Honoratus caught it on his own blade, was nearly forced to his knees, dropped the standard.

Wild eyed, spittle-flecked beard, the warrior screamed, lost in some battle madness. He lifted his reddened arms to finish this. Digging his heels into the dirt, Honoratus thrust. The blade was turned by the ribcage, slid along bone.

He was face to face with the chief. As they grappled, Honoratus twined his left leg behind the barbarian's right, shifted his weight in a wrestling move, let the bulk of the other man overbalance them both. Landing half on top of his opponent, Honoratus jerked out his dagger, plunged it into the man's groin.

The chieftain curled, clutching at his genitals. Honoratus grabbed his long hair, hauled back his head, and sawed at his neck. The knife scraped against cartilage and bone. No skill or science, Honoratus hacked away until the barbarian did not move.

Hands slippery with gore, Honoratus snatched his sword, used it to lever himself upright.

Ten men left. The Carpi closing to overrun them. A doomed last stand. The barbarians howling. The very earth vibrating.

And then, as if released from a spell, the Carpi turned and ran.

Swaying, the survivors clung to each other, trying to make sense of their reprieve.

The cavalry thundered through the chaos. Whooping, leaning from the saddle, as if after deer, they hunted down the barbarians.

Egnatius Marinianus pulled up by Honoratus.

'Revenge and victory. Pupienus and Balbinus and Gordian Imperatores. Victory!'

'Hail the Augusti and the Caesar,' Honoratus said.

CHAPTER 37

Dalmatia

The Town of Salona,
The Day before the Ides of June, AD238

The villa outside Salona had a terrace with a view of the harbour. Iunia Fadilla watched a big merchantman reach the breakwater at the mouth of the river, and prepare to set out to sea.

Bored waiting, she had finished *The Ephesian Tale* by Xenophon. Why had her cousin given her the novel? Had Fadillus thought it might distract her, or had he seen some parallel between the adventures of the heroine and her own? In the book, apart from twice being buried alive, Anthia had been forced into two marriages, repeatedly enslaved – by both pirates and brigands – and sold into a brothel. Despite all of which, she had somehow managed to persuade her various husbands, owners, and prospective clients to respect her chastity. Iunia Fadilla doubted the simpering Greek girl would have been as successful with her own husband Verus Maximus. All those tears would have just excited his lust. Why was Anthia always crying? And her husband, Habrocomes, was no better.

341

Men had no idea what women thought. Fadillus would have done better giving her a book of good poetry, or, if it had to be prose, something useful, something which would help her prepare to pick up the threads of her normal life in Rome and Italy. She had purchased a new property on the Bay of Naples before her marriage. When she returned it would need taking in hand. Varro or Columella's *On Agriculture* would have been helpful. Or perhaps *How to Manage your Slaves* by Marcus Sidonius Falx.

When she returned. She looked at the merchantman heading out into the Adriatic, and wished she was standing on its deck. She was comfortable enough. The villa provided by Claudius Julianus indeed was luxurious. But still the governor of Dalmatia would not give her permission to leave. One reason after another: the weather was threatening, the times unsettled, she was not yet recovered from her ordeal. It was as if she were a child.

At first she had been happy to be treated as a child. Her cousin and the soldiers had taken her hands and led her down from the cliff. They had made her wait for a carriage to take her back to the little town of Bariduum. There she had been agreeably lodged, and reunited with her maid. Restuta had bathed and fed her, put salve on her cuts and bruises. A local seamstress had run up new clothes. All the while Fadillus had fussed around her. No one was allowed to say anything which might upset her; no mention of the civil war, or her husband. Eventually – *when she was strong enough* – they had brought her down to Salona.

In truth she had behaved like a child. She had refused to believe that either Gordian or his father were dead. Claudius Julianus was kindly, but insistent. She would not accept it. What proof did he have? Finally he had shown her. The honey had not completely preserved the head. It was blackened, a little decomposed. The sweetness of the honey mingled with the stench of decay. Yet there was no doubt it was Gordian the Elder. A messenger had been intercepted taking the grisly trophy from Africa to Maximinus. Put to the question, he admitted that, although the body later could not be identified, he had seen Gordian the Younger cut down on the field of battle.

She had collapsed then – wailing, floods of tears, incoherent, no more resolve than the heroine of a Greek novel – but that was many days ago. Now she was recovered. She was herself, and she wanted to leave. She had requested this meeting with Claudius Julianus so she could demand to leave. She was not a prisoner, and she would not be treated as such.

Restuta came out onto the terrace. Keeping her promise, Iunia Fadilla had manumitted her. Now a freedwoman, Restuta deserved a greeting. As a slave she could have been ignored. Sometimes Iunia Fadilla found it hard to remember her maid's change of status.

'The litter is ready.'

They crossed one of the five bridges, and went up through the town towards the Forum.

Iunia Fadilla left the hangings open. The passers-by gawped, but all her life she had been used to people staring.

Claudius Julianus was waiting in a broad, airy room in the Basilica off the Forum. Her cousin was with him. Somehow they both made her uncomfortable, and she knew that they always would. Every time she saw Fadillus, she would be reminded of her flight, of the mountains, and her fear. Claudius Julianus may have been a lifelong friend of Gordian, but now he would remain the man who had shown her the severed head of her lover's father.

'Wine?'

'Thank you, yes. You know why I asked to see you.'

Claudius Julianus looked embarrassed. Fadillus would not meet her eye.

343

She would go no matter what objections they raised.

'There is news from Aquileia.' Claudius Julianus spoke carefully.

Iunia Fadilla forced herself to be calm.

'Your husband is dead. Verus Maximus was killed with his father in a mutiny.'

Her heart leapt.

'Then there is nothing to stop me returning to Rome.' Some of her wine had spilled on the floor; a libation to freedom.

Neither of the men would look at her.

'You can return to Rome, but . . .' Claudius Julianus' words trailed off.

'But?'

'Our Emperors, the noble Augusti Pupienus and Balbinus, have promised your hand in marriage to Marcus Julius Corvinus.'

It took a moment for her to understand who was meant. *My name is Marcus Julius Corvinus, and these wild mountains are mine.* She had the brooch he had given her. She had wanted to run to him. But now . . .

'I have no wish for another husband.'

'It will not be like Verus Maximus,' Fadillus said. 'The Emperors have promised Corvinus a house in Rome, and villas on the Bay of Naples and Sicily. You will have some independence.'

She already possessed that quality, and had her own houses in Rome and on the coast.

'You cannot coerce a woman into marriage. It is against the law.' She sounded weak and pedantic to herself.

'The Emperors must keep their promises,' Claudius Julianus said, his words weighty and considered, fitting the dignity of the governor of a province. 'The will of the Emperors is law.'

Damn them to Hades. No man would be forced into such

344

an arrangement. Claudius Julianus would continue to serve in safe posts across the empire, accruing the profits, untroubled by a wife left on his estates. Fadillus would return to Rome, to his indulgences and ridiculous novels, to life as a bachelor. The world was unfair. Damn all men to Hades.

PART X:
ROME

CHAPTER 38

The Temple of Concordia Augusta,
The Ides of June, AD238

Pupienus Augustus eased himself onto the ivory throne, Balbinus Augustus to his right, the Caesar Gordian his left. He looked down at the hundreds of Senators massed in the great chamber, and they gazed up at their rulers on the dais. The setting could not have been more fitting: the Temple of Augustan Harmony. Togate and grave, whatever tensions or animosities flickered behind their serious faces, for this act of theatre the two Emperors and their Caesar embodied imperial unity and the majesty of Rome.

The painting of Marsyas – naked and hanging in agony – caught his eye. It was less than three months since he had studied it as the news was broken that the Gordiani were dead in Africa. Then it had seemed that all their hopes had come to nothing, that everyone in the temple might share the fate of Marsyas. So much had happened since. Then he had been a Senator – one among six hundred – now he was Emperor. All his deep-laid plans had come to fruition, even the one that had seemed unthinkable. He did not let himself think about his father. Power did not come without a price. The throne was not won without suffering.

A Quaestor – one of the favoured, a candidate of the Emperors – was to read the imperial oration. It followed precedent, and it had solved a problem. Pupienus and Balbinus shared power equally. Neither could have made the speech without seeming to assume precedence. Pupienus almost allowed himself to smile as he imagined the alternative: both Augusti chanting the words together, perhaps with young Gordian adding a contralto backing.

Balbinus had been delighted when Pupienus suggested the Quaestor should be one Valerius Poplicola. The young patrician symbolized the change of regime. Maximinus had executed his uncle and grandfather. Balbinus had close links to the family, and saw Poplicola as a protégé. Balbinus was a fool, who mistook the trappings for the reality of power.

'Conscript Fathers, rejoice! By the will of Jupiter Optimus Maximus and all the immortal gods, and with the agreement of all mankind, the Senate invested us in the purple to save the *Res Publica*, and rule it in accordance with Roman law. We bring you good news. The provinces, once torn in pieces by the insatiable greed of the tyrant, are restored to safety. Only two governors in all the provinces in the North and the West have yet to acknowledge our beneficent rule. Crispinus, the hero of Aquileia, has been despatched to administer the oath of allegiance to Decius in Spain. The noble Rufinianus has been appointed governor of both Africa and Numidia. Here in Rome Sextius Cethegillus will replace Rufinianus as Prefect of the City. The oaths of loyalty have yet to arrive across the expanse of sea from the East, but we repose full confidence in our envoys Latronianus and Cuspidius.'

Jupiter Optimus Maximus, we give you thanks.

A deep, rhythmic acclamation rose from the assembled Senators.

'Civil strife is at an end. The legions and the auxiliaries march back to their stations on the frontiers. The Praetorians are returned to their camp here in Rome, the 2nd Parthian Legion to the Alban Hills. To celebrate the felicity of our times, we have issued a new denomination of coin, twice the value of the *denarius*.'

Pupienus Augustus, we give you thanks.

This acclamation was more muted. Senators had little sympathy for gifts to the troops.

Balbinus Augustus, we give you thanks.

A crowd of off-duty Praetorians thronged the open doors of the temple. Their demeanour also was less than enthusiastic. The new coins had not been well received. Pupienus made a mental note to raise the issue again at the next *consilium*.

Gordian Caesar, we give you thanks.

'The grain fleet from Alexandria has been sighted off Puteoli. Soon it will dock in Ostia, the public granaries will be full, and hunger a thing of the past.'

Pupienus, Balbinus, Gordian, may the gods keep you.

Timesitheus was standing among the Praetorians in the doorway. For now the little Greek remained *Praefectus Annonae*. Pupienus had new plans for him. In the hard duties of *negotium*, in politics and war, you had to use the instruments that were to hand, even if they were distasteful.

'The joys of peace are founded on the travails of war. While the soldiers of Rome have turned on each other in fratricidal conflict, the savage arrogance of the barbarians has grown. A conspiracy of the tribes threatens the lower Danube. The Persians have overrun Mesopotamia. Emperors should not rest in tranquillity while other men fight for the safety of the *Res Publica*. In the East, Pupienus Augustus will

351

humble the vaunting conceit of the Sassanids. The gods willing, he will sack Ctesiphon, and lead Ardashir in chains through the streets of Rome in triumph. In the North, Balbinus Augustus will bring ruin on Cniva and the horde of Goths and Sarmatians who follow in his train. For the good governance of Rome, Gordian Caesar will reside on the Palatine.'

No voice will ever be so strong, no speech will ever be so happy, no talent will ever be so fortunate, as ever adequately express the blessedness of your reign.

Like a theatre claque, the Senators called out their well-rehearsed happiness.

Pupienus was satisfied. It was all his doing.

Rome would be safe. The boy Gordian, when not enduring the censorious lectures of his dreadful mother and ape of a tutor, could return to his toys. Better to be a slave boy than suffer a childhood at the hands of Maecia Faustina and Gallicanus. Loyal men would watch over the seven hills for Pupienus. The new Prefect of the City, Sextius Cethegillus, was his brother-in-law. One of the Praetorian Prefects was Pinarius, once his adoptive father. The other, Aedinius Julianus, owed his position to Pupienus.

After the neglect of the reign of Maximinus, the East demanded the presence of an Emperor. New governors, right thinking men of probity, needed to be appointed. A victory over the Persians would bring Pupienus immeasurable wealth, and the glory of Alexander.

It had not been easy to make Balbinus agree to shoulder his duty. Only an appeal to his vanity had prised him away from his indolent vices. The Emperors were equal in honour. It was not fitting that one should win a reputation for military virtue and not the other. Balbinus was more of a child than Gordian. If neither the climate nor the natives dealt with him, if neither the gods nor the soldiery struck him down, that task would fall to the returning conqueror of the Sassanids. Balbinus was a glutton. A dish of mushrooms had translated Claudius into a spurious divinity. Another banquet had ridded Nero of an inconvenient brother.

When Pupienus returned to Rome, wreathed in the laurels of victory, perhaps graciously he would allow Gordian to retire into private life. Of course if the boy proved unwilling some other arrangement would have to be made.

'Tomorrow we declare open the Capitoline Games. To the five days of chariot racing in the Circus Maximus, athletics in the Stadium of Alexander, competitions in music and poetry in the Odeum, in our generosity we have added beast fights and gladiatorial shows in the Flavian Amphitheatre.'

Pupienus' thoughts were already running on the work that needed to be done.

'Conscript Fathers, put off the Roman toga, and clad yourselves in a Greek mantle. Put aside the cares of office, and enjoy the *hilaritas* of our reign. Conscript Fathers, we detain you no longer.'

Pupienus Augustus, Balbinus Augustus, Gordian Caesar, you have struck down the tyrant. You have restored Roman laws, justice, mercy, and morality. You have restored peace and happiness. May the gods preserve you. So fare Emperors wisely chosen, so perish Emperors chosen by fools.

CHAPTER 39

The Caelian Hill,
Three Days after the Ides of June, AD238

'You want to live forever?'

Timesitheus did not reply.

'The blood runs thin with age, nothing but a fever can warm the body of an old man. Sex is a forgotten memory. His nose drips like an infant's, his voice trembles as much as his limbs, he mumbles his bread with toothless gums. One illness after another, and then he forgets the names of his servants, his host at dinner, his own children. If he keeps his wits, he sees urns filled with the ashes of those he loved.'

Tranquillina had not finished. 'Old age is perpetual grief, black mourning, a world of sorrow.'

Timesitheus picked up a glass. 'The past tells against an equestrian who would be the power behind the throne. Sejanus was called partner by the Emperor, and Sejanus ended dragged by a hook. People took their slaves down to the Tiber to witness them kicking the corpse of the traitor.' He drank, his hand was steady.

'Better a few years of glory than a lifetime of obscurity.' Tranquillina prowled the bedroom. 'Is the limit of your ambition to lord it over some sleepy rural backwater, inspecting weights, giving orders for the destruction of short-measure pint-pots?'

'Cleander, Perennis, Plautianus, none of them came to a good end,' he said.

She ignored him. 'Felicio is embittered by his dismissal. He will go with you. Maecius Gordianus can keep the *vigiles* off the streets. We will see if Serapamum can ensure the 2nd Legion does not intervene. You must act quickly before the Urban Cohorts or German Guard can be summoned.'

'Someone thrust a few hairs in his daughter's face: *Behold your Plautianus*.'

Tranquillina came and stood close. 'This was *your* suggestion. Were you a man yesterday, and not today? A cat that would eat fish, but not wet its paws? I could find another.'

Timesitheus would not rise. 'It is not lawful to execute a virgin. Before they killed her, the executioners raped Sejanus' daughter.'

'You will not use Sabinia to frighten me.' Tranquillina looked into his eyes. 'The executioners would not be needed. Before that happened, I would kill our daughter myself.'

Timesitheus arranged his face.

'I would not live as a coward in my own estimate,' Tranquillina said. 'Nor would a man such as you.'

Timesitheus pulled her to him, rested his chin on her head.

She was silent while he thought.

'If it is to be done, it is best done quickly. All Rome is distracted by the Games, all discipline relaxed. One throw of the dice – *Venus* or the *Dog*.'

'I will come with you.'

'No, you will stay at home.' Timesitheus ruffled her hair. 'We are not barbarians. Roman soldiers will not follow a

355

woman, not even you. Keep Sabinia close. You will know our fate by the time the lamps are lit.'

The Praetorian Camp

'*So fare Emperors wisely chosen, so perish Emperors chosen by fools.* That is how they regard you – fools and simpletons.'

Timesitheus and Felicio had moved through the barracks, talking to the men in twos and threes. Now they stood on the tribunal, a sea of faces gazing up at them.

'They killed the Emperor that you chose. Maximinus was a soldier, one of you. They had a barbarian kill him. They cut off his head, trampled his corpse, treated him with contempt. They hate you for choosing him. They despise you for keeping your oath to him. They think you are fools.'

Some murmured in agreement, but Timesitheus had not won the majority over yet.

'Maximinus always shared your labours and your dangers. He rewarded you, doubled your pay. They cowered far from the battle, safe behind the marshes of Ravenna and the walls of Rome. They promised you a donative in *denarii*, but they paid you in these.' He flourished a coin. 'They tell you this new coin is worth two *denarii*. They must think you are simpletons. Even the stupidest slave can tell this coin weighs no more than one and a half *denarii*.' He tossed the coin to the ground.

Now more were coming around. The avarice of soldiers was unbounded.

'Your existence is an affront to Pupienus and Balbinus. To look at you reminds them of their treachery. Why do you think Pupienus did not send those German barbarians back to their dismal forests? Why bring them here to Rome? You know the answer in your hearts. You will be dismissed, replaced with hairy savages from the North.'

Timesitheus paused to let the thought have its effect.

'They will strip you of your arms and your honour, but you will have your lives. If only they intended to extend that clemency to their own Caesar. Once the Praetorians are disbanded, how long do you think they will suffer young Gordian to live? Already they plot against him. Torn from the safety of his ancestral home, he is at their mercy on the Palatine. Who have they appointed his tutor? None other than Gallicanus, the Senator who led the mob against your camp, the Senator who incited the plebs to the murder of your wives and children. The boy is all alone in the Palace. He cries out for your protection. Only you can save him.'

Drag them. Swords were drawn. *Drag them. Drag them.* More took up the chant.

'Wait!' The ranks of the soldiers parted.

A rustic figure approached the tribunal. Pinarius was wearing just a tunic. His hair was wild, and he looked as if he had been roused from sleep.

'It is best you leave,' Felicio said.

'I will not.' Stiff-legged with age, the old man climbed the steps.

'Get back to your garden.'

'Praetorians, do not listen to the lies of this little Greek.'

'I am truly sorry about this.' Timesitheus drew his sword.

Pinarius tried to defend himself. The first blow cut into his forearm. He doubled up in pain, clutching the wound. Timesitheus chopped down. The blade bit into the back of the neck. The old man collapsed in a welter of blood.

'So perish the creatures of tyranny.'

Timesitheus pointed his reddened sword at the corpse.

'Praetorians, you have a choice. Abandon me to the tyrants. Watch me be crucified, thrown to the beasts. Leave young Gordian to be murdered. Or follow me to the Palace, and save the young Caesar.'

To the Palace! To the Palace!

357

CHAPTER 40

The Hippodrome at the East of the Palatine Hill,
Three Days after the Ides of June, AD238

'Are these the best maps in the imperial libraries?'

'This one is from the *Parthian Stations* of Isedore of Charax,
and the other I had specially drawn from the *Commentaries*
of the Emperor Trajan.' Iulius Africanus looked a little put
out.

Pupienus studied the Itineraries: the straight, black lines
of the roads, the little drawings denoting towns and forts,
the distances between carefully marked. The mountains of
Armenia were depicted in the North, the Red Sea at the
South, the Euphrates and Tigris snaking down to the latter.
There were no other natural features. If an army was forced
to leave the roads, it would be lost.

'The divine Trajan campaigned in the East over a century
ago. When was Isedore writing?'

'At about the same time, Emperor.'

It was close on three hundred years since Pompey had
first reached the Euphrates with a Roman army. Later Crassus

had blundered to disaster in Mesopotamia. After Trajan, various Emperors had fought in the East; Verus and Severus with success, Caracalla, Macrinus, and Alexander less so. Yet these were the best maps that a diligent imperial librarian could produce.

It was only when you sat on the throne that you fully realized the limitations of the Roman empire. When you proposed to invade Persia, you found no maps, no military or diplomatic archives, no specialists in the affairs of the East. Strategic debate in the imperial *consilium* was little better informed than the conversation at any senatorial dinner party. Pupienus would put that right.

'Next year, when we march East, like Alexander the Great, we will include geographers and map makers in our entourage. Being Roman, we will also take land surveyors as well. On our return, Iulius Africanus will collect their works in a special section in the Pantheon library. No future Emperor fighting in the East will be uncertain of the line of march of his forces.'

'But, Father, after your conquest, there will be no further need for campaigning.'

Pupienus looked at his younger son. Marcus Africanus had always been the more arrogant. Yet since his own elevation both had developed an unappealing haughtiness of manner.

'You mistake my intention.' Pupienus let his tone add the word *again*. 'I am not minded to add new territories to the empire. This will be a just war. The Sassanids have broken the treaty with Alexander, and attacked our provinces. I will lead an expedition down the Euphrates. The gods willing, I will defeat the Persians, and kill or capture the faithless Ardashir. Having sacked Ctesiphon, I will crown Tiridates of Armenia as King of Kings. As an Arsacid, he has a better claim to the throne than any Sassanid. Chosroes will succeed

359

his father as King of Armenia. On our return, we will leave behind two friendly Kings as a bulwark to our provinces. The prestige of Rome will be restored throughout the East, our cities in Mesopotamia recovered, and our baggage train laden with gold.'

The twelve men summoned to the *consilium* made quiet, dignified noises of approval.

'Emperor, if I may speak?'

Pupienus gave permission to Fulvius Pius.

'Will you retake Carrhae and Nisibis in Mesopotamia before or after the march down the Euphrates?'

Pius was the scion of a noble family, but he was far from a fool. He did not attend the council merely because of his exalted descent.

'I envisage three armies in the field. While I lead the main force to Ctesiphon, Lucius Virius will operate out of Armenia. With the support of the warriors of Tiridates, he will descend on the Persian province of Media Atropatene. At the same time, Valerian will enter Mesopotamia, and besiege the cities lost to the Sassanids.'

Again the muted sounds of approbation.

'Emperor, if I may speak?' The query of Tineius Sacerdos was tentative. Once you had assumed the purple, even your oldest friends could not speak to you openly. Any criticism was constrained. The throne was a lonely eminence.

'The plan is not dissimilar to that of the late Emperor Alexander,' Sacerdos said.

'That is true, but the strategy is sound.' Pupienus kept any reproof from his voice. 'The armies of Alexander were weakened by disease, and undermined by that Emperor's cowardice. We will insist on discipline on the march and cleanliness in our camps. In all the commands I have held, in a long career with the armies, no reproach was levelled against my courage. It will not desert me now I am Emperor.'

The *consilium* was almost indecorous in the vehemence of its denial that such a thing was conceivable.

'With three armies operating independently supplies will be a concern.' Pupienus turned to the Master of Admissions who stood by the doorway to the garden. 'Where is Timesitheus?'

'The *Praefectus Annonae* was summoned. His wife sent his profound apologies, he is unwell.'

Pupienus considered what Sanctus had said. Only a bad ruler would demand a sick man attend him. No one but a tyrant would find fault with the man who gave unwelcome news. Sanctus discharged his duties with the expertise of long experience. He had served as *Ab Admissionibus* under Alexander and Maximinus, and now controlled who was allowed into the presence of the new Augusti. It argued both for competence and a talent for survival.

'We will discuss logistics on another occasion, when the *Praefectus Annonae* is recovered. There were no complaints when Timesitheus oversaw the supplies in Alexander's campaigns, and there were no shortages in the North when he still had charge of Maximinus' baggage train.'

'Emperor, we should worry about manpower rather than food and fodder. With Balbinus Augustus on the Danube, and three forces in the East, where are the soldiers to be found?'

The bluntness of Sextius Cethegillus caused a stir of embarrassment in the chamber. Yet Pupienus was not displeased. A good Emperor was a first among equals. He should allow his advisors to speak their mind with freedom, at least within reason.

'The Persians are a greater threat than the Goths.' Pupienus spoke with certainty. 'Apart from an honour guard of Praetorians, my co-Emperor must make do with those troops stationed along the Danube. The rest of the Praetorians, all the Equites Singulares, the 2nd Legion, and the German Guard will accompany me to the East. They will be augmented by detachments drawn from the armies on the Rhine and in Britain: two thousand from each legion, and a proportionate number of auxiliaries.'

And from Spain and Africa too, Pupienus thought. As soon as we have those provinces under our control. The more troops under his eye, the safer an Emperor was from some governor daring to revolt.

Cethegillus spoke again. 'The northern frontiers will be exposed, if there are barbarian raids.'

There was free speech, and there was impertinence. This fell just short of demanding a rebuke.

'For a year.' Pupienus spoke decisively. 'We will only be in the East for one campaigning season.'

From outside came the sounds of an altercation.

'The Emperor has taken his seat.' Sanctus sounded outraged. 'The *consilium* is in session. No one is to be admitted.'

'Who is it?' Pupienus said.

'It is me, Praetextatus.'

'Let him in.'

Pupienus' heart shrank at the sight of the ugly face. Praetextatus was as foolish as he was ill-favoured. He might be father-in-law to one of his sons, but that did not mean Pupienus would welcome his company, let alone ever seek his counsel. The daughter had inherited the looks of her father. Marcus Africanus had done his duty, and got her pregnant. That would have been a task few would have envied.

'The Praetorians . . .' Praetextatus was dishevelled, panting.

Pupienus and the others waited.

'The camp is in uproar. They are rioting, tearing down the imperial portraits.'

'You saw this?' Pupienus said.

'No, someone told me. But I heard the noise.'

Inured to the vicissitudes of fortune, the members of the *consilium* waited to fit their reaction to the Emperor's response.

An unreliable witness, bearing second-hand news. It was the Capitoline Games. The city was full of disturbance. This secluded garden in the Palace was one of the few places that enjoyed any peace.

'This report should be investigated.'

'As Praetorian Prefect, that is my duty,' Aedinius Julianus said.

'Carry on.'

'Emperor, in case there is any truth in it, let me go and summon the Urban Cohorts for your protection,' Cethegillus said.

'It is true!' Praetextatus exclaimed.

Pupienus silenced him with a look.

'No, the Urban Cohorts are scattered throughout the city controlling the crowds. In any event, they and the Praetorians detest each other. In the licence of the Games, most likely they would come to blows: cause the riot they are intended to prevent.'

And the Urban Cohorts would lose, Pupienus thought. The plebs called them *sporteoli*, and the 'little-bucket-men' were even less real soldiers than the Praetorians. Unlike the latter, they never served on campaign.

Menophilus spoke for the first time. 'Let me fetch the German Guard. They are quartered just outside the city. It will take some time. For safety, best I leave now.'

The Germans were a different proposition from the Urban Cohorts. Fierce fighters, bred to war, they treated oaths, such as that they had sworn to the Emperors, with deadly earnestness.

'Fetch them.'

'Emperor.' It was that fat fool of a patrician, Valerius Priscillianus. 'I should inform your co-Emperor, the noble Balbinus.'

'Yes,' Pupienus said. 'Valerian, you might see that the Caesar Gordian is not alarmed.'

If the danger turned out to be more than some wild rumour, Pupienus would not have his sons caught up the tumult. 'Africanus, your wife is near the time of her confinement. You should go and make sure she is not disturbed. And,' he turned to his elder son, 'Maximus, our family home on the Esquiline is quite near the camp, go and see that all is well there.'

'I will go with him,' Praetextatus said.

'Please do.'

The *consilium* was much reduced. Pupienus knew he must set an example in unconcern. It was not difficult after a lifetime of self-control and subterfuge.

'Now, we must turn to the question of money. I am informed that the new denomination, the Antoninianus, is unpopular. Licinius Rufinus, you once served as *A Rationibus*, you understand the imperial finances. Advise me what measures we should enact. No war was ever fought without money.'

CHAPTER 41

The Aula Regia at the West of the Palatine Hill,
Three Days after the Ides of June, AD238

On a hot summer day the Sicilia courtyard lost some of its
appeal. With no breeze, it was stifling under the porticos, and
the sunlight, glinting off the pool and reflected by the marble
cladding, was painful to the eyes. At the last moment Balbinus
decided they really would have to go somewhere else.

Although clad for the festival in an informal Greek tunic,
Balbinus led the entourage slowly and with due pomp. An
Emperor should never hurry. As they passed the entrance
to the network of tunnels and covered walkways that ultimately led to the Capitoline, he looked with longing at its
dark shade. But Sophists could not perform before their
Emperor in a passageway, and the main audience chamber
should be as cool as anywhere.

Balbinus sat on the throne. From the apse behind him,
larger than life and sculpted in marble, his own image, along
with the statues of Pupienus and Gordian, gazed out over
his head.

Culture and power were his birthright. One of his ancestors had been deified as Zeus Eleutherius Theophanes, as much for his literary compositions as for advising Pompey the Great on the organization of Rome's eastern provinces. A more recent forebear, Herodes Atticus, had been acknowledged as the equal of the ten great orators of the Athenian past. Balbinus intended his would be a reign of culture, which in posterity would outshine that of his kinsman the divine Hadrian. Let dour, timeworn Pupienus labour over accounts and troop rosters. Balbinus Augustus would preside over a court of poets, artists and orators.

Balbinus had thought to reintroduce competitions in Greek and Latin oratory to the official programme of the Capitoline Games. His old friend Rufinianus had strongly argued against it. Apparently the contest had been removed from the festival after the fall of its originator, the Emperor Domitian of evil fame. It was not good to remind the populace of a tyrant, even one from generations before. Today would be a private event.

Balbinus sometimes wondered if he heeded the advice of others too readily. Perhaps in four years' time, at the next staging of the Capitoline Games, orators might appear. He had half a mind to reintroduce races for girls. They would follow the Spartan custom. The thought was appealing. Their young bodies oiled and naked, their embarrassment as they were exposed to the crowd; their firm, rounded buttocks, budding breasts. The competitors would be chosen by imperial command. It would be good to order the daughters of his enemies stripped for public enjoyment. A pleasant fantasy, no more.

It was still too hot in the Aula Regia. The open doors and great window that led onto the balcony admitted not a breath of air. The tall columns of Phrygian marble and the high, shadowed ceiling gave a false impression of coolness. The purple tunic clung damply over the Emperor's paunch.

The two Sophists and the select audience were in place. Balbinus had given the occasion some thought. The contest needed an edge of danger. Nothing crass like Caligula having the loser thrown in the river, or Heliogabalus making him lick the ink from the papyrus of his published speeches. It was Balbinus' choice of orators that added an element of personal rivalry, even animosity. Apsines of Gadara was a friend of Philostratus, while Periges the Lydian was a pupil of Cassianus, the bitter enemy of Philostratus. And, of course, the victor would be handsomely rewarded, while the vanquished would forfeit his exemption from taxes.

Balbinus studied the two speakers. Both were sweating like gladiators about to go into the arena. Well they might. Extempore display oratory, where there was no forewarning of the subject, was the most difficult of all forms of rhetoric. Balbinus pondered a theme. *Demosthenes, after breaking down before Philip, defends himself from the charge of cowardice.* It would be fitting for an imperial audience. *Should the islanders revolt from Persia when their children have been murdered?* No, he had thought of something better.

'*Should the Athenians revolt from Alexander while he is in India?* Apsines will speak first.'

The chamber was silent with an air of expectation.

Apsines stood very still, looking down at his feet.

The tension gathered. Apsines had charmed audiences as diverse as the educated men of Athens and the barbarian Maximinus. The Phoenician had to produce an outstanding performance to make the transition to favour in the new regime.

Very suddenly Apsines stood straight, tossed his artfully curled locks, thrust out an arm, and began to declaim.

'The same sun shines down on India . . .'

Some of the audience murmured applause. A true Sophist was master of delivery and appearance as well as words.

'More distant than Hercules, further than Dionysus, the Macedonian has crossed the Indus . . .'

Balbinus was disturbed by a man pushing through the crowd, approaching the throne.

'Emperor.' It was Valerius Priscillianus.

'Not now.'

'Emperor, I must speak to you.' Valerius' face was far too close, heavy jowls dripping with sweat.

Balbinus waved a hand to stem the flow of Apsines' words.

'What?' Valerius had been a companion since childhood, but this was unforgivable presumption. An Emperor can choose new friends. Everyone wanted to be *amicus* to the Augustus.

'Praetextatus has just told the *consilium* that the Praetorians are tearing the imperial portraits from the standards in their camp.'

After the first stab of alarm, Balbinus calmed himself. Praetextatus had always been a credulous fool, and one with a nervous disposition. Most likely it was nothing but a wild rumour.

Valerius leant yet closer. His breath hot and offensive in Balbinus' ear. 'Pupienus has sent Menophilus to fetch the German Guard.'

Now Balbinus' innards shifted with fear. A lifetime in Roman politics had attuned him to suspicion. Praetextatus' hideous daughter was married to one of Pupienus' sons. Menophilus and Pupienus had conspired together to kill Maximinus' Prefect of the City. Menophilus had beaten Sabinus to death with his own hands. Pupienus had brought the German Guard to Rome. The barbarians were said to be devoted to him, to have sworn outlandish oaths.

'Emperor—'

'Silence. Let me think.'

The Praetorian Prefect Aedinius Julianus had been

appointed by Pupienus. If it had any reality, the Praetorian riot was nothing but a pretext to bring the Germans to the Palatine. Once in the Palace, they would obey any command issued by Pupienus. The barbarians would have no compunction in killing an Emperor.

Balbinus seized the front of Valerius' tunic. 'Intercept the Germans. Countermand the order. Lead them back to their quarters. Make sure they remain outside the city.'

'But—'

'That is an imperial command.'

Panic-stricken, Valerius blundered away.

Balbinus composed his face. With a gesture, he summoned Acilius Aviola to his side.

'Go and see what is happening in the Praetorian camp. If there is trouble, offer them a donative in my name and that of Gordian. Just our names, no mention of Pupienus.'

Acilius had more about him than Valerius. He left without demur.

So Pupienus had shown his hand. All his pressing talk of campaigns in Germany and the East, of both being harnessed together in duty, had been subterfuge. Balbinus had put a stop to this scheme, but now he must put his mind to ridding himself and young Gordian of their treacherous partner in the purple.

Balbinus did not know how much of the whispered conversations the others in the chamber had heard. An Emperor must not show weakness. He smiled gracefully.

'We regret the interruption. All is resolved. Apsines, when you are ready, please continue.'

CHAPTER 42

The Quarters of the German Guard in the Gardens of Dolabella,
Three Days after the Ides of June, AD238

'So you are back then?'

'I am back,' Ballista said.

'Enjoy the *baths*?' Calgacus pronounced it as if the word itself was reprehensible.

'The Baths of Caracalla are very big, very impressive.'

'Proper little Roman now you have stopped being Dernhelm and become *Marcus Clodius Ballista*.' The old Caledonian affected the belief that a change of tone, as if he were thinking out loud, made his asides inaudible. 'Probably got yourself buggered senseless, like a Roman would.'

Ballista had not enjoyed the baths. He loathed drawing attention, at least when he was out of his element. Although he spoke Latin well enough, his height, pale skin, and long fair hair had made him stand out from the crowd in the baths. He was still young enough to find it hard to hide his acute embarrassment when stared at by strangers. And,

370

Calgacus had a point, some of his fellow bathers had shown too much interest in his physique.

'I am going to rest,' Ballista said. 'You might as well go and do whatever it is you do for amusement; perhaps inflict yourself on some poor whore under the arches of the Circus.'

'And when would I find time to get my leg over, working my fingers to the bone morning, noon, and fucking night looking after you?' Calgacus continued his shrewish complaints as he left the room. 'Ungrateful little fucker.'

Ballista lay down. It was very hot, far hotter than he had ever known at home. The sounds of the camp came through the open window. There would never be quiet where two thousand Germanic warriors were quartered. Shouts, boasts, snatches of songs, men practising with their weapons; Ballista found the sounds soothing. It was good to be among his own people. The Guard was drawn, by treaty or money, from many northern tribes. Yet they shared both language and a way of looking at the world. Ballista tried to enjoy it while he could. In a few days he and Calgacus were ordered to go and live in the imperial school on the Palatine.

Ballista closed his eyes, and thought of Kadlin and the brothers he had loved. Froda was dead, Eadwulf in exile, and Kadlin lost to him. And his father had cast him out. Lines of poetry came into his mind.

> *I had to bind my feelings in fetters,*
> *Often sad at heart, cut off from my country,*
> *Far from my kinsmen, after, long ago,*
> *Dark clods of earth covered my gold-friend;*
> *I left that place in wretchedness.*

The usual wheezing and coughing, and very audible muttering, announced that Calgacus was returning.

So this world dwindles day by day,
And passes away; for a man will not be wise
Before he has weathered his share of winters
In the world.

'Get up. The Praetorians are going to kill the Emperors in the Palace. Not that I for one give a fuck.'

Ballista swung off the bed, went to get his mailcoat.

'No time. We need to go now.'

Calgacus handed him his sword-belt, buckled on his own.

'You have taken no oath to the Romans,' Ballista said.

'I took one to your father. Isangrim scares me more than these soft southerners.'

Ballista recognized the Senator standing in the middle of the gardens. Menophilus still looked ill from the arrow he had taken at Aquileia.

'I saw you at the siege,' Menophilus said. 'You were leading the assault.'

'I was too busy running to see you.' There were no more than two or three hundred warriors assembled. The rest would be scattered through the city; drinking, whoring and gambling. Some would be insensible through drink. One or two who had appeared were reeling.

'We cannot wait any longer,' Menophilus said.

'Over here, Emperor-killer.' The tone of the Alamann was mocking, but not unkind. 'Today, Angle, you will learn how a real man fights – with a sword not a stylus.'

The nearby warriors laughed.

'Glad you brought that ugly Caledonian. His face alone should scare the Praetorians.'

'Fuck you,' Calgacus said.

'Remind me to show you how to beat your slave later.' The Alamann was in high spirits. They all were. Fighting was their reason for existence. For many the storm of spears held no fear. If they fell, the shield-maidens of the Allfather would take them to Valhalla. There they would fight and feast with the gods until Ragnarok, and the end of time.

Ballista wished he shared their confidence. He fiddled with his weapons; half-drawing his sword, then snapping it back, doing the same with his dagger. *Allfather, do not let me disgrace myself in the eyes of the fighting men.*

Menophilus led them out onto the Via Appia.

A crowd milled in front of the Porta Capena. A wagon had shed a wheel. It was wedged under the arch, blocking the gate. At the sight of the barbarians the throng melted away.

'Stand back, Emperor-killer.'

Ballista did as he was told. He was big for his years, but could not match the strength of the older warriors.

'One, two, three.'

They lifted the wagon by brute force. First a yard, then another. Gradually they hauled it clear.

The bed of the wagon was stacked with amphorae. A warrior jumped up, and opened one. He drank. Soon every man had wine.

'No time for drinking.' Menophilus was near beside himself. 'Follow me.'

Sword in one hand, amphora in the other, they surged after the Roman.

The tall façade of the Septizodium loomed ahead. Ballista could not understand this Roman habit of putting up buildings that were not buildings. What was the point of a frontage with no rooms behind, no hall in which a ruler could eat with his warriors, hand out gold?

As they turned into the Via Triumphalis, the first warriors, too full of wine, fell out to be sick.

At their approach, the civilians fled. Drunk barbarians, sword in hand, rampaging through the streets of Rome. It was the stuff of Roman nightmares. One day, thought Ballista, one day.

'Halt!'

Just before the Claudian aqueduct, a fat man was stood in their way. Obviously unaccustomed to running, his chest was heaving.

'Halt by order of the Emperor.'

The warriors stopped. One or two more spewed wine onto the street.

'What is this, Valerius?'

Menophilus had to wait as the other fought for breath.

'The order is countermanded. The Germans are to return to their camp.'

'On whose authority?'

'By order of the sacred Augustus Balbinus.'

The Alamann nudged Ballista. 'You understand more Latin than me. What are they saying?'

'They are arguing.'

'What about?'

'The fat one says Balbinus has ordered us back to the gardens. The other is saying he takes his orders from Pupienus.'

The Alamann took a drink. 'These Romans are shit. Imagine a war-leader who has no trust in his own people and kin, has to recruit a hearth-troop of nothing but outlanders.'

'There are warriors from many tribes in my father's hall.'

'But most who feast in Hlymdale are Angles. We should go back. I have little wish to die for these Romans.'

'We swore on our swords to defend them.'

The Alamann snorted. 'Those oaths were not freely given. You are as much a hostage as me. What does it matter to us who rules these southerners?'

'The Alamann is right,' Calgacus said. 'Fuck them all.'

'No,' Ballista said. 'Even an enforced oath is still an oath. If we break our word, we are no better than them.'

'Did not stop you finishing Maximinus, Emperor-killer.'

Ballista had no answer to that.

'Follow me!'

When the fat Senator went to detain Menophilus, he was shoved aside.

'Follow me!'

The warriors looked at each other.

Ballista stepped up next to Menophilus. He turned and addressed the men of the North in their own language. 'We gave them our word. They give us gold. We must do what is right.'

The Alamann came and stood at the shoulder of Ballista. 'The young Himling may be right. Anyway, it is too long since we killed any Romans.'

Hoom, hoom. The warriors liked the sound of that.

'It is not far,' Menophilus said. 'Pray to the gods, we are not too late.'

CHAPTER 43

The Hippodrome at the East of the Palatine Hill,
Three Days after the Ides of June, AD238

'Wars cost money. Only a tyrant, like Maximinus, resorts to unjust confiscations and stealing the treasures from the temples. The adulteration of the coinage may be unpopular, but the Antoninianus must stay.'

The remaining six members of the *consilium* had managed not to look at the door while Pupienus was speaking.

'Is there anything else?'

'Just one thing, Emperor.' Fulvius Pius spoke hurriedly. Obviously he wanted to be gone as much as the others. 'May I urge that the Board of Twenty continues?'

As a member of the *XXviri Reipublicae Curandae*, Pius had an interest in its continuance. Every mark of status was important to a Senator.

'A good Emperor should take advice from men of experience. The Board will remain.' Pupienus paused, thinking. 'With myself and Balbinus elevated to the throne, there are two vacancies. One already is promised to Catius Clemens.

It is fitting to the spirit of freedom in our reign that the other be filled by an open election in the Senate.'

It is right, it is just, the councillors murmured.

'Then, if that is all, we will detain you no longer.'

It was beneath the *dignitas* of Senators to scramble and push, but the pavilion emptied with rapidity. In moments Pupienus was alone with Fortunatianus, his secretary, and Sanctus, the *Ab Admissionibus*, at the door.

Where was Menophilus with the German Guard?

Pupienus went outside.

His brother-in-law, Sextius Cethegillus, was waiting.

'I thought you might like the company.'

'That is considerate, old friend.' Considerate and brave.

The sunken garden was quiet. No noise penetrated from the rest of the Palace, let alone the city beyond.

The Emperor Alexander had kept his aviaries here. Was it twenty thousand doves? Pupienus had liked the gentle noise they made. It was typical of that ineffectual Emperor that he had issued proclamations boasting of the revenue from the sale of the eggs. And all the while his avaricious mother had stripped the treasury bare.

Where was Menophilus?

'We should go and see Balbinus.'

The four of them climbed the steps.

The great entrance hall to the Palace was unnaturally empty as they passed. There were no more than a dozen petitioners. All were down at heel, a couple looked as if they were not in their right minds. Yet the Praetorians and imperial slaves were at their posts. The soldiers saluted smartly enough, and the members of the *familia Caesaris* bowed.

Pupienus wondered if he should order the doors bolted and barred. Yet that simple precaution might induce panic. Every act of an Emperor was symbolic.

Coming out into the Sicilia courtyard, Pupienus was

dazzled by the sunlight flashing off the walls. The distinctive cadences of a Sophist declaiming issued from the open doors of the Aula Regia. Having no desire to listen to extempore oratory, Pupienus took the arm of Cethegillus. They walked under the porticos, the other two respectfully followed.

This place had seen the first act of the revolution in Rome. Pupienus remembered the corpse of Maximinus' Praetorian Prefect lying abandoned by the fountain; the white toga in the pool of blood, the squalidness of violent death. Vitalianus had not been a bad man; nothing more than an equestrian functionary promoted above his capabilities. Yet to unseat the tyrant it had been necessary that Vitalianus die. Menophilus had acted with decision that morning. There was no reason to suppose that he would do less today.

The summoning of the Germans might be unnecessary. Praetextatus was an anxious fool. His report of unrest in the Praetorian camp might prove unfounded.

A ripple of applause from the audience chamber. The sound of Balbinus delivering his verdict. An effete voice, but strong. You would have thought it would have been weaker after a lifetime of excess.

Louder applause, its sycophantic nature clear even beyond the threshold.

It was time to enter.

The audience turned and acknowledged the entrance of Pupienus. Out of the corner of his eye, he saw young Gordian peeping around the inner door that led to the *lararium* and the stairs to the rooms up under the roof. The boy was no sooner glimpsed than gone. More likely he was hiding from his ghastly mother than worshipping the household gods.

'Health and great joy.' Balbinus was particularly pleased with himself.

'Health and great joy.'

The result of the contest was evident. Apsines of Gadara

was preening himself like a peacock. Periges the Lydian was thoroughly downcast. Perhaps, Pupienus thought, he could put his co-Augustus to work filling the imperial coffers by removing the tax exemptions from all the myriad Sophists and their like. The gods knew he was fit for nothing else.

Pupienus addressed the audience. 'We will detain you no longer.'

As they began to file out, he spoke softly to Balbinus. 'You heard from Valerius Priscillianus about the unrest in the Praetorian camp?'

'Yes.' Balbinus did not look at him, but gazed over his shoulder at the niches with the statues of the gods.

'Menophilus is bringing the German Guard.'

Balbinus smiled, as if he knew some important secret. 'Do you follow those philosophers who believe power is indivisible, or are you motivated solely by ambition?'

'What are you talking about?'

'I countermanded the order.'

'Why?'

An expression of great cunning appeared on the face of Balbinus.

'Why?'

Balbinus leant close. His breath reeked of stale wine, and other hard to define but unpleasant things. 'Your sons will not inherit the throne.'

Balbinus had spoken too loudly. Those who had not left stopped.

'Are you drunk?'

There was no sound in the lofty hall, only the hush of great fear.

Pupienus pitched his voice to carry. 'Gordian has been proclaimed Caesar. He is our heir.'

'Not if he is tragically killed, along with me, in an uprising by your barbarians.'

Through the open windows, from down towards the Forum, came a confused roaring, like the crowd in the arena.

Pupienus strode across the hall, and out onto the balcony.

Armed men – Praetorians – were emerging from under the arch, running up towards the Palace.

Pupienus rounded on Balbinus. The porcine face was white with terror. This was not Balbinus' doing. He was incapable.

The Aula Regia was almost empty. Even Cethegillus was gone. Only Fortunatianus and Sanctus remained.

'The tunnel to the Capitol.' Balbinus blundered back across the room.

Pupienus would not let his *dignitas* desert him now. 'Fortunatianus, slip away, save yourself. You too, Sanctus.'

Even in this extremis, Pupienus would not run.

When he reached the door, it was blocked by the bulk of Balbinus. Beyond he saw the first soldiers.

Pupienus stepped back into the centre of the hall. All was not lost, not while he maintained his self-control. They were common soldiers. He was an Emperor. Imperial majesty and eloquence could yet return them to their duty.

Balbinus was cowering behind a column.

Pupienus drew himself up straight.

The Praetorians stopped a few paces away, perhaps over-awed by their surroundings, and the still figure facing them.

Pupienus bared his throat.

'My death at your hands is of no great consequence. I am an old man, and have lived a long and distinguished life. Every man's life must come to an end some time.'

A wall of hostile faces. The little Greek Timesitheus among them.

'You are the guardians and protectors of the Emperors. For you of all people to become murderers, to stain your hands with the blood of a citizen, let alone an Emperor, is an act of sacrilege.'

One or two were looking unhappily at the floor.

'You have taken the most sacred of oaths. I have kept faith with you. There is no way in which I have harmed you. I am yours, and you are mine. Return to your oath.'

Some went to sheath their swords.

'If you are still upset at the death of Maximinus, that was none of my doing. If you demand justice for his murderers, they will be arrested and delivered to you in chains.'

Balbinus came out from behind the pillar. 'There will be no recriminations. We will reward you if you hand over the ringleaders.' He thrust a fat, bejewelled hand at Timesitheus.

The little Greek stepped forward. With the pommel of his sword, he hit Balbinus hard in the face.

Balbinus reeled back, blood seeping between his fingers.

The soldiers rushed at Pupienus. If he had been wearing a toga, he would have pulled it over his head like Julius Caesar. A soldier punched him in the stomach. He doubled up.

'You cruel, miserable old bastard.' The soldier hit him in the ribs.

More blows from all directions. His legs were knocked out from under him. He was on the floor. They were kicking him. He covered his head with his arms. Boots thumping into his body, his arms, his head.

'Not a beating, kill them.' Timesitheus was shouting. 'Finish them.'

'Have some fun first, sir.'

Hands were tearing at Pupienus' tunic, ripping off his under things.

He was hauled to his feet.

Across the hall, Balbinus likewise was naked. Great rolls of flesh juddering, as he stumbled this way and that, as they pricked him with the points of their swords. Red grazes and nicks blossoming on the white skin.

A soldier grabbed Pupienus by the beard. 'You will not be needing this where you are going.' He yanked out a handful of hair. The others laughed. More reached in to pluck clumps from his beard.

'Off to the camp with them, boys. Teach them the meaning of suffering.'

Pupienus was manhandled through the corridors of the Palace. Nearby he could hear Balbinus pleading and sobbing. The fat fool deserved everything. This was his fault.

'Kill them.'

'All in good time,' a soldier said to Timesitheus.

There were more soldiers outside. They too were determined to beat the fallen Emperors. Pupienus was sent sprawling. A ring of boots and legs. They spat on him as they kicked and stamped.

There were broken teeth in Pupienus' mouth, the taste of blood. Self-control. He would not beg like Balbinus. His body was nothing. The sound of screaming, his own. Self-control.

Pupienus heard and felt a rib break under a hobnailed boot. He did not deserve this. He had done no wrong. All his life he had served the *Res Publica*. It had been no crime, no impiety to help his father out of this world.

'The Germans are coming!'

Was it true?

The beating stopped.

Menophilus would save him. Then he would deal with these treacherous bastards. They would know the meaning of suffering.

Pupienus was rolled onto his back.

A bearded soldier looking down the length of his sword. The point at Pupienus' throat.

'So perish Emperors chosen by fools.'

The soldier put his weight into the thrust.

*

'Wait!'

Already the Praetorians were leaving, heading back down the path to the Forum.

'Wait!' Timesitheus shouted again.

'The Germans are coming,' one of the soldiers said. 'We need to get back to the camp.'

'They can do nothing. The Emperors are dead. They will go home.'

The nearest Praetorians stopped and regarded him.

'The thing is not finished. Search the Palace. Find Gordian. You must not let the boy get away.'

EPILOGUE

Rome

The Palace,
Three Days after the Ides of June, AD238

The young Caesar threw his cavalry across the river. They were brightly painted, and wonderfully detailed. Having better toys was one of the advantages of being Caesar. There were not many.

Gordian, as Junius Balbus now had to call himself, hated living in the Palace. It was too big, full of hushed and sinister passageways. And there were always people watching you, even more than in the *Domus Rostrata* of the Gordiani, let alone the relative obscurity of his father's house. At least he had found this secret place up under the roof with its views out over the city. What was it his tutor Gallicanus called it? A *coign of vantage*. Gallicanus was very stern, but he was full of funny expressions.

Sounds of raised voices echoed up from somewhere below. The *Silentarii* would deal with them. That was what they did. Gordian went back to his game. His mother did not approve. Now he was the head of the family, he must act like a man.

He tried to keep out of his mother's way. She did nothing but nag, or cry. Gordian was never sure which of the dead she was mourning: his dead father, or his grandfather or uncle.

The commotion increased. It was coming from directly outside. Gordian went and looked. A mob of Praetorians was pulling along two men. The men were old and naked. One was very fat. The Praetorians were beating and kicking them, pulling at their hair and beards. It took Gordian a moment to realize the victims were the Emperors Pupienus and Balbinus. There was an eddy in the crowd. Steel flashed in the sunshine. The soldiers were running; most down the hill, some out of sight back into the Palace. They left behind in the street the two naked, mutilated corpses.

Noises coming closer. The boy had nowhere to hide. Where was Gallicanus? Where was his mother? Hobnailed boots coming up the stairs. Gordian drew the child's sword his uncle had given him. If he was going to die, it would be like uncle Gordian; blade in hand.

The Praetorians burst in. Gordian felt the piss run hot on his thighs. The soldiers laughed. They pulled him along with them. They smelled of leather and garlic. There was blood on their hands and arms.

'Where are you taking me?'

The rough man holding his arm laughed. 'To your birth-right, lord – the throne of the Caesars.'

HISTORICAL
AFTERWORD

Time and Distance

The Roman Empire was huge. From Rome to Samosata, the easternmost location in this novel, was some fifteen hundred miles *as the crow flies*. On land using the *Cursus Publicus*, the imperial posting service with its relays of remounts, a man might expect to travel at about fifty miles in a day, rising to some hundred and fifty if there was an emergency. But such figures are misleading. Most travel was far slower, and the weather, state of the roads, availability of food and fodder, and attitude of traveller and those encountered conspired to make all journey times unreliable. Travel by sea could be very quick – Sicily to Egypt in just seven days – but it was even less reliable than ashore: a message sent by Caligula from Rome to Syria took three months to get there.

All this, and much more, is set out with wonderful clarity in two books by Lionel Casson, *Travel in the Ancient World* (Baltimore, and London, 1974); *Ships and Seamanship in the Ancient World* (2nd ed., Baltimore, and London, 1995).

In this novel the reader will often know of events long before characters on the frontiers.

MAXIMINUS THRAX

A new biography, *Maximinus Thrax: Strongman Emperor of Rome*, will be published this year. The author, Paul Pearson, was kind enough to send me an advance copy. The book is an engaging popular account, although the attempt, in the face of over a century of scholarship, to revive the theory that the *Augustan History* (see Afterword to *Blood & Steel*) was the work of six men around AD300, not one author about a century later, might not convince.

MINOR SOURCES

Three Latin historians writing in the second half of the fourth century cover the years AD235–238. Aurelius Victor and Eutropius have been translated into English by H.W. Bird, both volumes published in the Translated Texts for Historians series (Liverpool, 1993; and 1994). The anonymous *Epitome de Caesaribus* is available on the internet in the translation of T.M. Banchich (www.roman-emperors.org/epitome.htm).

All three accounts are very short and very unreliable. Their numerous verbal similarities, and shared errors and idiosyncrasies, lead almost all scholars to consider that the texts drew the vast majority of their information from one, no longer extant, Latin history written some time earlier in the fourth century. The latter usually is called the *Kaisergeschichte* ('Imperial History'), the name given it by A. Enmann, the German scholar who in 1883 first argued for its existence.

The late Greek historians, although also brief and inaccurate, are independent of the Latin tradition. The fifth-century Zosimus is translated by R.T. Ridley (Canberra, 1982), and the twelfth-century Zonaras by T.M. Banchich and E.N. Lane (London, and New York, 2009).

Reading for Herodian was given in the Afterword to *Iron & Rust*, and for the *Augustan History* in *Blood & Steel*.

The Twelfth *Sibylline Oracle* ends with the death of Alexander Severus and the Thirteenth begins with the reign of Gordian III, thus we are deprived of their extraordinary mix of popular history and invention masquerading as prophecy for the reign of Maximinus and the tumultuous year AD238.

Senatorial Debates

For the meeting places and procedure of the Senate, see R.J.A. Talbert, *The Senate of Imperial Rome* (Princeton, 1984).

Rome

Occasionally a book changes the way history is studied. *The Power of Images in the Age of Augustus* by Paul Zanker (English translation Ann Arbor, 1988) put visual images and the built environment of the city at the centre of Roman political and intellectual history.

The best book to have to hand when thinking about the ancient city while walking the modern is *Rome: An Oxford Archaeological Guide* by Amanda Claridge (2nd edition, Oxford, 2010).

Invaluable in the library is *A New Topographical Dictionary of Ancient Rome* by L. Richardson (Baltimore, and London, 1992).

Aquileia

In Roman times a city with a population perhaps approaching a hundred thousand, Aquileia now is a quiet village of some three thousand souls. Most of the site is unexcavated, but it is easy enough on the ground to explore the Forum and docks, and walk the lines of the walls in the footsteps of Menophilus.

For this novel, the Temple of Belenus is placed where the Basilica now stands.

I have not discovered any useful studies in English. Those with Italian might start with A. Calderini, *Aquileia romana* (Milan, 1930).

STOICISM

The philosophy of Menophilus owes a lot to Marcus Aurelius' *The Meditations*, as translated by M. Staniforth (Harmondsworth, 1964), and Seneca, as recreated by James Romm in *Dying Every Day: Seneca at the Court of Nero* (New York, 2014).

More technical guidance was drawn from various essays in *The Cambridge Companion to The Stoics*, edited by B. Inwood (Cambridge, 2003).

CHRISTIANS

Introductions that are a pleasure to read are *Christianizing the Roman Empire* by Ramsay MacMullen (New Haven, 1984), and *Pagans and Christians* by Robin Lane Fox (Harmondsworth, 1986).

Students of the early Church will note that I have diverged from the commonly accepted chronology of the bishops of Rome. This has been done purely to fit the story. Yet, in mitigation, the sources are unreliable and divergent. My version can be made to fit that of Eusebius in *The History of the Church*.

Mark Edwards of Christ Church, Oxford, was kind enough to create a reading list for me on Christian rituals. As a novice I found particularly helpful the sources and commentary in *Early Christian Worship* by Paul Bradshaw (London, 1996).

PROSTITUTION

'Sex for Sale: Prostitutes', Chapter 7 in *Invisible Romans* by Robert Knapp (London, 2011), provides a popular introduction to the subject, *'Quae Corpore Quaestum Facit'* by Rebecca Flemming, *Journal of Roman Studies* 88 (1999), 38–61, a scholarly one.

There are two extended studies by T.A.J. McGinn: *Prostitution, Sexuality, and the Law in Ancient Rome* (Oxford, and New York, 1998), and *The Economy of Prostitution in the Roman World* (Ann Arbor, 2004).

Much of the backstory and thought world of Caenis was constructed from Alciphron, *Letters of Courtesans*, and Lucian, *Dialogues of the Courtesans* (both are translated in the Loeb Classical Library).

SIEGE WARFARE

An overview of this topic by the author will be found in *The Encyclopedia of Ancient Battles*, edited by Harry Sidebottom, and Michael Whitby (forthcoming in 2016).

In this novel the narrative draws on additional material from the later sieges of Aquileia by the armies of the Emperor Julian (Ammianus XXI. 11. 2–12.20), and Attila (Procopius, *Vandal Wars* 3.4.30–5; Jordanes, *Getica* 219–21).

QUOTES

Ovid, *Tristia* III.3; and *Ep. Pont.* III.1 in Ch.11; and *Ep. Pont.* I.3; and *Tristia* V.7 in Chapter 24 are recalled by Honoratus in the translation of Peter Green (London, 1994).

Menophilus in Chapter 14 brings to mind the words of Epictetus, *Handbook* 37, in an English translation as revised by Robin Hard (London, and Rutland, Vermont, 1995).

The speeches of Crispinus and Maximinus' tribune in Chapter 16 are adapted from the translation by C.R. Whittaker (Cambridge, Mass., 1970) of the words given to them by Herodian VIII.3.4–7.

In Chapter 29 Apsines has quoted Virgil, *Aeneid* 5.438-442, in the translation of Frederick Ahl (Oxford, 2007).

Pupienus is right that the speech of Apsines in Chapter 33 smells of the lamp and textbook. It is slightly rewritten from the guide to addressing an Emperor by Menander Rhetor, translated by D.A. Russell, and N.G. Wilson (Oxford, 1981).

The poem that comes to Ballista in Chapter 42 is *The Wanderer*, in the translation of Kevin Crossley-Holland, *The Anglo-Saxon World* (Woodbridge, 1982).

HOMAGES

Writing a novel from multiple points of view is a challenge. It seems a good idea to learn from the best. All my novels contain homages to previous writers. *Fire & Sword* contains echoes of E.L. Doctorow, *The March* (2005), Sebastian Faulks, *A Week in December* (2009), and Hilary Mantel, *A Place of Greater Safety* (1992).

THANKS

As ever it gives me pleasure to thank the people whose affection and encouragement, criticism and forbearance, make it possible for me to write.

Family: my wife Lisa, sons Tom and Jack, mother Frances, and aunt Terry.

Friends: Katie and Jeremy Habberley, Peter and Rachel Cosgrove, Jeremy Tinton, Michael Dunne, Imo Dawson, and Vaughan Jones.

Professionals and friends: James Gill at United Agents; Cassie Browne, Kate Elton, Roger Cazalet, Liz Dawson, Ann Bissell, Charlotte Cray, Damon Greeney, and Adam Humphrey at HarperCollins; Maria Stamatopoulou, and Perry Gauci at Lincoln College.

Finally: Richard Marshall, for all his meticulous work preparing the Glossary and List of Characters, and for his kind words about the novel. This one is dedicated to him.

FIRE & SWORD
GLOSSARY

The definitions given here are geared to *Fire & Sword*. If a word or phrase has several meanings, only that or those relevant to this novel tend to be given.

1st Cohort Ulpia Galatarum: First Ulpian Cohort of Galatians, unit of auxiliary infantry originally recruited by the Emperor Trajan from Galatia (central Turkey), now stationed in Aquileia.

A Cubiculo: Official in charge of the bedchamber.

A Rationibus: Official in charge of the Emperor's finances.

Ab Admissionibus: Official who controlled admission into the presence of the Roman Emperor; sometimes translated here as Master of Admissions.

Achaea: Roman province of Greece.

Acropolis: Sacred citadel of a Greek city.

Ad Palmam: Oasis on the margin of the Lake of Triton (Chott el Djerid), south-west of Africa Proconsularis.

Adiabene: Ancient region corresponding to north-eastern Iraq.

Aequum est, iustum est: Latin, 'it is right, it is just'; imperial acclamation for Pupienus and Balbinus, recorded in ancient sources.

Aesontius river: The modern Isonzo river, flowing from the Julian Alps into the Adriatic.

Africa Proconsularis: Roman province of central North Africa, roughly modern Tunisia.

***Ahuramazda* (also *Mazda*)**: 'The Wise Lord', the supreme god of Zoroastrianism, chief religion of the Sassanid empire.

Alamann: From a confederation of German tribes living along the upper Rhine. The name probably means 'all men', either in the sense of men from various tribes or 'all real men'.

Alban Hills: Volcanic region ten miles south-east of Rome, site of the legionary camp of the 2nd Parthian Legion.

Alexandria: Capital of the Roman province of Egypt; second city of the empire. Point from which the grain fleets set sail for Rome.

Allfather: Epithet of Woden, the supreme god in Norse mythology.

Altar of Jupiter Optimus Maximus: An outdoor altar in front of the Temple of Jupiter Optimus Maximus on the Capitoline Hill.

Altar of Peace: Altar standing in the Forum of Carthage, dedicated to the Peace brought by the Roman Emperors; its remains are now in the Louvre.

Ambitio: Latin, 'ambition'; also has connotations of vanity.

***Amicus* (plural *amici*)**: Latin, 'friend'.

Amor Mutuus Augustorum: Latin 'the shared love of the Emperors'.

***Amphora* (plural *amphorae*)**: Large Roman earthenware storage vessels.

Angeln: Land of the Angles.

Angles: A north German tribe, living on the Jutland Peninsular in the area now occupied by southern Denmark and the German state of Schleswig-Holstein.

Antonine dynasty: Adoptive family of four 'good' Emperors of Rome, who ruled from AD138–192.

Antoninianus: Silver denomination of Roman coinage; notionally worth two *denarii*, it was debased on introduction and rapidly lost value.

Apollo: Greek god of music and culture.

Apollo Sandaliarius: Famous statue of Apollo in the Street of the Sandal-makers, north-east of the Forum.

Apulia: Modern Puglia, the 'heel' of Italy.

Aquileia: Town in north-east Italy.

Aquitania: Roman province of south-western and central Gaul, an area of modern France.

Arabia: Roman province covering much of modern Jordan and the Sinai peninsula.

Aramaic: Ancient language spoken in much of the Levant and Mesopotamia.

Arch of Septimius Severus: Monumental arch in the north-west corner of the Forum, commemorating the victories of the Emperor Septimius Severus and his sons over the Parthians in AD195 and 197–199.

Arch of Titus: Monumental arch between the Roman Forum and Flavian Amphitheatre, commemorating the re-conquest of Jerusalem in AD70 by the Emperor Titus.

Argiletum: Clay Street, leading from the Subura to the northern side of the Forum, passing between the Senate House and Basilica Aemilia.

Armenia: Ancient buffer kingdom between Rome and Parthia, occupying much of the area south of the Caucasus mountains and west of the Caspian Sea; much larger than the modern region of Armenia.

Arsacid: Dynasty that ruled Parthia 247BC–AD228.

Asia: Roman province in what is now western Turkey.

Atheling: Old English for Lord.

Atrium: Open court in a Roman house.

Augustus **(plural** *Augusti***)**: Name of the first Roman Emperor, subsequently adopted as one of the titles of the office.

Aula Regia: The audience hall of the imperial palace on the Palatine Hill; built by the Emperor Domitian, its ceiling was thirty metres above the floor.

Ausonian: From the Italian peninsular, originally a Greek term.

Autochthonous: From the Greek, literally meaning people sprung out of the earth.

Auxiliaries: Roman regular soldiers serving in a unit other than a legion.

Ave: Latin, 'hail', 'hello'.

Babylon: Major city in ancient Mesopotamia, lying in modern Iraq to the south of Baghdad.

Bacchant: Worshipper of the god of wine, Bacchus.

Bactria: Ancient region lying north of the Hindu Kush and west of the Himalayas.

***Ballistae* (singular *ballista*)**: Roman torsion artillery firing a bolt with great force and accuracy.

Bariduum: Ancient town in modern Croatia; its exact location is now lost.

Basilica: Roman court building and audience chamber.

Basilica Aemilia: Court building on the north-east side of the Roman Forum, originally built in 179BC and restored on several occasions in antiquity.

Baths of Caracalla: Giant bathing and leisure complex dedicated by the Emperor Caracalla in the south of Rome.

Baths of Titus: Large suite of baths built by the Emperor Titus on the flank of the Esquiline Hill.

Batnae: Town in south-eastern Turkey; modern Suruç.

Bedriacum: One of two decisive battles fought in northern Italy by rival Emperors in AD69.

Belenus: Celtic sun god and patron deity of Aquileia.

Bistua Nova: Town in Bosnia and Herzegovina; modern Zenica.

Bithynia: Ancient region lying on the southern shore of the Black Sea.

Bithynia-Pontus: Roman province along the south shore of the Black Sea.

Board of Twenty: see *XXviri Reipublicae Curandae*.

Borysthenes: Maximinus' horse, named from the god of the river Dnieper in Greek mythology.

Bucolic: Ancient genre of poetry dealing with rural themes, from the Greek 'cowherd'.

Byzantium: Greek city lying between the Black Sea and Sea of Marmara; modern Istanbul.

Caecuban: A highly prized sweet white wine grown in the coastal region south of Rome.

Caelian Hill: One of the seven legendary hills of Rome, lying south-east of the Roman Forum.

Caesar: Name of the adopted family of the first Roman Emperor, subsequently adopted as one of the titles of the office; often used to designate an Emperor's heir.

Caledonian: Inhabitant from northern Britain beyond the Roman provinces; roughly modern Scotland.

Campus Praetoria: Literally 'Praetorian Field'; parade ground in front of the Praetorian camp in north-eastern Rome.

Capax imperii: Expression originally used by Tacitus to designate those men 'capable of being Emperor'.

Capitol: One of Rome's seven hills; the ancient citadel of the city, location of the Temple of Jupiter Optimus Maximus.

Capitoline: See Capitol.

Capitoline Games: Quadrennial games celebrated in honour of Jupiter Optimus Maximus, held in the early summer and instituted by the Emperor Domitian, originally with a scandalous Greek element to the festivities, including nude athletics.

Cappadocia: Roman province north of the Euphrates.

Carinae: Literally 'the Keels', fashionable quarter of ancient Rome between the Caelian and Esquiline Hills; now San Pietro in Vincoli.

Carpi: Tribe living north-west of the Black Sea.

Carrhae: Roman frontier town recently captured by the Persians; modern Harran in Turkey.

Carthage: Second city of the western Roman empire; capital of the province of Africa Proconsularis.

Cataphracts: Heavily armoured Roman cavalry, from the Greek word for mail armour.

Catii: The Catius family.

Cella: The main hall of a temple.

Centurion: Officer of the Roman army with the seniority to command a Century.

Century: Roman regular army unit of eighty to a hundred men, commanded by a Centurion.

Cephalonia: Island off the west coast of Greece.

Chryselephantine: From a Greek term meaning gold and ivory, the two materials used to make major cult statues of the gods.

Circumvallation: From a Latin term meaning ringed with ramparts.

Circus: Roman term for a horse-racing track.

Circus Maximus: The great chariot-racing stadium in Rome; it could seat one hundred and fifty thousand spectators.

Classis Moesiaca: Latin, 'Moesian fleet'; the Danube river patrol.

Claudian aqueduct: Major aqueduct built by the Emperor Claudius; once it reached north-eastern Rome, it ran in a south-westerly direction, crossing the valley between the Caelian and Aventine Hills.

Cohort: Unit of Roman soldiers, usually about five hundred men strong.

Collegium (**plural** *Collegia*): Ancient Roman trade guilds and funeral clubs (members of the latter paid a regular fee for the club to arrange an appropriate service when they died); well-organised, they often fell under the sway of powerful politicians, and were responsible for much of the mob violence in the city.

Concordia: Deified abstraction of Imperial Accord; worshipped as a goddess and playing an important role in imperial propaganda.

Conscript Fathers: Honorific form of address used before the Senate.

Consilium: Council, body of advisors, of a senior Roman magistrate or an Emperor.

Consul: In the Republic, the highest office in the Roman state; under the Emperors, a largely honorific and ceremonial position. There were two Consuls at any one time, and under the Emperors, two types: Consuls Ordinarii (singular Ordinarius), who began the year in office (the most prestigious position, giving their names to the year), and Suffect Consuls, men appointed after a Consul Ordinarius had stepped down.

Consular: A former Consul.

Contubernia: A squad of around eight soldiers, from the Latin term to share a tent.

Corcyra: Greek name for the island of Corfu.

Corinthian: From the ancient city of Corinth in the Peloponnese, notorious for its luxurious living and prostitutes.

Cosmos: The universe as conceived of by the Greeks, an orderly, harmonious system, often thought divine in itself.

Crenulations: From the Latin term meaning 'little notches'; the protective battlements of a fortified wall.

Ctesiphon: Capital of the Persian empire, lying on the eastern bank of the Tigris river, twenty miles south of modern Baghdad in Iraq.

Curia: The meeting house of the Senate in Rome (and of town councils in the Latin-speaking provinces); the building erected after a fire in the later third century is still standing.

Custos: Latin, literally 'a guardian'; a male attendant would accompany an upper-class woman, in addition to her maids, when she went out in public.

Cybele: Originally an Asian goddess, brought to Rome and known as the Magna Mater (Great Mother) in Latin. Her most dedicated worshippers were expected to castrate themselves, though this was frowned upon at Rome.

Cynic: The counter-cultural philosophy founded by Diogenes of Sinope in the fourth century BC; its adherents were popularly associated with dogs (the name itself is from the Greek for 'dog') for their barking and snapping at contemporary morality and social customs.

Dacia: Roman province north of the Danube, in the region around modern Romania.

Daemon: Supernatural being; could be applied to many different types: good/bad, individual/collective, internal/external, and ghosts.

Dalmatia: Roman province along the eastern shore of the Adriatic.

Decii: Members of the Decius family; P. Decius Mus and later his son both dedicated their lives and those of the enemy to the gods of the underworld, sacrificing themselves in the thick of battle to ensure victory.

Decimation: Archaic Roman military punishment, very occasionally revived under the empire, involving the execution of every tenth man of a unit, chosen by lot regardless of personal guilt.

Decus et Tutamen: Latin, literally 'honour and safeguard'.

Delphic Apollo: The god Apollo as worshipped at Delphi in Greece.

Delphix: From the tripod tables, originally designed in Delphi, that furnished imperial dining rooms.

Demiurge: In some Greek philosophical systems, the divine figure which fashioned (but did not necessarily create) the cosmos.

Denarius (plural denarii): A Roman silver coin; originally a day's wage for a labourer, though by this period much debased.

Deucalion: In Greek mythology, the son of the god Prometheus, saved from a flood sent by Zeus to punish the arrogance of humanity.

Dignitas: Important Roman concept which covers our idea of dignity but goes much further; famously, Julius Caesar claimed that his *dignitas* meant more to him than life itself.

Dionysus: Greek god of wine; in his youth, toured the East as far as India, introducing its peoples to the cultivation of the vine.

Diplomata (singular diploma): From the Greek term for a letter folded in two; in the Roman empire, an official pass given to persons travelling in the provinces.

Disciplina: Latin, 'discipline'. The Romans' insistence on a high level of military discipline was a core contributor to the effectiveness of their armed forces. In more general terms, possession of this quality was thought by Romans to mark them off from other peoples.

Diva Paulina: Latin, 'The Divine Paulina', title of the wife of Maximinus, deified after her death.

Domina: Latin, 'lady', 'mistress, 'ma'am'; a title of respect.

Dominus: Latin, 'lord', 'master'.

Domus Rostrata: Originally the home of the Republican general Pompey in the fashionable Carinae quarter; decorated with the ramming beaks (Rostra) of the pirate ships he captured, and from which it took its name. Now the seat of the Gordiani.

Donative: Cash reward distributed to soldiers or the plebs by grateful Emperors on their accession, or following victories, notable anniversaries, etc.

Drauhtins: Gothic term for a military or tribal leader.

Druidess: Priestess of Celtic religion.

Durostorum: Roman fortress on the south bank of the Danube; modern Silistra in Bulgaria.

Eclogues: Title of a collection of poems by Virgil; from the Greek *ekloge*, 'extracts'.

Edessa: Frontier city periodically administered by Rome, Persia and Armenia in the course of the third century; modern Şanlıurfa in southern Turkey.

Emona: Modern Ljubljana in Slovenia.

Emporium: From the Latin term for a market or trading post.

Ephesus: Major city founded by Greek colonists on the western coast of modern Turkey.

Epilogue: In ancient rhetoric, the conclusion of a speech; from Greek 'to say in addition'.

Epiphany: The visual manifestation of a deity.

Equestrian: Second rank down in the Roman social pyramid; the elite order just below the Senators.

Equites Singulares: Mounted unit protecting the Emperor.

Erato: The muse of lyric poetry, the genre concerned with personal feelings, love, etc.

Esquiline: One of the seven hills of Rome, rising east of the Roman Forum.

Eternal City: Nickname given to the city of Rome.

Etruria: Region of Italy to the north-west of Rome; roughly modern Tuscany.

Falernian: Very expensive white wine from northern Campania, particularly prized by the Romans.

Familia: A Roman household; for the well off, this included slaves

403

and other dependents; that of the Emperor, the *familia Caesaris*, comprised both servants and the imperial bureaucracy; largely staffed by slaves and freedmen.

Fasces: Bundles of rods for beating malefactors tied around an executioner's axe; symbol of a Roman magistrate's or Emperor's authority.

Festina lente: Latin, 'hurry slowly!'; origin of the English expression 'more haste, less speed'.

Fides: Latin term encompassing good qualities such as trustworthiness, conscientiousness, and protection. A common imperial slogan.

Fides Militum! Romae Aeternae!: Latin 'The faithfulness of the Army'; 'Eternal Rome'; imperial propaganda, often used on coins.

Fidus: Latin, 'faithful'.

Fiscus: Originally the Emperor's privy purse; took over the functions of the state and provincial treasuries.

Flavian Amphitheatre: Giant arena for gladiatorial fights seating sixty thousand spectators; now known as the Coliseum, in antiquity known after the Flavian dynasty of Emperors who built and dedicated the structure.

Flora: Roman goddess of flowers and spring. Her festival was held between April and May.

Fortuna Redux: The Roman goddess of safe returns from long journeys or military campaigns.

Forum Transitorium: A monumental thoroughfare built by the Emperor Nerva, replacing the southern end of the Argiletum as this street approached the original Forum.

Forum: Central square of a Roman city, site of the market place, and government, judicial and religious buildings. In Rome, the oldest and most important public square, originally the scat of the government, littered with honorific statues and monuments going back to the early Republic. Surrounded by temples, court buildings, arches, and the Senate House.

Fratricidal: From the Latin term to kill one's own brother.

Frumentarii (**singular** *frumentarius*): Military unit based on the

Caelian Hill in Rome; the Emperor's secret police; messengers, spies, and assassins.

Furies: Goddesses of vengeance in Greek and Roman religion.

Gallia Lugdunensis: Roman province of north-western and central France.

Gallia Narbonnensis: Roman province of southern Gaul, roughly the French region of Provence.

Gardens of Dolabella: A large estate on the outskirts of Rome where German soldiers were stationed in AD69; its original location is unknown.

Germania: The Roman provinces of Germany, but also used of the lands where the German tribes lived, 'free' Germany beyond direct Roman control.

Germania Superior: More southerly of Rome's two German provinces.

Gordiani: The Gordianus family; in English, Gordian.

Goths: Confederation of Germanic tribes.

Graces: In Greek and Roman religion, a trio of goddesses, the daughters of Zeus.

Graeculus: Latin, 'little Greek'; Greeks called themselves Hellenes, Romans tended not to extend that courtesy but called them *Graeci*; with casual contempt, Romans often went further, to *Graeculi*.

Gudja: A Gothic priest.

Gulf of Tergeste: From the ancient name for Trieste, lying on the northernmost shores of the Adriatic.

Hades: Greek underworld.

Hadrumetum: City on the eastern coast of Africa Proconsularis, modern Sousse in Tunisia.

Haliurunna: A Gothic witch.

Hatra: Independent city state in northern Iraq, fought over by both the Romans and Persians in the early third century.

Hatrene: Inhabitant of Hatra.

Hearth-troop: From the Old English, a warband bound to a particular leader through ties of personal loyalty.

Hecatomb: In Greco-Roman religion, a sacrifice to the gods of a hundred cattle; from the Greek for one hundred.

Hedinsey: An island in the Baltic known from the Norse sagas, here identified as Zealand.

Heliades: In Greek mythology, the daughters of Helios; grieving for their brother Phaethon, they were turned into poplars and their tears into amber.

Helios: Greek sun god.

Hellene: The Greeks' name for themselves; often used with connotations of cultural superiority.

Hellenic: From Greece, a term from the Greeks' name for themselves.

Herakles: In Greek mythology, mortal famed for his strength who subsequently became a god.

Hercules: Roman name for Herakles.

Hierasos river: Greek name for the Alkaliya river, flowing into the Black Sea in eastern Ukraine.

Hilaritas: Latin, 'good-humour', 'cheerfulness'.

Himling: Fictional dynasty ruling over the Angles from the island of Hedinsey.

Hippodrome: Greek, literally 'horse race'; stadium for chariot racing.

Hipposandals: Metal plates secured under the hooves of horses by leather straps; used before the introduction of horse shoes in the fifth century AD.

Hlymdale: Literally, Valley of Uproar, a place name mentioned in the Norse sagas and here given to the ancient settlement excavated at modern Himlingjoe on the island of Zealand; home of the Himlings on Hedinsey.

Hostis: Latin, 'enemy' (usually implying an enemy of the state).

Hydra: In Greek mythology, a serpent with many heads, each of which grew back when cut off.

Hymen: God of marriage in Greek and Roman religion.

Iazyges: Nomadic Sarmatian tribe living on the Steppe north of the Danube on the Great Hungarian Plain.

Icon: From the Greek term for an image.

Ides: Thirteenth day of the month in short months, the fifteenth in long months.

Imperator: Originally an epithet bestowed by troops on victorious generals, became a standard title of the *Princeps*, and thus origin of the English word 'emperor'.

In absentia: Latin, 'while absent'.

Infamia: Latin, 'shame, disgrace'. Prostitutes, who were subject to *infamia*, lacked most basic rights and protections in Roman law.

Intempesta: Meaning 'unwholesome, unhealthy'; name given to the dead of night by the Romans.

Interfectus a latronibus: Latin 'killed by bandits'; around thirty such inscriptions are known from Roman tombs.

Iota: Ninth letter of the Greek alphabet, the smallest and simplest to draw (I in the Roman alphabet).

Istria: Ancient town originally settled by the Greeks, located near the mouth of the Danube on the shores of the Black Sea.

Itineraries: Ancient Roman catalogues of journeys, naming towns and the distances between them; often displayed graphically as rudimentary maps.

Ixion: In Greek mythology, Ixion murdered his father-in-law after refusing to honour a wedding contract, and was punished by being tied to a fiery flying wheel for eternity.

Jupiter Optimus Maximus: Roman king of the gods, 'Jupiter, Greatest and Best'.

Kalends: The first day of each month.

Lake of Curtius: Archaic monument in the middle of the Roman Forum taking the form of a sunken pool with statuary; the Romans themselves did not know its origins.

Lararium: Roman household shrine.

Latrones: Latin, 'bandits'.

Legate: From Latin *legatus*, a high-ranking officer in the Roman army, drawn from the senatorial classes.

Legion: Unit of heavy infantry, usually about five thousand men strong; from mythical times, the backbone of the Roman army; the numbers

407

in a legion and the legions' dominance in the army declined during the third century AD as more and more detachments served away from the parent unit and became more or less independent units.

Legionary: Roman regular soldier serving in a legion.

Libation: Offering of drink to the gods.

Libertas: Latin term for freedom or liberty; a political slogan throughout much of Roman history, though its meaning changed according to an author's philosophical principles or the system of government that happened to be in power. Also worshipped in personified form as a deity.

Liburnian: Under the Roman empire, name given to a small warship, possibly rowed on two levels.

Lictors: Attendants assigned to senior Roman magistrates as bodyguards and ushers; often ex-Centurions.

Logos: A Greek philosophical term meaning 'reason'; in many ancient theological systems, the divine mind said to govern the universe.

Ludus Magnus: Gladiatorial school located to the east of the Flavian Amphitheatre.

Lusitanians: From Lusitania, Roman province of the eastern Iberian peninsula, covering much of modern Portugal.

Lydian: From Lydia; ancient region of western Asia Minor, today western Turkey.

Magna Mater: See Cybele.

Mamuralia: Festival held on the *Ides* of March or the day before; possibly an archaic celebration of the new year, which in the old Roman calendar began in March. Ancient authorities were unsure of its significance; commemorated by ritually beating an old man tied in an animal skin.

Mansio: Rest house run as part of the imperial postal service.

Mappalian Way: Road leading out of Carthage.

Marcianopolis: Roman city in Moesia Inferior; modern Devnya in Bulgaria.

Marcomannic hordes: German tribal confederation only defeated by the Emperor Marcus Aurelius after a series of campaigns lasting more than a decade.

Mars: Roman god of war.

Marsyas: In Greek mythology, a satyr who challenged Apollo to a music contest and was flayed alive for his arrogance.

Master of Admissions: See *Ab Admissionibus*.

Media Atropatene: Persian province on the south-west shores of the Caspian Sea.

Memento more: From Latin, literally 'remember to die'.

Mesopotamia: The land between the rivers Euphrates and Tigris; the name of a Roman province (sometimes called Osrhoene).

Misenum: Base of the Roman fleet on the western shore of the Italian peninsular, modern Miseno.

Moesia: Ancient geographical region following the south bank of the Danube river in the Balkans.

Moesia Inferior: Roman province on the south bank of the lower reaches of the Danube, bounded by Moesia Superior in the west and the Black Sea in the east.

Moesia Superior: Roman province on the south bank of the upper reaches of the Danube, bounded by Pannonia Inferior to the north-west and Moesia Inferior to the east.

Moorish: Belonging to the Mauri tribe that gave its name to Mauretania, western North Africa.

Mos maiorum: 'The way of the ancestors'; fundamental Roman concept that theoretically governed most aspects of public and private life.

Mother Goddess: See Cybele.

Myrmillo: Heavily armoured Roman gladiator, recognisable by their crested helmets; usually men of stronger but less nimble physique.

Naptha: Greek term for liquid petroleum, in the ancient world usually sourced from Mesopotamia.

Narbonnensis: See Gallia Narbonnensis.

Natiso: Ancient name for the Natisone river, flowing between Italy and Slovenia.

Necropolis: Greek term for a cemetery; literally 'city of the dead'.

Negotium: Latin, 'business, both private and public'; literally, not *otium*.

Nemesis: Greek goddess of divine retribution.

Nisean: Ancient Iranian horse breed, prized in antiquity.

Nisibis: Border town that frequently changed hands between Rome and Persia; modern Nusaybin in south-eastern Turkey.

Nobilis: Latin, 'nobleman'; a man from one of the elite families, one of whose ancestors had been Consul.

Nones: The ninth day of a month before the *Ides*, i.e. the fifth day of a short month, the seventh of a long month.

Noricum: Roman province to the north-east of the Alps.

Novus homo: Latin, literally 'new man'; someone whose ancestors had not previously held senatorial rank.

Numidia: Roman province in western North Africa.

Numidian: Inhabitants of the Roman province of western North Africa.

Odeum: Venue for poetry and music competitions constructed by the Emperor Domitian, taking the form of a small theatre.

Odysseus: Legendary Greek warrior and traveller, famed for his guile.

Olbia: City originally founded as a Greek colony on the shores of the Black Sea at the mouth of the Hypanis river, now the Southern Bug in Ukraine.

Oligarchy: From the Greek 'rule by the few'.

Optio: Junior officer in the Roman army, ranked below a Centurion.

Orations: Work by Dio Chrysostom; a set of some eighty essays on various moral and philosophical subjects survive, originally presented as speeches.

Orator: Latin term for a professional public speaker.

Osrhoene: Roman province in northern Mesopotamia.

Ostia: Ancient port of the city of Rome, located at the mouth of the Tiber.

Otium: Latin, 'leisure time'; the ability to indulge in this set the Roman elite apart from the labouring classes.

Ovile: Settlement in the Thracian highlands, named from the Latin for sheepfold.

Palatine: One of the fabled seven hills of Rome, south-east of the

Roman Forum. Site of the imperial palaces; the English term is derived from their location.

Palestina: Palestinian Syria, Roman province.

Palmatis: A Roman village; possibly modern Kochular in Bulgaria.

Palmyra: Important 'free' city in the Roman province of Syria, governed by native rulers.

Panegyric: Formal speech in praise of something or someone, usually an Emperor; sycophantic and cloying for modern tastes, but a highly prized genre in antiquity.

Pannonia: Roman territory to the south of the Danube, split into two provinces.

Pannonia Inferior: Roman province in the central Balkans, straddling the upper reaches of the Danube.

Pannonia Superior: Roman province north-west of Pannonia Inferior, roughly corresponding with western Hungary and northern Croatia.

Pantheon library: Library attached to the Pantheon, a colossal domed temple dedicated to all the gods; rebuilt by the Emperor Hadrian, it is one of the best-preserved buildings to survive from ancient Rome.

Parricide: From the Latin, literally 'relative killing'.

Parthian: From the region of north-east Iran; seat of the Arsacid dynasty, its name came to be synonymous with their empire.

Patrician: People of the highest social status at Rome; originally descendants of those men who sat in the very first meeting of the free Senate after the expulsion of the last of the mythical kings of Rome in 509BC; under the Principate, Emperors awarded new families patrician status.

Phaethon: In Greek mythology, the son of Helios, the sun god; begged to drive his father's sun chariot, but when this ran out of control, was killed by Zeus to prevent the earth's combustion.

Phalanx: Ancient term for a dense formation of heavily armed warriors, pioneered by the Greeks.

Phoenician: From Phoenicia, an ancient region lying in the Roman provinces of Syria.

Phrygian: From the ancient region lying to the west of central Turkey.

Piquet: A soldier or small unit of soldiers placed in a forward position to warn against an enemy advance.

Pisae: Ancient name for the town of Pisa in northern Italy.

Plato's Academy: Plato's original school of philosophy, named after the grove of Akademia in which it met, north of the city walls of Athens.

Plebeians: See Plebs.

Plebs urbana: Poor of the city of Rome, in literature usually coupled with an adjective labelling them as dirty, superstitious, lazy, distinguished from the *plebs rustica*, whose rural lifestyle might make them less morally dubious.

Plebs: Technically, all Romans who were not patricians; more usually, the non-elite.

Poliorcetic: From the Greek, 'things belonging to sieges'; the science of besieging a city.

Pons Sonti: Ruined bridge spanning the Aesontius river on the main road to Aquileia.

Pontifex Maximus: Most prestigious priesthood in Roman religion, monopolized by the Emperors.

Porta Capena: Gate through which the Via Appia entered south-east Rome, near the Caelian Hill.

Post House: See *Mansio*.

Praefectus Annonae: Prefect of the Grain Supply. Title of official in charge of the grain supply of Rome.

Praefectus Urbi: see Prefect of the City.

Praenomen* and *nomen: Most Roman citizens had three names, a *praenomen* (first name), *nomen* (clan-name) and surname (often a nickname). Accordingly, anyone given Roman citizenship adopted three names as a sign of their new status, usually taking the *praenomen* and *nomen* of the person who made the grant. So Dernhelm, nicknamed Ballista in Latin, became known as Marcus Clodius Ballista after he became a Roman citizen.

Praetor: Roman magistrate in charge of justice, senatorial office second in rank to the Consuls.

Praetorian camp: Barracks of the Praetorian Guard, encircled by massive brick walls, located in north-eastern Rome.

Praetorian Guard: Unit of elite soldiers, organised into ten Cohorts, each with a thousand troops; the Emperor's personal guard in Rome, though detachments also served alongside the Emperor with the field armies campaigning along the frontiers.

Praetorian Prefect: Commander of the Praetorians, an equestrian; one of the most prestigious and powerful positions in the empire.

Praetorians: Soldiers of the Praetorian Guard, the Emperor's bodyguard and the most prestigious and highly paid unit in the empire. Unfortunately for the Emperors, their loyalty could be bought with surprising ease.

Prefect: Flexible Latin title for many officials and officers.

Prefect of Egypt: Governor of Egypt; because of the strategic importance of the province, this post was never trusted to Senators (who might be inspired to challenge the Emperor) but was always filled by equestrians.

Prefect of the Camp: Officer in charge of equipment, supply, and billeting.

Prefect of the City: In Latin, *Praefectus Urbi*. Senior senatorial post in the city of Rome.

Prefect of the Fleet: Equestrian officer commanding one of the Roman fleets at Ravenna or Misenum.

Prefect of the Grain Supply: See *Praefectus Annonae*.

Prefect of the Horse Guards: Officer commanding the Equites Singulares.

Prefect of the Watch: Equestrian officer in charge of Rome's *vigiles*.

Priapic: Like Priapus, a Roman rustic god usually depicted with giant genitalia.

Primus Pilus: The most senior Centurion in a Roman Legion.

Princeps Peregrinorum: Officer in command of the *frumentarii*; the Emperor's spymaster.

Procurator: Latin title for a range of officials, under the Principate typically appointed by the Emperor to oversee the collection of taxes in the provinces and keep an eye on their senatorial governors.

Prometheus: Divine figure, one of the Titans; variously believed to have created mankind out of clay, tricked the gods into accepting only the bones and fat of sacrifices, and stolen fire from Olympus for mortals.

Proskynesis: Greek, 'adoration'; given to the gods and during the course of the third century AD, increasingly demanded by Emperors. There were two types: full prostration on the ground, or bowing and blowing a kiss with the finger tips.

Providentia: Latin, 'providence, foresight'; an abstract deity playing an important part in imperial propaganda, guiding the actions of the Emperor for the benefit of his subjects.

Puteoli: Coastal city in Campania; modern Pozzuoli.

Quaestor: Roman magistrate originally in charge of financial affairs, senatorial office second in rank to the Praetors.

Quantum libet, Imperator: Latin, 'whatever pleases, Emperor'.

Quies: Latin, 'peace', 'lethargy'.

Quirites: Archaic way of referring to the citizens of Rome; sometimes used by those keen to evoke the Republican past.

Ragnarok: In Norse paganism the death of gods and men, the end of time.

Ravenna: Base of the Roman fleet on the Adriatic Sea in north-eastern Italy.

Reiks: A Gothic chief or warlord.

Res Publica: Latin, 'the Roman Republic', the free state usurped by the Emperors, under whom it continued to mean the Roman empire.

Retiarius: Type of lightly armoured gladiator armed with a net and trident.

Rex: Latin, 'king'.

Rhetorician: Professional public speaker from the Greek 'rhetor'; equivalent to an orator in Latin.

Rider God: A provincial deity worshipped in Pannonia and Moesia, based on elements of Roman and local religious traditions.

Romae Aeternae: 'To eternal Rome'; a political slogan found on coins of the Gordiani.

Romanitas: Roman-ness; increasingly important concept by the third century, with connotations of culture and civilization.

Rostra: Speaking platform at the western end of the Roman Forum; took its name from the beaks (*rostra*) of enemy warship with which it was decorated.

Roxolani: Nomadic barbarian tribe living on the Steppe north of the Danube and west of the Black Sea.

Sabine: From Sabinium, an ancient region in the central Apennines north-east of Rome, famed for its agriculture.

Sacramentum: Roman military oath, taken extremely seriously.

Sacred Way: At Rome, a processional route running below the northern flank of the Palatine and passing south of the Temple of Venus and Rome, ending at the Roman Forum to the west; at Ephesus, main road paved with marble passing the Library of Celsus and leading down to the major shrine of the city.

Saecular Games: Games notionally held once every hundred years, marking the passing of one age (measured by the supposed maximum length of a human life) and the beginning of a new one; the Emperor Claudius wished to have the honour of holding the games despite an interval of barely sixty years having passed since the last celebration, and two competing cycles were thus adopted; most recently celebrated by Antoninus Pius in AD148 and Septimius Severus in AD204.

Saldis: A small town in the Salvus valley, located in modern Croatia.

Salona: Roman capital of the province of Dalmatia, sited near modern Solin in Croatia.

Salus: Roman god of safety and health.

Salutatio: An important Roman social custom; friends and clients of the wealthy and influential were expected to wait on their patrons at daybreak, being admitted into the atrium to greet them and see if they could be of any service in the day's business.

Samnite: Type of gladiator, who fought with a short sword and large rectangular shield. In addition to a closed, high-crested helmet, only the left leg and right arm were armoured.

Samosata: City on the right bank of the Euphrates in south-eastern Turkey protecting an important crossing point; now flooded by the Atatürk Dam.

Sarcophagus: From Greek, literally 'flesh eater'; a stone chest containing a corpse and displayed above ground, often highly decorated.

Sarmatian: Nomadic peoples living north of the Danube.

Sassanid: Name for the Persians, from the dynasty that overthrew the Parthians in the 220s AD and was Rome's great eastern rival until the seventh century AD.

Satyr: In Greek and Roman mythology, half-goat half-man creatures with excessive sexual appetites.

Scamander: River flowing across the plain of Troy, personified as a god in the epic poetry of Homer.

Sciron: In Greek mythology, a divine-born bandit living on the Isthmus of Corinth, who enslaved travellers and disposed of those he tired of by throwing them into the sea. Fittingly, he met his own end in the same manner.

Scythian: Term used by the Greeks and Romans for peoples living to the north and east of the Black Sea.

Selene: Moon goddess of Greek religion.

Senate: The council of Rome, under the Emperors composed of about six hundred men, the vast majority ex-magistrates, with some imperial favourites. The richest and most prestigious group in the empire and once the governing body of the Roman Republic; increasingly side-lined by the Emperors.

Senate House: See Curia.

Senator: Member of the Senate, the council of Rome. The semi-hereditary senatorial order was the richest and most prestigious group in the empire.

Septizodium: Purely decorative monument built by Septimius Severus at the foot of the Palatine Hill, fronting the Via Appia.

Servitium: Roman town whose name literally means servitude, slavery. Modern Gradiška on the northern border of Bosnia Herzegovina.

Sesterces: Roman coin denomination; used as standard in ancient accounts.

Seven hills: Metonym for Rome, from the seven hills on which the city was said to have been built; ancient lists, however, do not agree on their identity.

Shahba: Village on the border of Syria Phoenice and Arabia; some miles north of the modern town of Bosra on the southern Syrian border.

Shrine of Abundance: Minor temple situated on the Capitol; sacred to Ops, the goddess of abundant harvests.

Sicilia: Monumental courtyard in the imperial palace on the Palatine Hill, named after Sicily, decorated with panels of reflective stone, surrounding a lake with an island at the centre.

Silenus: In Greek mythology, the chief satyr.

Silentarii: Roman officials who, as their title indicates, were employed to maintain silence and decorum at the imperial court.

Simulacrum: Latin, 'imitation'.

Singara: Highly fortified eastern outpost of the Roman empire in northern Iraq; modern Balad Sinjar.

Sirmium: Strategic border town in Pannonia Inferior; modern Sremska Mitrovica in Serbia.

Sophist: A high-status teacher, usually of rhetoric; the Sophists often travelled from city to city giving instruction and delivering speeches for entertainment.

Speculatores: Roman army scouts and spies.

Sporteoli: 'Little buckets'; mocking name for the *vigiles*, who carried buckets of earth or water to put out fires.

Stadium of Alexander: Monumental running track at Rome, originally built by the Emperor Domitian following Greek models; restored by the Emperor Alexander after a fire, it was subsequently known by his name.

Statue of Victory: Statue of the goddess placed at the far end of the Curia; before each meeting of the Senate, rituals were performed at the accompanying altar.

Stoic: Ancient school of philosophy; followers were instructed to believe that everything which does not affect one's moral purpose is an irrelevance; so poverty, illness, bereavement and death cease to be things to fear and are treated with indifference.

Street of Saturn: Thoroughfare in an upmarket residential quarter of Carthage.

Street of the Sandal-makers: Street in ancient Rome running behind the Forum of Augustus and Temple of Peace.

Stylus: Pointed implement of metal or bone, used for writing in wax.

Styx: River marking the border of Hades in Greek mythology; impassable to the living, the dead were rowed across, but only if they had been buried, usually with coins to pay the ferryman (typically placed in the mouth).

Subura: Poor quarter in the city of Rome.

Succurrite: Latin, 'help me, save me'.

Suebian Sea: Ancient name for the Baltic.

Symposium: Greek drinking party, adopted as social gathering of choice by the Roman elite.

Syria Coele: Hollow Syria, Roman province.

Syria Phoenice: Phoenician Syria, Roman province.

Tartarus: In Greek mythology, a dungeon underneath Hades for the punishment of the wicked.

Telamon: Modern Talamone on the north-west shore of Italy.

Temple of Concordia Augusta: Also known as the Temple of Concordia or Temple of Augustan Concord; sited at the western end of the Forum in Rome, and dedicated to the deified abstraction of a harmonious Roman society under the Emperors. Its symbolic associations led to its occasional use for meetings of the Senate, particularly when agreement on a difficult issue was needed.

Temple of Cybele: Sited on the south-western corner of the Palatine.

Temple of Jupiter Optimus Maximus: Largest and most sacred temple in Rome, sited on the top of the Capitol; often used to hold the most important meetings of the Senate.

Temple of Minerva: Dedicated to the Roman goddess of wisdom and the arts; located at the northern end of the Forum Transitorium.

Temple of Peace: Monumental building with planted courtyard north-east of the Roman Forum.

Temple of Venus and Rome: Temple designed by the Emperor Hadrian with back-to-back shrines for Venus, Roman goddess of love, and Rome, a deified personification of the city. In Latin, Roma (Rome) spelled backwards is *amor*, love. Situated east of the Roman Forum on the north side of the Sacred Way.

Tepula aqueduct: Possibly given this name because its water was tepid. It ran across north-east Rome near the Praetorian camp; not usually considered fit for drinking, in calmer times it was used to fill baths and water gardens.

Terpsichore: One of the nine muses; the goddess of dancing and choral poetry.

Tervingi: Gothic tribe living between the Danube and Dnieper rivers.

Testudo: Latin, literally 'tortoise'; by analogy, a Roman infantry formation with overlapping shields, giving overhead protection.

Thalia: One of the nine muses; the goddess of comedy and idyllic poetry.

Theatre claques: Organised group of professional applauders; in the ancient world, these gangs were hired by performers or politicians to sway an audience in favour of themselves or against a rival.

Thessalian persuasion: Ancient proverb of obscure origins.

Thrace: Roman province to the north-east of Greece.

Thracian: People from the ancient geographical region of Thrace, the south-eastern corner of the Balkans. Also name of a type of gladiator, armed with a small shield and curved sword.

Thysdrus: Town in central Africa Proconsularis; modern El Djem in Tunisia.

Tibur: Ancient town north-east of Rome popular as a hill resort; modern Tivoli.

Toga: Voluminous garment, reserved for Roman citizens, worn on formal occasions.

419

Toga virilis: Garment given to mark a Roman's coming of age; usually at about fourteen.

Togate: Wearing a toga.

Tomis: Roman port on the Black Sea; modern Constanta in Romania.

Tresviri Monetales: Literally, 'Three men of the mint" board of junior magistrates responsible for the coinage.

Tribune: Title of a junior senatorial post at Rome and of various military officers; some commanded auxiliary units, while others were mid-ranking officers in the legions.

Trierarch: The commander of a trireme, in the Roman forces equivalent to a Centurion.

Trireme: An ancient warship, a galley rowed by about two hundred men on three levels.

Triumvirate: 'Three men'; term made notorious by two pacts to share control of the Roman government between three leading citizens that precipitated the end of the Roman Republic and ushered in the Principate.

Tropaeum Traiani: Roman town named after a triumphal monument built by the Emperor Trajan; modern Adamclisi in Romania.

Troy: City on the southern shore of the Dardanelles, scene of the legendary siege recounted in Homer's epic poem.

Tutor: Guardian legally necessary for a child, imbecile or woman.

Ultio: Latin, 'revenge', 'vengeance'.

Urban Cohort: Military units stationed in major cities to act as a police force; at Rome, they also counterbalanced the Praetorian Guard.

Valhalla: In Norse mythology, the hall in which selected heroes killed in battle would feast until Ragnarok.

Venus: Roman goddess of love; also name for rolling sixes in a game of dice.

Vesta: Roman goddess of the hearth.

Vestalia: Festival sacred to Vesta, celebrated by the baking of special bread cakes to give as offerings to the goddess.

Via Appia: Ancient road linking Rome to the south of Italy.

Via Flavia: Roman road running east–west across the Istrian coast to Dalmatia.

Via Gemina: Ancient road linking Aquileia and Emona.

Via Julia Augusta: Ancient road leading north from Aquileia to Noricum.

Via Tiburtina: Ancient road leading from Rome to Tibur, exiting the city near the Praetorian camp.

Via Triumphalis: Named from the route taken by triumphal processions; ancient road running along the eastern flank of the Palatine towards the Flavian Amphitheatre.

Victimarii: Attendants who conducted Roman animal sacrifices, usually slaves or freemen.

Vigiles: Paramilitary unit stationed at Rome for police and firefighting duties.

Villa Praenestina: Lavish country residence of the Gordiani, situated on the Via Praenestina three miles outside the city of Rome.

Vindabona: Ancient city and legionary fortress in the Roman province of Pannonia Superior; modern Vienna in Austria.

Volaterrae: Ancient name for Volterra, a town north-west of Rome.

XXviri Reipublicae Curandae: Commission of twenty men selected for the care of the State.

Zacynthos: Or Zante, an island off the western coast of Greece.

Zeugma: Greek city named after a bridge of boats crossing the Euphrates; now mostly submerged by the Birecik Dam in southern Turkey.

Zeus: Greek king of the gods.

LIST OF
CHARACTERS

The list is organized alphabetically. To avoid giving away any of the plot characters usually are only described as first encountered in *Fire & Sword*.

Ababa: A druid woman called to the court of Alexander Severus and patronized by Maximinus.

Abanchus: A Sarmatian from the Iazyges tribe, held hostage in Rome to ensure his people's good behaviour but freed by Menophilus.

Abgar: Son of Manu, notional Crown Prince of Edessa.

Acilius Aviola: Manius Acilius Aviola, patrician Senator; his family claimed descent from Aeneas, and thus the goddess Venus, they first rose to prominence under the Emperor Augustus and an ancestor held the consulship in AD24; cousin of Acilius Glabrio.

Adiutor: See Flavius Adiutor.

Aedinius Julianus: Marcus Aedinius Julianus, a Senator and governor of Gallia Narbonnensis.

Aelius: A young equestrian, linked to Timesitheus.

Aelius Lampridius: A young tribune serving in the field army of Maximinus.

Aemilius Severinus: Lucius Aemilius Severinus, also called Phillyrio; commander of the *speculatores*, loyal to the Gordiani.

Aesop: Name of the author given to numerous collections of fables in antiquity; supposedly lived in the sixth century BC.

Africanus: Iulius Africanus, a noted scholar probably from Syria Palestina; entrusted by the Emperor Alexander Severus with running the library of the Pantheon, some of his writings still survive.

Iulius Africanus: See Africanus.

Albinus: Clodius Albinus, rebelled against Septimius Severus from the provinces of Britain and Gaul in late AD196 but was defeated in battle in early AD197.

Alcimus Felicianus: Gaius Attius Alcimus Felicianus, an equestrian official with a long record of office-holding, now procurator in charge of the Flavian Amphitheatre and its gladiatorial school; a friend of Timesitheus.

Alexander: Alexander Severus, last Emperor of the Servian dynasty; born AD208, he ruled from AD222 to AD235.

Alexander: The Great, King of Macedon, conqueror of much of Asia in the fourth century BC.

Ammonius: An equestrian army officer irregularly promoted by Maximinus to be governor of Noricum.

Andromache: Wife of the Greek hero Hector.

Antheros: Bishop of Rome, succeeded Pontianus.

Anullinus: Praetorian Prefect commanding a detachment of the Praetorian Guard with Maximinus' field army.

Apsines of Gadara: Valerius Aspines, Greek rhetorician from Syria, *c.* AD190–250, secretary of Maximinus.

Aradius: Quintus Aradius Rufinus Optatus Aelianus, recently appointed governor of Syria Coele.

Ardashir: The First, founder of the Sassanid empire, ruled AD224–242.

Aristotle: Greek philosopher, lived 384–322BC.

Armenius Peregrinus: Tiberius Pollienus Armenius Peregrinus, a Senator and adopted son of Pollienus Auspex; enemy of Timesitheus.

Arrian: Legate of the Gordiani in Africa; especial friend of Sabinianus.

Ascyltos: Innkeeper in the Subura at Rome.

Augustus: First Emperor of Rome, 31BC–AD14; known as Octavian before he came to power.

Aulus: A Praetorian guardsman.

Avidius Cassius: Rebelled against Marcus Aurelius, ruling Egypt and Syria for three months in AD175, but was murdered by one of his own centurions.

Axius: Quintus Axius Aelianus, an equestrian, procurator of Dacia, an associate of Timesitheus.

Balbinus: Decimus Caelius Calvinus Balbinus, a patrician Senator, claims kinship with the deified Emperors Trajan and Hadrian via the great Roman clan of the Coelli; Consul Ordinarius with the Emperor Caracalla in AD213; among his many political friends are Acilius Aviola, Caesonius Rufinianus, and Valerius Priscillianus. Member of the Board of Twenty.

Ballista: Latin nickname of Dernhelm.

Barbius: Elder son of Barbius, a tribune fighting on the side of Maximinus in the 4th Legion Flavia Felix.

Barbius: Equestrian landowner and local magistrate at Aquileia; father of Barbius and Marcus Barbius.

Brutus: Marcus Junius Brutus, assassin of the dictator Julius Caesar.

Caenis: A prostitute working in the inn of Ascyltos in the Subura at Rome; originally called Rhodope.

Caerellius: Military tribune stationed in Carrhae; son of a friend of Censorinus.

Caesar: See Julius Caesar.

Calgacus: A Caledonian slave serving Dernhelm.

Calidius: Prefect of the 2nd Cohort of Thracians, serving under Capelianus in Africa.

Caligula: The popular name of Gaius, notoriously deranged Roman Emperor AD37–41.

Capelianus: Caius Iulius Geminius Capelianus, governor of Numidia, personal enemy of Gordian the Elder.

Caracalla: Roman Emperor AD211–217.

Cassianus: Of Antioch, a leading Sophist and enemy of Philostratus.

Cassius: Gaius Cassius Longinus, assassin of the dictator Julius Caesar.

Castricius: Gaius Aurelius Castricius, a young man of uncertain origins engaged by Menophilus to assassinate Maximinus.

Catiline: A noble accused by Cicero of plotting revolution; the threat he really posed seems to have been magnified for Cicero's political purposes.

Catius Celer: Lucius Catius Celer, a Senator, Praetor in AD235; younger brother of Catius Priscillianus and Catius Clemens; a friend of Timesitheus.

Catius Clemens: Gaius Catius Clemens, helped to place Maximinus on the throne and appointed governor of Cappadocia; brother of Catius Priscillianus and Catius Celer.

Cato: Statesman of the late Roman Republic; a Stoic philosopher and upholder of traditional Republican values.

Celsinus: Clodius Celsinus, a Senator and ex-Praetor in financial difficulty.

Chosroes: Prince of Armenia, son of King Tiridates II; serving with the Roman army in the East as a hostage for the good behaviour of his father.

Cicero: Roman orator and statesman, 106–43BC.

Civilis: Gaius Julius Civilis, leader of a revolt in Germania Inferior in AD69.

Claudius Julianus: Senatorial governor of Dalmatia, son of Appius Claudius Julianus; friend of the Gordiani.

Claudius: Roman Emperor AD41–54.

Cleander: Marcus Aurelius Cleander, a Roman freedman and favourite of the Emperor Commodus, promoted to command the Praetorian Guard but blamed for a food shortage in AD190; to stop the rioting, Commodus had his head thrown to the mob.

Clemens: See Catius Clemens.

Cniva: A Goth from the Tervingi tribe, held hostage in Rome to ensure the good behaviour of his people but freed by Menophilus.

Columella: Lucius Iunius Moderatus Columella, Latin author of the first century AD who wrote on agriculture.

Corvinus: Marcus Julius Corvinus, leader of bandits in the eastern Alps, despite his equestrian status.

Crassus: Roman statesman and disastrous general, slaughtered with much of his army at the Battle of Carrhae in 53BC.

Crispinus: Rutilius Pudens Crispinus, an equestrian army officer risen into the Senate and eventually to the consulship; friend of Pupienus, now in charge of the defence of Aquileia with Menophilus. Member of the Board of Twenty.

Croesus: King of Lydia 560–547/6BC; his wealth was proverbial in antiquity.

Cuspidius Flaminius: Cuspidius Flaminius Severus, a *novus homo* in the Senate, an ex-Consul and friend of Pupienus.

Davus: A slave in the household of Gallicanus.

Decius: Gaius Messius Quintus Decius, from a senatorial family owning wide estates near the Danube, an early patron of the career of Maximinus, now governor of one of the Spanish provinces.

Demosthenes: Athenian statesman and orator of the fourth century BC.

Dernhelm: Son of Isangrim, war-leader of the Angles; a diplomatic hostage in the retinue of Maximinus, given the Latin nickname Ballista by his Roman comrades.

Didius Julianus: Bought the empire at auction and ruled for two months as Roman Emperor in AD193.

Dio Chrysostom: Greek Sophist and author from Prusa, active in the late-first/early-second century AD; his surname in Greek means 'golden-mouthed'.

Diogenes: Notorious Cynic philosopher of the fourth century BC; lived for a time in a wine barrel.

Domitian: Roman Emperor AD81–96.

Domitius: An equestrian, Prefect of the imperial camp under Maximinus and murdered by Timesitheus.

Domitius Valerianus: Marcus Domitius Valerianus, recently appointed equestrian governor of Arabia.

Eadwulf: Half-brother of Dernhelm.

Egnatius Lollianus: Lucius Egnatius Victor Lollianus, recently returned to Rome after serving as governor of Bithynia-Pontus; a friend of the Gordiani, brother of Egnatius Marinianus and brother-in-law of Valerian.

Egnatius Marinianus: Egnatius Victor Marinianus, a senatorial envoy and ex-Consul, sometime governor of the military province of Moesia Superior, brother-in-law of Valerian and brother of Egnatius Lollianus.

Epictetus: Greek Stoic philosopher, AD55–135.

Euripides: Greek playwright, *c.* 480–406BC.

Fadillus: Lucius Iunius Fadillus, cousin and tutor of Iunia Fadilla.

Faltonius Nicomachus: Maecius Faltonius Nichomachus, governor of Pannonia Inferior.

Felicio: An equestrian client of the Gordiani put in charge of the Praetorian Guard at Rome.

Fidus: Senatorial governor of Thrace; friend of the Gordiani.

Firmanus: Primus Pilus of the 3rd Legion Augusta.

Flavius Adiutor: Equestrian commander of 1st Cohort Ulpia Galatarum, stationed at Aquileia.

Flavius Vopiscus: A Roman Senator from Syracuse in Sicily, helped to put Maximinus on the throne and serving with his field army; fond of literature, especially biography, and much given to superstition.

Fortunatianus: Curius Fortunatianus, secretary of Pupienus.

Froda: Older half-brother of Dernhelm.

Fulvius Pius: Senator, descendant of the grandfather of Septimius Severus, Consul Ordinarius in AD238. Member of the Board of Twenty.

Gallicanus: Lucius Domitius Gallicanus Papinianus, a Senator and member of the Board of Twenty; of home-spun and hirsute appearance, sometimes thought to resemble an ape, much influenced by the philosophy of Cynicism. His particular crony is Maecenas.

Gaudianus: A freedman in the *familia* of Maecia Faustina.

Gnaeus: A young equestrian, linked to Timesitheus.

Gnaeus: A Praetorian guardsman.

Gordian the Elder: Marcus Antonius Gordianus Sempronianus, came to Africa Proconsularis as the governor but following his son Gordian the Younger's murder of Paul the Chain, proclaimed joint Emperor.

Gordian the Younger: Marcus Antonius Gordianus Sempronianus, came to Africa as a legate of his father but proclaimed Emperor with his father Gordian the Elder after the murder of Paul the Chain, adopting the titles Romanus Africanus; devotee of Epicurean philosophy; sometime lover of Iunia Fadilla.

Gunteric: Son of Tharuaro, high chief of the Tervingi.

Hadrian: Roman Emperor AD117–38.

Hannibal: Carthaginian statesman and general, 247–c. 182BC.

Harpagus: General of Astyages, King of the Medes 585–550BC; in revenge for the death of his son, betrayed the kingdom to Cyrus the Great of Persia.

Hector: Legendary Greek hero of the Trojan War.

Heliogabalus: Derogatory nickname for the Emperor Marcus Aurelius Antoninus, AD218–22. Said to be remarkably perverse.

Herodes Atticus: Greek Sophist of noble birth and great wealth; AD101–77. Entered the Roman Senate and became the first of his countrymen to hold the consulship.

Hjar: King of the Angles, great-grandfather of Dernhelm.

Homer: According to ancient tradition, the epic poet and father of Greek literature.

Honoratus: Lucius Flavius Honoratus Lucilianus, a *novus homo* in the Roman Senate, helped to put Maximinus on the throne. Now governor of Moesia Inferior; a man of ridiculous good looks, others often comment on his perfect teeth.

Horatius: Horatius Cocles, legendary Roman officer of the Early Republic who single-handedly defended a bridge over the Tiber, saving Rome.

Hormizd of Adiabene: A Persian Prince, the younger son of Ardashir I.

Iaculator: A gladiator loaned to Timesitheus.

Isangrim: The King of the Angles in the far north (modern Denmark); his son is held hostage for good behaviour by Maximinus.

Isedore of Charax: Ancient geographical writer active in the first century BC or AD; his work gave distances and towns on the caravan route from the city of Antioch on the Orontes in modern Turkey to India.

Iulius Africanus: See Africanus.

Iunia Fadilla: Great-granddaughter of the Emperor Marcus Aurelius; estranged wife of Verus Maximus, the son of Maximinus, and sometime lover of Gordian the Younger.

Javolenus: Bodyguard of Maximinus, originally a legionary in the 2nd Legion Parthica.

Julius Caesar: Roman general and statesman, assassinated for aiming at monarchy in 44BC.

Julius Capitolinus: An equestrian officer commanding the 2nd Legion Parthica; spends his leisure writing biographies.

Julius Julianus: Equestrian Prefect of the 1st Legion Parthica.

Junius Balbus: Governor of Syria Coele executed for treason by Maximinus; was the husband of Maecia Faustina and thus brother-in-law of Gordian the Younger.

Junius Balbus: Marcus Junius Balbus, son of Maecia Faustina and Junius Balbus.

Kadlin: A young Angle; lover of Dernhelm.

Laco: Prefect of the Ravenna fleet, appointed by the Gordiani.

Latronianus: Marcus Flavius Latronianus, senatorial envoy in the East; an ex-Consul, once patron of a young Menophilus.

Licinius Rufinus: Gnaius Licinius Rufinus, an equestrian who began his career under Septimius Severus, holding numerous secretarial and administrative roles including *A Rationibus*, before being rewarded with entry to the Senate and a Suffect Consulship. Member of the Board of Twenty.

Lucius Verus: Co-Emperor with Marcus Aurelius from AD161–169.

Lucius Virius: Lucius Virius Lupus, elderly Senator and Consul in AD232; father of Virius Lupus, close friend of Menophilus.

Ma'na: Son of Sanatruq II, Prince of the Hatrene royal family; serving with the Roman army.

Macrianus: Veteran centurion serving with the *frumentarii*.

Marcus Sidonius Falx: Author of *How to Manage Your Slaves*, as imagined by Jerry Toner (London, 2014).

Macrinus: Roman Emperor AD217–18; unrest over his inability to defeat the Parthians helped shorten his reign.

Maecenas: Senator and intimate friend of Gallicanus, member of the Board of Twenty.

Maecia Faustina: Sister of Gordian the Younger, daughter of Gordian the Elder, and widow of Junius Balbus, executed for treason by Maximinus. Her son is also called Junius Balbus, after his father.

Maecius Gordianus: A young equestrian, second cousin of Maecia Faustina and kinsman of the Gordiani; Prefect of the *vigiles*.

Manu: Son of Abgar VIII, titular King of Edessa, but left without real power after Caracalla incorporated the kingdom into the Roman empire in the early third century AD.

Marcus: A Praetorian guardsman.

Marcus: Son of Honoratus; died accompanying his father to Moesia Inferior.

Marcus Africanus: Marcus Pupienus Africanus Maximus, younger son of Pupienus, married to the daughter of Praetextatus.

Marcus Aurelius: Roman Emperor AD161–180.

Marcus Barbius: A young equestrian and younger son of a town councillor of Aquileia, serving against Maximinus with the senatorial forces of Menophilus.

Marius Perpetuus: Lucius Marius Perpetuus, Consul Ordinarius in AD237, son of a past governor of Upper Moesia, Maximinus' old general.

Mark Antony: Roman statesman and partisan of Julius Caesar, schemed and fought with Octavian for mastery of the Roman World, committed suicide in 30BC.

Masculus: Commander of the Watch at Ostia.

Massa: A soldier serving with Menophilus at the siege of Aquileia.

Mauricius: Son of Mauricius; a wealthy landowner and town councillor at Thysdrus and Hadrumetumin Africa Proconsularis, friend of Gordian the Younger.

Maximinus: Gaius Iulius Verus Maximinus, known as Maximinus Thrax (the Thracian); proclaimed Emperor by the northern armies in AD235 though only an equestrian officer.

Maximus: Tiberius Clodius Pupienus Pulcher Maximus, a Senator and ex-Consul, eldest son of Pupienus; brother of Marcus Africanus.

Menophilus: Tullius Menophilus, Senator originally serving as Quaestor of the province of Africa Proconsularis and sent by the Gordiani as an envoy to the Senate; subsequently made responsible with Crispinus for the defence of Aquileia against the forces of Maximinus.

Micca: Bodyguard of Maximinus from the days when both were young.

Montanus: A freedman in the *familia* of Maecia Faustina.

Musalia: Prostitute working in Ascyltos' bar in the Subura quarter of Rome.

Narcissus: Gladiator loaned to Timesitheus.

Nero: Notoriously degenerate Roman Emperor, AD54–68.

Niger: Pescennius Niger, hailed as Emperor by the eastern legions in AD193, but defeated by Septimius Severus in AD194.

Nummius: Marcus Nummius Umbrius Secundus Senecio Albinus, Suffect Consul in AD206, thereafter devoting himself to pleasure; first husband of Iunia Fadilla, now deceased.

Otacilius: Marcus Otacilius Severianus, governor of Syria Palestina, brother-in-law of Priscus.

Ovid: Roman poet exiled for impropriety by the Emperor Augustus; 43BC–AD17/18.

Paccius: Optio of the 1st Cohort Ulpia Galatarum, serving in the defence of Aquileia.

Parthenope: A mistress of the younger Gordian.

Patricius: Roman engineer, serving in the defence of Aquileia.

Paulina: Caecilia Paulina, wife of the Emperor Maximinus; killed by conspirators two years previously and afterwards declared a goddess.

Perennis: Tigidius Perennis, commander of the Praetorian Guard under Marcus Aurelius and Commodus; was executed by the latter in AD185 on charges brought by his rival, Cleander.

Periges: Greek Sophist; instructed in rhetoric by Cassianus, his only pupil.

Perpetua: Friend of Iunia Fadilla and widow of Serenianus.

Philip: Philip II of Macedon, attacked in a series of fiery speeches by the Athenian politician Demosthenes.

Philip: Marcus Julius Philippus, brother of Gaius Julius Priscus; born in Roman Arabia and serving as a legate to his brother on the Eastern frontier.

Philostratus: Greek orator and biographer of the Sophists (*c.* 170–250AD); in the early third century, introduced at the court of Septimius Severus at Rome.

Pinarius: Pinarius Valenus, adoptive father of Pupienus; a retired head gardener.

Plautianus: Gaius (or Lucius) Fulvius Plautianus; commander of the Praetorian Guard under Septimius Severus, his daughter was married to the future Emperor Caracalla, but the unhappiness of the match led to his downfall in AD205.

Polybius: Greek historian of the rise of Rome to superpower status; lived *c.* 200–*c.* 118BC.

Pompey: The Great, statesman of the Roman Republic; incorporated Syria into the Roman empire and reorganised the eastern provinces; murdered in 48BC.

Pontianus: Sent to the mines in Sardinia for professing the Christian faith; formerly Bishop of Rome.

Porcius Aelianus: Equestrian Prefect of the 3rd Legion Parthica, serving under Priscus in the East.

Praetextatus: A high-born Senator and ex-Consul, friend of Balbinus. Member of the Board of Twenty, and father-in-law of Pupienus' youngest son Marcus Africanus.

Priscillianus: Sextus Catius Clemens Priscillianus, governor of Germania Superior; elder brother of Catius Clemens and Catius Celer.

433

Priscus: Gaius Julius Priscus, equestrian governor of Mesopotamia, born in Arabia; brother of Philip and friend of Timesitheus.

Pupienus: Marcus Clodius Pupienus Maximus, a *novus homo* of very obscure origins, brought up in the house of a kinsman in Tibur; now a patrician, twice Consul, and Prefect of the City before being replaced by Sabinus; father of Pupienus Maximus and Marcus Africanus; brother-in-law of Sextus Cethegillus. A member of the Board of Twenty. His friends in politics include Tineius Sacerdos, Cuspidius Flamininus and Crispinus.

Restuta: Maid of Iunia Fadilla.

Reverendus: A freedman in the *familia* of Maecia Faustina.

Romulus: Legendary founder of Rome.

Rufinianus: Lucius Caesonius Lucillus Macer Rufinianus, a patrician Senator; Suffect Consul *c.* AD225–30; a friend of Balbinus. Member of the Board of Twenty.

Rutilus: Second cousin of Maximinus, serving with Honoratus in Moesia.

Sabinia: Furia Sabinia Tranquillina, the young daughter of Tranquillina and Timesitheus.

Sabinianus: Well-born legate of Gordian the Elder in Africa Proconsularis; a deserter to Capelianus.

Sabinus: Senator and ex-Consul; appointed Prefect of the City by Maximinus and killed by Menophilus.

Sanctus: Experienced functionary in the imperial household.

Scipio: Scipio Africanus, Roman statesman and general, famous for defeating Hannibal; 236–183BC.

Sejanus: Praetorian Prefect under Tiberius; his daughters were raped before execution, to avoid a legal bar on the killing of virgins.

Septimius Severus: Roman Emperor AD193–211.

Serapamum: Legate of the 2nd Legion; client of the Gordiani.

Serenianus: Licinius Serenianus, senatorial governor of Cappadocia executed for treason by Maximinus; once a friend of Pupienus and Priscus.

Servilianus: Flavius Servilianus, equestrian officer given an ad hoc appointment to command the militia at Aquileia.

Severus: See Septimius Severus.

Sextius Cethegillus: Senator and ex-Consul; brother-in-law of Pupienus.

Socrates: Greek philosopher forced to commit suicide by the Athenian courts; *c.* 470–399BC.

Solon: Athenian statesman of the sixth century BC; drew up a legal code for the city, then stepped down from power.

Spartacus: Leader of Rome's most serious slave revolt, 73–71BC.

Sporakes: Bodyguard of Priscus.

Statius: Equestrian landowner and local magistrate at Aquileia.

Sulla: Roman statesman, *c.* 138–78BC; resigned the dictatorship in 81BC after instituting sweeping reforms, and died of natural causes in retirement.

Tacitus: Marcus Clodius Tacitus, governor of Moesia Superior.

Tacitus: The greatest Roman historian, AD56–117.

Tharuaro: High chief of the Tervingi Goths, father of Guntcric.

Thrasea: Thrasea Paetus, Roman Senator and Stoic, opponent of the Emperor Nero; forced to commit suicide in AD66.

Tiberius: Dour Roman Emperor, AD14–37.

Tiberius Gracchus: Roman politician and champion of popular causes; killed by a mob of Senators in 133BC.

Timesitheus: Gaius Furius Sabinius Aquila Timesitheus, extremely ambitious equestrian official, but now a captive and being led to his execution.

Tineius Sacerdos: Quintus Tineius Sacerdos, Senator and Consul Ordinarius in AD219; father-in-law of Pupienus Maximus. Member of the Board of Twenty.

Tiridates: The Second, King of Armenia from AD217; as a member of the Arsacid dynasty overthrown by the Sassanids, lays claim to the Parthian empire.

Trajan: Roman Emperor AD98–117.

Tranquillina: Wife of Timesitheus.

Tynchanius: From the same village in Thrace as Maximinus, his personal attendant since early days. Killed protecting Maximinus' wife in the mutiny that led to her death.

Valens: *A Cubiculo* of Gordian the Elder.

Valerian: Publius Licinius Valerian, Senator and ex-Consul married into the family of the Egnatii; serving as legate of the elder Gordian in Africa when the Gordiani were declared Emperors, was sent to Rome to act as their envoy. Member of the Board of Twenty.

Valerius Poplicola: Lucius Valerius Poplicola Balbinus Maximus, a young patrician, son of Valerius Priscillianus; one of the Tresviri Monetales.

Valerius Priscillianus: Lucius Valerius Claudius Acilius Priscillianus Maximus, patrician Senator, Consul Ordinarius in AD233, son of Valerius Apollinaris and brother of Valerius Messala, both executed by Maximinus, and father of Valerius Poplicola.

Valerius Valens: Prefect of the Misenum fleet; the base of a statue erected in his honour still survives.

Varro: Marcus Terentius Varro, prolific Latin author of the last century BC; the first three books of his *On Agriculture* survive.

Vertiscus: Servant of Iunia Fadilla.

Verus Maximus: Gaius Iulius Verus Maximus Caesar, son of the Emperor Maximinus and Caecilia Paulina, designated heir to the throne and awarded the title Caesar.

Verus: See Lucius Verus.

Vespasian: Roman Emperor, ruled AD69–79.

Virgil: Roman national poet, lived 70–19BC.

Vitalianus: Publius Aelius Vitalianus, distinguished equestrian official and Praetorian Prefect under Maximinus, executed by Menophilus on the orders of the Gordiani.

Volcatius: Gaius Julius Volcatius Gallicanus, a Senator from Gaul accompanying Maximinus on campaign.

Volo: Marcus Aurelius Volo, Maximinus' *Princeps Peregrinorum*, commander of the imperial spies.

Vopiscus: See Flavius Vopiscus.

Xenophon of Ephesus: Greek author of the extant novel *An Ephesian Tale*.

Younger Gordian: See Gordian the Younger.

Zeno: Of Citium, Greek philosopher and founder of Stoicism, c. 334–262BC.

Zeus Eleutherius Theophanes: From Mytilene, became one of Pompey's most trusted advisors and was granted Roman citizenship; after the death of his patron, retired to the land of his birth to be greeted like one of the heroes of myth.

Zeuxis: Greek painter active in the fifth century BC, famed for the realism of his pictures.